Barren Waters

JULIA SHUPE

DEDICATION

For my lovely sister, Erin

For her strength, elegance, and beauty

ACKNOWLEDGEMENTS

Special thanks to my amazing husband, Nat. No other man would support me the way you have, and do. This level of support reaches beyond the norm: the hours I spend crouched over the computer, the dishes in the sink that don't get done, the dust that gathers in the corners of rooms.

Thank you for being my partner and inspiration, for being my best friend and confidant. Nothing means more than your love.

Readers, thank you so much. Writing this book has been the most thrilling experience of my life. Putting my innermost feelings on paper is like breaking a piece of my heart from the whole and baring it for the world to see. I hope you enjoy it, as well as my some of my other works.

I have many more stories to tell.

PART 1

I really don't know why it is that all of us are so committed to the sea, except I think it's because in addition to the fact that the sea changes, and the light changes, and ships change, it's because we all came from the sea. And it is an interesting biological fact that all of us have in our veins the exact same percentage of salt in our blood that exists in the ocean, and, therefore, we have salt in our blood, in our sweat, in our tears. We are tied to the ocean. And when we go back to the sea—whether it is to sail or to watch it—we are going back from whence we came.

—John F. Kennedy

CHAPTER 1
Present Day

"Samantha. Sam, wake up." Cursing himself, he shook her bodily, "Sam, come on. Come back to me."

Though he poked and prodded her, she remained unresponsive. This was his fault, his failing. He laid a cool cloth across her forehead and cursed aloud. How could he have been so stupid? So reckless? He'd known she was low, but hadn't listened to the whispering voice inside his head. He'd been foolish, imprudent, doggedly persistent. Why hadn't he heeded his carefully honed instincts? The voice in his head sometimes managed to make sense, but it was a voice that also seemed quieter each day. And for a moment, he wondered: had he finally lost himself? Somehow, after this pain and torment, somewhere along this agonizing journey, had he left a vital piece of himself behind?

Wanting them to make it as far as Huntsville in a week, he thought he'd feel better once they crossed the

Alabama border. But what would be the point? To say they had done it? To say they'd gone an extra fifty miles? To prove they could cross a state line within a month? What was he trying to do? To prove? And to whom was he trying to prove it? When all was said and done, whose agenda did they follow? He set the boundaries. He made the rules.

And rules are easily broken, he told himself, frowning as he regarded her motionless body.

"Sam. Come on, Pike. Open your eyes."

When he ran his hand along her scalp, his fingers came away damp. Not good. He should have known better. He knew all the signs. By now, he was a master at recognizing them. About thirty minutes ago, she'd begun to appear fuzzy. Fuzzy, he remarked. Fuzzy in the head. That's how he'd always described it. She'd stare off at nothing, her eyes unfocused, muscles in her face gone slack. After that, she'd become irritable and cantankerous, or worse, emotionless, impassive, and distant. Those were the times when he preferred an irritable Sam. Irritable, at least, was considered an emotion. It was the dullness that frightened him so, the flatness, the times when the edges of her smile bled to a frown, when her face went blank and the sheen left her eyes.

These past few days, he'd been pushing her too hard. And while he had to admit they'd made excellent progress, they'd been blessed with a fair amount of luck along the way.

Luck.

Jeremy frowned. Did he really believe in that?

Luck was a double-edged sword. Good luck could easily turn bad. And fast. It was something he knew too well. Personal experience was the best of teachers.

But, he reflected, of late they'd been fortunate. In Knoxville, fate had delivered them the bikes. Though it had been her idea, he reminded himself. He had to give credit where credit was due. Perhaps it wasn't fate after all.

Her idea had been nothing short of brilliant. They'd been following the sleek curves of Neyland Drive, which clung to the contours of the Tennessee River, when somehow, despite the odds, she'd seen the sign for the University of Tennessee. It was remarkable she'd seen it at all, he mused. Weeds and tall grasses had expelled it from the earth, ejecting it like it was a cancerous growth. It was leaning on its side, its base bent and corroded by rust. The lettering had long since faded by then, and the paint had chipped and worn free. Fungi crawled over its every nook and cranny, and had begun a slow digestive process.

"Wouldn't there be bikes at a university?" she'd queried.

"Probably rusted heaps of metal by now, Sam."

She'd frowned at that, tiny wrinkles creasing her brow. "You're such a pessimist. You don't know that for sure. We should at least check it out. What do we have to lose?"

And so they had. And she'd been right. After picking through the rusted heaps of metal, still chained to the racks at the edge of the campus lawn, they decided to search the domiciles. And after glumly inspecting more than thirty or so rooms, they finally hit pay dirt. He'd hoped to find discarded old clothing, made of fabric that wasn't moth-eaten or pilled, or perhaps a hidden bottle of water, seltzer, or soda, or a fresh pair of tennies that weren't split at the soles.

But damn if fortune hadn't smiled that day— smiled, and shown a bit of teeth. Against insurmountable odds, in one of the supply closets behind a pile of old suitcases, they found a row of bikes with gleaming polished frames: reds, blues, silvers, bright oranges, with glinting steel spokes and firm tires. Flat tires, mind you, but firm and usable, made of rubber that was thick, with deep treads. The tires had needed air, of course, and the chains a bit of oil, but it was a treasure trove of good fortune. He was thankful. As nothing had in weeks, the sight had lifted Jeremy's battered spirit. He'd taken the gift and run with it, so to speak.

The bikes had been in such excellent condition that he'd hated taking only two of them. Who knew when the tires would pop or run flat, or when the brake pads would disintegrate into dust. But thankfully he'd ignored his insufferable negativity. Best to not think about things in those terms—like a pessimist. Right?

She was always right.

Besides, he told himself, by then—for both of them—desperation had begun to sink in.

Before the bikes, they'd been walking for weeks, and he'd started feeling the beginning stages of panic. And it wasn't the walking that slowed their progress. Ironically, the cart was responsible for that, the vessel that was their livelihood, their sustenance, which contained what they needed to make this journey. The ark, so aptly named, was a burden. But it was also a necessary one. A vital one. Without their supplies, they'd be dead in a matter of weeks.

Even with the bikes, you won't make it, the voice hissed. Not with enough time to spare. You know that.

The thought, when it came, sparked renewed panic, and he refocused his attempts to rouse her.

"Come on, Pike," he said, ignoring the sinister voice as he shook her. "Time to return to planet earth."

He peered beneath an eyelid, lifted her arm, examined the numbers that glowed at her wrist. Forty-eight. That was better. She was coming out of it. Lifting her head, he tried to coax juice into her mouth, though most of it dribbled down her chin. Shit. She'd come out of it soon, he promised himself. She always did. But even that didn't save him from feeling like a heel. He should have been more thoughtful and attentive, and he shouldn't rely on the things she said. She often lied.

Her diet was unstable, her sleep unpredictable, her stress levels beyond what was normal for her age. This, a trifecta of conditions for most, was downright dangerous for a struggling diabetic. Even with the disk in place, she could experience unpredicted highs and lows, particularly after periods of intense physical exertion, which was something that couldn't be helped. Not yet. He was doing his best with what he'd been given. But there was light at the end of this tunnel. He was certain. He would push her toward it with his last dying breath. It was there. He could feel it. He knew it without a doubt.

Are you certain? the little voice sneered in his head.

Yes, he sneered back. I'm certain. Shut up.

It had to be there—that light, that hope. It was the point of this journey—to bring her peace and stability. He only wished stability wasn't so far away.

Lifting her arm, he inspected the numbers. Fifty-two. She should be waking by now.

"Sam," he whispered. "Can you open your eyes?" He massaged her hands and rubbed arms, regarded the boniness of her elbows and knees. She was far too thin.

He pushed the thought away.

Her eyes fluttered, and with a sudden twitch of hands, a lazy smile spread across her face. "Sam?" she muttered. "Who the hell is Sam? The name's Pike. I've told you that ten thousand times."

"Yeah. Right. I forgot." He heaved a sigh. "But are you sure about Pike? Wouldn't you prefer Albacore, or Orange Roughy?" He tucked a sweaty lock of hair behind her ear. "Pike is a boy's name, Sam."

She allowed him to lift her and prop her against his thigh, where she held her juice with trembling hands. "It's not a boy's name," she admonished him lightly. "I just like it. It suits me. It's a solid choice. You chose Carp, of all things. Carp sucks. It's a terrible choice. Doesn't suit you at all. You're more of a Bass, or a Salmon, or an Eel."

"An Eel? Hell no." He smiled in spite of himself. "I'll take Carp, thank you very much. Or Thresher. What do you think of Thresher? You have to admit, Thresher sounds kinda cool." Inhaling through his nostrils, he offered an astute analysis. "So here's the deal. Listen up. Salmon is a nerd's name. Bass is a girl's name. Eel is a pervert's name, so I'm definitely not an Eel. So that leaves Carp. Final answer. Deal with it." He supported her neck and pushed the cup toward her mouth. "Drink up. We're stopping. We're done for the day."

"We're done?" He watched thoughts spin through her head. "Where'd you come up with Thresher, anyway? What kind of fish was that?"

He pulled a kerchief from a pocket of his cargo pants. "Wasn't a fish. Threshers were sharks. Though I'm afraid they went extinct a long time ago—extinct like everything else that swam."

A bubble of laughter escaped from her throat. "A thresher was a shark? Then you're definitely not a Thresher. You were right the first time. Carp is better." She dismally pushed clumps of hair from her face and peered toward the side of the road, where her bike had fallen to the ground in a heap. "Was I bad? Did I fall? Did I ruin the bike?"

"Nope. Caught you before you fell. Saw it coming. You got fuzzy again. Knew it would happen."

Crinkling her nose, she set down her cup. "I hate that word. Don't say it like that. People don't get fuzzy, Carp. That's a terrible description."

She lifted her shirt to inspect the meter, which lay two inches from her navel. When Jeremy saw it, his belly clenched painfully.

"Thirty-eight percent," she called out, lifting her head. "That's why we're in such a hurry, isn't it? We're running out of disks, Carp. Tell me the truth."

The lie came easily to his lips. "No, we're not. We're not running out of disks, Pike. I swear to you. We're not."

"Okay. Then show me how many we've got left."

Lifting his fist, he shook it in her face. "How about I show you a knuckle sandwich instead?"

Groaning, she rolled her eyes and pushed herself to her feet. She bounced on her heels to test the strength of her legs. "Fine. Don't tell me. But you know I'm not stupid. I'll just look inside your pack when you're sleeping."

He sighed, thought his hand reflexively moved to his pocket, where he traced the outline of the disks against his thigh. The familiar shape brought immediately comfort.

"How far did we make it, anyway?" she asked.

He stood up and dusted off his jeans. "Not far. If you didn't get fuzzy, you'd remember."

She ignored that. "Didn't make it to Huntsville, I presume?"

"Nope. Not even close. We're somewhere outside Chattanooga, I think."

"Chattanooga?" She lifted the tail of her shirt and used it to mop the sweat from her brow. The gesture reminded him of his own discomforts. Ignoring them, he peered westward. Though the sun had slipped beneath the horizon, it was still hot as hell. Unnaturally hot. Or was this the new natural? He supposed it was. This was summer, autumn, winter, and spring: the thickness of the heat; the alien fungi—the species that seemed to have taken over the world. It claimed everything with its greedy lithe fingers. This was the new climate now, the new standard. There was no escaping this heat.

And the heat, of course, was the least of their troubles. What of the thinner air that occasionally caused intense moments of panic? Every now and then, if they pushed themselves hard enough, they would succumb to dizziness and poor coordination, and to the curious black spots that preceded unconsciousness. The planet's oxygen levels were much lower now, and the death of the oceans was the cause. And discomfort wasn't relegated to the highest elevations, either. Not anymore. It was everywhere now. Thinner air. Intense heat. God how he missed the mountains.

"Let's set up camp by the river," she suggested, lifting her bike and kicking the stand down.

"I'm warning you, Sam. It's gonna stink down there."

"No it won't. It won't be that bad. Not after you get used to it. Don't you find that you get used to certain smells? If you give them long enough, you don't notice them anymore." She shouldered her pack and then swayed beneath its weight.

He eyed her warily. "Stop right there. We're not going anywhere until you eat something first."

Searching through his pack, he found a bottle of water and an old Balance Bar, and leaning against a rotting old tree, he took comfort in watching her eat it. What was this fascination she'd developed with the river? It had been her idea to follow it. And it really did stink—even from here. Not of fish, or of plants, or of common river tang. There were no fish. Not for decades now. It smelled of something worse, something chemical and caustic, an acetic and corrosive perfume reminiscent of bleach, fertilizer, or pesticide. It lifted with the delicate breeze and burned the nose. It tickled the throat and watered the eyes.

"You get used to the smell," she repeated around a full mouth. "Besides, I don't care if it stinks. I like looking at it. Sue me. I've never seen naturally flowing water before. I just like it, okay? I wonder where it goes. I mean I know where it goes, but it's kind of amazing. It runs for hundreds of miles, cutting through hard-packed earth and rock. It carves its path over time." She shrugged. "It earns its path with hard work, I suppose."

It earns its path with hard work? He couldn't help but smile. "Where the hell do you learn this stuff?"

"Found a Grand Canyon brochure at the last house."

"So you like to imagine where it goes," he

8

prodded.

"That," she said as she sipped her juice. "And I like the sound it makes. It sounds like mom's old sound machine, the one she used to fall asleep to. Remember? She'd scramble to find batteries that worked, and then set it on white noise and try to fall asleep. When she finally did, I'd change it to babbling brook."

Of course he remembered. How could he forget? He clenched his fists and wiggled his toes, his thoughts threatening to slither to a much darker place, where memories of home crouched and waited in the dark. Not good. Shake it off. Don't think about that. He tried to paste a smile across his face.

"You ever see the Grand Canyon before?" she asked, her voice suddenly soft and dreamy.

"Yep. Long ago. I was a boy at the time. But I remember it well, though I saw it from a distance. I was in an airplane, high up in the sky. I remember it being so big and so vast, though it may have seemed big because I was so small. It was breathtaking, though. That I remember."

"And a river made that?"

"Yep. A river made that. But it took that river millions of years to get it done. Something that beautiful can't be created overnight."

"No," she murmured. "I guess it can't. Something that beautiful can't be created overnight. But it sure as hell doesn't take long to destroy it."

He didn't have an answer for that. No one did. He ignored it and rifled through his pack. From it, he removed the air pump they'd found in that UT supply closet, and made his rounds to test the firmness of their tires. Given the weight and pressure of their supplies, he constantly worried about the longevity of the rubber. Back at the college, when they'd discovered the bikes, he and Sam had crafted hand-made panniers out of any materials they could find, which they'd tied as securely as they could to the bikes. And from the cart, they transferred as many supplies as they could cram into those roughly sewn pouches.

It had been one of the most difficult decisions Jeremy had ever made. Take the bikes, reach their destination faster, or continue to walk and push their heavily laden cart. Initially, the idea of abandoning their supplies was inconceivable to him. But so was deserting the bikes, he'd concluded. Who in his right mind would pass on that? The vehicles were just as important as the supplies. So they'd made the best of a difficult situation, brought as much of the cart along with them as they could. Though now he worried that they'd brought too much, that it was too much weight for the slim tires to bear. Pursing his lips, he squeezed a tire. There was nothing he could do about it now. Move on.

"Are you ever gonna tell me where we're going?" she asked. He could hear the exasperation in her tone.

"Can't. Told you. It's a surprise." Straightening, he peered into the purpling sky. "Come on. Let's move off the road. It's getting dark. We need to find a place to make camp."

He lifted his bike and turned from the road, slipping into the forest that hemmed the river's bank, where the trees seemed thicker than they'd been back home, though not thick enough to offer proper camouflage. Acid rain had flayed their bark, choking them of vital nutrients, and as a result, they'd shed most of their leaves, like an aging man fighting a losing battle for his hair. Some of the pine trees were still lush and full. The tall deciduous species were the first to succumb. At the bases of these, decaying logs littered the ground, wrapped in thick moss and furry fungi. He stepped around them.

At least it's green, he thought despairingly. The forests back home had gone gray and brittle. He pushed through the rotting debris at his feet, while searching for a place to hide the bikes.

Behind him, Sam, marked her passage with the

snapping of twigs and hollow branches. "So," she asked him again. "Why Carp? Did it taste good or something?"

She sounded short of breath so he reflexively slowed his pace. "Don't know, actually. I never tasted carp, though once I was lucky enough to try a piece of smoked salmon."

"Smoked salmon? That sounds disgusting."

"It was. But it was all we had. Smoked or dried was all that was left. I was lucky. Most people never tried fish at all. My father saved a packet just for me."

As were most days he had spent with his father, Jeremy recalled that day fondly. They'd been sitting on the deck of their cabin in the woods, overlooking the Smokey Mountains of Tennessee, and enjoying the spectacular view in silence. He remembered—even then—that the air had been thin.

"We've got to eat it now," his father had said, pulling a knife from his pocket and snapping open the blade. He slipped it between the folds of plastic. "If we don't, it's gonna go bad." The package had opened with a tiny popping sound, and a curious tangy smell had lifted from within.

"Smells funny," Jeremy had said, pinching his nose.

"Not funny, Jeremy. Fishy. Go get an encyclopedia from the house—the one with the 'S' on the spine, if you would. Go on. Off you go."

Jeremy remembered running to their family's small library and pulling the heavy tome from the shelves. He loved to hear his father tell stories about fish. To be fair, he loved hearing his father tell stories about anything, really, but tales of the once-glorious oceans were his favorite. Sliding from his chair, his father crossed his legs on the deck's smooth planking, and with the tome in his lap, sifted through the yellowing pages.

"There," he pointed out. "That's what it looked like."

Eyes narrowed, Jeremy peered at the strange but beautiful creature on the page. "I thought fish were supposed to be small. That one's big."

"Salmon were fairly big," said his father. "At least they were back then. In the 1980's, they were actually quite large."

Jeremy traced the oblong silhouette. It was beautiful and majestic, covered with silvery scales. His father handed him a piece of pale orange meat, which he warily tasted before spitting onto the deck.

"Ick. It's gross. It tastes like smoke."

His father's laugh had been warm and hearty. "It's an acquired taste, I suppose. Though it's one you'll never develop, I'm afraid."

Jeremy nearly tripped over a fallen log, and turning, peered over his shoulder at Sam. "This is as far as we can get with the bikes. Let's leave 'em here. We'll camp close by. It's getting too thick up ahead."

She nodded then pointed toward a pile of branches, still thick with the remains of decaying leaves. It was as good a place as any, he supposed, and the two of them worked in a companionable silence. Jeremy had always found the tending of repetitive tasks peaceful. And repetitive was an apt description of their lives. Diligently following a routine was important. They had to remain maniacal about it, deliberate in every facet of their lives. Survival meant a deep commitment. There were many dangerous gangs wandering the streets, and if he or Sam— or their supplies, for that matter—were found, they'd be killed or robbed. Or left to suffer the elements without supplies, which was often the same as being killed, he supposed. It was a dangerous scenario for anyone, though for Sam, it would be a death sentence.

Having shrouded the vehicles beneath a mound of dead foliage, they moved through the thick underbrush to the edge of the river, where they wordlessly stared and scrunched their noses. The sight sickened Jeremy. He suppressed a gag, wondering again why she'd wanted to come down here. Though it wasn't as damaged as some other bodies of water he had seen, it wasn't a place you'd want to bathe or take a drink. And though the water ran relatively clear in this spot, the smell was truly revolting. Along the bank, algae bloomed in fingerlike patterns: reds and greens like long twisting ribbons. He could detect an unnatural sheen to its surface, a rainbow brilliance of oil and chemicals, like a layer of rotting skin across a wound.

Behind him, Sam was clearing the forest floor, settling their tarp on a blanket of dead leaves. "What should we eat?" she asked, her voice light, as if this were a Sunday picnic.

He dropped to his knees, shrugged the pack from his shoulder, and from it, selected a box of whole grain crackers and an old can of beans.

Smiling, she pulled a small lighter from her pocket and ignited the collection of wood at the edge of their camp. "I like the beans. They're sweet. But you know I like them best when they're hot."

He nodded and pushed himself to his feet, returned to the bikes to retrieve their small cooking pot. When he returned, she was flat on her belly, on the tarp, gnawing on crackers and pointing to their map, drawing a line across the page with a purple marker.

"So, Chattanooga you say? Right here?"

"That's right."

"Huntsville's next," she said, "It's not far. Barely over a hundred miles from here. By my estimate, we can make it in less than two days." She lifted her head. "Where to after that?"

Jeremy worked the rusted opener around the can. "Southwest toward Mississippi, then on to Arkansas."

"Can we follow the Mississippi river?" she asked excitedly.

"Hell no we can't. Absolutely not. We'll have to cross it, but we're sticking to the roads and the bridges. Far

13

away. We're not getting anywhere near that dump."

He could sense her disappointment and see it on her face, but he didn't anticipate the words that came next. Sometimes she was like that. She kept him on his toes. And sometimes, she took him off-guard completely.

"I wish Mom were here. Things would be better."

"Yeah. So do I. I know what you mean."

Eyes downcast, she swirled the beans with a smooth stick. "What name do you think she would have chosen for herself?"

"Mom? Hmm. That's a tough one. Maybe Angler? Guppy? Or Perch?"

She shook her head. "You're terrible at this." Biting her lip, she stirred the pot. "Starfish or Minnow. Either one would have worked."

It broke his heart to see her like this, and to hear her speak of her mother in the past tense.

"Searobin," he suggested.

She smiled. "Searobin. It's beautiful—beautiful and perfect, like she was." She met his gaze and nodded her approval. "Not bad, Carp. You usually suck at this."

Shifting on the tarp, he did his best to lighten the conversation. This particular subject led to nothing but despair. "Will you read to me tonight?"

"Not tonight." She pursed her lips. "I'm not in the mood tonight."

"Okay." And with that he knew she'd fallen into a mood, and once she had, there was little he could say or do to lift her out of it. She was a girl who had recently lost her mother. He was a man who had recently lost his wife. She deserved her moods, and then some. He let her be.

They ate in silence, an unnatural silence, something that was freakish for this part of the country. She'd been right, he remarked. The purling water was calming. But the absence of ambient sound still bothered him. Jeremy remembered his childhood and the cabin, the woods, and their shelter in the mountains of Sevierville,

Tennessee. They would sit on the deck, late into the evening, surrounded by the sounds of an animate forest. Back then a rich diversity of species still existed. Well, he corrected himself, not rich. Just more. More than existed today. And there'd been insects, too, a chorus of voices: singing cicadas and chirping crickets, the occasional croaking forest toad, none of which existed today, of course. Or if they did, they could rarely be heard.

This riverbank seemed devoid of life entirely. What was the thing people used to say? Something about insects inheriting the earth? Not so, after all. Not even close. Insects—like everything else—died with the oceans.

"I wish we were still back at home," Sam said.

"Yeah. Me too." He scrutinized her shadowed face in the dark, and the outline of her body, set aglow by their small cook fire. "Sam, we don't have to sleep outside, you know. How many empty homes did we pass along the way? How many side streets and private cul-de-sacs? How many large houses with white picket fences? It was your idea to sleep out here. We can leave if you want, find something better. To be honest, that's probably a good idea. It's not safe out here. It makes me uncomfortable."

"Just one more night," she said softly, a plea. "I swear, after that, I'm done. I'm finished with the river, with all of it, now. I just wanted to see it one time, is all."

Pushing her bowl aside, she curled on the blanket. When she slept, she would always put her back against his, because she said it made her feel safe and protected. He could see she was tired—physically and mentally, and for the thousandth time, their changed lives amazed him. Things had gone sour in such a short amount of time. When the three of them were a family, they would stay up late. Jeremy and Susan would drink wine from the ark, while Sam would read to them from Harry Potter books. Or the three would play cards or Monopoly by candlelight. They'd lived in a perfect sanctuary, on a mountain. But that was gone, now, and they were constantly moving. Rest

15

and peace were remembered possessions. Life had turned upside down. Jeremy had always considered himself a night owl. He'd always gone to bed late, and risen even later. But things were different now. He was different. His body was different. He matched nature's circadian rhythm. The rising and setting of the sun was his alarm clock. In truth—though he was loath to admit it—he slept more soundly than he had in years.

He settled on his back, made a trough of the leaves, and peered into the star-speckled sky. "So," he asked her. "What's the verdict? Now that you've seen the river, what do you make of it?"

She murmured her reply in a sleepy voice. "It's lovely, really. It's peaceful. I'm trying to imagine the way it was before."

The silence was complete until her voice cleaved it. "I'd like to know where we're going, Carp. You know I don't care for surprises anymore."

"Give me your number first."

She answered with a groan, but raised herself on an elbow and held her arm before the light of the fire. "One hundred seven," she called out irritably.

Instantly at ease, he smothered their fire, while she settled back onto the tarp. It was never a good idea to sleep beside a fire. A fire was a beacon to those who roamed the night. It broadcasted latitude and longitude to dangerous people, drawing miscreant travelers from their various tortured paths.

"I'm waiting," she whispered. "Where are we going?"

"To San Diego, Sam."

He felt her flinch. "To the ocean?"

"Yep. It's what you said you wanted."

He wouldn't tell her the real reason they were going, or that her life depended on him getting her there. And he definitely wouldn't tell her the truth: that they were running out of time, and quickly. He would keep that information to himself a while longer.

"Yes," she replied. "It's what I said I wanted. I'm just surprised is all, surprised you'd take me there." Suddenly pensive, she let the silence stretch between them. "Is it really dead though? I mean, really? How can something so big actually die? Weren't there millions of fish in the sea?"

"Not millions, Sam. Trillions of fish. Hundreds of trillions. Trillions upon trillions of trillions. Such a large number you couldn't imagine it."

"And you're certain all of it's dead?"

"Afraid so."

"San Diego's a long way, Carp."

She was right. Nodding to the face of the moon, he answered, "Yep. It is. But we can make it. Slowly but surely, we'll make our way there. Fifty miles a day. That has to be our goal."

"Has to be our goal?"

She didn't miss a beat, though he chose not to answer that particular question. He knew she'd work out his plan eventually. Sooner or later, she'd discover his motives. As her breathing evened, he held his own, but just when he thought she'd finally dropped off to sleep, she spoke.

"We're running out of disks, aren't we, Carp? Tell me the truth."

"Yes, Sam. We're running out of disks."

"It's Pike."

"Yes, Pike. We're running out of disks."

She said nothing in response and his heart skipped a beat. He worried at the boldness of the harsh revelation. With so many miles yet to travel, it was much too soon for her to panic. Peering at her through the dark, his throat suddenly tightened. She deserved more than this, more than he was giving her. But wasn't that the goal of this journey? He felt her move.

"Was the ocean beautiful when you saw it?" she

asked.

"No," he replied. "It was terrifying. It was dark, lonely, barren, desolate."

"Okay," she murmured. "I'll go with you, Dad. I love you."

"I love you too, Sam."

But in a way you can say that after leaving the sea, after all those millions of years of living inside of the sea, we took the ocean with us. When a woman makes a baby, she gives it water, inside her body, to grow in. That water inside her body is almost exactly the same as the water of the sea. It is salty, by just the same amount. She makes a little ocean, in her body. And not only this. Our blood and our sweating, they are both salty, almost exactly like the water from the sea is salty. We carry oceans inside of us, in our blood and our sweat. And we are crying the oceans, in our tears.

—Gregory David Roberts

CHAPTER 2
55 Years Prior

She slipped her hand into his and grasped it firmly. "Olivia Abner. Pleased to meet you."

"Liam Colt. So this is your boat?"

With fondness, her eyes swept the Goblin's vast silhouette. For a support ship, she was impressive, a sleek catamaran with an aluminum hull and wave-piercing bow. Olivia pointed toward the center of the stern where a large crane was suspended over a hangar. A two-man submersible, attached to length of cable, was secured to a winch by a heavy steel hook.

"Nope. Not mine. She's a loaner from the institute. She'll take us to the drop point, where we'll board the Savior III. We'll descend about ninety feet, give or take."

"Ninety feet," he repeated nervously, fumbling the files in his arms. "Okay. No biggie. I can handle ninety feet."

His hand moved to the back of his neck. If he were holding a kerchief, he'd be pressing it to his skin, like a preacher behind the pulpit on a hot summer day. Smiling, she gently touched his arm. "That's right. I forgot. You're not used to this. You're a lab geek from D.C., aren't you? Ever been in a submersible before?"

"Back in college. Older models though. Nothing as agile as this appears to be. But I consider myself one of the cool geeks, thank you very much." He seemed to relax as he turned to face the sun-glistening water. "I typically work the sidelines, crunch the numbers, that sort of thing. I'm usually analyzing samples in a lab, but these days...well." He sucked in a breath. "These days, I go where I'm needed, I suppose. These days, I try to check as many things off my bucket list as I can."

She nodded, unable to respond to that. These days, she tried not to think of her bucket list, though maybe she should. "Okay, cool geek. Works for me. Welcome aboard. Let's talk schematics." She turned and held out an arm, inviting him to board the Goblin's wide transom.

As he approached the craft secured to the crane, his eyes became round as saucers. "Beautiful vessel."

"She is—light too. She'll take us down swiftly. Nothing to worry about. We'll be topside again before you know it. Let me assure you, Dr. Colt," she added, stroking the smooth metal as she would a cherished pet. "The Savior was designed for robust missions—much more robust than this will be—and at much greater depths, I might add. So don't worry. She'll have absolutely no problem transporting the two of us." Olivia turned to a tanned man behind her, in white linen pants and a faded Pink Floyd T-shirt. "I'd like you to meet our captain for the day. Liam Colt, meet Captain Steve Pryon."

She watched the captain shake the scientist's hand, her eyes traveling over his inappropriate clothing. He certainly wasn't a seaman. He'd worn jeans for one. Olivia hated jeans. What horribly constricting garments they were, nothing more than attractively cut straight jackets for the legs. She'd never be caught dead aboard a ship wearing jeans. She much preferred khakis or loose, billowy linens. He'd also worn flip-flops, she noted with a frown. An experienced seaman would never wear flip-flops. Sneakers were better. Bare feet were best.

Other than that, she supposed he was handsome. He was pale, for sure, perhaps a little stiff. But his eyes were warm, and his hair...well...unique. Were it not for the topknot, crowning his head, she may have pegged him as somewhat uptight. These days, wasn't that called a 'man-bun'? She smiled. Maybe not a geek after all.

He plucked a Dramamine from his pocket and slipped it into his mouth. Great, she sighed. This should be good. She gave the captain a meaningful look. "Steve, we'll stay topside, if that's okay. Out in the breeze. Keep it fresh."

"Aye-aye, Liv," He tipped his cap. "Be ready in ten."

She led the scientist toward the bow and sat opposite him on the sofa-style seating. "So, tell me if I'm understanding this correctly. You've commissioned this vessel to take samples of the dead zone."

He laid his files across his lap, visibly trying to calm himself. Clearly he wasn't comfortable at sea. "I haven't commissioned this vessel, per se. My employer has. I'm here at the behest of Washington D.C., the D.C. Institute of Marine Sciences, to be exact."

"You're a government employee?" she asked incredulously. With a raised brow, she examined him anew. There was no way in hell she was buying that story. His style was too laid-back. Tiny rips and snags ran the length of his jeans. He certainly didn't look like a government agent.

"I said I was here at their behest." He waived a hand. "I'm not officially on the payroll. They've sent me to obtain water samples at various depths, to test my findings, and to then report back. Typically a dead zone collects at coastal areas, at the mouths of rivers or other waterways. They're caused by runoffs carrying fertilizer, sewage, and other industrial pollutants. These, in turn, cause phytoplankton blooms, which use up all the available oxygen in a given area, creating a dead zone for all wildlife—"

"I know what dead zones are," she interrupted him smoothly.

He coughed and smoothed strands of hair from his face. "Right. Of course you do. I won't dumb it down. I'm here to test this area for several specific elements, particularly nitrogen and phosphorous."

"That all?" She raised a skeptical brow. "Nitrogen and phosphorous? Nothing else? Not checking for sudden increases in oxygen?"

He blinked. "What exactly do you do, Miss Abner? Or is it 'Mrs.?'"

"It's Ms. or Olivia, if you prefer, and I'm not just here as your escort, Dr. Colt. I'm also a biological oceanographer."

The corners of his mouth lifted into a smile. "So I guess you're the brawn and I'm the brains."

She shook her head. "That's a common misconception. We're actually more alike than you'd think. You study the elements and properties of seawater, and I study the forms of life that make that water their home."

He nodded, casually crossing one ankle over the other. "You're right, I suppose. Though sometimes I admire what you do more than what I do. I've never been much for fieldwork myself. To be honest, I've never been much of a seaman, though I happen to love the sea. Go figure." He lifted his shoulders, humbling himself. "I chose a rather ridiculous profession for myself. Man suffers from seasickness then makes the sea his life's work. But I've made it work for me. That's what counts. I get to do what I love to do, and I get to make it my own." He cocked his head. "Still jealous of you, though. My lab is a white-walled building of concrete and steel, full of chemicals and test tubes. You get all of this." He gestured toward the water then lifted his face and squinted into the sun. "Whatever all of this has become, I suppose."

Sitting back, she tucked her legs beneath her, and looked him straight in the eye. "Are you able to level with me, Liam? Are you here to evaluate the recent Hail Mary? Are you here to see if they've fixed this disaster?"

"They?"

"The government, of course"

"Oh. Them." He peered across the peaceful waves, eyes unfocused, as if he could see something she couldn't. "It's not so much a Hail Mary, Olivia. The science is actually sound. A few months ago, in an attempt to stimulate life, they installed the oxygen pumps. And if you stop to think about it, it's quite a feat of geoengineering. If it works at the mouth of the dirty Mississippi, it might actually work at much larger sites. Think of the implications."

"Oh, trust me. I am. Don't get me wrong. I agree with you. It is quite a feat of modern science. The implementation of it doesn't bother me. It's the timing that sucks. They always get that wrong." She tilted her head. "Their attempts—at the beginning of the twenty-second century, to reduce the amount of waste being dumped into the river—failed, so now, they're turning to technology. Don't you find that a little insane? That a species as intelligent and resourceful as ours can't see fit to attack the problem at its source?"

"Can't see fit to, or won't?"

"Touché. And you elegantly made my point for me, Dr. Colt. As a species, we're excellent at treating the

symptoms, yet we shy away from examining the cause."
She sighed and folded her hands. "So, that's what you're
here to do, isn't it? Treat the symptoms. Take the samples.
See how well we're managing the problem."

He laced his hands over a knee. "I'm here to test
for signs of improvement, and to report my findings to
D.C.—that's all. May I ask what you're here to do—
besides pilot the submersible, of course."

She shrugged. "Same as you, though not officially.
Today, I'll be taking a few samples of my own."

"And what do you expect to find, Ms. Abner?"

She met his gaze and then quickly looked away. "I
don't expect to find anything, really. I expect the ocean to
be as dead and empty as it's been for a decade."

With that, she stood and checked her watch.
"Time to go. I need to check in with the captain." She
pointed. "And you need to change into your wetsuit."

"Wetsuit?" he groaned. "We're going into the
water?"

"Of course not. They're strictly precautionary."

Again, her gaze crawled over his attire and she
found herself stifling a grin. "I'm sorry, but you're not
descending these waters in my boat wearing jeans and flip-
flops, Dr. Colt."

He watched her rise from the white leather sofa,
and tracked her as she moved toward the stern of the boat.
A biological oceanographer? Her? She certainly didn't look
like a scientist. At least not any he'd seen recently.
Straightening, he slid to the edge of the bench, and peering
over the side of the boat, examined the water lapping the
hull. All of this is for show, he thought dismally. It's all just
a waste of time. But show or not, he'd do his part. He'd
take his samples. He'd do as he was told—not that he
expected anything to have changed. He agreed with
Olivia—though he hadn't said as much. Her point about

the timing was apt. How had she so eloquently put it? Oh. Right. That the timing had sucked. She was right. It was simply too late, and everyone knew it.

He remembered a time when the dead zones were seasonal. They would appear toward the end of spring and dissipate in early September, when the tropical storms swept ashore. But that was over a decade ago, and everything had changed in such a short amount of time. Now the dead zones covered a much larger area, so many square miles that they were present year-round. There were hundreds of them now, over 2,000, to be exact, and they weren't even the ocean's deadliest problem.

He rummaged his files and for his pH graphs. While on this excursion, he would test for something else. He was eager to study the oxygen levels, but also the water's acidity. In his office, he'd examined countless reports, but he wanted to take his own samples firsthand. The oceans faced myriad attacks. Scientists like Liam were looking for markers, specific signals that would herald the end. He hated acting like pessimist, of course, but for a long time now, he'd known what was coming. He'd read the signs and interpreted the data. The oceans, simply stated, couldn't be saved. Things were well past the proverbial tipping point—so far, in fact, that he'd started making plans. Detailed plans. Long-term plans. Plans that involved multiple lists, and supplies, stockpiles of food, and bottles of water.

He'd even settled on a specific place, high in the Tennessee Mountains. It was secure and secluded, surrounded by acres of uninhabited forestland. He'd even purchased a cabin in which to live, a comfortable home at the top of a rise, a cozy lodge with a bird's eye view, where one might sit and watch the end of the world.

"Liam?" Olivia called out. "We're ready." She held up a wetsuit, at which he groaned, but begrudgingly took below deck. Dressing quickly, he tried to calm his nerves, though his stomach was still tied into knots. He'd never seen a dead zone up close before, much less from ninety feet below the surface. It was exhilarating, to say the least, though terrifying, too. Gallons of emptiness, pressing atop him, curtains of blackness, a cold dead tomb full of bones and teeth: the anticipation was making him nauseous.

Olivia, on the other hand, was strictly business. When he returned topside, she offered her hand to help him climb into the submersible. She talked through various safety precautions and emergency procedures. She was patient, possessed of a calm bedside manner, and he barely noticed when the winch began to turn, until the submersible dipped below dark cloudy waters. A thick glass dome offered panoramic views of miles and miles of empty water. He watched it crest the top of the dome and forced himself to relax. This was a superb craft, he told himself, as he settled onto his black leather chair, and Olivia, of course, was an accomplished pilot. She was obviously comfortable in front of the controls. Despite his anxiety, he willed himself to breath evenly.

"I suppose—first—you'd like to collect samples at about thirty feet?"

Her voice crackled through the headphones, making him jump like a frightened schoolgirl. Shuffling his papers, he fumbled for the volume control. Dear God. He needed to pull himself together. He wiped his palms against the slick rubber of his suit, nearly laughing out loud at his foolishness. How ridiculous he must seem to her. He was a chemical oceanographer, for Pete's sake, a lifelong professional, a man who had always he loved the sea. It was, in his opinion, the planet's last uncharted territory. Forget deep space or the frozen Antarctic. Ocean life was largely undiscovered, and as alien as anything a Hollywood makeup artist could ever create.

He breathed to a count of ten then scrutinized his surroundings. The yellow glow of the submersible's lights cast a peculiar green haze to the environment, yet failed to reveal signs of life. The waters were barren and cold, save for small fragments of plant and debris, which spun with the movements of the tides—and the propulsion of the oxygen pumps, he presumed.

He peered at the depth gauge. Twenty-eight feet. An involuntary shudder shook his body.

Olivia placed a hand on his knee. "Everything all right?"

He cleared his throat. "It's fine. It's just a strange feeling, is all. It's actually quite uncomfortable. Eerie to see it in person, I suppose. There's absolutely nothing down here. It's dead. It's a giant tub of water we can't drink." He gripped his armrests and peered into the abyss. "There's nothing here at all. It's astounding. Look at this place. What have we done?"

Her voice was distant, her words edged with sorrow. "I know how you feel. It's inconceivable. We're piloting a craft through a giant bathtub. We may see a jellyfish or two, if we're lucky, but other than that, this world is extinct."

Leaning forward, he peered into the vast field of water. Endless and deep, it was an immense and massive maw, pressing onto them from all sides. The absence of life—in a strange sort of way—was more frightening than an underwater zoo could ever be. A nervous laugh bubbled from his lips.

"I feel like I'm starring in some lousy Jaws remake, like at any minute, a giant shark will come swimming out of the blackness to attack the sub."

"Trust me, Liam. That's not going to happen. There haven't been sharks in this part of the ocean for at least a decade, no fish for longer than that."

"Olivia, tell me. And please—be honest. In your opinion, are the oceans beyond saving?"

He bit his lip. Why the hell had he said that? Why did he have to be such an alarmist? No, he thought. Alarmist was kind. He was pretty sure he'd just sounded like a kook. He didn't want to bum her out, or sound like a crazed doomsayer wearing a tin foil hat. He'd never believed in outlandish conspiracy theories. He just wanted to hear her opinion on the matter, the opinion of someone objective and learned, someone with a background similar to his own.

She turned to him suddenly, caught him by surprise. How attractive she was, he marveled again, her face silhouetted in soft cerulean light. Her reply was soft and rich with emotion. "Unfortunately I do, Dr. Colt."

"Liam, please."

"Unfortunately I think we're past the point of no return, Liam. But I don't think it was one thing or another. It was a perfect storm of events, so to speak: the collapse of the Berkut oil platform, the increased levels of CO2, the pollutants, the contaminates, and the resulting acidification of the oceans."

She returned her gaze to the waters beyond the glass. "Think of it, Liam, of the political stage. China had become one of the world's most powerful nations—if not the most powerful nation—of our time. It nearly took the baton from the United States. A mere turn of fate handed the reigns back to us, a mathematical calculation they somehow got wrong. To put it simply, they overfished their waters, which resulted in three quarters of their population starving to death. And it was the same in Japan, South Korea, and parts of Africa, too. Add to that the destruction of the world's coral reefs, and well…it was too much to bear. The death of the reefs set off a chain reaction, and the rest is history, so to speak."

She was right. "It all began with the extinction of the whales."

"Yes," she said. "It did. Well, to be clear, it began with the plankton. But for the sake of argument, we'll go with the whales."

With a final look at the submersible's controls, she diverted his attention to the craft's metal appendage. "Okay. We're here. We're suspended at about thirty feet.

That mechanical arm will gather our samples. After that, we'll descend another thirty more feet."

He watched her work and admired her skill, the dexterity of her fingers as they traveled across the many buttons and levers. He hadn't meant to discuss the extinctions, but there was something about her demeanor that calmed him. He was curious about her. He wanted to know more. "If you don't mind me asking, Olivia, what attracted you to this occupation?"

She shrugged, though he caught the fleeting flash of a smile. "Once, when I was a little girl, my parents took me to Destin, Florida. I had never seen water that clear, or that blue, or sand that fine, or that white. I remember the way it felt beneath my feet. We made drip-sand castles, with tall spires and deep moats, and we collected beautiful shells along the shoreline. It was the first time I'd ever seen the ocean."

She hazarded a glance in his direction and smiled. "That was when that strip of the gulf was still habitable. The emerald coast was what they called it back then. And what an apt description it was. Emerald." Her wistful smile made him sad. "It was a place where water sparkled green beneath the sun. It was almost as if God had cast gems across the surface." Peering at him sidelong, she shrugged. "My love affair with the ocean began there, I suppose, and I haven't lost interest ever since."

She met his gaze and her smile broadened. He found himself staring at her teeth.

"That summer we took a tour on a glass-bottom boat, and I can't explain in words how beautiful it was: the colors and textures of the reefs, the vibrancy and variety of fish. It was as if a painter had used every available color on his palette, chosen at random, yet perfectly blended. I loved that it was at once haphazard and harmonious. That summer, it captured my heart and imagination, and it hasn't let me go since then."

When she exhaled softly, he realized he'd been

staring, long after she'd finished her story. He was mesmerized, and decided to press her further. He was probably bordering on kooky again.

"Olivia, do you think about the future? About what you'll do if the world collapses. More than it has already, I mean."

"No. I don't think about things like that. And in truth, I'm not a good planner. I'll level with you, Liam, there's a small part of me that still hopes humanity can make it through this. I still believe we can turn things around, dig ourselves out of this mess we've made. I mean, really." She lifted her hands in the air. "How can we let it all go? It's unthinkable. Not only that, it's shameful."

"It is. And though it's good to believe in happy endings, in times like these, one must also be prudent. One must consider the facts as they are." Glimpsing at her sidelong, he added. "I guess it's a good thing you met me, Olivia. I happen to be an excellent planner."

"Are you flirting with me, Liam?"

Damn right he was.

They collected their samples at thirty feet then descended to sixty and did the same. As they worked, they spoke of trivial things, kept the mood light despite the depressing landscape. They were isolated in a thick curtain of blackness, and were the only two living organisms for miles around. Liam had never felt more alone or detached, and though unnerving at times, it was an odd sort of peace: the whirring sounds of the submersible's engines, the purring of oxygen as it flowed through the vents. He couldn't take his eyes off the water. The ocean had been ailing since before he could remember, for more than a century, at least. It had been suffering a slow decline for ages. It was a patient fighting the rot of cancer, a victim falling prey to a deadly parasite. This strange world around him was suffocating.

Through heavy obsidian layers, the craft descended, until a sudden swirl of sand and silt began to obscure their vision. Liam pointed. "The pumps. Be careful. Don't get too close."

The mechanical processes were upsetting the water, which rocked the craft with the swell of the tides. Liam seized his armrests with talon-like fingers. To see the apparatus up close was unnerving. Gallons of water were being sucked into the pumps, treated and enriched, and then expelled from the rear. It was nothing short of remarkable.

Olivia angled the craft, shining the submersible's light on the enormous apparatus. Pipes and tubes, like a writhing pit of snakes, crawled across the sea floor, while sand billowed from both openings at the rear. It reminded Liam of a complex CPR device, attempting to rejuvenate a long-dead patient.

The craft rolled slightly to the right. Liam cried out in surprise. *Jesus,* he grimaced. *Get hold of yourself. You sound like a twelve year-old girl.*

Olivia responded by pulling the craft higher. "This is as close as we can get, I'm afraid. Any closer, and we'll be sucked into the business end of one of those tubes."

"Let's get our samples and get out of here."

"Works for me," she said, her jaw firm. As she worked the levers, the mechanical arm took samples from the turbulent waters, while the submersible's light exposed the ductwork below. Her eyes widened at the complexity of it. "It's huge. It must have cost millions," she breathed.

"It did. Billions, actually—if you include the labor cost to set it all up." He brought a hand to his temple and applied pressure. "I guess we'll find out if it was money well spent."

A green light flashed at Olivia's left hand. The samples had been taken. Time to leave. She folded the arm inside the submersible's body. Peering at Liam, her brow creased with concern. "You know this isn't scalable, don't you? The concept barely makes sense. Think about it. What's the long-range plan? To set this up across every dead zone? Who's going to pay for all of this?"

"Don't know. But I do know this: they won't pay for anything if it doesn't work." With a sigh, he took a last look at the man-made circulatory system. She was right. It didn't make sense. Synthesized life was no life at all. None of this belonged down here. He felt a sudden impulse to return to the surface. "We've got what we came for, Olivia. Let's go. I don't know about you, but I need a drink."

With graceful elegance and a whisper of silk, she slipped into the high-back chair opposite his.

"You're late," he noted. "But you look beautiful, so I guess I can find it in my heart to forgive you."

With a smile, she lifted her napkin from the table. "So tell me, Dr. Colt. What's the verdict?"

"You're certainly not one for small talk, are you?"

"Nope. Not when it comes to this. So spill it. You've already tested the samples, I'm sure. If it were me, I know I would have. So out with it. I've been waiting all day. Put me out of my misery. Are the pumps working? Have they saved humanity? Has technology finally saved the world?"

Leaning forward, he inspected the deep cobalt of her eyes. Such an unusual color they were. So unique. How he hated to mute their sparkle. He took a breath. "You tell me, Olivia. What do you think? Do you believe technology can save our species?"

After briefly meeting his gaze, she looked away and lifted her glass of Pinot to the light. He waited. Her reply, when it came, was devastating.

"No. I don't. Though I once did, perhaps. I don't know anymore. Once, I believe there was a chance for us, a chance to recover a small piece of what was lost. But I don't think so anymore. I was wrong. I think that time has come and gone."

"You're right."

"I'm right?" she repeated, crestfallen.

"I'm sorry."

She straightened in her chair. "Then tell me everything. And don't sugarcoat it. I need to know the truth"

"The pumps aren't solving the issue. The Gulf dead zone—for the foreseeable future—will remain quite dead, I'm afraid. Unless another solution can be found."

Sitting back, she visibly collected herself then scanned the room and lifted a finger. "Excuse me," she called out to the waitress. "Scotch, please."

"Two," he added. "Please make that two."

Several times, as the evening progressed, Liam caught himself staring at her. Her green dress was enchanting and simple, the color vibrant against bronzed skin. She had tied her hair back in a loose and messy bun, knotted at the crown of her head. Wispy tendrils had fallen to her shoulders. She was sophisticated in a way that left him breathless.

Though he tried his best to keep the conversation light, the ominous truth bore down on their shoulders. They were scientists, after all, he reminded himself, professionals with the same background and education. They had too much in common to discuss other things. And the truth was unbelievable, too surreal to imagine. The world was falling to pieces around them, and they clung to each other as they slogged through the facts. She was a kindred spirit who shared his beliefs. End-of-the-world notwithstanding, he remarked, he was enjoying the evening immensely.

"So tell me, Liam, what's next for you?"

"Well," he replied, reaching under the table. "Back to D.C. in the morning." He pulled a slim case from the bag at his feet. "To present my findings to the committee. After that, I'm off to the Far East."

"Okay. And what do you think the committee will do with your findings?"

He popped the glucometer into the tip of his finger. "Oh, I'm sure they'll schedule more think tanks, summon more scientists and specialists, try to implement a few fresh ideas. I'm impressed they've rallied to the cause. That's promising. And I'm moved that they care about finding solutions. It's just a shame they reacted so late."

She smiled. "You mean to say that their timing sucks."

"Yeah." He grinned back. "Their timing sucks."

He read the glucometer then twisted the dial on his pen to 4.

"Type 1?" she asked, as he dosed himself.

"Yep. Since I was twelve."

"So, what grand adventure awaits you in the Far East?"

"More investigative testing, I'm afraid. I'm off to the coast of Japan, this time. To Komatsu, to be exact."

She leaned forward excitedly. "You're being sent to investigate the giant jellies, aren't you? The recent bloom off the coast of Japan."

"That's right." He raised an appreciative brow. "You certainly know your current events. They're sending me to Echizen to investigate the bloom. The jellyfish are capsizing fishing boats there, and destroying what remains of a dying ecosystem. I've been asked to run tests to determine the cause."

"But you already know the cause," she scoffed.

"True. But I'm going anyway. I do what I'm told. These days, most of what I do is busy work. And yes—I'm certain I know the cause. It's the water's pH, in my opinion. My latest tests have revealed a startling range, somewhere between 7.6 and 7.9."

Whistling low, she sat back in her chair. "That's a perfect breeding ground for the jellies."

"It is. Pair that with the extinction of predatory fish and you have yourself a tough situation. The jellyfish are running amuck in that area. I'm not sure what to expect."

She reached across the table and touched his hand. "I want to see it, too. Take me with you."

Leaning forward, he rested his elbows on the table while trying to suppress a shit-eating grin. "Let me get this straight. You want me to take you halfway around the globe to see a runaway population of giant jellyfish. Am I getting that right?" He lifted a brow. "How incredibly romantic. What an amazing second date that'll be."

"It will." She smiled. "It's my kind of romance, at least. Besides, I've got way too much vacation saved up at work. I can't think of a better way to use it."

It is a curious situation that the sea, from which life first arose should now be threatened by the activities of one form of that life. But the sea, though changed in a sinister way, will continue to exist; the threat is rather to life itself.

—Rachel Carson

CHAPTER 3
7 Years Prior

FEBRUARY 8TH, 2169
SMOKEY MOUNTAINS
TENNESSEE

She shook her head, her hands fluttering in the air.

"We can't do it, Jeremy. It's not clean." She glanced wildly about the room. "I've changed my mind. We can't do this to her."

As he gazed into his wife's frightened eyes, Jeremy was sure his heart would break. Tears had pooled and were leaking down her cheeks.

"Susan, we talked about this. We have to. We have no choice. The insulin we have won't last much longer. Every year, the pills are less and less effective. In the long run, this is the only way to keep her alive. This might be her last chance to live a normal life. We've done the research. We know the facts. And we know that this is our best shot."

"But look at this place. It's not sanitary."

He tracked her gaze as it flitted around the room, from heaps of old newspapers, to stacks of dated books, to dirty laundry, piled high on the divan. Several days worth of dirty dishes had been left to soak in the sink. The cabin was cluttered, untidy even, but that wasn't the same as unsanitary. It wasn't unclean—so to speak. That was true. But it wasn't a hospital; that was the issue. Over the years, they'd grown accustomed to hospitals, but hospitals had failed a long time ago. Hospitals weren't an option anymore. Their halls had long gone ghosted and silent. The sick and dying now fended for themselves.

Jeremy ground his molars. They were lucky to have located such a specialized doctor, luckier still that he'd agreed to perform this surgery—though agreement had come at a price, he thought, and it had been a very expensive price. Doctor Jack had agreed perform this procedure in exchange for a list of supplies, and though the list was long, Jeremy had gladly obliged. The negotiation was more than he or Susan had dared hope for. It was an answer to a problem that had haunted them for years.

He turned to her, suddenly doubting his convictions. "Susan, if you really want to leave, we can. This has to be a unified decision. I won't make it alone. I can't have that on my conscience. But if we choose to leave, we have to devise an alternative plan. The insulin we have won't last. And it's not just the quantity I'm worried about. You know as well as I do, it's the quality that matters. The pills are becoming less potent each year. They'll spoil eventually. They already are. As time goes by, a higher dose will be needed to achieve the same effect. And what will we do when that happens? What will we do when we run out entirely? We've foraged for years, and what have we gained? A mediocre-sized stash that decreases in value as the years go by. We can forage 'till we're blue in the face, if we want, but it won't change the quality of the product we find. It doesn't matter how many

39

caches we find in an old shoebox or behind a dusty curio. Not if what we find is useless to her." Lifting his wife's chin, he kissed the tip of her nose. "My father sacrificed his life for Sam. I'd like to honor that gift, Suse. Let's do what we came here to do. Let's be bold. Let's give her the opportunity to live a long and healthy life—whatever that life may be."

She snaked her arms around his neck, and laid her head on his shoulder. "Don't misunderstand what I'm saying. I'm thankful for your father, for the sacrifices he made—more thankful than you ever could know. I'm just afraid, is all, afraid of what could happen." Raising her head, she waved her arm around the room. "And afraid of this crazy idea. This surgery is difficult in the best of conditions. But here? Now? In this shitty mountain cabin? The risk of infection is that much worse. What are the chances she'll heal without complications?"

He pursed his lips. She was making good points. "But my father considered that as well, did he not? Susan, we may be the luckiest people in the entire country. We may even be the luckiest people on earth. Even the good doctor said so himself. Listen to me Susan, and listen to me well: had the circumstances been different, I would not have allowed that man into our home. In truth, we can't trust anyone. Hell, he's her doctor and I don't even trust him. I just didn't have a choice. I did what I had to do." Jeremy ran a hand through his hair. He needed to get her beyond this fear. As he laid out his arguments, his beliefs solidified. This was something they just had to do. "Susan," he said gently, "Don't fear infection. If there's one thing we have plenty of, its bottles of antibiotics. Come on. Let's do this. Let's follow our plan. We'll keep her sugars low, give her a steady stream of antibiotics. We can get her through this. Together, we can. This is just a one-time thing. If we get her the implant, she stands a fighting chance."

As he held his breath, he watched his wife slowly

come around. She rounded her shoulders and firmed her chin. She wiped her eyes and cleared her voice. She'd never let Sam see her cry. It was something Jeremy admired her for, something he'd always respected her for.

"Okay," she said weakly. "Let's do it. Let's get her the implant and get back home. Let's plant the garden like we promised her we would. Let's put this whole damn thing in our rearview mirror as fast as humanly possible."

Kissing her again, he drew strength from the warmth of her lips, and the two of them moved into the doctor's living room, where Sam was seated in an overstuffed chair. A picture book was splayed across her lap. She looked so innocent, so young and fragile. Her legs, unable to reach the ground, swung back and forth like an ominous pendulum. She raised her head and examined their faces, though Jeremy couldn't read her expression.

"So," she said. "do I get the disk player?"

Susan frowned. "Stop calling it that. It sounds so barbaric when you say it like that."

Jeremy moved to the chair, lowered himself in front of it, and gathered his daughter into his arms. "It's official, robot-girl. You're getting the disk player."

She playfully pinched his nose. "And I'll be able to play music from my belly, right?"

"Wrong. It's not that kind of disk player, kiddo." He swung her around before burying his face into her neck.

"But I won't have to swallow those icky pills anymore?"

Nodding, he cradled her against his chest. The pills were so weak she'd been forced to consume more. And lately, the doses were more and more frequent. She was tiring of the loathsome routine.

"Yep. That's the plan," he reassured her, "no more pills. How does that sound?"

"Sounds good. But will it hurt? I really don't want it to hurt."

"It won't hurt. You'll sleep through the whole thing. Just like a rock."

"Rocks don't sleep, Dad. They're inanimate objects."

"True." He smiled. "But if they did, you'd be sleeping like them." Setting her back to her feet, he caught her hand in his. "And guess what else we're planning to do? When you're better, we've decided to plant the garden."

"Really?" Her eyes lit up. "Says who?"

"Says Mom."

She clapped her hands. When Mom said it, it was real. As he watched her, his breath caught in his throat. He dared not speak, lest his voice falter or crack. He didn't want her knowing how frightened he was. God, how he loved her—how he loved them both. He was good at pretending to be strong in front of Susan, but Sam had always seen right through him. His knees felt weak. He broke out in a cold sweat. Beneath his calm exterior, he was little more than a cowering child. He'd be lost if something happened to her—to either of them, for that matter.

Releasing her hand, he moved to the front door, where beyond, the mountain air felt crisp on his face. Inhaling its piney scent, he tried to calm himself. It was now or never. He bolstered himself.

Parked on the front stoop was a large cart, full of supplies, items the doctor had picked by hand. There were hundreds of canned goods, packages of crackers, large bags of rice, piled high and bundled with thick rubber bands. There were even—though he loathed parting with a single one—three small canisters of sardines. But there was something missing: water. Water was where Jeremy drew the line. He would never use it as a bargaining chip. It would never be part of any negotiation he would make.

Setting his hands to the cart, he shivered as he recalled his first meeting with the doctor, a month ago.

When Dr. Jack had first seen the room—or the ark, as Jeremy's family called it—his eyes had gone wide, his expression one of awe. Water was gold—no—more precious than gold, and Jeremy—as the doctor had learned—was wealthy.

He recalled every moment of the encounter as if it had happened only yesterday. Doctor Jack had looked upon the neat rows of bottles with unbridled envy, practically salivated down his chin as he did. Pints and liters, gallons and ounces: for years, Jeremy's father had stockpiled all he could.

"Incredible!" the doctor had exclaimed out loud. "How many cases will you trade?"

"Not a one." It wasn't that Jeremy hadn't anticipated the question. He'd expected it, of course. He'd known it would come, just as soon as the man crossed the threshold, in fact. He'd suggested a meeting in a neutral location, where the doctor could make selections from a list of items. Jack had refused. He hadn't made it easy.

"If you get to see where I live," he had said, "then I should get to see where you live, as well. It's only fair, Jeremy. I'm sure you understand. Though we're both honorable men, we're not fools. If there isn't an equal risk to us both, this transaction doesn't make sense. I'm sorry, but that's the best I can do. It's the only offer I'm willing to make."

It was a dangerous gamble for both men to make. But the doctor's requirements had been clear. If Jeremy had refused, he could have lost him. It was a risk he hadn't been willing to take. And so he'd complied with the doctor's demands, with every single one—except for the water, of course.

The doctor had seemed an honorable man, for once he saw inside the ark, he could have set an unreasonable price. He could have ransomed Sam's health for whatever he wanted. And as desperate as Jeremy was, he would have paid it. He and Susan would have given anything. Thankfully the doctor had settled on a portion of supplies, and though the portion was large, it was only a portion.

"No cases of water, I'm afraid," Jeremy had said, in a voice that sounded more confident than he'd felt. "I don't trade water. Not ever. Choose whatever items you want from the aisles. Fill this cart to the brim, if you want. But I'm sorry: the water's off limits."

He was thankful they'd reached an agreement, but scrutinizing the lot beneath the pale morning light, his stomach did a nauseating flip. He wouldn't delude himself. It was a large portion of what they had left. What he and Susan were doing was risky. Though few humans inhabited this world, those who remained were dangerous and unpredictable. In this harsh new reality, one was either predator or prey. Jeremy wondered which one he'd become.

Taking a breath, he picked up a stone, and used it to prop open the cabin doors. It was truly massive, this cart Jack had chosen. It was one of those canvas laundry caddies they had used in hospitals and prisons, with a sturdy wood cover and four wheels at the base, and it was filled to the brim with life-sustaining supplies—his family's life-sustaining supplies. With a sigh, he kicked the metal brakes off the wheels, rolled it past the threshold, and through the double doors.

By the time he pushed it inside, the owner of the cabin had entered the room, and with unconcealed glee, looked upon his new wares. He bowed to Jeremy, his freshly washed hands held awkwardly in front of him.

"She'll be fine, Jeremy. I know what you're thinking. My setup might not look like much, but it'll get the job done, and she'll be better for having done it. I'll insert the unit, and inside, a fresh disk, and I'll give you the rest of my supply. I have twenty-three insulin disks left, for which I have no use anymore. I can't see myself performing this surgery again. So at the end of today, you'll have two year's worth of insulin. I'll give you a list of locations, as well, places you can scout for more disks. There are gangs out there that'll trade for other wares, and I'd be happy to give you their names and locations, but I strongly urge you to seek other means. Find your own replacements, if you can. Be smart. You don't want other people knowing what you have." He struggled to pull plastic gloves over damp hands. "The unit will supply her with a steady dose of insulin, but that doesn't mean she shouldn't monitor herself. Monitoring her sugars if a part of her life, and always will be, regardless of the disks. Physical exertion causes blood sugar levels to spike. Stress does as well. Be wary of both. I'm sorry Jeremy, but this is the best I can do. Once she has the unit in place, it'll be your job to maintain it, to feed it. For the rest of her life, she'll need to seek additional product."

Jeremy quickly glanced at Susan, a wordless plea for her approval. He watched her terror-stricken eyes behold the doctor, from his faded white coat, to his inappropriate pants, to the dirty sneakers on his feet. She was barely keeping it together. So was he.

She shifted uncomfortably then crouched beside her daughter. "How bout it pumpkin? What do you say? It's your body. Tell me what you want."

Sam's innocent voice broke Jeremy's heart, and reminded him of the weight of this decision. A parent holds his child's life in his hands. With a trusting smile and a confidence that was well beyond her years, Sam reached out and touched her mother's face, thumbed away a fallen tear, and said gently, "You always know what's best for me, Mom. What do you think? Should I become robot-girl?"

Gathering her precious daughter into her arms, Susan let loose a quiet sob. "I do, baby. I really do. And we'll be here when you wake up. Both of us. I'm sorry to say, but you're stuck with us for life."

Jeremy moved to his wife's side and clung to her

with desperate hands, and together, they watched the most precious thing they'd ever created be taken to the bedroom of an old mountain cabin to undergo pancreatic surgery. It was madness. He wanted to tear his hair out. What the hell was he doing? Thinking? He could figure this out. He could find another way. Couldn't he? Shouldn't he? He owed it to Sam.

His mind began to race, as he doubted himself. They could bike to the public library one more time; try their luck among the stacks—try to find a different solution. Though they'd practically torn the place apart, who knew? It was possible they'd missed something important.

For months, they'd searched the drafty building, rummaging through information by candlelight, but it was impossible to know if they'd seen everything. There were thousands of books on the subject of diabetes. Maybe they should try another week of solid research. They had the time, didn't they? They still had the pills: bottles and bottles, inside the ark.

He recalled sitting vigil by the library entrance, Glock G43 in his hand, while a bleary-eyed Susan combed the endless shelves, tossing reject after reject into the growing pile in the center of the room. She was doggedly persistent, frustratingly so, and would only switch places when her eyes gave out.

The books—unlike the rest of the burnt-out building—had luckily remained pristine. Books weren't desirable to people anymore. Information wasn't something people traded things for. Food was the currency, and water the coinage. Data and biological facts were useless. A wealth of information had been waiting for them.

For weeks and weeks, they went home empty-handed, for all of the reference materials had led to the same unfortunate conclusions. The first to die in a world without medicine were the diabetics and the chronically ill, or those unfortunate enough to require life support systems to live. Insulin simply wouldn't last. Without electricity and proper refrigeration, or production and careful maintenance, all liquid forms were lost in a matter of weeks. Technology had introduced the pills, of course, which were infinitely better than liquid. The encapsulated delivery system kept the insulin fresh for longer periods of time, but as Jeremy soon discovered, even the pills had their limitations. Pills weakened over time. It was unavoidable. Sam had only lived this long because of certain sacrifices Jeremy's father had made.

Watching his daughter disappear with Doctor Jack, Jeremy remembered the feelings of dejection, the endless hopelessness, the depression that followed weeks of fruitless research. He should be thankful, he reminded himself, for this rare opportunity being presented to them. He and Susan should be kissing the doctor's feet. They'd spent countless hours inside that library. Days became weeks, weeks became months, and after a while, despair had set in. Despite their efforts to think positive, the situation had become hopeless.

Until one night it wasn't.

Susan had been the one to make that discovery. It was a night Jeremy would never forget. He was stationed at the library's entrance, once again, staring at the sky and picking at his nails. It had been a long evening after many long evenings when he heard her calling from the darkened building.

"I found something!" she'd yelled, and he'd squinted into the dark.

"Show me later. Put it in the pack. It's late, Susan. We need to get back to the cabin."

Her scowl had been audible from his position by the door. "Jeremy, get over here. Now. You can leave the door for five freaking minutes. There's no one coming. We're the only ones here."

He'd let the door fall behind him with a frown.

She'd summoned him like this, several times before, and just like before, it was probably nothing. With each passing day enthusiasm was harder to find. And though he hadn't wanted to burst her bubble, he was starting to believe they'd never find a solution. There had been too many disappointments thus far, when his spirits had been lifted and then dashed to the ground. Every book had led them to the same frustrating conclusion: science hadn't worked this out yet—this particular problem affecting millions of people.

With a frown, he stooped beside her. "Susan, it's late, and I'm tired. Let's get back to the cabin before Sam wakes up. We've been gone too long already."

His wife's eyes glittered in the wan candlelight, and her fingers trembled as they flew across the pages. "Jeremy," she pointed out, "Look here. There was a new device they were testing back then. It was already in production before everything collapsed. No." She shook her head, correcting herself, her thoughts coming faster than her mouth could shape the words. "It was released to the public before the collapse, but we didn't hear about it because we'd already gone to ground."

Leaning forward wordlessly, he tried to make out the odd-looking device on the page, while refusing to let his excitement surge.

"It was fully vetted," she continued. "It passed all human trials. Before the collapse, people were already starting to use it. It's an implant, Jeremy. It delivers insulin in a different way. They were planning its widespread release before everything fell to shit. That's why we never heard of it before—why most people didn't, in fact." She pointed to the page. "Insulidisk. That's what it was called. It's nanotechnology, Jeremy. The insulin is encapsulated so it lasts much longer, like the pills only better, more advanced. The delivery is slow and consistent." She set her hand atop his and squeezed, and for a moment, he dared to let hope blossom. "This is the answer we've been looking for. These disks won't spoil for decades, maybe longer."

She flipped the page and pointed. "Look here. It's a list of doctors who can perform the surgery, people who were trained before the collapse. There are three right here in Tennessee! All we have to do is find a legitimate doctor, and see what he's willing to trade."

They'd spent the remainder of the evening side-by-side, combing through manuals, and reading about of the fundamental concepts of nanotechnology. The device—if it lived up to the studies that were written about it—offered Sam unprecedented freedom, and before long, Jeremy was drinking the Kool-Aid. The plan was easy. Find man. Make trade. And for a man of Jeremy's considerable means, the trading part would be easy.

He remembered, a wistful smile on his face, something his father had said. "Before society collapsed, I wasn't a rich man—not by traditional standards. It took an apocalyptic event for me to become a man of means." And now, all of that wealth had passed to Jeremy. He could have anything he wanted in this world—end of the world notwithstanding, of course—but what he wanted most was to have a healthy daughter.

When the door to the spare bedroom closed and locked, Jeremy squeezed Susan's hand. Anxiety was a parasite, slithering beneath his skin, a leech, sapping him of strength, leaving him weak. The waiting, he knew, would be a torment. They tried to busy themselves by walking the paths of old hiking trails and aged roadways, now impassable by vehicles, other than bikes. What foliage had survived the death of the oceans had pushed through the pavement, thrusting it upward, leaving behind a green and black patchwork quilt. Not that it mattered. Not anymore. Road maintenance was of little concern now. Cars were useless without a viable source of gasoline, and what little remained had long ago been pillaged. Gas stations had been raided; the covers of tanks pried up and tossed aside, and the contents drained with hand-held pumps. What little was left had long spoiled. Jeremy's cabin was equipped with a generator, of course, but even that had ceased to operate years ago.

Having negotiated the winding paths as many times as they could make themselves do it, they returned to the cabin to pace its halls. Susan busied herself by cleaning Jack's kitchen and unpacking his brand new collection of supplies, and Jeremy did his best to occupy his mind by delving into the man's considerable medical library. It was hard to focus, to keep his head to task, and to keep his feet from pacing the room. When the door finally opened, the sun had dipped below the mountaintops, which were a jagged line across a pink-speckled sky. He had fallen into a fitful sleep, yet shot to his feet at the sound of the door, his knees nearly buckling at the sight of the doctor. Blood dappled the man's lab coat. Unable to breathe, Jeremy watched him carefully. He pulled his mask from his nose and mopped his brow, pulled off a glove with a startling snap.

"It went well," he said, his voice calm. "She's a fighter. She's strong. The device is in place and the stitching looks good." He removed the other glove. Powder rippled through the air. "She'll be waking in a few short hours, so I suggest you take her home as soon as you can. Get her comfortable before the pain meds wear off." He glanced at the neat rows of supplies that lined his kitchen counter. "I see you've emptied the cart for me. Take it with you when you leave. Wheel her home in it. It's yours. You don't even have to bring it back. Don't suppose I'll need it after this."

Jeremy was grateful Susan managed to find her voice, for he was much too emotional to find his own. "Jack," she began with a cough. "We can't thank you enough: for the disks, for everything, for making this easy, for doing what others probably wouldn't, for taking an unnecessary risk...for all of it. I can't find the appropriate words to say."

Jack nodded, a smile playing on his lips. How good it must feel to be a doctor again, to feel needed, competent, proficient in a field. "Happy to, Susan," he said with a grunt, collapsing into the nearest chair and resting his head against the cushions. "Suppose—if I'm being honest—it felt good to do something productive again. It felt good to help my fellow man. And," he added, "I sorely needed the supplies." He heaved a sigh, looking suddenly haggard. "This is the way of the world, I suppose: bartering and trading, using one's skills, providing a service in exchange for goods. To be honest, I'm thankful to have met the two of you, thankful you'd let me do this at all. If you hadn't, I'd have had to find a another solution to my food and beverage problem." He massaged his temples and raised his head. "I threw in a little something extra, for good measure, a blood sugar counter on the inside of her wrist. It was the newest technology available at the time. Not many people received them. The concept is simple and it's easy to use. It's a display unit, powered by the body's metabolic processes. You can read her current blood sugar any time. And it never needs replacing, winding, or recharging. If she's got one now, she's got it for life."

Jeremy felt himself slowly relax, despite the gore that smeared the man's cheek. "Amazing," he breathed. "Thank you, Doctor." He was suddenly as heavy as a ton of cement bricks. "I suppose you're right, Jack. Trading and dealing is the future now—the only way to survive this new world. And you've got a skill men would give their eyeteeth for." He peered around the room, as if seeing it for the first time. "I don't mean to pry, but are you alone up here?"

"Lost my wife a few years back. Buried her up on the hill." Shaking his head, he scrutinized his hands as if digging her grave had been a betrayal he hadn't yet forgiven them for. "I couldn't run tests or diagnosis her officially, but I'm fairly certain it was cancer that got her."

Jeremy cringed at the horrific images. It was something he'd often had nightmares about. What if Sam or Susan contracted a life threatening illness? What if he did, for that matter?

"Toward the end, there was nothing I could do," Jack continued. "Besides keep her drunk on scotch, that is. I ran through all the pain pills I could find: Percocet, Valium, even Advil and Tylenol. In the end, all I had to offer was good old-fashioned alcohol. I scoured the neighborhood for as much as I could find. It might surprise you to know how many folks keep a bottle of vodka in their underwear drawer." He lifted his head and offered a weak smile, before his eyes lost focus as he reached for the memories. "I did everything I could think to do. But her pain became completely unmanageable. God, Jeremy, it felt so barbaric. At one point, I considered finding a leather strap for her to bite down on."

He sighed and dropped his hands his sides. "Her death was a miracle of mercy, if you ask me. I was so broken-hearted to see her go, yet relieved to see an end to her suffering. Crazy, isn't it? Never thought I'd feel that way."

Jeremy's heart went out to the lonely Doctor, but a deeper part of him, a much darker part, the shadow self that resides in us all, sprang and hissed. Get the hell out of here, it said. Go now. Get your family and run from this cabin, from the ghosts that reside in this house. Get away from this pain and this misery, from the phantoms that shuffle these empty hallways, from the ghosts that curl in these stone-cold beds.

He knew it was a sudden and irrational fear. It wasn't like Jack's misfortunes were contagious. Death wasn't an oily film that multiplied and spread like a virus. His fear was childlike, not based in reality. But it was real enough, and it pushed him to his feet.

"We've taken enough of your time already. I'm

sure you're quite tired after what you just did, and it's a long way home for us to walk, particularly when pushing a cart." He lifted his hands. "I don't know what to say. Like Susan said, we can't thank you enough, for your hospitality, for your bravery when it came to my daughter. Ten carts of supplies couldn't repay this debt." Stepping forward, he thrust out a hand. "Doctor Jack. Our best to you. Always. If you need anything, you know where to find us."

Jack struggled from his chair to clasp Jeremy's hand. "Don't be a stranger. You hear me? We don't live that far from each other, you know. Seems to me, in this day and age, those of us who're left ought to seek one another's company."

He let Jeremy's hand drop, and Jeremy felt a sudden stab of guilt. Where did this impulse to run come from? Why did he always want to seclude his family? Perhaps the doctor was right about neighborly ties. Jeremy wasn't a psychologist, but humans didn't flourish in isolation and confinement. Was making a friend so bad?

"Perhaps we will, Jack. We'll give it some thought."

Turning to Susan, he gave her "the look", the wordless gesture only married people understand. She gave him a nod and crossed the room, and together they lowered Sam into the cart, swaddled her in blankets, and began the long journey home.

For over three hours they walked in silence, negotiating the cart across a broken terrain, while jostling it as little as possible. They weaved between overgrown grasses and fallen trees, and the disintegrating fragments of man-made structures, and after a while, Jeremy realized something important. He felt happier than he had in years, like a man who could contemplate the depths of a problem and work out a viable solution. He'd given his daughter a chance at a real future. Smiling, he walked in a strange sort of peace, his gaze fixed on the purpling sky and his sights set on the glorious future.

At the press conference for the film he impressed everyone with his complete sincerity and innocence. he said he had come to see the sea for the first time and marveled at how clean it was. someone told him that, in fact, it wasn't. 'when the world is emptied of human beings' he said, 'it will become so again.

—Werner Herzog

CHAPTER 4
Present Day

As always, they arose with the dawning of the sun. Of late, mornings had become his favorite time of day, even more so now that they had the bikes. He'd come to cherish these brief moments of comfort before the sun beat down on their backs. With the wind in his face, and the satisfying burn of physical exertion in his muscles, and the radiance and solitude of a world that belonged only to them, Jeremy found a strange sort of peace. Wasn't it remarkable, he thought, in awe, that the soul could find beauty in the worst of circumstances?

Cupping a hand to his brow, he scanned the strip of highway that had once been US-64. It was nothing but a stretch of black pavement now, with washed-out lines and faded oil stains: remnants of decades of road traffic. The blotches and smears of car lubricants and old grease felt like a crime scene to Jeremy, like the cadaverous remains of a large-scale mass murder, the likes of which hadn't happened for millions of years. The world, he considered as he peered at the fungi-covered foliage, had effectively been delivered back to the plants. It was as if the plants moved with purpose now, as if they deliberately pushed at manmade structures in an effort to extinguish humanity from their home. For Earth, humans were a hiccup in time, a setback or hindrance, a brief nightmare. The planet was recovering from years of abuse. It was trying to move on. But could it?

Jeremy wondered if that was even possible. Humans were resilient. He'd seen it firsthand. What he'd seen over the past decade—what little contact he'd had with others, of course—was nothing if not dichotomous. He'd seen the best and worst of his species. There were moments of brilliance, ingenuity, and compassion, but also of savagery and unspeakable brutality. And what of himself? What of his own actions?

What of the boy, his inner voice sneered.

Yes. What of the boy? What about all of that? Was he better than anyone else? Than those who had torn his family apart? Sam didn't know the details of his cruelty. His actions had been unbelievably dark, yet he hadn't been man enough to own them yet. Shrugging off the debilitating thoughts, he refocused his attention on the bright new day, and realized suddenly how much he missed the birds. Only the music of their whistles and warbles could further enrich this glorious morning. But like most wildlife, they too, had died.

Pedaling faster, he caught up to Sam.

"How goes it up here?"

"Not bad," she yelled back.

Lately, she had wanted to take the lead, and lately, he'd seen no reason not to let her. The risk seemed minimal. After all, they hadn't seen another living soul for weeks. Not since after the fire, he thought. Not since the mother and her boy. His thoughts dared to linger on that innocent face, which made his skin prickle and his neck begin to itch. Shaking his head, he attempted to scatter the ominous memories.

"How many more miles on this road?" Sam called out.

"A little over seventy. We won't make it tonight, so I've planned a short stop along the way."

"Where to?"

"Scottsboro."

"Scottsboro? What's in Scottsboro?"

"A Walmart."

Though she rolled her eyes, Jeremy wasn't fooled. Sam loved foraging a Walmart—though most were completely ransacked by now. The shelves would most likely be empty, but he'd learned long ago that it was always wise to check.

"The population of Scottsboro, at its peak, was only around seventeen thousand people. So I'm hoping we'll find something useful," he said. She didn't respond to that so he enticed her further. "Scottsboro also had a public library."

She lifted a brow at that. "Is that so? There's a book I want to read. Perfect timing."

"Yeah? You're finally tired of Harry Potter? What about Twilight? What are we today? Team Edward or Team Jacob? I need to know where I stand."

"Don't make fun," she scowled over her shoulder. "You liked it, too. Admit it. It's good."

"Never!" He yelled out. "So what's the book?"

She swerved around a hollowed-out tire. "Twenty Thousand Leagues Under the Sea."

"Jules Verne." He nodded appreciatively. "A classic. I'm impressed. We'll find it." Eying the shapes of rusted cars in their path, he pulled in front of her to take the lead.

"Sam," he said gently, "While we're in Scottsboro, I'd also like to locate a nursery."

"A nursery?" He heard her front tire skid against a patch of sand. "Oh, no, Carp. I'm not stepping foot inside a nursery. What do you expect to find in there? I'm a bit too old for diapers and binkies."

"Not a baby nursery, Pike. A garden nursery. A place where plants and seeds were once sold. I was thinking, once we get to San Diego, we could choose a large home in the hills of Point Loma, something that overlooks the bay. What do you think? And I was thinking we could plant a new garden there, too."

He awaited her reply while holding his breath. When she spoke, her voice was thick with emotion. "I think Mom would have liked that."

"Me too. So I'm thinking, first, we find a nursery, if we can, stock up on seeds, things like that. Anything grows in San Diego, Pike."

"Anything grew in Sevierville, too."

Yeah. It did. She had a point.

He knew this wound was still fresh and tender. It would likely fester for the rest of her life, just as it would for him. He frowned. There were times when he feared she might never recover. Leaving home had been the most difficult thing they'd ever had to do. They'd had it all in Sevierville. Everything they'd needed, anything they'd desired—thanks to Jeremy's father, of course.

But Jeremy had become too comfortable there, and comfort can lead to complacency. He'd begun to believe them invincible, untouchable in a world that was dead and decaying. His confidence was their undoing. He'd thought they were safe, that they lived inside some impenetrable bubble that could keep the claws of extinction from reaching them. Despite the thin air and the foulness of the rain, despite the spoiling food and the failing power grids, their family had remained and flourished for years, defiant in the face of annihilation. It was the type of confidence that accumulated over time, solidified by years and years of routine.

But he'd been wrong, dead wrong, and they'd paid a steep price.

That cabin was the only place Sam had ever called home. She was born there. She'd lived and thrived there. It was the place that connected her to her mother. Perhaps he was hoping to recreate those feelings in San Diego, in a home on a cliff, by the sea. And maybe the garden would be the first step. Planting it had brought their family closer together. It was one thing to read books beside a warm fire, but another to work alongside another person, shoulder-to-shoulder, bringing life back to the earth. Those memories were treasures Jeremy kept close to his heart, riches that were more valuable to him than money ever had been.

"Not like that," Susan corrected him gently, after he scattered spinach seeds across the rich, black soil.

In his memories, Sam's laugh had the resonance of a finely crafted wood chime. It was a sound he hadn't heard in a long time. "Dad, don't do that. If you throw them across the soil like that, they won't settle in and grow roots. They'll just blow away in the wind, right, Mom? He's doing it wrong."

In his mind's eye, he watched his daughter correct his mistake. She gathered the tiny seedlings and crouched beside small mounds of earth to press each one beneath the top layer of soil.

He crossed his arms and appraised her with pride, a small smile pulling at the corners of his mouth. "Yep. You're way's better, kiddo. I stand corrected."

He and Susan had overturned the soil and trenched long rows down the side of the hill, but Sam had done all the planting. She'd planted each seed on her own, while they watched.

"Now," Susan said. "All we have to do is wait for it to rain."

"Wait for it to rain? But what if it doesn't rain? What happens then?"

"If it doesn't rain, pumpkin, then nothing will grow. Sorry to say, but that's just how it works."

Jeremy remembered Sam running out the door, morning after morning, bare feet scampering across the warm earth. She'd drop to her hands and knees, inspect the soil, clap her hands if she saw any sprouts. "Look," she'd call out, "We've got baby broccoli!" They'd follow her, point, ooh and aah, and then smile. Against all odds, their garden had grown. The delicate buds had pushed through the soil, struggling to thrive in a dying environment and bathe in the sun's morning light.

It had been one of those bright fresh mornings when Jeremy first mentioned the laundry cart to Susan. They'd been standing shoulder-to-shoulder, coffee cups in hands, watching Sam dart between the rows and prop up tomato plants with sticks.

That particular morning, smoke curled on the horizon, from an explosion that had happened the night before. It was still visible over the peaks of the mountain, a reminder that people were uncomfortably close. He hadn't meant to scare Susan, but true to form, had done it.

"I've been thinking about the cart," he had mumbled to her. "We're not using it for anything specific right now, and I have an idea. Let's fill it with supplies, wheel it to the base of the mountain and leave it there."

"Whatever for?" she queried softly, her eyes tracking her child.

"I don't know. A security measure, I guess." He shrugged. "After what happened last night, it just seems—"

"But we don't know what happened last night."

"True," he allowed, "but we can certainly guess. That wasn't a natural fire, Suse. It was an explosion. Nature doesn't create explosions. There are people on that hill. People who—in my opinion—are uncomfortably close to our home."

"What does any of that have to do with the cart?"

He swallowed. She wouldn't like this. "I think we should fill it with a ration of supplies and leave it somewhere in the woods. We should hide it somewhere where nobody else can find it, where no one knows where to look but us. And I think we should camouflage it with big green tarps, weatherize it inside a thick casing of plastic."

Her brows knit together as she connected the dots. "You mean like a get-away cart, Jeremy? You think we'll be driven from our home?"

He shrugged non-committedly, in an effort to take the edge off her alarm. "I don't know. I mean, I guess that could happen. The way I see it, it's just sound planning. What could it hurt? We've got plenty of supplies, and the cart's just sitting there. I think it's sound planning. Don't you?"

"Perhaps. But if we do it," she said slowly, "we do it late at night, after Sam goes to bed. I don't want her thinking that could happen to us. I don't want her thinking such a thing is even possible."

And thank heavens they'd eventually done it. Because soon enough they had needed it, and it had ended up saving their lives. Like so many others, they became vagabonds, refugees who were thrust from their home. They eventually lost their perfect life in the mountains, the one they'd grown to love and cherish, and were forced to brave the discomforts of a new one.

Sadly, I am one of a growing chorus of people who believe that, yes, it is too late to turn things around. So many species are in such low numbers, and habitats are so badly damaged, that restoring them to their original splendor is simply no longer possible. I believe that our only option now is to decide how much we value what we currently have, and to decide what we are willing to do to maintain it -- or at least slow down its disappearance. But honestly, can you really see all 7 billion of us agreeing on that?"

—Dr. Lisa-Ann Gershwin

CHAPTER 5
55 Years Prior

SEPTEMBER 13TH, 2121
INSTITUTE OF MARINE SCIENCES
TEMPORARY BASE OFF THE SHORES OF ECHIZEN
SEA OF JAPAN

He watched from across the room as she poured herself another glass of juice. He admired the way her nightgown skimmed her curves. The bed was warm where she'd left it, his skin chilled in places where their bodies had touched.

"I think I might need another glass after this," she muttered to herself with a giggle. "Particularly after the day we just had."

"No wine?" he queried, trying to catch her hand.

A twinkle lit her eyes. "No wine. Not tonight."

As she crossed the room and slipped beneath the covers, he marveled at her effortless beauty. Her white silk gown whispered against the cotton sheets, and he immediately curled his legs around her body.

"I'm still in shock, as well," he agreed, easily reading her body language. "I've never seen a bloom that pervasive before. Hell, I've never seen a nomura jellyfish in person before. It's jarring, to say the least. They're huge. They're like something out of a science fiction movie."

She nodded. His skin prickled at the memory. The day had been truly extraordinary. The event was another nail in Earth's proverbial coffin. The crew of the Kazunoko had barely spoken English, but the language of fear was universal. Those sailors were frightened— frightened for their lives.

They'd sailed forty knots off the coast of Echizen, where they immediately encountered the bloom, and the size of it had taken Liam's breath away. For the rest of the day, the crew had worked tirelessly to keep the ship upstream of hundreds of tangling bodies.

When he first saw the swarm, Liam had reached for Olivia's hand, and the two had stood in silence and wonder, surveying the field of jellies around them. These were not the jellyfish Liam remembered as a young boy, swimming the murky waters off the Jersey Shore. No. These were Nomura's jellyfish, the stuff of monstrous nightmares. The specimens were massive. Their bells, in some cases, reached a length of seven feet. Olivia had estimated the weight of each at around 450 pounds. But it was more than the size of any one specimen that had turned Liam's stomach to acid. It was the sheer size of the bloom itself. There were hundreds upon hundreds of sliding bodies, a tangle that reached as far as the eye could see. They clustered and braided in a large floating mass.

"It's happening," he'd muttered to himself, horrified, as knots of poisonous tentacles weaved through the water. It was impossible to see where one jellyfish ended and the next began, and with a squeeze of her hand, Olivia had agreed.

"I'm here to test the composition of the water," he had told her, "but I don't think I need to run the tests at all. I can plainly see what's happening here."

"It's a multitude of things," she had breathed beside him. "And the result is absolutely remarkable. There's overfishing for one: the larger predators are all but extinct in this area, which is allowing the larva of these jellies to thrive at undocumented levels. There's nothing left to eat their young. Large predators gave this ecosystem its balance. But now that delicate balance is out of whack, which has allowed the jellies to overrun these waters. This area has effectively become another…" She shook her head.

"Another dead zone," he finished quietly. "Dropping her hand, he pulled a map from his pocket and pointed to the outline of China. "I think, chemically speaking, the root of the problem originated here. The runoff of fertilizers and sewage from China's coastal waters contributed to a bloom of phytoplankton."

She easily picked up the thread of his logic. "And the phytoplankton begat zooplankton, which is an ample supply of food for giant jellies."

"The temperature of the water increased," Liam added, "which increased the rate of polyp reproduction."

"Correct," she said. "And don't forget: jellyfish reproduce asexually. The warmer the water, the more they reproduce. Warmer temperatures only increase the speed at which they develop."

Liam had sighed and refolded the map, slipped it into his pocket and run a hand through his salty hair. "So if I follow this logic—using your biblical lexicon, of course—the water pollution begat the zooplankton, and the zooplankton begat the polyps. Warmer waters and a lack of natural predators begat the giant jellies. So." He took a deep breath. "What will the giant jellies beget?"

She cocked her head. "Umm…the end of sushi restaurants?"

"Cute." He smiled. "Very cute. And though I hate to admit it, you're right. The poisonous tentacles of these giant jellies will kill any fish that swims into their path. Imagine what happens when they're caught up in fishing nets. Nothing could survive but the jellies themselves."

She'd agreed and taken his logic one step further. "It's why entire catches have been lost. These jellyfish can eat ten times their weight in a single day. Their existence alone is wiping out large fish populations."

The afternoon, if nothing else, had been surreal. They watched the swarm of mindless carnivores while Liam took his samples. It was another stop on his worldwide tour of environmental devastation. Over the past few months, he'd journeyed from one disastrous event to the next, first to Sweden to study the moon jellies, which had cost the country millions of dollars, particularly after a large bloom had clogged the pipes of a nuclear power plant. The event had shut down half the country's power grid. After that, he'd been sent to Florida, and next to Cape Town, Africa, both of which were suffering deadly blooms of Box jellies and Irukandji, the two most toxic stings known to man. Those beaches had been closed permanently. Liam didn't expect them ever to open again.

Yes, he reflected, the day had been difficult. He fluffed the pillows behind his head. The jellyfish problem was one of many problems, but though significant, it was only an economic one. Liam was concerned about chemical issues.

"Olivia," he ventured cautiously. "I've done what I came here to do. I'm done. I've taken my samples. We're headed home tomorrow. Have you given any thought to what you'll do when we get back?"

The moment they'd arrived in Japan, members of the United States army had whisked them to the institute amid crowded streets of homeless refugees, displaced by hard economic times. These people had depended on the oceans for food and work. In as little as two decades, Japan had fallen hard. Once a technological giant, it had devolved into a third world country. It was difficult to witness firsthand. And after seeing it, Liam couldn't help but wonder what third world countries had become. Barren wastelands, he supposed. He didn't want to find out. The situation in Japan was grave. Liam wanted to leave as soon as possible.

Olivia untangled herself from his legs and sat cross-legged on the bed. She swirled her juice as if she wished it were wine. "What will I do next? Hmmm. I don't know. We did all we could in D.C." She shrugged. "We've done all we can here, too, I suppose. We've visited every natural disaster with a biological element. So there won't be many more that require my expertise. I suppose I'm no longer needed." She stared at her glass and then raised her head, meeting his gaze through lowered lashes. "But I'd like to stay with you, if I can."

As he stared into her deep blue eyes, he found himself wanting to voice his plan. It was a plan he had hatched weeks ago. Well, to be fair, it was one he'd put into motion several years before that; he just hadn't expected to be sharing it with someone else. The original blueprint of his post-apocalyptic life had lacked the element of companionship, and sitting here now, he found that startling. Had he envisioned for himself a life of solitude? He had planned so carefully. He'd thought of everything. He'd drawn maps, made lists, placed large orders with bulk suppliers, built vast storerooms with floor-to-ceiling racks. He'd purchased generators and weaponry, stockpiled water, medicines, and food. Yet what was life without a partner to share it with? Now that he'd gotten to know Olivia, a life without her seemed unimaginable. He couldn't just pack things up and abscond to the mountains by himself.

Peering into her glass of juice, he decided to lay his heart on the line. At this point, what did he have to lose? "Olivia," he risked, "I think I've fallen in love with you."

When she flinched, he immediately second-guessed his words. It was sudden, he knew. They barely knew each other. Would she think it too soon for such sentiments? But time, he reasoned, was a luxury they didn't have. He needed her to see the truth. Now. And fast.

"Before you say something, just listen," he said, his back stiff with anxiety. "Olivia, I think this is the beginning of the end."

When she opened her mouth, he held up a hand. "Wait," he said. "Hear me out. I don't want to sound like a lunatic here, but I'm not a fool either. Neither are you." Her mouth closed with a snap. He continued. "Liv, I think the time has come for me to go to ground." He shook his head to silence her objection. "I don't mean completely off the grid. Not yet. I just mean that it's time to make a change. It's time to select a place that meets certain criteria. It should be an isolated place, remote, with acres of wilderness and forestland to spare. It should be temperate, too, a place that could easily support plant and animal life, where despite the lower oxygen levels, plants could grow roots and flourish. It can't be arid or swampy. And it can't be overly-populated, or near a popular travel destination."

"Liam," she whispered, "What are you saying? Are you saying you're planning to leave me? I know we haven't been together that long, but…"

"No." He gathered her into his arms and pressed his mouth to her ear. "No. I'm asking if you'll come with me. Look around you, Liv. Look at this place. Society is crumbling around us. We need to get out of here, return stateside, move to an isolated place. Don't you get it?"

Pushing away from his chest, she met his gaze. "You think it's that bad already?"

"I do."

"Okay. Then tell me. What are the facts?"

He blew out a breath. "Jellyfish blooms notwithstanding, of course, the real problem lies in the chemistry. The oceans are becoming anoxic, Liv. I ran tests in Sweden, off the coast of India, in Wales, and here in Japan, as well. There's no fixing this issue. It's too late for that. We've reached the point of no return. It's time to make personal decisions. I'm afraid it's time to thinking selfishly. In D.C., the rumors have been circulating for months: the United States is planning to close its borders—permanently. For good this time."

He plucked the glass from her hand and set it on the nightstand. "Countries are beginning to close ranks. There are too many refugees seeking asylum, too many for any one country to support. The situation is every bit an economic one as it is a political one." Dropping her hands, he gathered his hair into a low ponytail at the base of his neck. "It's the anoxia that'll finally do us in. It already is. The Polar Regions are warming at a faster rate than the water at the equator, which has decreased the temperature differential between both regions. It's been happening for decades, but we're just beginning to see the effects. This temperature differential is what drives ocean circulation, and since that circulation has become less pronounced, the currents are shutting down altogether. Think of it, Liv. Think of what's happening. Without ocean circulation, the water won't turnover anymore. The currents shut down. Things become still. Oxygen no longer mixes with water, and bacteria takes over. Do you see what I'm saying? The oceans are becoming…" He searched for the right word.

"Stagnant," she finished dully.

"Yes. Stagnant. And what did you mother always tell you about stagnant water? Think about the effect a stagnant ocean would have on the world at large. If the oceans become stagnant pools of stinking water, how that would affect our planet?" Her eyes became round as saucers. "In a world like that, those who haven't planned will ultimately perish. Large-scale production of food will cease. Nothing new will be developed.

"Our country is rich in supplies," he continued. "There's a convenience mart or grocery store on every block, in every city, from coast to coast. But how long will those supplies last us? And how will people treat one another to claim the rights to them? It's a vision of a world I don't want to be a part of. It's a world we need to sequester ourselves from—until the worst of things pass, that is. I'm not suggesting a complete withdrawal from society. I'm not even suggesting the collapse is imminent. I only submit that we set up safety nets, that we sketch out a diagram of a possible new life—should the one that exists fail us." He gently took her hands in his. "Liv, I'm asking you to join me."

"Join you?"

Her eyes were wide. He had her full attention. And though he hadn't meant to say the words out loud, he found them spilling from his lips just the same.

"Liv, I'm asking you to marry me."

"Marry you?"

As her mouth dropped open, gooseflesh crawled across his arms and legs. It was too damn soon. He must sound like a nut. "You don't have to answer right away," he stammered, trying to backpedal but failing miserably. "There's no rush. I'm just posing the question. Just think about it. Take whatever time you need. It's just an idea. Just something to think about."

She placed a finger on his mouth to silence him, then replaced it with her lips and spoke softly against his mouth. "I don't need to think about it, because my answer is yes."

Inhaling her scent, he kissed her deeply. He'd never been so happy in his life.

"So, Colonel Custer," she smiled brilliantly. "Have you considered where we'll make our last stand?"

"Considered?" He shook his head smugly. "I haven't considered anything, Mrs. Colt. I've actually purchased it already."

She gasped. "Okay. Do tell. Where will I be living out my last days on this planet?"

"Sevierville," he said, "Sevierville, Tennessee. I purchased a cabin in the Smokey Mountains, a spacious home on the crest of a large hill, surrounded by thirty-seven acres of forestland."

She set down her juice, slid her body beneath his and snaked her bare legs around his waist. Her throaty whisper set fire to his body.

"A spacious one, huh? Spacious is good." She kissed his ear and the base of his throat. "Does it have a nursery?"

"A nursery?" He nearly choked.

Her lips curved into a smile against his mouth. "Yeah. A nursery. Come on now, Liam. You know how much I love my nightly glass of wine. Why do you think I'm drinking juice?"

Courage is not having the strength to go on; it is going on when you don't have the strength.

—Theodore Roosevelt

CHAPTER 6
1 Year Prior

MAY 17TH, 2175
SMOKEY MOUNTAINS
TENNESSEE

"I'm telling you," Jeremy warned his daughter, "Professor Snape's a Death Eater! He's fooling everyone, even you."

"But he isn't," Lifting her chin, Sam stared down the bridge of her nose. "He's not, Dad. I swear. If Dumbledore trusts him, then so do I."

Eyes twinkling, Jeremy turned to his wife. "Care to weigh in on this? What do you think?"

"Oh no." Susan showed him a palm. "I'm keeping my opinions to myself on this. It's early yet. The jury's still out for me. We've got a whole book left to read. Who knows?" She swirled the wine in her glass and frowned. "Enough wine for tonight. How about some hot chocolate?"

"Extra powder," Sam said, her nose buried in her book.

Balancing their dirty dishes in the crook of her

arm, Susan carried them back to the kitchen. In the morning, she'd take them out back, to the stream, to wash them in the water and dry them in the sun. The water was more acidic than it should be, of course, but for things like washing and bathing, it was harmless. And though it wouldn't kill them to strain, boil, and drink it, Jeremy preferred that they drink from the bottles in the ark.

"So," Susan asked as she banged around in the kitchen. "After we finish book seven, what's next?"

Sam closed the thick tome and gathered her hair into a messy bun. "The Twilight series, I'm thinking. Yes?"

Jeremy couldn't help but grimace openly. "You're gonna to put me through months and months of teen romance? That's cruel, Sam. I'm not ready for that. And to be honest, I'm not sure you're ready either."

"But I'm old enough, Dad. I'm thirteen now. I'm a teenager. What's the problem?"

She was right. It was the same argument they'd had several times before, every time she asked him for the books. She drummed her fingers against the book in her lap, and he fought the lump that was rising in his throat. She was staring him down, daring him to disagree. She held him in the palm of her hand and she knew it.

But he had his reasons for withholding those books. For as long as he and Susan had been able, they'd steered her away from the Twilight series. Not because she was young or immature. Quite the contrary, in fact. She was actually well balanced, self-possessed, mature for her age. The subject matter wasn't over her head. Sam's maturation didn't make Jeremy nervous. His weren't the fears that commonly plagued other fathers. His was a different kind of dread, a deeper fear, not of an abundance of unworthy suitors, knocking on their door to take her out for the evening, and not of sexual experimentation. His was a fear of the void awaiting her. Like a gaping maw it was, a deep and bottomless pit. Anxiety would choke him if he imagined her future. It was a cave where loneliness crouched and waited. Jeremy would give anything for her to enjoy the kind of puppy dog romances he had when he was a boy, but it wasn't in the cards for her. It wouldn't happen. Their family hadn't seen another living soul for years. To find additional sources of disks, he and Susan had ventured into the world, and on those trips, had encountered other people. But Sam hadn't accompanied them on those missions. For her, the world was all but empty.

Jeremy's father had built this cabin and equipped it with the best supplies money could buy. He'd planned for every possible need; given them a chance at life while millions of others had surely faced death. And he'd included the basics to live that life: food, water, shelter, and medications. But what of companionship and love? What of intimacy, affection, and warmth? Jeremy and Susan rarely spoke about the future, but there would surely come a day when things would change. Sam would be forced to provide for herself. It wouldn't be for decades, of course, God willing, but that day would undoubtedly come. Jeremy and Susan would grow old and die, and Sam would be left to fend for herself. But would her life be a life worth living? For what, Jeremy wondered, was life without the spice of human interaction to season it? Would Sam live out her days alone in this cabin, tending her gardens and reading her books? It was a lonely set of images, which he and Susan didn't openly discuss.

Peering at her delicate face, he felt a clenching in his gut. These were the reasons he withheld the books. He didn't want her comparing fiction with reality and realizing how strange her life really was. Though fiction, the sentiment behind the stories was real, and it broke Jeremy's heart to imagine her pain and the time she would spend yearning for something she'd never have. But he also couldn't protect her from certain truths forever. Perhaps it was time to get it over with. He watched his wife prepare mugs of powdered chocolate to heat over a flame. Would Sam ever experience the kind of love he felt for Susan? Marriage had given his life meaning. Susan brought him direction, hope, and love.

He felt himself caving, and with a sigh, turned to Sam. He was only postponing the inevitable, he supposed. He couldn't withhold the books forever. At some point she'd read them. Why not now?

"Okay, Sam," he said. "You win. We'll tackle the Twilight series next."

She smiled.

"Sucker," Susan murmured from the kitchen.

Yeah. He was.

A knock at the door drained the blood from his face, spiked his adrenaline, and set his feet in motion. It was such a curious sound to hear: the hollow rap of a fist against wood. It was the sound of a visitor, of another, and he found himself jumping from his chair with alarm. His eyes were wild and immediately sought Susan's.

"Jeremy?" she whispered, frozen mid-step, mugs of cold chocolate held awkwardly in front of her.

He whirled around and peered at Sam. She was standing, sword-straight, arms wooden at her sides. The book had spilled from her knees to the floor, and fear was coiling in her eyes like writhing snakes. It had to be after nine o'clock, possibly even ten. Something wasn't right. It was too late for visitors.

"Dad?" she whispered.

"Hide," he hissed, his voice sounding harsher than he'd intended it to. "Get behind the chair. Susan, stay in the kitchen."

As Susan moved for a gun in the cabinet, Jeremy moved for the door. He watched her widen her stance and remove the safety, and when she finally appeared ready, he peered through the peephole.

"Doctor Jack," he exclaimed, his heart pounding.

Although the image was tunneled and small, tension was visible in the man's posture and bearing. His lips were pressed into a thin line, and the muscles in his face were pulled taut. A thin trail of blood tracked the left side of his face, beginning at the hairline, just above his forehead, and running over the curve of his cheekbone. What the hell was he doing here?

"Jack," Jeremy spoke through the door, "What's happened? Why are you here?"

Jack shifted nervously from foot to foot. He was acting strange. Something was off. His gaze slid to the right and back, and his voice, though muffled, was clear when he spoke.

"Jeremy," he said, "I need help. Please. I'm hurt. I've had…an accident. I think I'm badly injured… internally I mean."

Jeremy's hand was still frozen on the knob. If the man had sustained an internal injury, how had he made it to their house in the dark? Something about the story rang false. The voice in his head hissed a warning. He tensed.

"Jack, how did you get here? How did you make it this far? Did you walk?" Confused, he shook his head and posed a different question. "How did you get that cut on your head?"

Jack lifted his palms to his temples and squeezed his eyes shut as if enduring a private torture. "I can't remember what happened exactly…I…I fell on the way over here, I think. It's all muddled up in my head. I fell down. I was knocked unconscious. I think I have a concussion, Jeremy."

Jeremy lifted his gaze to the piece of concave glass, and though he couldn't see through it, he felt naked beneath Jack's appraising stare. Jeremy's mind spun. What would he do? Though he wanted to help Jack, something wasn't right. For this, he had learned, was a strange new world. One could trust another, but only by degree, and certainly not in the dead of night. Before he could respond, Jack posed a different question—the question Jeremy had dreaded the most.

"Jeremy, please. Will you let me in? Can I come inside for just a moment? I need someone to watch over me for a while, take care of me while I gauge the severity of this wound. I shouldn't sleep alone. I mean—I shouldn't sleep at all. Not with an injury like this."

Jeremy glanced from the peephole to Susan. He was deeply conflicted, torn in two. This man had practically saved his daughter's life. How in good conscience could he turn him away?

"Susan?" he queried, lifting his hands from the door.

He needed her opinion to make this decision, but her eyes held the same uncertainty he felt. She shook her head slowly as she dithered, as yet unable to find her voice. An inappropriate laugh suddenly bubbled from his throat. "God, Susan. What have we become? Has it been so long since we've seen another person that we've forgotten simple things like neighborly courtesy?" Sweat gathered beneath his arms. "It's Doctor Jack, Suse. What are we doing? Are we being overly cautious here?"

When she spoke, her voice cracked. With a cough, she cleared it. "Okay. Let him in, but I'm not putting down this gun. Are we clear?"

With a nod, he returned his gaze to the peephole. "Jack, I'm opening the door. Slowly. We do this my way if we do it at all. Take three steps back, away from the door. Hold your hands in the air. Do it now."

Jack obeyed, but his movements were awkward and jerky. His gaze slid to the right once again, a doe caught in a Mack truck's headlights. Jeremy tracked him as he backed away from the door. When his field of vision was somewhat larger, Jeremy strained to see to each side of the man, but the peephole set frustrating limits to his view. There wasn't a backpack or rucksack in view, no supplies or gear with which Jack had traveled. Had he forgotten those too? How was that possible? Or did it, in fact, give credence to his story? If he'd sustained a head wound, it made sense. For who in his right mind would walk through the woods in the dead of night, without a bottle of water or a scrap of food? Maybe he really needed help.

Jeremy peered in his daughter's direction. He could see her shadow in relief against the wall as she crouched behind her chair. To someone else, she might be unnoticeable. It was the best they could do in a pinch, he decided.

"Jack," he said, disengaging the lock. "We do this slowly if we do it at all." Setting his hand to the knob, he opened the door, and peering through the blade-thin aperture, said, "Keep your hands up, Jack. Here's what we're going to—"

—Time seemed slower, though several things happened at once. Three men burst into his field of vision, throwing him backward as they leaned against the door. The door, when it opened, was ripped from Jeremy's hands, and with guns raised, two men rushed into the room.

"Hands up," one shouted. "Up where I can see 'em."

Jeremy could see Susan peripherally. There hadn't been time for her to run, or hide. He willed himself to stare straight into the man's eyes. "I'm unarmed," he choked, lifting his hands above his head.

Two of the men pushed farther into the room, while the third dragged Jack through the door and jostled him into a chair. When he met Jeremy's gaze, the doctor seemed to wilt. "I'm sorry," he whispered, guilt thick in his voice. "I'm so damn sorry. Should've let them kill me."

One of the men raised the barrel of his gun and leveled it on Jeremy's temple.

Susan flinched.

The gunman unfortunately caught it and spun. "Drop it, lady," he said, his tone businesslike, well practiced. It was as if he'd done this several times before. He was close to gaining the upper hand and motioned

Jeremy to sit on the sofa. Susan made an animal sound in her throat.

No! Jeremy screamed inside his head. Don't you dare drop that gun! Stay strong!

Over and over again, he willed her strength. She mustn't show weakness to these predatory men. Not while their family still had a fighting chance. They were three adults against three adults. All wasn't lost if one of them still had a gun.

Her eyes darted between the three strange men, snagged on Doctor Jack's head and widened. Her resolve was crumbling. Jeremy could feel it. He could see it, even from here. She wasn't ready for something like this. None of them were and it was Jeremy's fault. He'd never thought to prepare them for this.

Susan set her gaze on the gun that was pointed at Jeremy's temple. Beaten, she let her weapon fall from her fingers, clatter to the floor and spin away from her foot. When she raised her hands above her head, the man with the gun gave an approving nod. "So, Jeremy," he said almost comfortably, the only threat in the room now neutralized. "It is Jeremy, isn't it? Pleased to make your acquaintance, though I feel like I know you so well already." He glanced at the fire and the book on the floor. "What a pleasant evening you're having tonight. So tell me: where's this room I've heard so much about?"

Jeremy struggled to find his voice. "Room? What room?"

The man shook his head. "Uh-uh. Don't do that. Don't lie to me, Jeremy, or you'll learn that I'm not a patient man. I'm talking about your supply room."

With two of the men covering Jeremy and Jack, the third moved for Susan and grabbed her by the shoulders, and after pushing her down to the sofa beside Jeremy, paced a slow circle around the room. With eyes as wide as saucers, he beheld his surroundings. For the first time since they'd entered his home, Jeremy noticed how disheveled they were. Refugees of a dying world, their clothing was tattered and soiled, mismatched, and their shoes were split at the soles. They had the look of bandits, both thin and scraggy, in hand-me-down garments and stolen shoes; spoils from a world in which nothing new would ever be made.

Jesus, he thought miserably, this place must seem like a Vegas penthouse to these guys.

"This place is amazing," the third man muttered, as if plucking the thought from Jeremy's head. Coming to a stop in front of the fireplace, he examined the portraits on the mantel. Jeremy tensed. He was too close to Sam's hiding place. "This place is something else, Sturgeon," he said to one of his colleagues, extending his hands over the fire and rubbing them briskly. "Like a place I'd like to call home."

The man—apparently known as Sturgeon— returned his piercing gaze to Jeremy. "I asked you a question. The supply room. Where is it? The ark. Tell me where it is. Right now."

The ark? Jeremy shot an accusatory glance at Jack. The doctor had ratted his family out! To save his own skin, the traitorous Judas had betrayed a family of three. How could he have done that? It was disgusting, unthinkable, something Jeremy would never do. Jeremy tried to center himself. He lifted his shoulders, took a deep breath. Think about Susan. And Sam, he told himself. Stay strong for them. Just get them out alive. We'll figure out what to do later.

"Down there," he motioned with a nod of his head, the words dripping from his lips like acid. "End of the hall."

The second man took Sturgeon's place, and Sturgeon disappeared down the hall. Shit. That door was locked. He forgot to tell the man about needing a key. Jeremy always kept the ark locked down at night, and though he didn't want these men getting inside, he didn't want to anger them, either.

As expected, Sturgeon reappeared within seconds, and with the butt of his gun, struck Jeremy's head, connecting painfully with the side of his face. "Forget to mention something?" he hissed. "Don't fuck with me, Jeremy. I don't have time for this."

The coppery taste of blood flooded Jeremy's mouth, sharpening his thoughts and centering him. His mind raced as he considered his options. The cart at the edge of the forest, he thought, his mind grasping the edges of a plan. There was no way in hell these men were letting him keep the cabin. Not after they saw what was inside the ark. He and his family would be turned out or killed. He would do what he must to ensure it was the former. He'd appeal to this man's sympathies, if he could—if this man had sensitivities, of course.

Seizing the tenuous thread, he pulled. "Sir, if you let my wife go, I'll help you. I'll even—"

"The key, asshole. Where is the key? All I want to talk about now is the key."

"Okay. Right. And I'll tell you where it is. But first I want to know what you plan to do with us. I'm only asking for something small, for you to allow my wife to leave the cabin. It's a simple request. She can't possibly—"

In a rush of movement, he advanced three steps, raised his gun and squeezed the trigger. The report echoed loudly in the room, bouncing between wooden beams that crossed the cabin's vaulted ceiling, though it failed to mask Sam's piercing scream. Jeremy inspected the angle of the gun, as strange images danced behind his eyes. He'd expected to feel a sharp pain, a punch in the gut, or the hot burn of metal cutting skin. Curiously, he felt nothing at all. Maybe he was just in shock? In a strange sort of daze, he tracked the path of the gun, the acrid smell of gunpowder sharp in his nose. The trajectory was off. Had it been a warning shot? The weapon wasn't pointed in Jeremy's direction. It was pointed left of him. He didn't want to look. His neck was frozen, sparing him the pain of what he knew to be true.

Breaking his paralysis, he forced his head to turn.

There she sat, his beautiful wife, clutching her gut, blood oozing through her fingers. It was running onto the legs of her pants, one of the many pairs of khakis she'd inherited from her mother-in-law. His voice failed him as he took it all in. Her eyes were scrunched against her pain, and her breath was coming fast and shallow. Jeremy had never been shot, but he knew a bullet to the stomach was an excruciating death. Death? He shook his head incredulously. No. Susan wouldn't die. This wasn't over yet. He would get them out of this. There was more to be done.

Propelling himself into motion, he fumbled for the key in his pocket. The barrel of the gun swung ominously toward his head.

"No," he called out breathlessly. "Don't shoot. Please. The key. I've got it right here, in my pocket."

The man called 'Sturgeon', of all the crazy things, allowed Jeremy to pass him the key, while the third man— as yet unnamed—pulled Sam from behind her reading chair.

Dear God. Not Sam. Please not my baby girl.

Jeremy fought an anxiety attack as he beheld his daughter's stricken face. She'd gone ghostly white, her mouth agape as she beheld her mother's wound.

"I'm okay baby," Susan managed to say through clenched teeth. "Everything's gonna be alright. Do as the man says and we'll be okay."

As if the man had no heart or soul, Sturgeon turned from Jeremy's ailing family and motioned his partner to follow him to the ark. Jeremy sat stupidly, eyes pinned to his wife. But when he heard the key in the lock, he flinched. This is it, he despaired, the end. With no supplies and no place to go, his family would be thrust into the night, defenseless.

When the door to the ark opened, Jeremy heard the men gasp in unison. The man guarding Doctor Jack craned his neck, called out to his partners, took a step forward, ranging farther from his position by the door. "What is it, Sturg?" he called out. "Is it good? Cuda? What've they got?"

Cuda? Jeremy though. Had he just said Cuda? As in Barracuda? Had these men named themselves after long-extinct fish?

From the corner of his eye, Jeremy caught a twitch of fingers. He slowly moved his gaze to Doctor Jack, who nodded and lunged for the gunman without warning, and with a grace Jeremy hadn't thought possible for a man of his size and bearing, caught hold of the man and spun him to the ground. Jeremy dropped from the sofa to the floor, and rolling closer, clamped his hands across the intruder's mouth. When Jack wrestled the gun from his fist, he brought it to bear on the man's forehead. A tear tracked the side of Jack's face while he fought. Guilt was an anvil, crushing his spirit. He would shoot the man if Jeremy didn't stop him first.

"No!" Jeremy whispered. "Don't fire it, Jack! It's too loud! Stop! The others will hear!"

Jeremy held the intruder's head between his knees, holding firm like a vise as he avoided gnashing teeth.

"Strangle him," Jack spat, peering nervously over his shoulder. "Do it. Before they come back."

Strangle him?

Jeremy swung his head toward Susan. Strangle? Really? Her rosy skin had gone waxy and gray. Cold sweat dotted her forehead. She was trembling with unconcealed agony. She was dying. She'd already lost too much blood. It pooled around her body in ghastly red ribbons. She wasn't going to make it. Jeremy tried to catch his breath.

"Susan?" he whispered. "Strangle?"

He desperately needed her approval on this. Should he kill this man? This monster? This man who had entered their home and effectively stolen their future? Should he kill this man in front of their daughter? And should he do it with his own bare hands?

Briefly opening her eyes, Susan nodded. "Do it, Jeremy. You have to do it."

Jeremy's eyes slid to Sam and lingered on her stricken face. She wasn't aware of her surroundings right now. Her eyes were fixed on her mother's reddening shirt, and her hands were clenched, balled into fists. She was strangely stoic, tense but not crying. He returned his gaze to the man between his legs, and slowly closed his hands around his neck. It was scrawny, corded, not what he expected. As he squeezed, he was dimly aware of ambient sound: blood rushing in his ears, the snapping fire, the tiny throbbing pulse on the side of his face.

The robber's eyes grew wide with alarm, and he began to struggle against the pressure on his throat. The fighting was intense, but the doctor was there, holding the man's legs and feet in place. When the kicking and grappling reached a pinnacle, the doctor threw himself across the man's kicking legs, and in a valiant effort, stifled the sounds of battle.

Jeremy was surprised by how long it took to kill a man. He would have thought it just minutes. It wasn't. It was difficult too—the strength required, the tension one must keep in the fingers and hands, the tautness and rigidity of muscles and tendons. The minutes ticked by, impossibly slow. Jeremy worried it would take an eternity. As he lifted his gaze, his pulse began to race. He was certain he wouldn't complete the task in time. The men would return, catch him in the act.

But they didn't. And he did get it done.

The man's struggling waned then ceased. Doctor Jack moved closer to his face. Touching two fingers to the man's inflamed neck, he leaned closer and listened for the sounds of breath.

"Not breathing," he whispered, "but that doesn't

mean dead. We need a knife,"

"A knife? Why?" Jeremy's heart skipped a beat. "Are you sure he's not dead?"

"We can't be sure. One can come back from this, particularly if the windpipe isn't ruptured." His gaze was intense. "A knife, Jeremy. We need a knife. Now."

In his pocket was Jeremy's handy pocketknife, but would it be useful in this situation? "This is all I have, Jack," he said, handing over the tiny weapon.

Snatching it from his hand, Doctor Jack flicked open the two-inch blade and moved for the suffocated man with purpose. Clenched in a bearish fist, the knife looked ridiculously small. What the hell could he do with that? Jeremy used that knife for opening packages, cutting twine, or cleaning his nails, nothing as robust a slicing a man's throat. But before he'd even finished the thought, Jack had set the blade to the man's throat and sliced, opening an artery in one smooth stroke. Thick, syrupy blood leaked onto the floor, pooling around Jeremy's knees. He felt sick. Dropping the man's head, he scuttled backward like a crab. Revolted, he tried to collect himself. Strange, he thought, that I feel like this. After all he'd seen and done this night, it was this that somehow crossed a line.

But at that moment, the men reappeared in the doorway. Sturgeon's hawk-like gaze scanned the carnage. What now? Where would they go from here? What would be done? As the precarious moment hung in the air, Jeremy's thoughts became incoherent and scattered.

Doctor Jack was the first to move. Lunging across the floor, he propelled himself toward the gun in the kitchen. Of course! Jeremy thought. Susan's gun! While Jack crawled toward the weapon, Jeremy pitched himself back toward the sofa. Guns were hidden all over this house, strategically placed, in various locations. In his haste he'd forgotten about that. Jeremy threw himself toward the sofa, desperately, and thrust his hand beneath the cushions. He pushed past dust bunnies and used Kleenex, his grip finally closing on the FN Herstal.

A shot fired behind him.

He froze.

No, he thought, panicked. Not again. I can't bear it. Who is it this time? Susan again? Sam?

Without thinking it through, he pushed himself to his feet, raised the gun in front of him and squared his stance. The shot had been fired at Doctor Jack, and though the man had been hit in the back of the thigh, he'd reached Susan's gun and now held it in his hands. The barrel quivered with the waves of his pain.

Sturgeon dared a step forward. Jeremy fired. Though only a warning shot, it stilled the man. "Not another step," Jeremy growled. "Freeze."

Sturgeon leveled his gun on Jeremy. The two locked gazes and Jeremy held firm. "Well," Sturgeon said, maddeningly calm. "Now what? It seems we've reached an impasse, Mr. Colt. Gun for gun, man for man."

Impasse? The word sounded strangely astute on the tip of Sturgeon's lips, too educated and civilized for the tense situation.

"Seems so," Jeremy spit from between clenched teeth. "Get out of my house. Go now, or I'll shoot."

The man smirked at that and shook his head. His tone was dangerously soft when he spoke. "You know that's not going to happen, Jeremy. This is my house now. I'm not going anywhere."

Doctor Jack dragged himself across the floor, eyes fixed on Sturgeon's gun. "I shouldn't have brought you here," he hissed. "I should've just let you kill me instead."

Sturgeon eyed the pool of blood at Jack's feet. "Oh, I wouldn't worry. We've successfully done that."

Jeremy realized it was time to think strategically. It was time to be realistic, no matter how much the truth hurt. There was no way out of this, no keeping his home. The doctor was as good as dead. So was Susan. He quailed.

There was only one thing left to do. For what offense could he effectively wage with a thirteen-year-old girl attached to his hip? He stepped forward, bravely, while summoning his courage. "All right. You win. The house is yours. I only ask that you let my family leave. It's a fair price to pay for what you've done."

Barracuda spoke, his eyes crawling over Susan. "Let 'em go, Sturg." he said. "They won't make it very far. Not out there. Not with her like that."

Sturgeon turned his gaze to Susan. He seemed to be considering Barracuda's advice, for the disgust in his eyes was unmistakable. It was as if she were nothing but a piece of rotting meat on a spit, an unpleasant job he'd have to tend to later, once she died on that couch. "Get out of here," he breathed. "Get out of here now. Get out of here quickly before I change my mind."

"Get the girls," Jack hissed. "I've got this, Jeremy."

Moving to his wife, Jeremy dropped to a knee, while trying to keep his gun trained on Sturgeon. At some point, Sam must have broken her trance, for she was sitting on the couch, cradling her mother's head, crying quietly, tears streaming down her face. Jeremy crouched and grasped his wife's clammy hands in his.

"You ready, Suse?" he whispered. "You've got this."

His wife's chin quivered. Tears pooled in her eyes. "I can't do it, Jeremy. You know I can't do it."

"Mom," Sam choked through a wrenching sob. "It's time to go. You have to get up. They're letting us go. We have to leave."

Lifting a trembling hand to her daughter's face, Susan smiled thinly. A trickle of blood spilled over her bottom lip. "Go on, honey," she breathed. "You have to go with Daddy. I love you so much, but right now, you need to go."

"We can't." Sam shook her head violently. "We're

not leaving without you, Mom. The Doctor can make you better, like he made me better." Jeremy watched her stand and sway, his heart breaking as she lifted Susan's limp arm. "I'm not kidding, Mom. Get up. We're not leaving without you. We can't." She glanced at Jeremy, daring him to disagree. "Isn't that right, Dad? Tell her. We're not leaving here without her. Make her get up. You have to make her get up." Kneeling, she placed a gentle hand across her mother's wound, and sobbing, bent to tie her shoes. "Please, Mom. Please don't do this to me. Not now."

"Sam," Jeremy whispered, pulling her closer and gathering her in his arms. Words failed him, for in this situation, none would suffice.

"I'm waiting," Sturgeon said.

Jeremy flashed a hateful glance. "We're going," he snarled. "Give us a minute." Lifting Sam's chin, he thumbed a smudge of blood from her cheek. "We have to go, honey. I'm sorry. I know it's difficult to understand, but you have to come with me. We have to leave."

Cradling his child as best he could, he bent and kissed his wife's trembling lips. His heart broke in two. This couldn't be happening. Was he actually considering leaving Susan behind? Was he really doing this? Or was it a terrible nightmare?

"Susan," he gasped. "It's always been you. There's never been another and there never will be." Touching his forehead to hers, he whispered, "If I were stranded on a deserted island, you're the only one I would want by my side."

She smiled. It was something they often said to one another, an implausible scenario that had somehow become real. Fresh tears spilled over her cheeks. "I love you, Jeremy. Take care of our daughter. Be strong. You can do this. You know what to do." She kissed him once more. "Now go. Get out of here. For the love of God, Jeremy, before something worse happens, before she gets hurt."

He nodded and pulled Sam's arm. She resisted, though her hand found his and clenched it painfully. There was nothing left to say and the three of them knew it.

"Mom," Sam breathed.

"I know, baby, and it's okay. I love you. Remember that. You're the best thing that ever happened to me. Take me with you on your next adventure. Listen to your Dad, but take me with you. This is only the beginning of something new, Samantha. Daddy will take care of you now. Go."

Sturgeon thumped his gun against his palm, and Jeremy tore his gaze from his wife. But as he moved for the door, he heard her call out.

"Wait," she said. "Jeremy, come back." Dropping Sam's hand, he rushed to her side. "My pocket," she whispered. "Check my left pocket."

He plunged his hand into her pocket, and there, deep within the folds of cotton, were the shapes of seven small disks. The insulin. The intensity of emotion nearly choked him. She'd somehow remembered to bring what he'd forgotten, and she'd saved their daughter's life in the process. She amazed him. He pressed his lips to hers, palmed the medication, and then ran to his daughter and grabbed her hand. Doctor Jack pushed himself to his feet, hung his head, and followed them into the dark silent night. It was surreal, like a dream, the edges bright and jagged. They scampered down the winding path, down the stairs that led to the garage.

"Stop," Jack said. "Please, Jeremy. I need to rest."

Eyes flashing, Jeremy spun to face him. He was breathless and pale. He'd lost a lot of blood. Jeremy thought he might throttle the man, beat him, smother him, cut, or maim him. He should make him pay for what he had done. But as he stared at the man's haggard face, he felt strangely hollow. He pitied the doctor. Look at him. He was dead on his feet, not a chance in hell. Without proper care, a gunshot wound would fester. In a matter of days, infection would set in, and that, or the blood loss, would kill him.

"I'm a liability," Jack whispered, and Jeremy didn't disagree. "I can barely make it down this hill, much less through the woods at night. Go without me. Go. I've already lost too much blood."

Jeremy nodded. He couldn't argue with the man. Turning around, he peered at his cabin, at the curling smoke, lifting from the chimney, at the orange and yellow light, flickering from the windows, at the large picture window overlooking their precious garden. He was angry, furious, his body sick with it. His mind tripped over everything he had lost and a white-hot blade of anger twisted his gut. This wasn't fair. It wasn't right. He pictured the life these men would live, the years they'd spend inside his home, the comfortable nights they'd sleep in his beds. He imagined warm nights they'd spend in front of his hearth, feasting on his supplies, gorging themselves, making salads with his daughter's spinach and kale.

"No," he whispered fiercely. "This isn't happening."

He couldn't allow this to happen. He wouldn't. He wouldn't permit them these unearned luxuries. Not after Susan, the brutality, the savagery. These men had built nothing. They hadn't earned this. They were pariahs, thieves. They didn't deserve these opulent spoils. Resolve hardening like a vise in his chest, he clamped his teeth together. He would stop this. Now. He wouldn't let them enjoy this life—not if he and his family couldn't. He refused to spit in his father's face, wouldn't allow them to soil his father's legacy. If Jeremy couldn't have this, no one could. It was as simple as that. And though he knew the sentiment was childish, Jeremy allowed himself to feel it fully, just the same.

He wordlessly dropped his daughter's hand and sprinted for the garage, for a door at the rear, a fake stone to the left. Unlocking the door, he slipped inside, headed straight for his workbench and tools. His eyes traveled over neat rows of tools, gloves, hats, shovels, and household cleansers. Bucket in hand, he grabbed bottles of any kind of solvent he could find: nail polish remover, drain cleaner, gasoline, any aerosol cans he could get his hands on. Alone, each chemical was easily combustible, but when mixed together, were poisonous and toxic. He howled inwardly at his cleverness, while simultaneously being shocked by the depth of his savagery. He wanted them to suffer, he realized. He wanted to inflict as much pain as he could. They would escape, of course; they weren't idiots. They wouldn't sit inside a burning house and die. But maybe Jeremy could inflict a bit of pain, injure them while they waivered. They'd be sitting in the ark right now, gorging themselves, and once the fire took hold of the house, they would dither over which supplies to take and which to leave behind.

When the bucket was full, he grabbed a box of matches, and fleeing the room, began running up the hill.

"Dad?" Sam asked him as he ran past her. "Dad! What are you doing? Where are you going?"

Peripherally, he saw her push past the Doctor's clutching arms, sprint up the hillside behind him, and scream. "Dad! Did you hear me? What are you doing? Stop!"

What was he doing? His wife was in there. No, he told himself. She's not in there. She's dead. She's gone now. Do what needs to be done.

Even now, he could imagine the men sitting in the ark, bags of chips and cookies scattered carelessly around them. He could envision them popping the tabs off of cans of beer, corking bottles of wine from his west-facing wall. And he could imagine his wife, dying alone on the couch, perched beside a dead man, light dimming from her eyes. The images only kindled his rage further.

He dropped his pail at the edge of the lawn and

ripped the tops from various cleaners, splashing the contents up the sides of his cabin. He spattered the door with nail polish remover and the window frames with rubbing alcohol. Around and around the cabin he raced, while Sam's feet churned billowing clouds of dirt behind him. He was only dimly aware of her sobs, until his pail was empty and he finally stopped. He fished out the matches and held one aloft.

"No." She shook her head. "Dad. You can't. Mom's in there. You can't do this."

He wasn't aware, until that moment, of his tears, streaming down the sides of his face. Salt was tight against his cheeks when he spoke. "She's not, Sam," he whispered. "She's not in there. Not anymore." Crouching beside her, he placed a hand on her chest. "She's not in that house anymore, Sam. She's with you."

And with that, he stood and beheld his family legacy, the lodge that had been the only home he'd ever known. Detached, he struck the first match. Moving for the door, he tossed the match against the wood, where it lit with silent and deadly force. Sam's hand found his, and together they watched the inferno climb the walls. It was odd, he realized, the frailness of it. It had taken his father years to build this cabin, while Jeremy could destroy it in an instant.

He pulled Sam's arm. He had to get her out of here. But he was a man on a mission, wouldn't allow himself to stop—not until the plan was fully executed. Together they sped around the house, lighting matches and flinging them onto the wood siding. Before long, the cabin shone brighter than the moon. Asphyxiating smoke began curling into the air.

"Enough!" Sam screamed, her voice penetrating the maelstrom in his head. "Dad, that's enough! Let's go!"

She'd screamed the last word. And she was right. Time to go. The men would be running outside at any moment. In no time, they'd puzzle out what he had done, and burst through the doors in pursuit. Not good. Jeremy knew a confrontation would be deadly.

He grabbed her by the hand and they sprinted down the hill, toward Jack, who had obviously died. His eyes were glassy. They left him where he lay. Scooping his daughter into his arms, Jeremy ran for the trees as fast as he could. He knew where they would go. He'd known all along. With his daughter cradled against his chest, he melted into a canopy of trees, his trees, his forest, his thirty-seven acres of forestland.

The forest opened its arms to them, like a living, breathing organism, embracing family. He ran until the muscles in his legs burned with acid, until his chest heaved and his eyes blurred, until his arms and cheeks were covered in scratches. He ran toward the rising shape of a cart, covered by an army-green tarp and slick plastic, this awkward little wagon, this wheelbarrow on steroids, this sub-standard ark that would keep them alive.

PART 2

You must not lose faith in humanity. Humanity is like an ocean; if a few drops of the ocean are dirty, the ocean does not become dirty.

—Mahatma Gandhi

CHAPTER 7
Present Day

SEPTEMBER 24TH, 2176
SCOTTSBORO WALMART SUPERCENTER
2,058 MILES TO SAN DIEGO

"I wanna explore on my own," she mumbled, as she turned away from him and disappeared down an aisle of women's clothing and shoes. Her spirits were somewhat brighter, it seemed, but he knew, emotionally, she was astride a bucking mare. For the hundredth time that week he asked himself: would she ever know the carefree comings and goings a girl her age should?

She was thirteen now, but just barely so. Jeremy recalled himself at that age. By that time, his parents had moved to the cabin, but outside life hadn't completely imploded yet. He'd still attended public school, competed in sporting events, and played with friends. Sam's life, however, was different. She had him, no one else. She was isolated, lonely, always on edge. Jeremy tried to imagine her life and couldn't: day after day, night after night, with no one to talk to but her father. It would surely test anyone's patience, much less a young girl slogging through adolescence. So he'd let her be for a while, he thought. It was just as well. He had things to do. He wanted to visit the pharmacy, which was something he preferred to do alone. No need to remind her of her precarious health.

The pharmacy was usually a bust anyway. Rarely did he fine anything useful these days. Not after so much time had passed. Without proper refrigeration, the injectable forms of insulin would have spoiled. But still, he thought, it was wise to check.

He walked the darkened aisles alone, his footsteps echoing strangely. Sounds were odd in an industrial store, even worse in an empty industrial store; every noise reverberated off the ductwork and ceiling. The store was a mess, as were most places he and Sam visited lately. While Jeremy and his family enjoyed a secluded life, tucked away in the Smokey Mountains, protected from the perils of a crumbling society, thousands of unfortunate others hadn't. They'd foraged and scavenged, hunted and gathered. They'd become petty thieves and criminals. Neighborly hospitality and courtesy had died; the ties that bound communities had frayed.

Pausing a moment, he peered across the store, where he saw Sam's flashlight weaving about the aisles. She'd find few things of value here, as most of what was left was useless and frivolous: old hats, maybe, or school supplies, a variety of household vacuums and scrubbers, a collage of framed art or porcelain figurines. But maybe she'd find a new game they could play, several pairs of thick socks, a book, or magazine.

Something caught his eye to his left. He turned and nearly laughed out loud. There, on the floor, half-concealed by the lip of a metal shelf—in the bulk food aisle of all places—was a large box of lentils and a bag of dried peas.

"Score," he whispered, congratulating himself, though he had to admit: he wasn't surprised. Things like this happened frequently. People passed treasures like these all the time, favoring canned goods, boxes of crackers, or bags of chips instead. He weaved around a pool of rancid ketchup, which had dried, molded, and spread furry fingers across the dirty tiled floor. Righting an overturned basket, he smiled. Lentils were his favorite. They were rich in protein, fiber, and fatty acids. When cooked, a single bag could last he and Sam a week.

Approaching the pharmacy, he lifted the counter, approached a door marked Employees Only. There was a small yet opaque window set into the top, and it was dark as if covered with a piece of dark cloth. Fantastic, he thought. Someone covered it. With his luck, someone had claimed this room, sealed the door, and then died or gone crazy.

Lifting the gun from the holster on his belt, he crept closer, and placed his ear against the frame. As he slowly turned the knob, he held his breath. Locked. Yep. He should have known that. If he were a betting man, he'd have wagered on this, as well as the likelihood of a dead corpse inside. In many of the convenience marts they'd visited along the way, he and Sam had made similar gruesome discoveries, the remains of people who had made their last stand. They would stockpile as many supplies as they could, and then hole themselves up inside a tiny room like this, attempt to wait out the worst of the disaster. Bad idea. His father taught him that. That kind of logic would inevitably fail them.

"Jeremy," his father had cautioned him sagely. "Never confine yourself inside a public place. Select a private one, carve out a simple life."

Jeremy pulled the crowbar from his pack and wedged the claw between the doorframe and the knob. He'd become quite good at this, if he did say so himself. His weight against the shaft was all it would take. How silly, he thought. How trusting people were. For hundreds of years people had believed locks secure.

When he was able to successfully jimmy the door open, he was greeted by a stench so foul he nearly vomited. Oh yes. Someone had been here, all right. Been here, shat here, and died here, he thought—shat here repeatedly by the smell of it. He needed to be quick, so he set himself to task. It was a task he knew quite well. He was methodical about it, meticulous, if not overly so.

Beneath the pooled light of his flashlight, he began with the cholesterol medications and high blood pressure pills, before moving to pain management and antibiotics. Though the person who died here hadn't lasted very long, he'd managed to keep others from tearing the place apart, and though the medications were sparse and banged up, there were probably still a few items of use.

As was to be expected, all of the pain medications had long been pillaged. And the antibiotics had been taken, as well. Dropping to his knees, he peered beneath the lip of the rack, where he saw several bottles that had rolled beneath. After fishing them out, he held them aloft. Industrial-strength antacids. Useless. He tossed them. But a bottle of aspirin. Score! Double-score! While antacids were useless, aspirin was gold. The small bottle of pills had just made this stop worthwhile.

He continued down the aisle, past bottles of Cialis and Propecia, past other silly drugs he'd once heard about: pills that prevented unwanted emotional outbursts, medication for restless leg syndrome (that was a thing?). Rounding the next corner, he found a collection of birth control pills and diaphragms, and in the darkness of the room, a silvery memory arose: the moment Susan told him she was pregnant. It was an odd thing to recall inside a broken-down store. Both tender and frightening, it was one of his most precious memories. He and the woman he'd chosen to spend the rest of his life with had somehow created life. In a world claimed by death and decay, in the confines of a cabin on the side of a mountain, they'd come together and started something new. The memory brought tears to his eyes.

"Susan. Jesus. A baby?" he had asked.

"I know. Not ideal at a time like this. I know it'll be hard, another mouth to feed, another hopeless future to plan for." She'd hung her head and brought her hands to her face. "I'm sorry, Jeremy. It's a burden we don't need. Neither does your father, for that matter. Not now. Particularly not while we're still filling the ark. Not while we have so many things left to do." When she lifted her head, Jeremy could see she'd been crying. "The timing is terrible. I don't know what to say."

He'd dropped beside her, onto the sofa, his thoughts strangely calm, given the news. A baby, he remembered thinking: a family of his own. The idea was as mystifying as it was frightening. It was the left field thing of all time, in times like these. It was a fantasy a man in his position didn't allow himself to have. It was an indulgence Jeremy hadn't thought possible.

"Well?" Susan asked him. "What do you think? Say something. Please. Your silence is killing me."

He'd turned to her then, gathered her hands in his, and begun to speak slowly, almost carefully, picking through concepts that were foreign to him, like the images of a dream that would scatter too fast.

"I'm not upset, Suse. Not for reasons you'd expect. I'm just shocked, is all, but I like the idea." He squeezed her hands. "I like it a lot. I mean it. It's a gift. Don't you think?" He bumped her gently with his forehead. "It's lucky, too. For you, I mean. Imagine staring at this old mug for the rest of your life. Don't you think you'll get bored?"

"You're not mad then?" Relief shone golden in her eyes.

"Not mad. No. Worried, perhaps. Worried for you. For your health, for the birth, for the limited medical resources at hand…"

"But the ark," she interrupted. "We have what we need. Your father has everything we could possibly want, and the hospital is only ten miles from here. We could forage for anything we're missing. We've got seven months to prepare, maybe eight, if I'm calculating it right."

He held up his hands. "I know all of that. We have time. I'm just thinking ahead. I'm thinking about the possible complications of birth, about the pregnancy itself, and the eight long months, the vitamins and checkups you won't be receiving." Raising a brow, he glanced at her sidelong. "…and the labor at the end? What about that?"

"What about it?" Peering at him from beneath dark lashes, she blew out an exasperated breath. "Oh Jeremy, I'm not worried about that. Women have been giving birth for thousands of years, and they've done it without medication or pain pills. You're worried about afterward, aren't you? Be honest. You're worried about having a baby to tend to, about what his life will be like once he's born."

"Yes. There's that, but it's more than just that. It's about the life we'll be leaving for him." He met her challenging gaze, where he could see his concerns mirrored back in her eyes. "I'm not saying this right. Don't misunderstand. I want to be a father. I've always wanted that. But now that it's happened, I'm wondering if it's morally responsible to want it. What kind of life will this child—or any child—inherit? The world has reached a turning point, Suse, a point at which the quality of life is worse than it was for previous generations. For the first time in history, the world's future is murkier than it's past. I guess I'm just concerned about quality of life."

She'd gone suddenly rigid at his side. "What are you suggesting?"

"No." He shook his head. "Not that. Never that. I'm only speaking in hypotheticals here." He brushed a lock of hair behind her ear and tenderly kissed her cheek.

"But I guess we can't speak in hypotheticals anymore. So everything I'm saying is just wasted breath. Here's the truth, Suse: I'm happy, really happy. I'm happy, thankful, scared, nervous. I'm experiencing so many emotions right now that I'm not communicating them properly. I love you, no matter what happens. And I'll love our baby just as much."

He distinctly remembered gathering her to his chest, and smoothing her hair down her back as he held her. "We'll figure it out," he said softly in her ear. "We'll find a way to make it work. We always do."

By then, the power grids had failed the surrounding neighborhoods, and the water pumps had ceased supplying homes with potable water, but the pregnancy—despite the lack of these—had been wonderful. Jeremy dropped his gaze to his hands, to the plastic case of pills in neat little rows. Recalling the images, he smiled through his tears. The labor had been difficult, as he'd expected it would be, but in the end, they'd welcomed a perfect baby girl. Against insurmountable odds, two became three, and Jeremy and Susan had never looked back. It was only after Sam's third birthday that things began to change. With the onset of symptoms, their lives had taken a sharper edge.

Remembering his objective, he gently set the package of pills on the counter and continued down the aisle toward the medical devices. Blood pressure cuffs, syringes, home drug-testing kits: people had barely touched this area. And for good reason: all of these items were useless.

He turned the corner and nearly gagged. There, on the floor, in the back of the pharmacy, the store's single occupant had erected a tent. Blankets draped a rear window, and a collection of garden tools surrounded the man's feet. A decaying body was heaped in the corner, a long hoe clutched in a hand that had gone to mostly bone and bits of skin. Fighting his revulsion, Jeremy lifted a hand to his nose and squeezed. The damp heat of the current climate, and the closeness of the room were conducive to decay—and an accelerated decay at that. He looked away.

At the man's feet was a small Lego castle, partially built and crudely designed. Frowning, Jeremy moved past the cadaver, to the final aisle of the pharmacy. It was the aisle he'd come to inspect in the first place, but for some reason, he always saved it for last. Maybe he liked to savor the unexpected, or maybe he was a glutton for punishment. Who knew?

Despite his expectations, it was always the same. It began with rows of blood sugar testers and glucose tabs— of which there were usually none, of course—followed by pumps and a refrigerator of vials—all of which were usually spoiled. He sighed. Frustrated, he waived his arm across a shelf, scattering the collection of bottles near the back. He almost turned away, but something caught his eye. He lifted it and gasped. How was this here? A bottle of insulin pills? What were the odds?

Though the pills were weaker than the disks by far, he was incredibly lucky to have made such a find. The device in Sam's belly had been a luxury item, expensive, and for most people, hard to come by. The trajectory of the research he and Susan had discovered had pointed to a long-term marketing plan, but it was a plan that never came to fruition. The pharmaceutical companies had projected widespread distribution and use, with future releases, improvements and developments. The disks would become more advanced with time, culminating in a product that required replacement only once a year. But none of it happened. The world fell apart. People never received the implant, and so, were relegated to the pills. They were hard to come by.

He palmed the bottle with unbridled excitement, slipped it into his pocket and turned to leave. Sam was lucky enough to have an implant, luckier still to have the blood sugar indicator at her wrist. Jeremy knew the pills were weakening, but with the wrist indicator, he could monitor their strength. Too bad there was only one bottle.

Edging past the dead man's booted foot, he slipped back into the darkened store. And following Sam's beacon of light, he passed baby clothes and lawn furniture, picked up a box of plastic forks and then tossed them.

A short yet resonant blast stopped him dead in his tracks.

"Sam!" he yelled out as he ran toward her light. Had he just heard the sound of a whistle? "Sam, are you all right?" He crisscrossed aisles, wove between scattered debris.

"Back here!" she returned. "Dad, hurry!" She didn't sound afraid, but excited, the tone of her voice somewhat higher than normal.

His footsteps echoed as he ran. Where was she? He wove between cans of paint, bags of long-dehydrated garden sod, and useless home décor, and found himself in the sports equipment aisle, where soccer balls rolled down the linoleum path, disturbed from years of quiet slumber. Jeremy stopped short, his eyes wide.

"Sam?"

There she was, at the end of the aisle, crouched low, focused on something. Moving slowly, he squinted through the light. It was difficult to make sense of the oddly shaped shadows. The beam of her flashlight illuminated something that suddenly moved. What the hell was it? He couldn't make it out.

"Hey," he heard her say. "Do you want to come out?"

A person? No. Jeremy's heart skipped a beat. He took a step forward before stopping in his tracks, his heart pounding in his chest. There, in the depth of an empty shelf was a small cowering boy with eyes as round as saucers that darted back and forth like a trapped animal. Stopping immediately, Jeremy backed up.

"It's okay, son," he said, lifting his hands in supplication. "My name is Jeremy. This is my daughter, Sam. Are you hurt? Are you sick? Can we can help you find your parents?"

When he took another step, the boy flinched. Jeremy froze. He was small, too small, too frail, emaciated. He couldn't be older than eight or nine, and he was clinging to a wicked pair of sharp garden shears, the size and length of which only accentuated the slightness of his form. They were sharp and glinted in his trembling hands. Jeremy's pulse quickened.

"Sam, be careful."

"He won't hurt us, Dad."

Of course she'd think that. Nothing frightened her—which was often incredibly stupid.

Jeremy mimicked her non-threatening pose, dropped to his knees and crawled forward on his hands. He stopped just behind her left shoulder. The boy didn't appear well. His skin was dirty. His hair was matted. Jeremy cursed himself for leaving the food outside. How stupid. Wait. He wasn't empty-handed. He tore open the package of dried peas. It wasn't a Big-Mac but it would have to do. In a non-threatening way, he pushed the food toward the boy.

"For you, son," he said, cupping a hand to his mouth. "Are you hungry? Here. Have something to eat."

The boy's gaze darted from Jeremy to Sam, before zeroing in on the package of food. His lips parted. His eyes flashed with longing.

"It's okay," Sam encouraged him softly. "You can have it. We've got plenty. This is yours." Edging closer, she pushed the bag forward, offering it to him like she would a chest of gold. But the farther she moved from Jeremy, the more uncomfortable he became. She was too damn close to those blades. He tugged her boot.

"That's far enough, Sam. Slow down."

Peering over her shoulder, she chastised him.

"He's scared of you. Not me. You're like a bull in a china shop to him."

"I am? I'm scaring him? Are you serious? I'm not the one holding those blades."

With a scowl, she turned her back and shrugged. "Don't mind him. He's just a big wimp." Leaning forward, she pushed the food closer, until it came to rest near his toes. He flinched.

With a sigh, Jeremy rolled to his rump and watched, while Sam tried to reach him using a different tactic.

"Do you like Harry Potter?" she asked, and he nodded, his hand moving closer to the food. "Because I've got a few books in my pack. I can read them to you, if you like. Or we can pick up different books if you prefer something else. You could come to the library and pick out your own. Can you read?"

The boy nodded, his eyes fixed on the peas. His semi-clean clothing set a contrast with his grimy skin. Where, Jeremy wondered, would he find clean—

With a clumsy lurch, the boy leaned forward, snatched the bag of peas and scuttled away like a crab. He ripped into the package and scooped up the food, shoving as much as he could into his mouth. A Walmart tag was dangling from his shirt, while similar ones hung from his pants and shoes. So he'd been here a while, Jeremy realized. Long enough to exchange inferior clothing for new.

"Dad, do you have any water?" Sam whispered.

"Oh yeah. One sec. I've got one right here."

He slowly lowered the pack from his back, pulled out a bottle, and crawled forward. Reconsidering, he stopped and handed it to Sam. While the boy seemed somewhat comfortable with her, he didn't seem trusting of adults just yet. And those shears were still within reach.

"So," Sam ventured, matter-of-factly. Crossing her legs, she tossed her hair over her shoulder. "Got a name?"

The boy didn't answer so she pressed him. "Well, if you don't, what do we call you then? We can't call you Boy or Kid or Son. Not forever, at least. How about Kenneth or Tom or Jim?"

Jeremy noticed the boy relaxing. His shoulders dropped in response to her voice. Funny things happen to humans over time. When humans are sequestered from other humans, strange things happen to the psyche. As much as one desires companionship and love, the prospect of both can become just as frightening.

Jeremy cleared his throat, made to speak. He would play along with this crazy charade, see where it went and then decide what to do. "I don't think he's a Kenneth, Sam. Not a Tom or Jim, either. He looks like a Tiger or a Hippo to me."

As much as he fought it, the boy smiled.

"Yeah," Jeremy continued. "Hippo sounds right. I mean, look how fat he is! It only makes sense. He's downright enormous. Get this kid on a diet."

Sam burst into giggles and nudged the water forward. Braver this time, the boy plucked it from her outstretched hand. He stopped chewing long enough to clear his voice and speak.

"Seth," he said, his voice hoarse. "My name's Seth."

His unused voice was like gravel beneath the heel of a boot.

"Seth," Sam responded, with a meaningful nod. "Yeah. Okay. I can live with Seth, but you need a fish name." She pointed to her chest. "I'm Sam, but my name's really Pike. You see? And this is my dad. His name's Carp."

Seth pulled from lustily from the bottle in his hand then wiped his mouth with the back of his sleeve. "Why do I need a fish name?"

Why indeed. Jeremy frowned. What was up with this game? Why was Sam intent on honoring a tradition that had been passed to them by killers and thieves? The day she'd named herself had practically broken his heart.

"Because it makes you tougher," she explained. "That's why. It makes you part of a gang, or a crew. To be a gang member, you need a gang name. I'm sorry, but that's just how it works."

Seth crammed a handful of peas into his mouth and appeared to consider his options. "Great white?" he said finally.

Sam shook her head. "Can't be two words. Two syllables? Fine. But not two words."

"Then how about Cod, or Trout?"

"Nope." She pursed her lips. "Doesn't sound right." She peered at Jeremy from over her shoulder. "Any advice from the peanut gallery?"

Jeremy pretended to ponder the question. "How about Goldfish or Salmon? I still like Salmon. Or what about Kelp or Mullet?"

Shaking her head, she returned her gaze to Seth. "He's terrible at this. Those are awful ideas. And mullet?" She tossed Jeremy an exasperated look. "Ridiculous. A mullet was a horrible hairdo in the 1980's. A mullet was never a fish."

Strangely, it was.

Seth straightened, his eyes hopeful. "What about Jellyfish?"

"No jellyfish!" Sam and Jeremy laughed out loud.

"Well," Seth said, "Then I really don't know. I don't know many kinds of fish. I've never been to the ocean."

He dropped the package of peas beside his leg and curled his fist around a Lego. When he brought it to his chest and cradled it lovingly, Jeremy's stomach lurched uncomfortably. The toy brought to mind the dead man in the pharmacy. Enough chitchat. He needed answers.

"Enough about the names, guys. We'll figure it out later. Seth, how long have you been in this store?"

Seth lifted his face to meet Jeremy's gaze. "A long time, I think, but I'm not really sure."

Jeremy dared to ask the million-dollar question. "And are you here by yourself?"

"No." Seth's voice was small, like he didn't want to answer, and though his eyes welled with tears, he thrust out his chin. "No," he said, with more confidence this time. "I'm not by myself. I'm here with my Mom."

Jeremy's heart felt heavy. That was a woman back there? He took a deep breath to steady himself. "Then I guess we should find her, shouldn't we? After all, we can't leave you here alone. That wouldn't be right. Is there anyone else we can take you back to?"

He perked up at that, his body rigid. He was a rabbit that had caught the scent of a fox nearby. "You're leaving?"

"No." Sam turned to glare at Jeremy. "We're not leaving. But we can't stay here. And neither can you."

Seth's face crumpled. "I'm not leaving my mom."

"Okay," Jeremy conceded, "then let's find her. Your house must be somewhere nearby. Is that right? Can we help you get home?"

The direct line of questioning was stressing the child, and truth be told, it was stressing Jeremy, too. He had no time for this. They had to get going. Seth was a boy who could read and speak and hold intelligent conversations. The sky was darkening through the storefront windows, and Jeremy was yet to find a safe place for them to camp for the night. Never mind his pressing need to return to the bikes, which were hidden behind the parking lot along with all of their worldly possessions. He had tired of this game. Time to wrap things up. Crossing his legs, he moved closer.

"Seth," he began slowly, "I think I found your mom. Is she inside the pharmacy, in the back of the store?"

Though Seth ignored the question, Sam flinched.

Meeting Jeremy's gaze, she blinked, and when the truth settled in, she turned back to Seth.

"Seth, I think it would be best if you came with us. We've got plenty of food, and lots of water, and my Dad is taking us to a very special place. It'll be like an adventure. Will you come?"

"Sam," Jeremy said softly. "Come with us? What are you saying?"

"We'll talk about it later," she hissed back at him. "Let's see if he has a house. Let's start with that. If he does, then at least we have a place to stay for the night."

Jeremy sighed. She made a good point. A house would be a nice change of pace.

Seth's head was now buried in his hands. "Seth," Jeremy said, "I'll be honest with you. I saw your mother, back at the pharmacy. And son," he added, "I need to speak to you now—man-to-man, if you can let me do that. You're a big boy, right? I'm mean look at you. Look how well you've done in this store. You've been here, alone, for all this time, and you've obviously taken good care of yourself. You've done a great job to say the least. You're not little anymore. You're not a baby, right? You're an adult now, and adults tell each other the truth. Even when the telling is difficult to do." He inched closer, his steel-toed boots nearly touching Seth's neon sneaker. "Seth, your mother passed away, didn't she? She's passed on to heaven, and now you're here with us."

Seth raised his head from his hands. Tears had tracked twin paths down his face, like tribal lines had been painted his cheeks. Twice he tried to speak but couldn't, his mouth opening and closing like a fish out of water. Jeremy beheld his trembling hands and ill-fitted clothing with fresh eyes. Now that he was closer, he could see that the pants hung from his body in folds. They would hang past his shoes when he walked. The seams of his shirt fell well past his elbows. This was a boy who needed tending, care, and love. It wouldn't be proper to leave him here alone. Not after what had happened a few weeks ago…not after…

Jeremy caught his breath and pushed the thought aside. He refused to ponder that now.

Surprising himself, he opened his arms, and for an instant, Seth's features morphed into someone else. Beneath the flashlight's dancing beam, the bridge of Seth's nose seemed to narrow and lengthen. His brow seemed to deepen and furrow, and though Jeremy knew it was a trick of light and shadow, it was an effective one, and elicited a sharp response, a sudden blooming of shame and guilt. His decision was instant. There was no other path. He found his eyes brimming with tears. He was offering safe harbor, the promise of family, life to a person who surely faced death. But there was something else too, wasn't there? It was something Jeremy needed for himself: atonement, repentance, for past misdeeds. It had been nearly five months since he and Sam had been forced from their cabin, and so much had happened since then. He'd encountered others, and stolen from them. No, he cursed himself. He'd done much worse. He shook his head. How strange life was. It always seemed to circle back to the beginning. How similar Seth was to Peter. The situations were oddly parallel, weren't they? It was impossible to miss the symmetry. How long had it been since he'd last thought of Peter? A hour? A day? Maybe two at the most? Those memories were never far from his mind.

He wasn't sure Seth would respond to his invitation. But he did, immediately and viscerally. From deep inside, a sob tore from Seth's chest. He lunged at Jeremy, the shears spinning away from his foot. Throwing himself into Jeremy's lap, he curled himself there like a cat. He clutched Jeremy's shirt and wept freely, the heaving of his shoulder's matching Jeremy's own.

Time slipped away while Jeremy stroked Seth's hair. He wasn't sure how long they sat in the dark, until Sam slid closer and faced them. Balancing her elbows on her knees, she glanced from Seth to Jeremy. "You owe him this," she whispered. "This is healthy for you. You've needed to fix your karma for a long time now."

Jeremy lifted his tear-streaked face. "Karma?"

"For Peter. You know it's true. You know that's why you're upset."

His eyes searched hers. Dear God. She knew. She'd probably known all this time. Damn it to hell. How could she know? For all this time, had she known and said nothing? He readied himself for her anger and judgment. He prepared himself for her sharp accusations. To his relief, she had none to give. Saying nothing, she pushed herself up to her feet and peered down at him from the bridge of her nose.

"It's okay, Dad. I know. I've always known. What you did to Peter was unforgivable. I've struggled with it. You should know that. I've examined it from every possible angle, from every point of view, but there's no right answer. What you did was wrong, and I think you know it too."

Her hands were fluttering at her sides, nervously. He suddenly realized how hard this was for her. God, how he admired her strength. She was a marvel to him, much wiser than her age.

"Dad, I still haven't gotten past this. I can't seem to put a good spin on what you did. It was reprehensible, and will always be so." She gulped a breath of air. "But you did it for me. I know that now. I know that you did it for me."

Bending down, she reached toward his waist, where attached to his belt was a tiny figurine. It tinkled softly when she grasped it in her hand, a miniature stuffed bear with a collar around its neck and a tiny bell jingling at the side. It was grimy and faded. Jeremy startled when he saw it. She held it in an open palm, examined it closely then closed her fist. Spinning away, she slipped it into her pocket, picked up her pack, and disappeared down the aisle. Her last words lingered like an exotic perfume.

"I forgive you," she whispered as she rounded the corner, and with that, Jeremy's tears spilled anew.

After some time Jeremy managed to untangle himself from Seth's clutching arms. He carried him through the store, searching for Sam, and found her smelling an assortment of candles. The three of them took a final walk through the store. Good God, he marveled. How light Seth was. He couldn't weigh more than forty pounds.

They added a collection of items to their basket: a screwdriver that had fallen behind a shelf, Saltines, a dusty roll of Lifesavers. Nothing but junk. In the spice aisle, Sam found bottles of paprika and curry, useless to many, but valuable to her.

At Jeremy's insistence, they gave the pharmacy a wide berth, leaving the store without speaking about what was inside. Shoulder-to-shoulder, they stood beneath the stars, gulped the fresh air and marveled at the world. Jeremy set Seth to his feet, and after smoothing his shirt, wound a cord through the loops of his pants and tied a knot.

"That ought to get us as far as your house. You're bound to have a belt at home. Something that actually fits?"

Seth nodded and crinkled his brow. "What about my Mom? What do we do?"

Sam stepped forward, crouching low. "I've been thinking about that. How about this? Let's eat a hot meal, get a good night's sleep, and tomorrow, we'll come back and give her a proper burial."

Lifting her finger, she pointed toward the crest of a hill, where light from a crescent moon fell in silvery beams to the grass. "I saw some old shovels in the store," she added, "I say we bury her up on that hill, maybe say a little prayer, something like that. What do you think?"

Seth nodded soberly and offered her his hand, and

the three started walking toward the bikes.

"Wait." Seth stopped. "We can't go back to my house. Won't the bad men still be there? It's not safe."

Jeremy froze. Good point. "We'll approach it slowly," he said. "I'll go first. We won't go in unless it's safe. I promise."

He and Sam walked the bikes, while Seth led the way to his house. As he became more comfortable, he became quite chatty, telling the story of how he'd come to live inside an old Walmart store. His father had gone in search of supplies three years ago, but had never returned. After that, 'bad men' had ambushed their home, but the Christmas bells tied to the top of their door had jingled a warning and they'd gotten away. They'd lived inside that old Walmart ever since. Their family was the last on their block, Seth said, maybe even the last in their town, which his father accredited to structure and organization, and to the surface of their roof, which was flat, where they stored rainwater and grew various kinds of food.

Seth's father sounded much like Jeremy's own. He'd barricaded the house, set up rain catchers, planted fruits and vegetables in a series of planters. They'd had beans, nuts, root vegetables, citrus fruits, and even a compost heap for re-fertilization of the soil. All this Jeremy gathered in bits and pieces, from a breathless Seth as he trotted beside them.

"Mom said they set it up before I was born. I was an 'oops' baby, she told me." He laughed. "But that was okay, because Dad started saving supplies years before that. He said that's how we stayed alive while everyone else died." In the half-light of twilight, Seth lifted his gaze to Jeremy. "Where are all the people, Carp? People don't just disappear into thin air. So where did they all go?"

"You're right, Seth. They don't. This started happening years before you were born. You and Sam didn't go to school like I did. And even then things were falling apart. People just weren't prepared for this kind of catastrophe, and as a result, they starved to death. That slow starvation has been happening for decades."

"So we're the last people in the world?"

"No." The innocence of his question was disarming. "There are lots of other people out there, Seth, I'm sure. Many have claimed large plantations of land, in the Midwest and Southeast parts of the country, while others have remained in what remains of big cities. Most, though, have hunkered down and built quiet lives for themselves. Most are just trying to get by. It's the only way to survive nowadays."

Seth was silent for a speculative moment. As they walked down residential streets, past homes, Jeremy tried to ignore overgrown lawns and collapsing roofs, the remains of homes that had succumbed to the elements. The chains of their bikes buzzed like insects, and Jeremy marveled at how normal he suddenly felt. It was almost as if they'd been out for the night, at the movies, or down at the park.

"So," Seth reasoned, pulling Jeremy back to reality. "If hunkering down is the only way to survive, then what are you two doing here? Shouldn't you be hunkering down somewhere?"

Jeremy lacked the confidence to answer.

"We were," Sam said. "Hunkered down, so to speak. We've only been out here for about half a year."

"Not quite half a year." Jeremy corrected her gently. "Though it sometimes feels like longer, I admit."

"Half of an entire year." She sounded mystified. "But before that, we were hunkered down. We had everything we needed, but we lost it all." She turned her face toward Seth and met his gaze. "Bad men took our house too. They chased us from our cabin, left us with nothing but a cart we'd hidden in the woods."

"At least you had each other," he said. "So, technically, you didn't lose everything." His face was solemn and his voice had almost cracked.

"True," Sam admitted. "We did have each other. But we had more than that before the bad men came. Before them, we still had my mom."

Seth drew closer and leaned into her, and when she squeezed his shoulders, Jeremy's heart swelled with pride.

"We're the same," Seth whispered. "We both lost our moms. We both lost our homes and now we might die, too."

"Hey," Jeremy said. "Stop that. Nobody uses the 'D' word in front of me. Nobody's dying on my watch, guys. And besides, not everything is bad. We're not just wandering the countryside aimlessly. We're following a plan. We know where we're going. We're on our way to someplace new. When we get there, we'll hunker down and plant a new garden. We'll set up new supplies and build ourselves a home."

"Okay," Seth said. "So where are you going?"

"Not you." Sam corrected him. "We. It's where we are going, and it's to San Diego, California. What do you think about that?"

Seth frowned. "Isn't that far? What's in San Diego?"

Sam's answer was a breath on the wind. "The ocean. That's what. The ocean is there."

"That," Jeremy acknowledged, "and other things too: rich soil for planting, a more temperate climate. The list goes on. It's a good place to go."

Sam eyed him sidelong. "Is that all?"

"Meh." He shrugged. "Perhaps a few more things."

"Mmm-hmm," she mumbled before turning to Seth. "He won't tell us everything. He thinks he's got some big secret."

"So you're taking me to San Diego to see the ocean," Seth said, his tone introspective, like he was working out the details by saying them aloud. "That's really far, Carp. My Dad always said it's not safe to travel far. Why don't we just hunker down here? Try to rebuild my garden on the roof—only if the bad men are gone, I mean. Wouldn't it be safer if we just did that?"

"Yeah," Sam said, with a hint of smugness. "That definitely makes more sense. Wouldn't you say?"

"We're going to San Diego for other reasons, guys. We have to go that specific place, and we have to get there fast." He turned to Seth. "I know it's difficult to leave your home. Trust me—trust us. We know. But I wouldn't ask you if I didn't think it was best. Suffice it to say, we wouldn't be traveling that far if we didn't have to. But we don't have a choice. We have to. And we'd love it if you would come with us."

"It's going to be dangerous," Seth cautioned them sagely.

Jeremy ruffled his hair. "Perhaps. But it's safer than being alone. Don't you think? And it's definitely safer than living inside an old Walmart store."

"Besides," Sam added, "you're a gang member now. You're tough. You've got nothing to fear anymore."

Seth shook his head, "No, I'm not. Not yet. You said I can't be a gang member unless I have a gang name. I don't have one yet, so right now, I'm just Seth."

"Just Seth," Sam repeated, peering up, toward the moon. "Marlin," she said quietly. "Your name will be Marlin."

"Marlin? Okay. Like Merlin the wizard."

"Sure." Sam smiled. "Like that."

We know only too well that what we are doing is nothing more than a drop in the ocean. But if the drop were not there, the ocean would be missing something.

—Mother Theresa

CHAPTER 8
35 Years Prior

FEBRUARY 26TH, 2121
I-81 S, 72 MILES TO BRISTOL, TN
VIRGINIA

Olivia rolled her head toward the window, the sharp peal of a siren lifting her from the peaceful serenity of dreams. Peering out the window, she wiped the corner of her mouth with her sleeve. "Where are we?" she asked. She glanced at Liam when he didn't answer, and then flushed beneath his appraising gaze.

"Nothing's sexier than a woman who drools."

She dabbed once more at the corner of her mouth then scrutinized the puddle that had formed on her shoulder. "Sorry about that. I'm so damn tired I can barely keep my eyes open. This pregnancy thing is exhausting. So," she added, straightening in her seat. "Where are we? How far did we get?"

He tapped the map on the center console. "Just

about to cross the Tennessee border. In about three hours, I think we'll be home."

"Three hours, huh?" She peered at the long line of traffic in front of them. "I think that might be wishful thinking."

As she reached for the bag at her feet, her diamond caught the sun, reflecting a brilliant prism of colors. A smattering of dots splashed the interior of the car. Her engagement ring was absolutely beautiful, and though Liam moved fast, she refused to complain. She hadn't the luxury of time to complain. Nobody did. Not these days. But their courtship had certainly been faster than most.

Change, she mused. That was the correct word. What an apt word to describe her recent life. Though a simplistic term, and an overgeneralization, it certainly fit the circumstances. Olivia had made fast friends with new concepts, and though most of the changes in her life were voluntary, many were also unavoidable. Change had come fast and abruptly. She'd welcomed the marriage and the move from Richmond to Tennessee, but in many other smaller ways, everyday life frightened her. Liam had been right about everything, and for the hundredth time, she thanked God for putting her feet in his path.

Since returning from their trip to Japan, Olivia had noticed life crumbling to pieces all around her. The United States, along with many of the other world's super power countries, had closed its borders permanently—and shockingly, for the first time in history. Any country with abundant natural resources, or acres of land to support farming and animal husbandry had become a desirable location. Alternatively, any country whose primary source of food—or economic wealth—had come from the oceans, was starving to death, or was decimated. Refugees flooded the streets in unprecedented numbers. Millions starved while millions more spilled across the borders of countries like the United States and parts of Southern

Russia. People fled to Canada, New Zealand, and Sweden. Argentina, Brazil, and inland portions of China were inundated, putting strain on an already stressful situation. Resources were limited. Food was scarce. And before the borders were finally closed, the U.S.-Mexican and U.S.-Canadian borders were lines that had blurred. With no concern for law or authority, people had crossed borders openly.

But when martial law was declared, everything stopped.

And now here we are, Olivia thought, amazed: two people trying to start life anew while living in a slowly dying world, two people trying to survive amid panic and chaos. People everywhere were stockpiling resources, preparing for a life behind sturdy walls and locked doors. People were buying large quantities of food. Unfortunately, people were also stealing from others, and things had gotten ugly. Fast.

Olivia startled as an ambulance shot past them. She strained to see past the endless line of cars. "Must be an accident up ahead," she mumbled, while tearing into her second peanut butter and jelly sandwich of the day.

"You know," Liam pointed out sarcastically, "you could try something with a vegetable in it. Something with a piece of lettuce? A cucumber? Or a tomato?"

"Peanuts are vegetables."

"Peanuts are legumes."

Grimacing, she touched her swollen belly. "Nope. Can't. Peanut butter and jelly is the only thing that sounds the least bit appetizing. You don't want to have to pull over again, do you? So your wife can decorate the side of the road?"

Reaching over, he squeezed her thigh. "Wife. I like the sound of that."

"You better. Cuz the way things are going, it's just you and me. Forever. And ever. And a day after that." Frowning, she turned to face I-81 South. "As far as we know, we're the next Adam and Eve."

"So let me make sure I'm getting this right. If I'm the last man on earth, you'll have sex with me?"

Rolling her eyes, she scanned the road. They'd been on this road for approximately four hours, and the closer they came to the Tennessee border, the more fugitives they saw walking down it. People had abandoned failed vehicles on both sides of the road, and made the decision to press on. Small groups had decided to walk together, while others were clearly going it alone. Some had heavy packs slung over their shoulders while others had tied sheets around their waists, which they'd filled with supplies and other valuables. The luckier ones wore the kinds of packs with a multitude of pouches and zip-able compartments, or the kinds that were sewn onto sturdy metal frames, upon which sleeping bags and blankets could be mounted.

Luck, Olivia thought, considering the word. Liam didn't consider people lucky or unlucky. Luck wasn't a word in his lexicon. People, he said, created their own luck. People controlled their own outcomes. People either planned, or perished, she had learned. For in this world, failing to plan was planning to fail.

Setting the sandwich aside, she reached for her briefcase and the laptop within. For the past few months, she and Liam had done just that. They'd planned, planned, and made more plans. They'd started making detailed lists, which had eventually become complex Excel spreadsheets. They were compiling an inventory of specific items. To completely withdraw from a dying world, what were the things one would need to build a life? That was a question they had strove to answer. Liam, while alone, had made an excellent start, but two heads were always better than one. Olivia had provided a unique perspective.

In the beginning, she'd expected the task to be effortless. A list of necessities and essentials? Easy. An inventory of ingredients one would need to build a life?

Simple! Just consider what items one used in a day, write them down, and then purchase them. Right? Wrong. How wrong she had been. Considering how much broader her worldview had become of late, she nearly laughed out loud at the thought.

Ahead, the ambulance slowed and then stopped. Three hours, my ass, she thought, frowning. Settling into her seat, she let her mind wander. None of what she and Liam had done had been simple. It was more complicated than she'd ever imagined. Food and water were just the beginning. A very important beginning, mind you, and the things people think about first in these situations, but what about medical supplies and cooking utensils? What would they do when the power grids failed? What would they need to start a fire and cook food? And what about the luxuries we all take for granted: toilet paper, feminine napkins, dish soap, and laundry detergent?

Yes. She frowned. What about toilet paper? I mean really—what the hell about it? Such a simple thing to consider, yet also so important. A year ago, she never would have thought such a thing. She'd have never classified toilet paper as a luxury item, but she'd quickly learned that it was. That was the craziest thing about of all of this: the hundreds of personal discoveries like that.

Lately she'd been thinking about third world countries, about how people had lived in medieval times. Hell, why not take that one step further? What about toilet paper—yes—but what about in-door plumbing in general? What would happen when the plumbing systems failed? Where would they do their business? Would she and Liam prefer an outdoor privy, with 'his' and 'hers' butt-sized holes cut into a slab of wood? Or would they desire a simple outhouse? Would they hover over a hole above a hollowed-out shaft? Or might they prefer a pit latrine? And if so, how far should it be from their home? How deep should they dig it to avoid groundwater contamination?

Shaking her head, she bit her lip. These were the things that kept her awake at night. She and Liam agonized over such details, and toiletry was barely scratching the surface. Bathroom mechanics aside, every aspect of life was just as complicated, so much more than she'd ever envisioned.

In the beginning, the planning had been difficult. They'd sat, side-by-side, at the kitchen table, jumping from dilemma to dilemma. Their thinking had been nomadic and aimless. They'd flitted from concept to concept and solved little, and feared they were running out of time. It was Liam who'd suggested a better approach, a methodical way of cataloging supplies, and from there, they'd moved with purpose. It was an art form, she'd learned, this 'survivalism'. They would focus on a problem—like the bathroom issue—and vet it from all possible angles. They'd argue with one another, play devil's advocate, research and propose several different ideas, read books about life in the seventeen hundreds and then try to blend new technology with old philosophies. They'd considered which systems might fail, and when, and which could be replicated on a smaller scale at home.

But it wasn't just about the necessities. What about the things that made life enjoyable? It wasn't long before wine topped their list, followed soon after by coffee beans, chocolate, and spices. It was then that Olivia named the supply room the 'the ark'. And what an ark it was, she remarked. The cabin itself was magnificent. It was large and the view was spectacular, built high on the crest of a breathtaking peak. It was remote in a way that felt safe, soared high above the terrain in a way that felt strong. Liam had thought of everything, she mused. He'd picked the perfect location, the perfect climate. But it was the ark that impressed her the most. It was vast. Well, she reconsidered, as she imagined its shelves, boxes, and crates; it was vast the first time she'd seen it. Now that they'd doubled it in size, it was cavernous.

To maximize space, they'd hired contractors to expand the back wall of the cabin, and to extend the structure to the base of the mountain. They'd purchased industrial-sized shelving and cabinetry then alphabetized the shelves and measured out space. Half of the ark was earmarked for water, while the remainder was split between food, cans, jars, and boxes. Not that there wouldn't be water, of course. Though indoor plumbing would eventually fail, there would always be natural rainfall, and even though rain was trending acidic, it would still be potable for years to come. The water just gave them peace of mind.

They'd worked on the ark for months, it seemed, and this was the trip that marked its completion. She had sold her single-story home in Richmond, Virginia, and she and Liam were relocating permanently. The items in their car were the last of the load. This, she smiled, was the final leg of the trip, after which they could finally settle in. And once they were in, they could double their efforts, work on the ark full time. They had a plan in place, an experiment of sorts, something they were calling a 'dry run'. For an entire month they would seclude themselves, withdraw from society completely. For one full month they would test their efforts, live life with only the things they'd collected. They would use no utilities, plumbing, or gas, and absolutely no electricity. They would wash all clothing and dishes by hand, use the outhouse facilities exclusively, chop wood for the hearth, plant crops on the sweeping hills behind the cabin's deck, and make and grow their own food. They would go to ground, so to speak. For an entire month, society wouldn't exist. Their only contact with the outside world would be Olivia's prenatal doctor's appointments.

The dry run was a pilot study of things to come, and was set to commence in less than two weeks. Olivia was shocked by her exuberance. She was actually looking forward to it. Her! Olivia Abner! She of the silk dresses and laptop computers. She of the rolled up khaki's and Starbucks lattes. A few weeks from now, her entire world would change. Starbucks lattes would become brewed coffee, ground by hand. Television would become books and magazines, read by the soft light of candles, or board games played on the porch beneath the moon. Late nights on her computer would be late nights with her husband, reclining on chairs, drinking wine.

It was crazy. She'd never considered herself the type. She'd never thought she was made of strong enough stock, but she had to admit, the vision was romantic, like a set of images with filigreed edging. The cabin was life, while outside it was death, for life could be found in a well-appointed shelter. Death was out there, exposure to the elements, with one finger poised to pull a trigger. She felt lucky. "Roughing it" didn't sound like "roughing it" anymore. Or maybe she'd evolved past possessions and property. Maybe it eventually happened to everyone. Maybe once the noise was silenced and life's excesses were pared down to necessities, the human soul could take root and flourish. Perhaps only then could one find comfort in the simple treasures life had to offer. Olivia, thankfully, was ready for something deeper, something she and Liam would discover together, alone in their cabin at the top of their mountain.

It was something she was determined to embrace and love.

They would journal their experiences for thirty days and evaluate themselves after it ended. They'd keep a tally of items they wished they'd had, make of a list of items they hadn't used, and at the end of the experiment, re-join society, purchase what they needed and then try it again.

"We have time," Liam had assured her. "Let's make sure we get it right."

And Olivia wholeheartedly agreed. She actually found the process captivating. It was an exercise she wished she'd done as a much younger woman. To pare down her list of 'wants' to a concise list of 'needs' was humbling. She never realized how much she took for granted, how little in life was truly essential. It was a scrutiny of the self, a check of the ego, a much-needed exercise in maturity. But it was also something else: a tie that bound. It connected her to Liam in ways she hadn't expected. Never had she felt this close to a man. Most married people imagined growing old and retiring together, but she and Liam were planning for it, in a way that was most substantive.

Turning from the window, she observed him in profile. He had threatened to cut his hair twice this month, and twice, she hadn't allowed it. She loved his imperfect ponytail, and the way his left eye was slightly lower than his right. She loved the way he pursed his lips when pondering a thing, the way he pulled his earlobe when embarrassed. She loved that he'd immediately accepted her pregnancy. He'd be an excellent father. She was certain of that. And she loved that he took all of this planning so seriously. She admired his courage and forethought for having had it. He had read all the signs while so many others hadn't. He'd saved their lives. She was forever in his debt.

A loud thwack at her window made her jump, nearly forcing her out of her seat. Had she not been carrying an extra twenty pounds, she would have hopped onto the center console of the car. Liam cried out. She felt the car swerve. Outside her window five teenaged boys were ogling the half-eaten sandwich in her lap, and the boxed-up goods in the backseat of their car. Liam tried—in vain—to steer the car away, but there was nowhere to go. They were stuck.

"Stay calm," he asserted, between clenched teeth.

She barely moved as she watched them. They circled the car like a pack of starving wolves, and she peered at her surroundings maniacally. What could she and

Liam do to protect themselves inside this tin can? They were stuck in a car, in the middle of the road, like fish in a very small aquarium. A hundred yards ahead, the ambulance hadn't moved. Whatever event was unfolding up there was causing a bumper-to-bumper situation back here.

"What are they planning to do?" she breathed.

"What can they do? We're not exactly alone out here. We're surrounded by people who are stuck in their cars, behind police cars and emergency vehicles. They're just trying to scare us. Ignore them. Maybe in time they'll move on."

Ignoring his advice, she watched them carefully. The hairs on the back of her neck lifted. This was exactly what she and Liam feared for the ark, and the reason they'd taken such precautions while building it. Never had they let outsiders step foot inside their cabin. To ensure its secrecy, they'd taken drastic measures. They'd shopped for supplies in neighboring towns, sometimes in bordering states. They'd ordered from different online providers; spread things around, so to speak. Ordering bulk from a single retailer was stupid and careless, or so Liam had said. And when the contractors built the second half of the ark, she and Liam hid their supplies in the cabin's guest bedrooms.

"Planning to can jams and jellies," Liam had said, though not convincingly. He had always been a terrible liar. "This section over here will be the front counter of the store. We'll store the product in the back."

Dear God. Was that the best they'd been able to do? The contractor had peered around "the jam and jelly store", and frowned at the would-be "front of the shop" with no frontage access to streets or walkways. And forget about parking. Way up here? Theirs was a single-lane, private dirt road, cut into the side of a mountain, for Pete's sake. The only path that led to their home was a series of switchbacks and hairpin curves. The contractor must have thought them daft, or fools. Jam and jelly? What were they thinking?

The contractor had coughed his agreement into his fist, but he'd kept his opinions to himself. He'd had class. After all, their money was as green as the next man's, and they were paying it in cash. He wasn't a fool.

Despite the rocky start, the ark, when finished, was something to behold. It surpassed their every imagining of it. With proper organization, it was a vast reservoir, its capacity much larger than the needs of a family of three. And it was theirs, she thought with satisfaction. Theirs alone. They had put in the time to create it. They'd developed the plans and implemented them, liquidated their entire lifes' savings to make it happen. Never would they allow a living soul take it away.

Outside, the boys were still circling the car, pulling Olivia back to the present. She gestured wildly at the vehicle to her right, doing her best to catch the driver's attention. Stubbornly, he wouldn't take the bait. He was facing forward, keeping to himself, aware of the situation, but choosing anonymity.

"Hey man!" one of the boys cried out to Liam. He was reed-thin and dressed in torn jeans, wearing a shirt that was as dirty as his face. The tattoo of a great white conical snout was peeking around the curve of his throat. Olivia jumped when he pounded his fist against Liam's window. "How about you give us a hand, old man? Get us across the Tennessee border." His eyes flitted to Olivia's swollen belly and a slow smile spread across his face. "I'm not askin' old man. I'm tellin'. I'm giving you an order. Open the door. Sneak us across the border, or things will get very uncomfortable for your wife."

One of the smaller boys hopped onto the hood of the car, dropped to all fours, and peered through the window. Though Olivia was trying to keep herself calm, a sharp squeal slipped through her lips.

"Liam," she hissed, shrinking back in her seat.

"Sneak them across the Tennessee border? What the hell is he talking about?"

Without acknowledging her question, Liam reached beneath his seat and withdrew a small handgun. As he tapped it gently against the steering wheel, he bravely met the nearest boy's gaze.

Olivia sucked in a breath, dumbfounded. A gun? Liam? Since when? Swallowing hard, she jerked her gaze from the gun's sleek barrel to the boys who were eyeing it warily. After several moments, the weapon did its job, and the boys moved along to harass the next vehicle. Wrenching the rearview mirror to the right, she watched them move to the car behind Liam's, kick its tires, and tap on its windows. She allowed herself to take a deep breath. The world was full of desperate people like these, and desperate people were dangerous. A sudden anger clenched her fists. Was this the best those boys could do? Antagonize others to get what they needed? There would always be victims in life, she thought, and there would always be those who were victors. There were those who were feeble, and those who were strong, those who would achieve and those who would fail. It was unavoidable. It was just a part of life.

She turned to her husband, mouth slightly agape, and eyed the gleaming weapon in his hand. "Where the hell did you get that?"

Turning from the window, he loosened his fist, which was still wrapped tightly around the handle. "I…" He stammered, facing her. "I have many," he dared. "We. I mean we have many," he corrected himself. "Many guns, rifles, and rounds of ammunition. It's necessary, Olivia. We don't have a choice." He nodded toward the rearview mirror. "Don't you agree after witnessing that?"

She mopped her sweaty brow with the edge of her sleeve as an inappropriate laugh threatened to bubble from her lips. "I'm not complaining, Liam. Really, I'm not. I'm in shock, I guess. I didn't think you owned a gun. I'm surprised you've never shown it to me before."

"I didn't want you thinking about violence, I suppose. Or worrying about things, or feeling frightened. I didn't want you feeling unsafe." Turning awkwardly in his seatbelt, he added. "I want you to connect the cabin to feelings of security and confidence, Liv. I want you to think of it as a stronghold, not a place we'll have to defend."

She rubbed her belly in slow circles. "Like I said, I'm not complaining. And I'm not upset. I just wish you had told me, is all. Don't keep things from me. I don't like it. We can't afford to keep important things from each other—even if we find them uncomfortable to talk about. We've too long a life to live with none but each other to share it with. Let's not keep secrets, okay?" Putting the situation from her mind as best she could, she straightened and peered out the window. The situation ahead was growing closer by the moment. "And Liam," she said absently, "We will have to defend the cabin. Please tell me you know that, right? It's bound to happen. Those boys…" She shook her head. "Were nothing compared to the kinds of people who roam these parts, especially if things deteriorate further. Look at all of these homeless people! Look at these empty cars! What do you think these people will do? These are families, Liam: parents and children."

She was referring to the cars at the sides of the road, which had gasped their last breath and been abandoned. And it wasn't faulty mechanics or flat tires that had rendered them useless. They'd simply been deserted, left behind. People were spending the last of their money to flee as far west as they could, and may of these cars had simply run out of gas. Or battery power. Or electricity. These days, cars ran on many different fuel sources, though all were scarce and expensive. The government had raised the price of gasoline, which had made transportation a luxury item. People had driven as far west as they could and then resigned to continue on foot.

"You're right," Liam said quietly. "We'll have to defend the ark. We'll have to keep safe our belongings and our child. That's what the guns are for." He dropped his gaze to her belly, adding, "Are you angry with me?"

"Nope. I told you I wasn't. Just want to be part of the decision-making process. And I don't want you keeping important things from me. Come on." She tapped his knee. "We're starting to move."

The traffic was starting to inch forward again, the red and blue lights of police cars and ambulances growing steadily closer. Olivia could see some type of barricade ahead, where law enforcement officers had exited their vehicles and stationed themselves at the sides of each lane.

"They're stopping every car. What for?" she asked.

As they approached the scene, her tension increased. She could see policemen reaching through windows, examining driver's licenses and other paperwork. And she could see them turning people away. Her stomach clenched as she watched. Cars were making U-turns up ahead, the faces of drivers, grim. She watched an officer scrutinize a document, reach a decision, and then motion to his partner, who nodded and lifted the barricade. But others, she noticed, weren't getting through. A procession of drivers was being turned away, and being told to head back to the last exit. Unfortunately a concrete median was in their way, preventing them from doing it properly. Cars were weaving between pedestrians and stalled vehicles, trying to cut paths back to freedom. It was madness! Drivers were angry, red-faced and crying. An unsettling thought suddenly occurred to Olivia.

"Liam," she asked, "what state are you licensed in?"

Though his voice was calm, the lines around his eyes betrayed his anxiety. "New Jersey," he muttered. "Only New Jersey. I purchased the cabin three years ago, but only as a second home. I don't have a Tennessee driver's license."

She swallowed hard, her mind racing. "And the closing paperwork for the house. Do you have it?"

"I have it, but I don't know where. I don't have it on me, if that's what you're asking." He pointed. "Check the glove compartment. See if there's an old tax bill inside, or a copy of the insurance policy for the house, something with the address listed on it."

She rifled its contents but found nothing that would work. Car registration...New Jersey. Damn. Insurance bill...New Jersey. Not good. Nothing mentioning Tennessee whatsoever. Pulling her phone from her purse, she turned to Liam. "What escrow company handled the closing?"

"First United Title and Escrow."

Ahead, the situation was intensifying. More and more cars were being turned away, and more and more drivers were getting angry. What the hell was this about? Why were they doing this? Why prevent ingress at a state border? Was this even legal? And what about people who were simply passing through? Trying to reach other destinations?

Her pulse quickened as she dialed the escrow company's phone number, and when a recorded message reported the office closed, panic set her hands trembling. These days escrow companies were few and far between. People weren't purchasing homes anymore. Most were using what money they had left to stockpile food and other valuables.

Setting the phone down, she cursed aloud. They had run out of time, reached the front of the line. "What do we do now?" she asked Liam.

Leaning over, he buried the gun beneath his seat "Nothing we can do, Liv. I think we're about to be turned away. And if we are, we'll figure things out. Okay? No need to panic just yet."

Easier said than done, she thought, as she watched the verbal exchange in front of them. The driver of the car was gesturing wildly to a cop who was frowning, arms crossed across his chest. A body was slumped against the passenger door, but she couldn't make out the details. Liam slowly rolled down his window, and she cocked her head to hear what they were saying.

"Officer," the driver said, "my family and I are headed west, to Denver. We are not turning this vehicle around. I won't lose a day and a half because of this shit. Who's to say this isn't happening in other states, too?" He slammed a fist on the dashboard, shocking the cop. "How do you expect us to get out of here?"

The policeman shared a meaning glance with his partner, who took a step closer, lowering a hand to his hip. "Sir, please lower your voice," he said. "There are plenty of ways to get to Denver." He shook his head. "I'm sorry, but Tennessee is closed to anyone who isn't a resident. Without proper paperwork, I'll have to ask you to turn this car around."

The blond cop at the window suddenly narrowed his eyes. "Sir, is that your wife? Is she okay?"

The driver ignored the question, saying, "This is some kinda bullshit you're pulling on us. My family and I need to get out of here. Now. I am not turning this vehicle around. This is a public road. You can't do this. You can't stop people from using a public road."

The blond cop took a step closer. "Sir, I asked you a question. Is that your wife? Is she ill?" Olivia watched him set his hands to the sill. "Ma'am?" he asked, "Is everything all right? Do you need—"

With an abruptness that shocked Olivia, the driver thrust the door open and leapt out. The cop was thrown backward, slammed to the ground, where he landed hard against the pavement, and grunted. The driver pulled a gun from his waistband, and in a matter of seconds, officers swarmed the scene. Guns were raised and trained on the driver.

"Drop it, sir. Place your hands above your head."

Olivia shrank from the developing scene while Liam's panic was palpable. He threw himself across the center console, as much as his seatbelt would allow, in an effort to shield her body.

"Sir," the officer was saying, "the gun. Drop it. I won't ask you again."

The tense moment hung in the air, before a gut-wrenching sob tore from the gunman's throat. He lowered his weapon, though not completely, and cupped his knee with his free left hand. "Laura," he moaned. "My Laura."

With the man's attention focused on his feet, the policemen slowly edged closer. The blond cop who had fallen to the ground had scrambled to his feet and raised his weapon. "What about Laura, Sir? Does she need medical assistance?"

The man only shook his head and moaned. "My Laura. What have I done?"

The officers exchanged wary glances, while one moved cautiously for the door and peered inside.

"Ma'am? Can we offer you aid?" With a jerking motion, he pulled back his head. "Jesus," he said, cupping his nose. "I think she's dead. And there's a kid in there!"

A cop with salt-and-pepper hair moved for the door but didn't get far, for in a fluid motion the driver lifted his weapon, leveled it on the officer and pulled the trigger.

The sound of the shot disbursed through the air. Olivia screamed and pushed at Liam's chest. He was practically on top of her, twisting her painfully. Her voice was shrill as she struggled from his grasp. She had to free herself, to see what would happen, for the passenger door of the gunman's car was slowly opening, and a child was stepping onto the pavement.

"Let…me…see," she complained, pushing at Liam as forcefully as she could. "Get off of me. I'm fine!

Let me see!"

When he reluctantly released her, she craned her neck to see the child. He was thin and obviously frightened. He couldn't be more than three years old. He was clutching a blanket with a thumb in his mouth, and he was making his way to his mother's door. He fumbled at the handle and pulled.

Olivia's eyes darted to the officers. They'd been focused on the driver. They hadn't seen him yet. The salt-and-pepper officer was clearly dead, his body bloodied and crumpled on the ground. She tried to swallow, but her throat had gone dry. There was too much blood, carnage, and pain. The officers were tense and shouting.

"Drop your weapon, sir," the blond cop yelled. "Or we'll be forced to take you down. Lower your weapon. I won't ask you again."

Peering at the dead officer, the man began to quietly sob, "I can't do this by myself—not without her. I can't give him the life he deserves."

As he raised the butt of his gun to his temple, time seemed ponderously slow. The blond officer advanced half a step, pleading with the man, his voice soft and level. "Sir, trust me, you don't want to do this. Come with me. Please. We'll figure this out."

Olivia was amazed by his professionalism. Having witnessed the man shoot one of his own, he was still able to master his emotions. Unlike her, she thought savagely. Rage consumed her. Let the man kill himself, for all she cared. He was obviously crazy.

The blond officer continued to speak in even tones. "Drop your gun. We can figure this out. Just tell us what happened to Laura. Lower your gun, Sir. We can talk things through."

Olivia heard a faint click. The man had cocked his weapon, loaded the chamber. She quickly returned her gaze to the boy, who had somehow managed to open the passenger door and was tugging on his mother's sleeve, sobbing. She scanned the scene, trying to decide what to do, while a maternal instinct slowly took over. It was an overwhelming impulse, a force more powerful than fear.

Now, it said quietly. Go now.

Her fingers found the handle and pulled, and with a soft click, the door fell open. Leaning against it, she slid to the ground.

"What are you doing?" Liam cried out, crazed. The depth of his fear brought tears to her eyes. For a moment she was trapped; his eyes held her captive, while a myriad of consequences tumbled through her head.

"Liam, I—"

What? she asked herself. What can I say? What the hell am I doing? Her thoughts were wild and tempestuous, and she was barely able to find her voice. "The boy ..." she stammered, turning toward the child. "He's alone out there. I have to help him." Finding the resolve she thought she had lost, she pulled herself into an awkward crouch, the door her only shield from the violence outside.

"No," Liam hissed as he fumbled for his seatbelt. "Get back here, Liv. Get back here now. This is madness. You can't go out there."

Turning from him, she edged further from the vehicle, her eyes still fixed on the child. "Hey there, sweetheart," she called to him softly. "Over here. Can you make your way over to me?"

She motioned with her hands but kept her movements small. When she caught his attention, he turned to meet her gaze, but refused to let go of the hand he was holding. Revulsion was bitter in her throat, like acid, for the hand he held was heavy and lax, the pale skin veined with purple and blue. She swallowed hard and whispered to him. "Stay with her. It's okay. I'll come to you."

As Liam tumbled from the passenger door, Olivia crept closer to the front of their vehicle. "Olivia," he was saying, "Come back here. Now." She ignored his voice, taking a moment to assess the driver's mental state. He was bent at the waist, hands braced against his knees. Tears were streaming down his face. It wasn't good. Though he'd moved the gun from the side of his head, his knuckles were white where they clenched it. If he turned his head but a quarter of an inch, he'd catch her movements peripherally. She hunkered down and crept forward slowly.

One of the policemen dared to take another step. "That's it, Sir. That's good. Lower the gun. We'll help you if you'll agree to come with us. We'll sort this out at the station."

Blinking rapidly, the man shook his head. He was muttering to himself, in a voice that was pitched too high. "There's no fixing this. There's no going back."

"No," the officer persisted. "We can fix this. We will fix this if you come with us. Set your weapon down. Raise your hands above your head."

"My weapon?" the man murmured quietly. He raised his hand and peered at the gun, as if he'd suddenly forgotten it was there. "My weapon," he said, with more conviction this time.

For Olivia, the next few moments were hallucinatory, the images bright and jagged against her eyes. With smoothness and efficiency, unlike his previously erratic behavior, he lifted the gun and placed it firmly against his temple. She let loose a gasp that caught his attention. Turning to her, he met her gaze for just an instant, pulled the trigger, and was gone.

Olivia lunged for the boy in that moment. She somehow crossed the gulf between them, swept him into her arms and covered his face. Pushing him into the crook of her neck, she ran for the shoulder of the road. Liam followed, his footsteps thundering behind her.

It's okay, she thought. The danger has passed.

She carried the boy to the grass and set him down. He swayed and she caught him, ran her hands over his body. He was fine, uninjured, healthy, and whole—and utterly defenseless with big brown eyes. He was clinging to her pants, arms reaching for her, pleading for the shelter of her warm embrace, and she willingly obliged, nestling him to her breast.

"Do you think they were his parents?" she asked, turning to Liam.

"What? I don't know. Jesus, Liv. What were you doing back there? What were you thinking? You could have been killed." He was breathless and angry, his face red and blotchy.

"I'm fine," she insisted. "Everything's fine. We need to talk to those cops."

"No we don't. I'll do it. You stay here. I'll talk to the cops. Can I trust you to stay put for the next five minutes?"

"Liam," she objected, "the danger has passed. And that man," she added, covering the boy's right ear. "He's dead. He's stone cold dead. I hardly think we're in danger anymore. Let's figure out who that man was to this boy."

"No." Liam said, his jaw firm. "Let's get back to our car and head back to the last exit. What we need right now is a hotel room. Let's find our paperwork and get to our cabin. Let's cross the Tennessee border before we can't anymore."

Olivia pulled the boy closer to her breast. "I won't leave him, Liam. You know I can't do that. I'm sorry, but it's just not r—"

"Excuse me, ma'am?" The blond cop was staring at the child in her arms. Olivia recoiled from the blood on his face. "Ma'am," he repeated, "I can take the boy now. You and your husband can return to your vehicle. If you show me your papers, we'll let you move on."

He reached for the child, but Olivia stepped back. As if on cue, the boy held onto her tighter. He snaked his arms around her neck, locked his fingers behind her ears.

"I think, for now, if it's alright, he wants to stay with me."

The officer surveyed woman and child, and seemed to reach a quick conclusion. "Follow me." He turned to Liam. "I'll need to see your license and registration. The two of you may as well give us your statements."

They followed the officer behind a row of police vehicles, where an EMT was parked and waiting. Olivia perched on the edge of the bumper and positioned the child on her knees. She turned his face toward the EMT, while the blond officer crouched down beside them.

"Hello son," he said softly. "How're you doing? Were you taking a trip with your mother and father?"

The child's eyes were wide, his face pale. Olivia worried that he might be in shock. The EMT must have shared her concerns, for he draped a blanket around his slim shoulders.

Wrapping him in the folds, Olivia snuggled him closer. "I don't think we're going to get much out of him today." She peered at a paneled van, ten feet from where they were sitting, where several occupants were seated inside, hands bound and cuffed behind their backs. "Looks like you've had an interesting day, officer."

With a sigh, he lifted his hand to his brow. "Interesting is an understatement." Reaching for a pen and a pad, he asked, "Can you give me your names?"

Liam took over. "My name is Liam Colt. This is my wife, Olivia. We own a home in Sevierville, Tennessee, and once we get back, we're never leaving it again."

"Smart thinking," the cop said, returning his attention to the boy. "So, I'm guessing you don't know this child. Am I right?"

Liam met Olivia's gaze. "No," he answered softly. "Not yet. But I have a strange feeling we're about to know him better."

A third officer entered the conversation. "There were needles inside that woman's purse," he said. "Lots of needles. Look." His expression was sober as he opened his hand and lifted a small vial of liquid to the light. The contents gleamed silver in the sun.

The blonde cop furrowed his brow. "She's an addict? Okay. Is she dead?"

Olivia clutched the child closer to her breast. His mother was a drug addict? How could that be? Who could afford to do drugs these days?

"Dead, yes" the other answered, "But addict, no." Holding the small bottle of liquid to the light, he turned the label to face them.

"Insulin," the blonde said softly. "She's a diabetic?"

"Was a diabetic. Not anymore." Lifting a wallet from an evidence bag, he pulled a worn photograph from its folds. "Found this too," he said, handing it over.

When she saw the photo and the smiling faces, Olivia's heart tore in two. Centered in the frame was a family of three, smiling for the camera and holding onto one another, the setting sun bright behind their backs. Olivia felt her throat catch. Reaching for it with small hands, the child brought it to his chest and wept. She met the officer's compassionate gazes. "I think that answers everyone's questions."

"I don't suppose you'd come to the station with us, Ma'am."

Liam answered him boldly. "I don't suppose you'd let us cross the border without paperwork."

The blonde cracked a smile. "I think we can manage that. I suppose we can make an exception in this case. Stay here, with the boy, while we wrap things up. Let the EMT give you both a clean bill of health."

Together they watched the blonde return to the bloodstain in the middle of the road. The gunman's body had already been removed, which was somehow depressing to Olivia. The boy was now alone, no mother, no father. They'd been swept away as if neither had existed.

Crouching down in front of the boy, the EMT gently palpated his body.

"I think he's all right," Olivia offered quietly. "Physically at least." Lifting him from her chest, she set him on her knee, and when the EMT left, Liam took his place. "My name is Olivia," she whispered to the child. "And this is Liam. Can you tell us your name?"

He was staring into his open palm, where the picture of his parents lay crumpled and frayed.

Liam's voice was thick with emotion. "I'm sorry about your family, son. I'm sure your Mommy and Daddy loved you very much."

"I'm sure they did," Olivia agreed. "How could they not?" She squeezed his shoulders gently. "We have to take you to the police station now. Are you ready for that?" The boy raised his head, alarm in his eyes. Reaching out a hand, he caught her hair in his fingers. She swallowed past the lump in her throat. "We'll go with you," she promised. "We won't leave you alone." She pushed a fall of dark hair from his eye. "But I'm hoping you'll tell us your name. We've told you ours. It's only fair."

He met her gaze, answering bravely. "Jeremy," he said. "My name is Jeremy."

There's nothing wrong with enjoying looking at the surface of the ocean itself, except that when you finally see what goes on underwater, you realize that you've been missing the whole point of the ocean. Staying on the surface all the time is like going to the circus and staring at the outside of the tent.

—Dave Berry

CHAPTER 9
1 Year Prior

JUNE 20TH, 2175
JUST OUTSIDE OF KNOXVILLE
TENNESSEE

She pushed the food aside without saying a word. She hadn't spoken in over a month.

"Sam, you need to eat," Jeremy said. He caught her hand and turned it over to examine the meter at her wrist. "Your blood sugar is at sixty-two. That's far too low. You need to eat something."

Jeremy, though he was loath to admit it, was quickly losing his patience. He ladled a steaming cup of soup into a bowl, crumbled crackers upon it, and pushed it toward her. "Sam, what do you think mom would say? How would she feel about this? She sacrificed her life for yours, you know, but you seem bent on destroying her gift."

She snatched the bowl and turned away from him.

She had lost her patience with him as well, though he probably should have withheld that remark about her mother. He was using guilt to get what he wanted, which wasn't fair to her. Guilt wasn't the best treatment for loss and depression.

It had been thirty-four days since they'd been forced from the cabin, thirty-four days since Susan had died, thirty-two days since they'd last seen the smoke, lifting from the tops of the highest trees. In a macabre way, they had clung to those tendrils. They'd hugged their knees and stared, transfixed. First, the smoke had disbursed, lost its shape, before dissipating fully and blending with the clouds. It was difficult to watch it drift away. That sad sooty cloud had been the last of their home, and once it was gone, reality set in. They were alone, they two, homeless and hopeless.

Many times since that fateful night, Jeremy thought of the men he'd left inside the cabin. Had he put enough distance between them and Sam? They'd be angry, he considered. Infuriated, really. He tried to imagine their rage, and couldn't. To have survived this ailing wilderness for so many years, and then to have found his luxurious cabin, only to watch it burn to the ground? Oh, yes. Their wrath would surely know no bounds. If they ever crossed paths with Jeremy again, their retribution would be anything but swift. They'd make him pay, dearly, and painfully. But he refused to dwell on that now. There were other pressing matters to tend.

He poured from the ladle and moved to the couch. They'd found this abandoned house several weeks ago, and hadn't seen fit to leave it yet. They needed time to recuperate and heal. It was as much a mental break as it was a physical one. Jeremy needed time to formulate a plan, to take stock of their supplies and plot a course for their future. They couldn't stay here long term, he knew, but for now, it was as good a place as any to carve out a temporary life.

After emerging from the woods, thirty-four nights ago, battered and broken of spirit and body, he and Sam had followed Main Street westward. It was an easy road, both straight and wide, and they'd traversed it in silence, their heads hung low. He'd been eager to leave Sevierville proper behind, and had followed Main Street until it became US-441, which they followed on foot toward Knoxville. But from there, he hadn't really known what to do. Despite the planning he and Susan had done, and despite the brilliance of the cart in the woods, neither had considered a second destination. Why would they? What for? The idea was ludicrous. Losing the cabin was so farfetched that neither had created a contingency plan. The whole thing was absurdly implausible. What could force them from their private paradise? In what crazy parallel universe had a fire burned it to the ground? Yet here they were, vulnerable, exposed, with nothing but an industrial-sized laundry cart to keep them alive, and Jeremy was becoming increasingly concerned. Did they have the resources to make a new start? They were well equipped—yes—better prepared than most others he'd seen, but could they build a new life? More importantly, did they have the heart to?

Turning to Sam, he began his nightly ritual, speaking to her, yet receiving no response. "So," he said as he slurped from his spoon, "I was thinking that tomorrow we go to the library, pick out a few new books for you to read. What do you think about that?"

She didn't answer. Not that he was expecting her to. She hadn't spoken a word since that fateful night, though he'd vowed to never stop trying to reach her. He knew what she was feeling, having experienced it himself. Ever since that fateful night, his emotions were like a nauseating rollercoaster ride. First came the anger, a deep and bottomless rage, something that surged at unexpected moments. He'd been difficult to live with those first few days. He hadn't behaved the way a responsible adult should, the way a father should, and he'd known it. For a time, he'd withdrawn from her completely. He'd turned his rage inward and suffocated on it. It was then, he supposed—because of that rage—that she'd given up on him and stopped talking. At first, her silence had only fueled his anger. He'd lost his wife, his partner in life, his best friend and confidant, and now he'd lost her. The only person left in his life was refusing to acknowledge his presence. But why? It wasn't fair. How dare she shut him out? How dare she pretend that he didn't exist? Did she think his pain wasn't equal to hers? What had he done to deserve her taciturnity? Perhaps she blamed him, he wondered privately, held him accountable for the path their lives had taken. But how could she hold him responsible for this? For the actions of thieves and murderers?

He wasn't proud of his actions back then, or for the way he'd behaved in front of her. But by the time he'd thought to set things right, she'd already withdrawn inside herself. She'd needed him, and he'd failed her. He'd left her alone in a deep pit of grief, and now he wondered if he could ever forgive himself. It was his right to grieve; he'd lost someone too, but he could only do so in private, he'd concluded. It wasn't healthy to brood openly. Nor was it healthy to curse or scowl. He shouldn't be sharing his fears with her, or deliberating their next course of action out loud. Fathers held things together, stoically, with a steady hand and a compassionate heart. Sam had enough to worry about: where they would live, what she would eat, how she'd go on without her mother by her side. Jeremy would be a counterpoint to her sadness. He'd try to make the best of this tragic situation. He'd create hope and light, try to blanket her in it. He'd never stop trying to reach her. They didn't have Susan, or the cabin, or the ark, but they still had each other, and that had to be enough. For tonight, and for many more nights to come, they had food, water, a roof over their heads. Best to focus on that, he thought. Best to let the rest fall away for a time.

"At the library, maybe you'll find the Twilight series," he suggested spiritedly.

She slurped at her soup, eyes fixed on the highest window in the room, at the deep starry night beyond the glass. They were sitting in the living room of this beautifully appointed home, with its granite countertops and smooth tile floors. In the living room hung a massive—yet useless—wall-mounted flat-screen television. The beds were outfitted with clean furnishings, and the bathrooms with semi-clean towels. Worn-down slivers of soap were curled in the corners of the shower. It was safe, quiet, a good place to mourn. They'd been here a bit over two weeks now, and Jeremy had used the time wisely. He'd organized their supplies, made a list of things he wanted to scavenge, and though she hadn't spoken to him, she'd helped. She followed him quietly wherever he went, engaged in whatever activity he was doing. Since the fire, she didn't like being alone. He could understand that. He felt the same way.

Together they boarded the windows of the house and conducted a thorough search of its grounds. Why particular homes were ransacked and destroyed, while others remained unmolested was a mystery to him. It made no sense. There was no rhyme or reason. This house had been picked clean, though thankfully, not ruined. There were no scraps of food to speak of, of course, no bottles of water, no clothing, no shoes, but it was clean, safe, and somewhat remote. He was surprised no one had claimed it yet. It was centered on several acres of forestland; the nearest neighboring home was at least several miles away, which was the reason he'd chosen it in the first place.

That night, in a fog, they'd meandered down the road, searching for something, though they weren't sure what. They'd haphazardly turned down residential streets and followed dirt paths to remote areas. Years ago Jeremy had thought to pack an atlas inside the cart, and since losing the cabin, he'd put it to good use, plotting their path with a faded purple marker. They'd happened on this house by accident, really, while searching for a place to erect their tent.

"So," he urged, "how about it then? The Twilight series? The Hunger Games? Or maybe you've been thinking about something else instead?"

She finished her soup and lay down on her side, and without saying a word, curled into herself. The outline of her spine startled him. He hadn't realized how much weight she'd lost in such a short amount of time. Her vertebrae were visible through her thin T-shirt, and resembled a snake running the length of her spine. Grief, he said, to assuage himself. It was grief she suffered. Her sugars were fine.

With a sigh, he arose, stamped out the fire, and then stretched out beside her, clasping his hands behind his head. Though the house had four bedrooms, they hadn't occupied any, choosing instead to sleep in the living room, together. Neither could face a night alone.

He peered at her slim form, the moon silhouetting her body in soft silver piping.

"Sam," he said quietly, "you have to stop this. At some point, you're going to have to talk to me again. I know you blame me for what happened to your mother. And perhaps you should. Perhaps it was my fault. After all, I opened the door, didn't I? I didn't do my job. I didn't protect her. I failed you both. I lost the cabin."

She didn't respond, so he took a ragged breath. Something inside him felt different tonight. It was as if he'd weakened somewhat, as if a tender thread in his heart had broken. His emotions felt raw and close to the surface. Maybe he was lonely or his patience had thinned. Or maybe he was tired of pretending all the time, of feigning strength while crumbling inside. His voice shook when he spoke. He couldn't control it.

"I've been lying to you, Sam, pretending to be

strong. But I'm lonely. I need to hear your voice. I miss you. I'm weak. I've been trying to act strong, but I'm not. The truth is I'm the vulnerable one, not you. I'm the one who needs noise and laughter and books, and silly teenage talk about vampires and magic wands." He pulled the blankets up to his chin, like a child trying to comfort himself. "I miss you so much, and I feel so alone. I just wish you'd say something, anything—for my sake. Sometimes weathering a difficult storm is easier to do when you're doing it with someone else."

She rustled in her blankets but didn't speak. It hadn't worked.

Well, he thought sourly, I've done what I can. I've tried everything I can think of to reach her. I've laid my emotions bare. I've been brutally honest. I've done what I can with what little I have. He blinked into the darkness, a thought taking shape. Wasn't there one more thing he could do? One more thing he could share? To crack her protective shell, perhaps he'd have to do something a bit more drastic. He'd tried everything else; why not try this? He'd been considering it for several days now. He'd come to think of it as his last Hail Mary. But was it the right thing to do, he wondered? It certainly wouldn't win him any parent-of-the-year contests, but if it bridged the gap between them, so be it. Shared experiences often incite empathy.

"Sam," he began cautiously, "I know how it feels to lose a parent. It hurts. I remember the pain quite well. It hurts like nothing else I've experienced before. It leaves a deep and jagged scar, one that won't heal no matter what you do."

She scoffed, and the noise startled him. He tensed. He was accustomed to silence or his own ramblings. The sound of her voice seemed somehow alien. Her voice came ragged and low, but it came.

"No," she whispered hoarsely. "You don't understand. You have no idea what it feels like for me.

Your parents lived to be old and gray. They died of natural causes. It's not the same thing."

With that, she settled into her blankets and attempted to shut him out completely.

"I only wish that were true, but it's not. That's not the story of what happened to me. The grandparents you thought were my parents actually weren't. My real parents died long ago, when I was young." His belly did a nauseating flip. So much had changed in her life recently. Would this information send her over the edge? "When I was three," he continued bravely, "my father shot himself in the head."

Flinching, she sat up smoothly in her blankets, her body stiff and straight in the moonlight. She sat still for a moment, her gaze fixed on the wall, clearly pondering what he'd just said. After a time, she lay back, stiff as a board, her voice softer yet no less accusatory.

"You're lying to me. I know what you're doing. I'm not stupid, Dad. You're trying to make our situations sound similar. But they're not similar. You should stop right here. What you're saying doesn't even make sense. It's disgusting actually. You should quit while you're ahead."

He shrugged into the darkness, his eyes wide. "I'm not lying, Sam, and I think you're old enough to know the truth. Blame and condemnation are adult concepts. If you're going to adopt them, you should know the whole story. If you're determined to hate me forever, then I guess you should know who you're hating, and why. You should know everything there is to know about me. I'd like you to finally know the truth. Mom knew this story, and you should too. Adults make informed decisions, Sam, but not before they have all the facts. So if you're going to alienate me permanently, I'd like you to know who you're alienating first."

Without another word, he turned over and closed his eyes. Let her ponder on that for a time.

The next morning was bright and warm, and together they set out for the library. She hadn't said a word, but something felt different. He could sense her careful control, her restraint. It was just below the surface. The pressure was building. He'd lit a fire and he was watching it burn. And the best way to stoke a teenage flame, he had learned, was to pretend that it didn't exist.

"We'll go to the library first," he said casually, "then I'd like to rummage a few convenience stores, see if we can't find something useful."

His hand found the shape of his gun, loaded and holstered at his waist. Since they'd lost the cabin, they'd encountered few people, and he really didn't expect to see more. Without a convenient source of water nearby, these lands were practically useless. Not that there wouldn't be people out here, families hunkered down in these hills and valleys, in places where fresh water could still be pumped from wells. But they weren't likely to cross paths with anyone today. The gun was precautionary, a security blanket, one he wouldn't leave behind ever again.

She said nothing as they ventured down the road toward town. The gravel beneath their shoes and their huffing breath were the only sounds he could hear, and he found himself imagining a strange and lonely world, a world in which they two were the last people on Earth. A shiver ran through his body. That fantasy could easily become reality. They might never lay eyes on other people again. Other decent people, he corrected himself, people with whom they would welcome acquaintances. There would always be gangs, miscreants, and fools. They'd even seen a few of these and hidden like cowards, behind houses or deep in the woods. But they were yet to cross paths with decent folk.

Her voice split the silence, nearly making him trip. "So," she said, "Are you gonna tell me then? Or were you just planning to let me wonder what you meant?"

He raised a mocking brow. "About what?"

"About what?" Scowling, she stopped in her tracks. When he turned to face her, she'd dug her feet in, and was standing, arms akimbo, wearing an exasperated look. He almost laughed, but caught himself. He knew that look. It was one that thrilled him. How like her mother she was.

"I mean it, Dad. Don't play games with me. You told me that story to get me talking again. I'm not stupid. I'm talking. You win. I'm letting you win. But I want to know, now. You owe me an explanation. What you said doesn't make any sense. Your mother was Olivia, and your father was Liam. Either you've been lying to me for my entire life, or you're lying to me now. Which horrible one is it?"

Turning from her, he started walking again. "Olivia and Liam weren't my parents. They were the people who found me and took me in. They found me, saved me, and adopted me, but they weren't my biological parents."

"And you never thought to tell me? You didn't think it was important? Wait." She stopped to shake her head. "That can't be right. You have to be lying. Grandpa had diabetes—like me. You guys always said that I got it from him."

"You didn't. I'm sorry. Unbelievable, I know. But sometimes—as they say—truth is stranger than fiction. And yes, I understand: it's unlikely. What are the odds grandpa would share the same condition as my mother?" He shrugged. "But like I said: it's true. Your biological grandmother suffered from diabetes. You actually inherited it from her."

He allowed her a moment to reflect on things, while enjoying the warmth of the sun on his back. It was a lot for her to digest, he knew. Hell, it was a lot for him to digest. Susan had known, but they'd never told Sam. There hadn't been a reason to divulge it. It wasn't that they kept it from her deviously. It just hadn't come up, and the years had slipped by. Liam and Olivia were special to Jeremy, more like parents than adoptive parents. They were his parents in every sense of the word. They'd loved him, cared for him, planned for his future, and he'd returned that love intensely. Biology had nothing to do with it.

Besides, he mused, he could barely remember his biological parents, much less anything about the day they had died. There were flashes of red, and tactile impressions: the coldness of his mother's hand, the firmness of Olivia's round belly. He remembered the red stippling of blood that had feathered the policeman's cheek. But there was nothing more than that, nothing spoken, or heard. The memories were akin to sensations. They were smells and colors, loud bursts of sound. It was the day his life was saved, not destroyed.

Sam pressed him further, but her tone had softened. "So you said your father killed himself. Is that right?" She cleared her throat "Shot himself…in the head?"

"Yep. That's right."

"I'm sorry. That's…terrible. Can you remember much else?"

Jeremy sighed. "Not really. I remember Grandma Liv and Grandpa Liam, and the cops who were there, and the emergency personnel. I can't remember much about my parents."

"But what about your mother?" Sam's brow furrowed. "What happened to her? If your father killed himself, then how did she die? Why did you go with Grandma and Grandpa instead of staying with her?"

He stopped and turned, caught the edge of her sleeve. This was the reason he'd brought this story up. This was the message he was trying to convey. He swallowed past the lump in his throat and forced himself to see this through. Despite its melancholic nature, this was something she needed to hear.

"My father killed himself because my mother had died. She died in our car, on the road. Grandma once said he felt culpable for her death, that he may have been culpable. We'll never know for sure. But Sam." He took a deep breath and centered himself. "My mother died from her diabetes. Back then, the way Liam and Olivia told it, only the wealthy could afford medicine. Society was crumbling. Treatments were scarce. It became harder and harder to treat her illness. People were beginning to raid convenience stores as they fled inland, away from the oceans. They turned on one another, stole from one another to suit their needs. It was an ugly world. Millions of people starved, while millions of others died from disease. Understand, Sam, that cancer, diabetes, and heart disease are death sentences if not properly treated."

He suddenly sat in the middle of the road, pulling her down, though he didn't know why. He was heavy as a stone, cast into a pond.

She glanced to her right, and then to her left, as though she feared they'd be seen and mocked. "Dad, get up! What are you doing? You're sitting in the middle of the road!"

"I'm sorry, Sam. Am I embarrassing you? Are there cars coming by? Am I about to be hit?" Crossing his legs, he pulled her down beside him. "Let's make one another a pledge, shall we? Let's sit in the middle of this forgotten street and make one another a promise. But before we do, let's stop this silliness. Let's end this awkward silence between us. Guilt, though not an illness itself, can be a death sentence if allowed to fester. Look how it destroyed my biological father." He took a deep breath and captured her hands, smoothing them inside his own. "Sam, you blame me for your mother's death, and that's okay. I blame myself, too." When his voice threatened to break, he steadied himself. "Damn it, Sam. I fucked up. I never should've opened that door. I never should've let your mother put down that gun. Maybe I shouldn't have let Doctor Jack come into our lives in the first place. Who the hell knows? 'Should' is a rabbit hole with a bottom we'll never see. We can play the 'should' game till the cows come home, but in the end, it won't do us any good. The past is gone. We only have now. We can choose to move forward as best we can, or we can choose not to. In the end, it's up to us. We can get up every morning and move ourselves forward, or we can curl in the shadows and live in the past."

She pursed her lips before speaking evenly. "Move forward? How can you say that? I'm not just going to forget about Mom."

"Who said moving forward means forgetting? I loved her too, Sam. I loved her very much. I loved her since the day we met. But I won't do to you what my father did to me. I'd never do that. It isn't fair to you. If I quit trying, what will you do? If I roll over and refuse to speak, act, or eat, what's going to happen to you?"

The lines around her mouth tightened. She was deep in thought. Maybe, he hoped, she was beginning to understand. After a moment, she squeezed his hands. "Dad, you're wrong. I don't blame you. Not for her death. Not for anything, really. I'm just angry. I miss her. I feel lost inside. I wonder if I'll ever be happy again. What your father did to you was wrong. I'm sorry you had to go through that."

"It was wrong, Sam, on so many levels. He gave up on me. He abandoned me. But do you know what was worse? In the end, he gave up on himself. He didn't believe he had the strength to persevere. But perseverance is a big part of life. Sometimes when we persevere, when we push through the darkest and most difficult times, we find light at the end of the tunnel. Somehow we arrive at a better place than we were before. I'm not saying our lives will be better without Mom, or that the pain won't take a long time to heal. I'm just asking you to persevere. With me, if you can. If we don't give up, we could be happy someday. Life goes on. It's a choice we make. One day, when we least expect it to happen, we might find that our lives are pretty good."

She dropped his hands and stared at her open palms. "I can't imagine our lives being good. I'm not there yet, but I know what you're saying."

"Good. That's all I was hoping for."

"I'm sorry, Dad." She lifted her gaze. "I wish you had told me these things before, but I'm sorry to hear about your parents. I think your dad should've made a better choice. I think he should've tried harder, for your sake."

He held her gaze with the fierceness of a lion protecting his cub. He didn't want to scare her, but this was important.

"Samantha, part of persevering is having a plan. That's the best lesson Grandpa Liam ever taught me. He planned for every occurrence, every outcome. His approach to life was systematic, methodical. I think this—more than anything else—is the reason you and I are still alive." As he pieced together his scattered thoughts, he lifted his hands to massage his temples. "I'm not saying this very well, am I? What I'm trying to say, Sam, is this: you and I need to formulate a plan. And the core of that plan needs to be your illness. We lost so much in that fire. Too much. Your mother handed me the only disks she had, but they won't last forever. We have to figure something out. So I need you to cooperate with me. I need you to understand why I do what I do. I'm developing a plan, but I need your help. To protect you, Sam, I'd go to the ends of the earth. But that's something I can't do alone. I need your help to persevere. Can you do that for me? With me?"

He saw her eyes well with tears she was much too strong to shed. Instead, she leaned into him, circled her arms around his neck. "I will, Dad. I'll persevere. For you.

For Mom. I'll try harder. I promise."

"Good." He heaved a sigh. "Thank God. Now, let's get to that library and get you a book. I assume you still want to torture me with the teenaged vampires and werewolves?"

She pushed herself to her feet and dusted her kakis. "I guess we can pick those up. But I think I want to read Harry Potter again. Do you mind?"

He smiled. People often did that. They recaptured a moment by recreating it. It was a healthy part of the healing process, and one he was happy to oblige. "Yeah," he agreed with a nod. "I'd like that."

Humans could never accept the world as it was and live in it.
They were always breaking it and living among the shattered pieces.

—Robin Hobb, *Blood of Dragons*

CHAPTER 10
Present Day

OCTOBER 2ND, 2176
MEMPHIS, TENNESSEE
1,777 MILES TO SAN DIEGO

"How are you holding up, Seth?"

Jeremy watched the boy's feet pedal furiously. The bike they had found wasn't set to the correct gear. For some reason, it refused to shift properly. Tonight, when they stopped, he'd have to take another look.

But at least they'd found one. He was thankful for that. For some reason the fates had delivered them a third bike. Not that Jeremy believed in fate. In his experience, it didn't exist. Once you committed to looking for a thing, once you were focused on one specific item, it always seemed to appear faster. The bike had come from one of Seth's neighbors' houses, down the street, from a garage, to be exact. And even though it was a rare find, it was a bit too small for his growing frame. The tires had been flat, but thankfully whole, and when the wheels turned they made a horrible screeching sound, but Jeremy was able to make it work.

"Merlin," Seth corrected him from over his shoulder. "My name's Merlin now. And I'm doing just fine."

"Not Merlin," Sam corrected him. "Marlin. We talked about this. Get it right. Merlin was a wizard not a fish."

"But I like Merlin better!"

Jeremy groaned. He had tired of this familiar argument. "Pike," he called out, "number please."

She lifted her arm and peered at her wrist. "Eighty-eight."

"Good," he said. "Perfect." Increasing his speed, he pulled alongside Seth. It was time to discuss the next leg of the journey, and though he'd planned to address it casually, his pulse was thundering in his ears.

"Okay guys," he said. "Listen up. Here's the thing: we've crossed into Memphis, now, and in another three miles, I-55 crosses the Mississippi River. Do you feel like crossing it tonight, or tomorrow? If you're tired, we can stop, camp on this side of the river, then bike across it in the morning. What do you think?"

Sam's excitement couldn't be contained. "Are you kidding me, Carp? Tonight, of course!" She glanced at the sun, now low in the sky. "The sun won't set for at least two hours. I think we should do it tonight!"

Seth, unlike Sam, was reluctant, which was odd. It was rare for him to disagree with her. In the short week they had spent together, he'd already put her on a ridiculously high pedestal. He idolized her, and he didn't hide it well. Whatever it was she wanted to do, he was doing it, right alongside her. He was a little lost puppy, nipping at her heels. But curiously, this time was different. He was overly cautious, wary of something.

"A river? he asked, a slight tremble in his voice. "How will we cross it?"

"Easily," Jeremy reassured him. "On a bridge,

overhead. We won't get anywhere near that water. We'll be high above it, and dry, looking down. We'll cross it tonight, make camp on the other side."

Seth's brow was creased with concern. "But I'm not supposed to get close to water. Won't we get sick when we cross it?"

Sam slowed down and fell into place beside them. "It can't hurt us, Marlin, and we have no choice. We have to cross the River if we want to get to San Diego. Besides, it only makes you sick if you drink it."

Jeremy took the lead. It was now or never. "She's right, Marlin. We'll be fine. Let's do it now. Let's get it over with. We won't get anywhere near it. I promise."

Seth pursed his lips but kept pedaling. They'd been approaching the river for some time now. Jeremy had smelled it a few miles back. And it wasn't that he feared to cross it. It wouldn't harm them; Sam was right. It was harmless if not ingested. He just feared to look upon the devastation. The Mississippi River was one of the foulest bodies of water on the planet—or so he'd been told, and had read in books. It was responsible for killing all the wildlife in the Gulf of Mexico. For decades, it had been like a tumorous growth, leaking poisons into a healthy body. It would be difficult to behold in person. Much worse—he hoped—than the Pacific Ocean would be.

He blindly fished through his side pannier, palmed a granola bar, and pulled alongside Sam. "Pike, time to eat. Do you need to stop?"

"Nope." She smiled. "I'm an excellent multi-tasker."

She ripped into the plastic with her teeth while Seth watched. He was curious, of late, about her illness. "She's like a robot," he had said, that first night he saw the florescent numbers at her wrist. And when she'd lifted her shirt to show him her implant, he'd pulled back, startled, and then smiled.

"Yep," she'd said. "I'm a robot." She pointed to

her belly. "This keeps me alive."

And from that moment on, he'd made a game of her illness: guessing her sugars, giving her food, catching her when she got fuzzy.

"Does it hurt?" he'd asked once, his eyes lidded with sympathy.

"No. Not really. Just a bit sometimes, but only when we have to change the disk." She'd peered at her belly before meeting Jeremy's gaze. "Which I'm afraid we'll have to do soon, Carp. I'm at fourteen percent. This disk is almost empty."

"I know," Jeremy had said. "It's okay. In a few more days, we'll load you back up."

"Can I watch?" Seth asked, far too enthusiastically.

Jeremy didn't think Sam would let him do that, though it was endearing the way Seth doted on her. She was probably the first child he'd seen for many years, if ever, and she wasn't even a child anymore. But it was more than just admiration or mild curiosity; she was something new for him to focus on, something other than the death of his mother. Seth, though young, was strong for his age, but Jeremy knew he was still struggling privately. He hadn't yet told the full story of what had happened to him. Jeremy didn't know how long he'd been living inside that Walmart, with his mother's corpse on the opposite end of the store. But if her level of decay was any indication, it was longer than was healthy for a child his age. Not that he wasn't well adjusted, Jeremy thought. He was surprisingly resilient and levelheaded. His zest for life, and the buoyancy with which he tackled everyday tasks, bespoke of a strong parentage. He had obviously been loved, his character shaped and molded by devoted parents.

Before they'd left Scottsboro, Jeremy had conducted a brief but touching ceremony to honor Seth's mother. Seth had needed closure and Jeremy had wanted to give him that. He'd chosen a spot at the tope of a gentle rise, and the three of them had dug a shallow grave. It had been a quiet, sunny morning. Seth had grabbed a small hand shovel, which had done more to fill the hole than it had to hollow it out, but the morning had been strangely pleasant.

They'd wrapped her body in soft blankets, and Seth had draped her in her favorite shawl. They'd picked wildflowers: yellow celandines, purple dog violets. Sam had found clusters of baby blue eyes, while Seth argued fervently that dandelions were flowers, not weeds. Several sprigs of fuchsia foxgloves had made the meager collection seem ample. And together they'd gathered around the small grave. Seth had spoken of her love for her rooftop garden, and expressed his hope that she'd reunited with his father.

"I'd like to do a reading," Sam had said, rather proudly. "Something I selected from Jules Verne."

"All right." They'd finally made it to the Scottsboro library, and she'd somehow located Twenty Thousand Leagues Under the Sea, which she and Seth were now obsessed with. "Let's have it then, Sam," Jeremy said. "Carry on."

"The sea is everything," she began, soberly. "It covers seven tenths of the terrestrial globe. Its breath is pure and healthy. It is an immense desert, where man is never lonely, for he feels life stirring on all sides. The sea is the only embodiment of a supernatural and wonderful existence. It is nothing but love and emotion."

Lowering the book, she'd gazed at them expectantly. Jeremy coughed into his fist. Seth appeared confused.

"Hmmm," Jeremy said. "That's...interesting Sam. But I'm not quite sure it's relevant? It's a beautiful quote, but perhaps a bit obscure?"

"No it's not," she argued. "Don't you get it? When we die, we go to heaven. And for me, heaven is a sparkling ocean, with red, blue, and yellow fish. Like the book. See? Just like it says. Heaven is an ocean with life stirring on all sides."

"He was talking about the desert when he said that."

"What?"

"That part about life stirring on all sides—he was talking about a desert."

"Well…" she stammered before closing the book. With a huff, she scowled. Seth giggled behind his hand. "Well," she repeated, "I thought is was beautiful. Beautiful and apt."

"Oh, it's…beautiful, alright." Jeremy smiled. "It's perfect, Pike. Thank you for sharing it."

Remembering that day made him smile. They'd shared a laugh at the top of that hill, a bit of merriment despite an inauspicious occasion. And though it had been at Sam's expense, she'd been a good sport. He'd been proud.

"Dad, I think we're here," he heard her say. Pulled from his daydreams, he focused his attention on the entrance to the bridge.

"Ick!" Seth complained. "It smells terrible." He squashed his hand against his nose, and when that didn't help, lifted the neck of his shirt. "Why is it so stinky?" he asked, his words muffled through the fabric of his shirt.

Jeremy put on a burst of speed. "Because it's dead," he called out over his shoulder. "That's why. It's dead and rotting, but we need to get across it. Come on. Let's get this over with."

He led them to the foot of the bridge then stopped to behold the road ahead.

Seth came skidding up behind him and gasped. "It's huge!" he exclaimed.

"It is." Jeremy answered. "Too huge. Let's cross the damn thing before it gets dark."

He edged onto the timeworn ramp. Weeds hadn't completely destroyed the paving yet. At least the road was still wide and smooth. But when he peered at the immense body of water to either side, his stomach flipped nauseously. It was worse than he'd expected. Much worse.

"Oh my God," Sam breathed, pulling up behind him. Swerving, she nearly lost control of her bike.

"Sam, watch it, please," Jeremy said, halfheartedly, before pulling onto the ramp to take the lead. She was staring at the water, open-mouthed, her hand cupping her mouth. She pulled ahead but then veered off again, her front tire bumping the lip of the sidewalk. Frowning, Jeremy pulled to a stop. "Guys, pay attention to what you're doing. This is dangerous. If you can't keep your eyes on the road, we can't ride. We'll have to walk the bikes on the side of the road."

They silently agreed, hopped off their bikes, and wheeled them to the pedestrian lane in a fog, where they kicked down the stands and set their hands to the rail.

The water was nothing if not putrid. The three of them leaned over the edge to peer into its murky depths, but couldn't see past the surface level of scum.

"I can't see the bottom," said Sam.

"I can't see the water," Seth echoed her strangely.

Indeed, Jeremy thought. It was overrun with algae. The 'water' was a green field, its consistency similar to that of pea soup, and though he knew it wasn't warm to the touch, it appeared to bubble like a cauldron over a flame, like a curdling consommé of bacteria and other waste products. Streaks of an unknown red contaminant veined through the green, like blood. He likened it to an arterial pathway ferrying poisonous sewage to the vital organs of an ailing body. It was an agricultural soup one wouldn't want to eat. Clumps of dead grasses dotted the green, along with clusters of non-biodegradable plastics and other decaying matter.

It broke Jeremy's heart to look upon it.

Leaning out over the edge, Seth lifted a hand to his eyes, as if doing that would help him see the bottom more clearly. "Are there any fish in there?"

Sam huffed. "Of course not. There aren't any fish anywhere, you dope. But especially not in there." She crinkled her nose. "Dad, it smells funny, like trash, but also like something else."

She was right. It was affecting him, too. The acrid smell scratched the back of his throat and stung his eyes in a distracting way. He didn't want to think about the effects on their lungs. What was causing it? Bleach? Fertilizer? Pesticides? A combination of all three, perhaps? He abruptly backed away from the edge.

"Let's go guys. We need to get out of here. I don't think we should stay any longer than we have to."

Neither Seth nor Sam objected, and the three walked their bikes to the center of the road, where they wordlessly pedaled toward the far end of the bridge. Like a murky fog, silence fell upon them. He'd expected them to ask more questions than they did, but they must've been focused on their own private musings.

The journey across the bridge was unusually silent, save for the whir of tires and the creaking of the bridge as it shifted with the movements of the earth. When they passed a sign welcoming them to sunny Arkansas, Jeremy breathed a sigh of relief. Yet another state was behind them now. It was another small win, but it was also something else, something that saddened him greatly. They were another state farther from their home, another state farther from the place they'd lost Susan. It was another state he wouldn't visit again, not for the rest of his life, which was a strange and humbling thing to ponder, a curious stream of consciousness that led to thoughts of one's own mortality. One day, he mused, this bridge would tumble to the ground. One day, humans would be extinct. Humans would be gone. This bridge would topple over. It would plunge into the filthy river along with everything else man-made. As he peered at the bilge stretching north and south, he couldn't help but wonder if that was such a bad thing.

Just as the sun was dipping below the horizon, they reached the other side of the bridge. Jeremy felt like he could finally breath again. There was something satisfying about putting half the country behind him. They'd crossed the Mississippi River! They'd done it! They'd technically reached the western half of the United States. They'd make real, measurable progress. He sat up straighter, felt himself smile, and began to scout the road ahead for promising exits. He'd take them as far as Bridgeport, if he could, where he'd find an old motel. They'd never stayed in a motel before, and—

"Dad!" Sam shrieked, her voice shrill.

Jeremy was so startled he nearly fell off his bike. A glance over his shoulder made him clench his jaw. What the hell was Seth doing? He had set his bike to the pavement in a rush, and was picking his way down the polluted embankment.

"Seth!" Jeremy shouted, his voice an octave too high. "What are you doing?" In one fluid motion, he dropped his bike to the ground. "Sam, stay here. Don't you move from this spot. Do you understand me? Am I clear? You are not to move from this spot." She was wringing her hands, hopping from foot to foot. She had never hid stress or agitation very well. "Sam! Did you hear me? Did you hear what I said? Don't you dare move from—"

"I heard you!" she shouted, casting him an irritated glance. "What are you waiting for? Go get him!"

With a nod, he turned, and, "Marlin," he yelled, "you can't go down there. It's dangerous!"

Seth's voice rose from the depths of the ravine. "I saw something, Carp! I'll be right back. I'm just gonna see what it is."

Grinding his molars, Jeremy followed Seth's path down the slide. Although he was loath to touch anything, he was forced to use his hands to keep from slipping on the trash. Why on earth was Seth doing this? What could have peaked his interest enough to overcome his natural revulsion? The smell alone was enough to make one vomit.

He was forced to move carefully as he picked his way down. The water level was lower than it normally was, and it hadn't rained as often as it had in recent years. While one might think that would make descent easier, it somehow only made it worse. When the water receded, it left behind a rotten and rancid footprint. Algae-laced trash littered the embankment like fallen leaves, along with patches of dead grasses, unnatural in color and smell. Everything was damp and slimy and rotten.

He heard Seth scream and nearly panicked. He looked up. And after losing his footing, managed to keep upright by plunging his hands into a stinking mound of filth. A cloud of chemicals lifted and burned his nostrils. He fought to suppress his rising gorge.

Seth moaned, pulling his attention toward the edge of the river, where Seth was lying too close to the edge of the bank. He was on his side, clutching his leg, rolling around, clearly in pain. He was dangerously close to the edge of the water, and at the sight of bright blood, Jeremy's panic deepened.

From above, he heard Sam gasp at the sight. "No," he screamed. "Don't you even think about it! Do not come down here, Sam!" His tone challenged her to defy him, and he struggled to focus his attention on Seth. "Hold on Marlin, I'm on my way to you. Roll away from the water, son. Away from the water. You're too damned close to the edge. You cannot fall into that water!"

Having reached the bottom, he carefully padded his way toward Seth, his feet sinking into the mire as he went, the mud sucking strangely at the bottom of his boots.

"Seth," he breathed as he stumbled up beside him. "Dear God, boy. What the hell were you thinking?"

Seth gasped through obvious pain. He peered up

at Jeremy, eyes brimming with tears he refused to let spill. Man, Jeremy thought, this kid was brave.

"The mirror," he hissed through clenched teeth. "I wanted it. I just wanted to get it for her."

"The mirror?" Jeremy crouched, pulling Seth to his chest. "What on earth are you talking about? Good grief. Let me see what you've done."

Seth bit his lip but bravely lifted his hands from atop his wound. Jeremy sucked in a breath. It was bad. The cut was long and deep, but appeared clean enough. It began just below the knee and ended on the fleshy outer part of his shin.

Jeremy quickly pushed Seth's hands back over the wound. "Keep it covered for a moment," he whispered, and peeling off his shirt, replaced Seth's bloody hands with the fabric. He pressed down hard to tie a tight tourniquet and then lifted Seth into his arms. "You wanna tell me what this was all about?"

Seth's face was pale and pinched when he answered. "The mirror," he repeated, pointing a bloodstained finger at a shimmery object. "I just wanted to get Sam the mirror."

"What for?"

Seth's eyes darted to where she was standing. She was towering over them, at the top of the bridge, leaning over the edge, the wind whipping her blond hair in clouds around her face. Though she couldn't possibly hear what they were saying, Seth lowered his voice to something barely above a whisper.

"She told me she was ugly," he said quietly, "and that she hadn't seen her face in weeks. I just wanted her to see how beautiful she is."

"Oh, for Pete's sake." Jeremy took a deep breath. "Okay, Casanova. Let's get topside and take a look at that leg."

Slipping the broken mirror into his pocket, he clutched Seth closer to his chest. With Seth's added weight, the trip uphill was significantly more difficult. As he crested the ridge, Jeremy met Sam's gaze.

"You'll have to walk the bikes by yourself," he told her. "I'll take mine, and Seth will sit on my handlebars. He can't walk or ride by himself. He's in too much pain." Shaking his head, Jeremy reconsidered the plan. "No. Leave his bike. We'll get it tomorrow. Right now we need to find a place to sleep for the night. And we need to tend this wound. Fast."

Sam's eyes widened as she beheld the blood soaking his shirt. She paled and her fingers were trembling at her sides. "Is it deep?"

"No, Sam. He'll be fine."

"But Dad, it's so dirty down there. Won't it get—"

"Sam, stop. Do what I said. Get your bike. Seth will be fine, but we need to get moving. You and I are going to have to stitch this wound."

Seth's body trembled at the words, though stoically, he refused to complain. Jeez, Jeremy thought, he has it bad for Sam. Lifting him gently, he set Seth's body across his bike's handlebars. He would keep the leg elevated, as much as possible, and pedal with Seth propped up against his chest.

"You good, Marlin?"

"Yep. I'm okay. Let's go."

His voice was weaker than it normally was, and a lot of blood had soaked that shirt. His knuckles were impossibly white against the handlebars. Jeremy feared he would pass out soon. Putting on a burst of speed, he led Sam onto the flat plain of I-55, Westbound. At the end of this road were old inns and motels. He remembered seeing them on the map.

Though they pedaled fast, Seth's head began to droop. With each passing mile, his chin tucked closer to his chest.

"Look alive, boy. We're almost there," Jeremy

said, racing farther west and turning right on an old service road. East Broadway, he noted, reading the sign. "There," he called out to Sam, "Budget Inn. Just ahead."

It was a cheap-looking sign, the lettering faded and worn, the plastic warped and peeling. And the building wasn't much nicer than the sign. The left side of the roof had caved in years before, but the rooms on the right appeared solid enough.

It will have to do, Jeremy said to himself, skidding to a stop and lifting Seth into his arms. Letting the bike fall to the ground, he ran to the door. "Stay with me, Marlin." He kicked the door open. "Be strong."

"I'm okay, Carp," Seth muttered, though not convincingly.

Jeremy gently lowered him to the bed and propped a pillow behind his head. Sam, though timid, was soon resourceful. After passing Jeremy their first aid kit, she dropped to her knees beside him. Jeremy focused on the mess that had become Seth's leg. It didn't look good. It was bleeding profusely. Jeremy's makeshift tourniquet had soaked through. He gingerly peeled it away from the wound, wiped away fresh blood, and considered the trauma. The edge of the mirror had been sharp, thankfully. The cut it had made was clean, not jagged, which was one small thing to be thankful for. With a needle and a small bit of thread, it would mend, but it would hurt like hell when Jeremy did it.

Sensing his reluctance, Sam moving to Seth's head, lifted his pale hand and clasped it tenderly. "Merlin," she murmured, "You'll have to be strong now."

"Not Merlin," he gasped. "It's Marlin." Sweat had beaded along his forehead. "You said Merlin was wrong."

She pushed a lock of hair from his brow. "I think you may have been right after all. Merlin sound better. It suits you. Besides, you're kind of like a wizard, aren't you?" He nodded.

Jeremy pulled clean clothes from their pack, along

with an antiseptic, clean needle, and thread. "You ready up there? This'll hurt like hell. But we have to do it, Merlin. We have to clean this out. We can't let infection set in. Okay? Can you do it? Come on. Count to three. Are you ready?"

Jeremy didn't wait for him to answer. It was better, he supposed, to catch him off-guard. Before he could muster a reply, or say a number, Jeremy splashed rubbing alcohol into the wound, and in the small enclosure, Seth's scream was piercing. Jeremy worked as fast as he could. He cleaned out the wound then inspected it closely. He couldn't see dirt, or other foreign matter, but he feared the things he wasn't able to see: bacteria, mold, chemicals, pollutants, the things that had cast an unnatural sheen to those polluted waters. He worried that he hadn't been fast enough. But in these situations, only time would tell.

Pinching the two sides together, he reached a decision. He'd use tape instead of a needle, he thought, butterfly the ends together, if he could, and then watch it to see if it held. From the raw sounds coming out of Seth's throat now, he didn't think the boy could withstand much more.

"We're almost done, Seth! Stay with me. We won't stitch the wound for now, okay? We'll try a few butterfly stitches instead."

Sam was cradling Seth's head to her chest, while murmuring soft sounds of encouragement. He was weeping softly, his hands tangled in her hair. It could have been worse, Jeremy realized, but this was bad. They would need to talk about this. This kind of travel was dangerous, more dangerous than either of the children realized. They were having fun with this, but forgetting the truth. This was a race for survival—Sam's survival. They were apt to encounter many perils along the way, and some would be worse than this accident had been. As such, they would need to take this seriously. He would make them treat this process with more respect.

Jeremy was grateful for the laughs they had shared. Sam had been right. Seth was a blessing. The company of three was much better than two. And in a few short weeks, Seth had become an important part of their lives. He was, at times, a comic relief, while at others, a welcome distraction. He diverted their thoughts from Susan and the cabin, told them jokes, and asked them silly questions. But the truth of the mission still haunted Jeremy. The kids didn't know why they had taken it on. Maybe, if he told them, they would show it due respect. Maybe it was time he finally told them the truth. He hadn't told them yet as to not worry them. This was too big a burden for children to bear. He didn't want Sam dwelling on her illness—not until he was certain his plan would work. He still wasn't sure that in the end he could save her.

The thought sent shivers down his spine. His hand froze. Amid the chaos, he'd forgotten to check her meter. Peering up, his gaze fell to her belly. Her T-shirt was thin, the fabric worn to threadbare. He could just make out the faint numbers at her belly. Two Percent. He was hollow inside.

Two percent remaining and one thousand, seven hundred, seventy-seven miles yet to travel.

Two percent, and two disks remaining.

PART 3

She watched the gap between ship and shore grow to a huge gulf. Perhaps this was a little like dying, the departed no longer visible to the others, yet both still existed, only in different worlds.

—Susan Wiggs, *The Charm School*

CHAPTER 11
1 Year Prior

JUNE 20TH, 2175
JUST OUTSIDE OF KNOXVILLE
TENNESSEE

      The Walgreens sign was almost completely shattered. Thick pieces of the faded red background had cracked and fallen to the paving, exposing shattered florescent bulbs beneath. The front of the store was badly vandalized. Shattered windows and fractured doors had done little to protect the interior from the elements. Jeremy could see the alien fungi—the exotic stranger that had taken over the world—fingering it's way across the threshold, inching its way across the linoleum flooring.

      He just wanted to check the pharmacy. It was something he did everywhere now. He and Sam had become like the other refugees, like those who foraged and fought for what was left. Yes, he mused, he was luckier than most. He still had the disks Susan had passed to him that night, along with several others they'd hidden in the cart. But they wouldn't last forever. A solution must be found. Jeremy vowed to visit every damn convenience store, grocery store, or pharmacy from here to Kalamazoo, if it came to that. He'd do anything to keep Sam safe, anything to keep her alive.

Sam was walking behind him slowly, preoccupied with one of her new books. Funny, he thought, how he referred to them as new. The covers were cracked and dusty and faded, the pages yellowed and warped into curves, but they were new to her, and that's what mattered. It had been a successful trip to the library. The books he carried were heavy in his pack. She'd found all but two of the Harry Potter series, and the entire Twilight series, too—much to his chagrin, and already, she was immersing herself in the comfortable well-worn pages.

The morning had been pleasant. Dare he say enjoyable? Now that their silence had finally been broken, he hadn't realized how much he missed her companionship. And though a weighty sadness underscored her every word and gesture, he was certain they'd reconnected in a way that healed her. Her eyes were somewhat brighter than before, and she moved with purpose and vitality again. On their way to the library, she'd been downright chatty. Hell, he'd even seen her smile once!

It was a testament to the healing power of honesty. Hanging on to blame and anger and resentment hurts the self more than anyone else. Sam seemed lighter, as if unburdened, like she'd shed a winter cloak on a summer afternoon. Emotions, he had learned, were like that. He'd even experienced a bit of that himself.

He pushed through the Walgreens door, which was hanging half-open on a broken hinge, and waited for his eyes to adjust to the sudden darkness. He didn't expect to find anything of use, but it was important to check nonetheless. This particular store was at the corner of what had once been a bustling intersection, and thus, had been plundered so severely that he doubted a rat could find sustenance within. All of the windows had been smashed to bits and pieces, and most of the shelving had been turned on its side. Some senseless idiot who failed to understand the obsolescence of money had dashed the cash registers to the ground in a fury, a likely attempt to break them apart. Fool, Jeremy thought, shaking his head. The thief had probably ignored food and water, focusing instead on useless paper. Money had become worthless a long time ago. Water was the world's currency now, and food its coinage. Anything else was a waste of time.

Wading carefully into the mess, he stopped to peer over his shoulder. Sam hadn't followed. She'd stayed outdoors. He watched her sink to the curb, slowly, eyes pinned to the book in her hand. Sunlight streamed over her glossy hair.

"Staying behind?" Jeremy called out to her, though he already knew the answer.

She muttered her reply to the binding of her book. Good, he thought. Let her enjoy the freshness and warmth of the day. Let her lose herself in a fantasy world, imagine herself anywhere but here, in a place that was free from uncertainty and stress. For God's sake, let her know a moment of peace. God knows he wished for one too.

Alone, he turned, picked his way through the rubble. All convenience stores seemed to follow the same basic floor plan. The cash registers were always housed in the front, makeup, hair products, and other cosmetics to the right of the store, and household items to the left. The pharmacy was always at the back. With a frown, he scanned the wreckage, and seeing nothing but remnants of bedlam and chaos, decided to make his way straight to the back. He ducked beneath the pharmacy counter, absently kicking past trash and empty packaging. The bottles at the front were crushed or broken, and what medicines remained were long expired, or useless for his particular needs. There were myriad diet pills and appetite suppressants, which would remain untouched until the day humanity was officially extinct. Weight gain was no longer a leading cause of death in the United States. But diabetes was. He frowned and moved on, past over-the-counter medications and ointments, to the back of the pharmacy where he spotted the needles, the glucometers, and of course, the glucose tabs. Empty bottles littered these shelves. Not a one was full. There was nothing of use. With a resigned sigh, he pushed himself to his feet, turned to leave, and inadvertently kicked a small box across the floor. With a tearing sound, like the shearing of paper, it skated across the cracked linoleum. He would have walked past it altogether, he thought, were it not for the jingle of a something inside. Curious, he crouched to examine its contents.

Pills? Small trinkets? What the hell was this?

As he parsed the contents, his pulse quickened. There were two bottles of multi-vitamins, a bottle of Advil, and three containers of antacids next to these, and—whoa!—two bottles of insulin pills. A tiny stuffed teddy bear was curled in the corner of the box, nestled next to an old tube of Carmex. He lifted the toy, which was an old a keychain, and slid his index finger through the ring on its tail. A tiny bell, attached to its collar, jingled softly in his hands as he turned it around.

How on earth was this here? he wondered. Who had assembled this haphazard collection? Brow furrowed, he examined the randomness of things that were seldom found on the same shelves of a store. Someone had been here, recently, and with a rather discerning eye, ransacked this store, chose items he or she found worthy, and then assembled them inside this box. But then what had happened? It was left it behind? Treasures like these were forgotten in haste? Or did a gang interrupt this fruitful expedition and neglect to take the spoils for themselves? Both scenarios were highly unlikely. Ridiculous, in fact. It didn't make sense.

A thread of uneasiness rippled through his body, and the walls seemed suddenly closer. This had the hallmarks of a well-laid trap, and he had fallen into it without thinking. He held the box away from his body, as if it were a snake poised to strike. Sunlight spilled through the entrance of the store, where small motes of pollen and dust danced in the golden light. Sam was just beyond that door, far away, and unaware of the danger. For a moment he considered setting the box to the floor, but for some strange reason, he paused. Perhaps he should just take the insulin pills. He could palm the bottle and run for the door. How in good conscience could he leave them behind?

"Put that down," a voice hissed from behind. "Now. Set it to the ground and I won't pull the trigger." The voice, though raspy, was distinctly feminine, a voice worn thin by draught and dust. "Do it now," she repeated. "I won't ask you again."

Jeremy slowly sank to the ground, set the box to the floor, and then straightened. He lifted his hands above his head as he did. "I'll leave," he said softly, without turning around. "I'm no threat to you. I'm a father. I have a child outside. I'll just walk away from here."

He ventured a step toward the light and then paused.

"No," she said, "You'll do no such thing. You'll turn around slowly and face me. You'll turn around slowly and back toward the door, and you'll do it with your hand in the air. Am I clear? I need to see your hands at all times."

Jeremy's stomach performed a tumbling act, worthy of Barnum and Baily's. "Okay," he conceded. "I'm turning around now. Do you see? I'm doing it slowly." He lifted his hands higher. "Please don't shoot. I have a daughter outside. She—"

He was speaking the words as he turned toward the woman's voice, but what he saw when he faced her stole the breath from his lungs. He was unable to think, speak, or breathe. He was paralyzed. Dear God, he thought as he fought his rising gorge. This was his deepest fear manifest. This was his worst nightmare incarnate and standing five feet from where he stood. He struggled to keep his expression placid, as he looked upon the woman and her boy, but failed.

She was young, he observed, twenty-five, or twenty-six. Certainly no more than thirty. And her boy, sick as he was, was no more than six, though his illness made him seem much younger. He was gravely ill, emaciated, worn. But that wasn't the worst part, by far.

As Jeremy's eyes found the barrel of the gun, he took a breath to steady himself. Every instinct told him to flee from this place, and it took all his energy to fight it.

"My name," he ventured, "is Jeremy Colt. My daughter, Sam, is outside, on the curb. I mean you no harm. I'd just like to leave. I'll back away now, like you told me to. I'll leave you to your property and your business. We'll leave and we won't look back. We've business of our own to tend. I'm not interested in the affairs of others."

She nodded her assent and motioned with the gun, an efficient and militant dismissal. He didn't waste time, took two steps back, while carefully judging her reaction. She was alert, he observed, though obviously exhausted, worn despite a manic gleam in her eye. A deeply lined face and puffy eyes betrayed the depth of her fatigue, and as he looked upon her, his eyes betrayed him. His glance slid to the boy at her side, and then finally, to the small cache of medicines his mother had collected for him. A sharp panic knifed through his gut. This could easily be Sam, he thought. This was her nightmare future. He couldn't face this. His arms slowly lowered, against his will, while his fingers sought his nose, and pinched. He cast a nervous glance over his shoulder, toward Sam. Hopefully she was still engrossed in her book. He didn't want her seeing this.

In the heavy heat of early afternoon, the boy's stench was ghastly. Jeremy stumbled a few steps back. Though he wanted to leave, he was frozen in place. It was two-dozen steps to the door, if that, and he awkwardly pitched himself toward it. The woman's son was on his deathbed, sprawled on his back, in the base of a shopping cart, which was much too small to contain his long-limbed body. He was folded inside a stack of blankets that were dirty, his legs awkwardly dangled over the side.

And it was his left leg that betrayed his disease.

With a start, Jeremy realized he was mewling like an animal. He coughed into his fist and cleared his throat. He had to get away from this. Now. Away from this reminder of how things could be, of how things would be if he didn't devise a plan, if he wasn't able to find a solution.

He stuttered and tottered his way toward the door. "I'm leaving," he muttered. "I'm leaving right now."

The scene in front of him was a train wreck, and he was finding it increasingly difficult to look away. His eyes betrayed him again and again. The child, at this point, was all but unresponsive, probably unaware of his surroundings at all. One small blessing, Jeremy said to himself, his gaze settling on the boy's leg.

The gangrene, it seemed, had set in long ago, as it commonly did for untreated diabetics. The decay had originated in his foot. Four of his toes were blackened and curled, beyond regenerative healing capabilities. They were twisted and gnarled, and the skin was peeled back, which revealed a shiny and glistening rot. The rot seemed to crawl from the ankle to the calf, in a way that was similar to the fungi outside. It was staking its claim as if sentient and purposeful. Like a parasite it crawled across his leg, necrotizing healthy flesh as it inched its way along. It reached for his knee, longingly, lovingly, as if it knew that once it scaled that final bony hurdle, it would be free to feast on the abundant flesh beyond. There were faint patches of white bone in the deepest parts of that rot. Jeremy shivered. The pain was unimaginable.

He stumbled back, almost fell to his knees. He'd never let this happen to Sam. Not ever. Not in a million years, if he could help it. How could this woman have allowed this happen? How could she have neglected her son so completely?

Wait. He faltered. Neglect? Was that fair for him to say? Did he believe this woman had allowed this to happen? Why would she do that? How had it happened? Neglect was a conclusion he had no right to reach. Not without more information.

His gaze found hers and held her tightly. She was exhausted, drained, barely able to stand upright. Fear coiled in the depths of her eyes. She made no attempt to conceal it. She was doing all she could with what little she had. And didn't Jeremy know, firsthand, what that was like? His thoughts turned to Sam, then finally to Susan, and he knew a moment of crippling guilt. Would Susan have behaved as he was right now? Would she have jumped to such terrible conclusions? And furthermore, he wondered, would she abandon a sick mother and child in a store? Though he'd lost the cabin, Jeremy was still a rich man. He was wealthy in a world that was stricken by poverty. His resources were abundant. Would he truly walk away? Would he refuse to offer them aid?

He lifted his palms, held them out for inspection.

"I have a house," he whispered, "not far from this place, with food, water, and medicine." His voice sounded strained, almost hollow in his ears.

She shook her head slowly. It was the smallest of movements. "You seem decent," she breathed, "but I can't do that. You'd best be on your way, and you'd better do it fast."

"I will," he replied. "I am. I'm just saying. You look…" He paused. "You look tired. You look like you could use little help, is all. My daughter is—"

"Stop. You're lying to me. You have no daughter. Quit playing me for a fool."

"I do have a daughter," he objected. "You're wrong. She's sitting outside, on the curb, on the street corner. You can see for yourself if you look out the window." His words came faster as his thoughts coalesced. "She's reading a book. We just came from the library in midtown. She likes to read." He glanced at the boy. "She found Harry Potter books. Would your son like that? Come with us. Come back to our house. She could read it to him, and you could get some sleep. You could eat a hot meal. I have plenty of food: cans of beans, vegetables, rice, oats, and lentils."

He could see her hunger beginning to build, and he suddenly dropped to his knees. "I'll stay here," he whispered. "So you can go look. I won't come near you. I promise. Just look out the window, see for yourself."

She dared a step forward and he refused to move. Bolder, she crept to the nearest window, and with hands that shook, wiped it clean. Her grip on the gun had loosened, though slightly, and Jeremy held his breath as he watched her. Sunlight spilled across her hair and face. Perhaps she had once been pretty, he remarked. There may have been a time when she was beautiful. Her dark hair may have been lustrous and thick, though now, it was matted and clumped. It hung to her shoulders in twisting tendrils. She was thin, though her hips swelled suggestively, as though her womanly curves had been whittled with time. She captivated him as she stared out the window. The depth of her despair was etched onto her face, sadness so profound it took his breath away.

She must have seen Sam, for her mouth fell open. Jeremy's emotions stirred at the sight, and he instinctively knew she and her boy were alone. How strange it must be to confront another person after so much time, even stranger to encounter another child. He watched a tear slide slowly down her face, drop from her chin, and fall to the floor. Her voice shook, her words desperate and pleading.

"Dear God," she breathed as she slowly exhaled. "How badly I want to trust you. How badly I want that hot meal."

"Then take it."

"I can't," she whispered.

"You can. You should. Here's what I'm going to do. I'm leaving this store and I'm joining my daughter. We'll leave and walk back to our house. We won't look back. We won't turn around. You're welcome to follow us, see for yourself. You can watch us for a while, give it some thought, come back when you're ready, but we're moving on soon. Not right away, but soon." He ran a hand through his disheveled hair. "It's just the two of us, just my daughter and I. We lost my wife, Susan, and we're resting and healing, gathering our strength before me move on. You can have the house when we leave. It's yours."

He turned from her then, and walked toward the light.

"I'm Jeremy," he said, "and my daughter is Sam."

While he crossed the store, she didn't make a sound, until he finally reached the door and the light. Her reply, though faint, was discernible, full of hope.

"I'm Meghan," she said. "And my son is Peter."

The winds, the sea, and the moving tides are what they are. If there is wonder and beauty and majesty in them, science will discover these qualities... If there is poetry in my book about the sea, it is not because I deliberately put it there, but because no one could write truthfully about the sea and leave out the poetry.

—Rachel Carson

CHAPTER 12
Present Day

OCTOBER 6TH, 2176
LITTLE ROCK, ARKANSAS
1,679 MILES TO SAN DIEGO

"How are the lentils?"

"How are they supposed to be?" Sam replied. "Icky. They taste like cardboard."

"How do you know what cardboard tastes like?"

She was sprawled on her stomach, her bowl of food centered on of the map in front of her. "We've done well," she commented, as she drew the purple line that marked their progression westward. "About 140 miles in only three days. We're halfway across Arkansas already." She peered at Seth and raised a mocking brow. "Not bad for a klutz."

"I'm not a klutz!" he objected. "I just fell. It was hard to walk by the water. It was sticky and wet. And you should thank me, by the way."

"Thanking you?"

"Don't worry, big guy," Jeremy said. "She thanks you. But speaking of that incredibly graceful act, it's time to change your bandages."

Pushing himself to his feet, Jeremy moved to his backpack and rummaged the contents. He had to admit: he was proud of Seth. Over the past few days, the boy had shown pluck, not to mention bottomless resilience and determination. Despite his injury, which was nothing to take lightly, he had insisted they burn through the miles. He'd acclimated well to the physical demands that were being placed on him daily, to the acidic soreness of overworked muscles, to the weariness that resulted when strenuous activity was performed at lower than optimum oxygen levels, and to the ever-present heat that saturated the air. It was a mist that draped their backs like woolen cloaks. Jeremy tended Seth as best he could. He massaged his muscles, stretched his hamstrings, gave him extra rations of food. He'd even parted with a few precious Advil, though he feared, at this point, they were ineffective. They were over fifteen years old, and though they wouldn't harm him, they wouldn't help him much, either.

Lifting the first aid kit from his pack, he settled himself next to Seth. "Does it hurt?" he asked.

"It hurts," Seth answered, "but I'm tough. I can handle it." He hissed as Jeremy rolled back his pant leg.

"I know you're tough, but for a minute, pretend that you're not. Give me your pain on a scale from one to ten."

"Six."

"Six? Well. That's pretty good. Six is manageable." He lifted his gaze and caught Seth's attention. "You ready to make that a seven?"

As Jeremy poured rubbing alcohol onto a semi-clean cloth, Seth ground his teeth and prepared himself. He was a strong boy. There was no doubting that. Even now, he was trying to focus on something else. "So all that damage back there," he asked, "A tornado caused that?"

"Yup. Probably. Back in the day, this part of the country was known as Tornado Alley. But now, the storms, when they come, are more violent, and there's no one living here to put the pieces of towns back together again."

"And will a tornado happen now?" Seth asked, his voice trembling as Jeremy tended his leg.

"I suppose it could. No reason it couldn't. And if it did, it wouldn't be pretty. The weather has become increasingly volatile over time. In fact, I'd like to get out of here as quickly as we can. I don't want to linger, if we can help it." He lifted the corner of the bandage and frowned, then pressed a finger to the skin. It was warm. Warmer than it should be, verging on hot. "Seth, are you feeling alright?"

Seth glanced at Sam and Jeremy pursed his lips. The boy was so damned transparent. But all men are, aren't they? Even as boys? Always trying to impress a pretty girl. Always acting tough, gritting their teeth against pain.

"Sure," Seth lied, despite the beads of perspiration that dotted his brow. "I'm fine. Like I said: I'm tough."

"I know you are, but this doesn't look right. The skin feels warm. And it's a little red, too."

He removed the remainder of the bandage, carefully, without allowing the edges to pull at the wound. Seth made soft sounds of displeasure. Despite the severity of the wound, he'd been lucky. Things could have been much worse. He'd lost a lot of blood that day, and then spent an uncomfortable evening clenching his teeth against the pain. Jeremy and Sam had coaxed fluids into his mouth, and tried their best to get him to eat. They'd spent two days in that dilapidated motel room—two tense and restless days. Jeremy had been climbing the proverbial walls. It had been two days Jeremy knew they couldn't afford. But at this point, leaving Seth behind wasn't an option.

With a hiss, the bandage came free in Jeremy's hand. He frowned. Seth's skin was unquestionably flushed, though Jeremy couldn't see any puss. To his untrained eye, the edges didn't appear to be overly swollen, but the skin was warm, which didn't seem right. Jeremy's initial fear had been of blood loss, but the risk of infection was what worried him now. Who knew how much of that polluted water had seeped into the wound? How much of that chemically poisonous soup had found its way in, and festered there? Had Jeremy cleansed it thoroughly? Had he done it fast enough? Only time would tell.

"Here goes," he said quietly to Seth. "Be strong."

He took the antiseptic to the wound swiftly, and above him, Seth stifled a yell. His knuckles were white as he gripped his thighs, but he held his emotions in check. Jeremy made quick work of the entire process. After cleansing the wound, he replaced the bandages, careful to apply tape to the outermost edges.

"We need to keep an eye on this," he said tersely. "We can't risk infection." He ran a hand through his hair. "We still have antibiotics, but what we have has long expired. They're probably weaker than we'd want them to be. I don't want to take any chances."

Having cleaned and dressed the wound, Jeremy rolled down Seth's pant leg, and winced. The fabric was dirty and smudged with oil. The chain on the bike had soiled the cloth. And it was stiff with the sweat of hard work. Dirty fabric against an open wound? Fantastic. They needed to find a suitable place to wash their clothes, but it had been many miles since they'd last passed a stream, or a semi-clean river, or any body of water, and he refused to use what little they had left for anything other than drinking. They would have to make do for now.

"Number please," he called out to Sam.

She lifted her arm. "Three hundred and fifty-six."

Jeremy sucked air through his teeth. "Too high. Try taking another pill."

She rummaged for the bottle of pills in her pack. "Carp," she said, "they aren't any good. They're not strong enough anymore."

"I know. But they're not exactly worthless to us either. We're lucky to have them. Now that you've eaten, try taking two more. Let's see what happens. That's all we can do."

She dry-swallowed the pills. She was a pro at this. At the sight of the bottle, Jeremy felt a sudden stab of guilt. His conscience whispered, murmured a single name. Peter, it said, and he suddenly felt sick. The pain was an uncomfortable flickering of conscience, like a muscle that cramped or an annoying nervous tick. His gaze was drawn to Sam's waist, where the teddy bear keychain hung from a belt loop. Ever since they'd teamed up with Seth, she'd taken to wearing it again. But why? Did she blame herself for what had happened to Peter? No, he thought. That couldn't be true. It wasn't her fault, and she knew it. Was she wearing it to convey a certain message? To keep Peter at the forefront of Jeremy's mind? Ensure history didn't repeat itself? Jeremy owed a moral debt for that sin. He only hoped he would ultimately pay it.

Just six hours ago, the meter at her belly had fallen to zero percent, and Jeremy had decided to test the pills. He was running an experiment of sorts. He wanted to see how effective they were at raising her insulin before replacing her disk.

"So where are we off to next?" he asked her. "Where do we go from here?"

She pointed to the map. "The Caddo River. It's smaller than some of the other rivers we've passed, so I'm thinking we can use it to bathe." She tossed an empty water bottle in Seth's direction. "We need to wash. That guy stinks over there."

"No, I don't!" Seth tilted his head at Jeremy. "But

how will we get ourselves clean if we're washing with stinky river water? I thought you said the water was spoiled."

Jeremy spooned cold lentils into his mouth. "Oh, it's spoiled, all right. No doubt about that. But it won't be as bad as the Mississippi was."

Sam turned and rummaged through her pack, likely in search of the Prisoner of Azkaban. "Merlin," she said, "we can't drink the water, but we can boil it and use it to wash ourselves." Pulling the book into her lap, she sought the bent corner marking last night's reading. "Besides, some rivers aren't as bad as others."

"And none are as bad as the oceans are, right?"

"Ask Carp," she answered. "He's the only one who's ever seen the ocean."

Recollection slowly dawned on Seth's face. "That's right! You've actually been there. Haven't you? What was it like?"

"Before we get into any of that, give me your number, Pike. Let's figure this out." Until he'd gauged the effectiveness of the pills, he wouldn't be able concentrate on anything else.

She groaned and checked her arm. "Three hundred and one."

Jeremy cursed inwardly. "So, they work, but barely. It is what it is. They're not as powerful as I'd like them to be. Okay. That's it. Experiment over. Let's replace your disk before we do any reading."

Setting down the book, she crawled closer to him. Though her faced lacked expression, Jeremy knew how much she hated this. He fished one of the disks from his pocket, careful to avoid showing her how many were left. Seth watched her raise her shirt, eyes wide. Sam was a modest girl. Always had been. She rarely let others see the device. The fact that she was doing so now only proved that she was becoming comfortable with Seth. Jeremy suspected it was the first time he'd ever seen the unit up close.

Inching closer, he leaned in. "You said it was a disk player." He frowned. "It doesn't look like a disk player to me. Where does the disk go?"

"It's not really a disk player, Merlin" Sam said. "How would we get a disk into my belly?"

Jeremy lifted the small plastic disk to the flickering light of their candles. "See?" he said. "It's the case that makes it looks like a disk. The actual medicine is just a thin tube."

"It's an advertising gimmick," Sam added.

"A what?" Jeremy grinned despite himself. "Where do you come up with this stuff?"

"Its called reading, Carp. You should try it some time. If you did, you might learn something."

Palming the applicator, he leaned closer to her stomach. "Deep breath, kiddo."

"Will it hurt?" Seth breathed.

Jeremy answered in Sam's stead. "It's not pain in the conventional sense. It's more of a discomfort, or pressure. See that hole in her belly?" He pointed to a small circle of durable plastic, which marked the point of insertion. "We attach the applicator here and inject the tube. Simple as that." He demonstrated by touching the applicator to the small hole, and with a soft click, it snapped into place. He released his hand, left it attached to her body.

Seth cocked his head. "It looks funny. So you just leave it there? Now what do you do?"

Jeremy had a sudden thought. "Why don't we let you do it this time?" It was a good idea, he told himself. Training Seth how to tend Sam was just sound planning. At the very least, it wouldn't hurt anything.

Seth peered at Sam through lowered lashes. He was obviously embarrassed to touch her.

"Just do it," she snapped. "Carp's right. It doesn't hurt. It just feels strange, and it only lasts a minute. Just do it, already, scaredy-cat."

He gently wrapped his palm around the applicator, fit his thumb over the plunger, and paused. "Give me your pain on a scale of one to ten," he asked her quietly.

"Zero, you dope. Now do it."

His thumb turned white as he pressed the applicator.

"That's good," Jeremy encouraged him. "Be sure to keep it straight. Don't allow it to bend to either side. Hold it straight, and as it lowers, apply steady pressure."

As Seth pressed it down, a smile crept across his face. There was a low, satisfying click. "That's it," Jeremy encouraged with a nod. "You did it! Now remove the applicator, and watch her numbers rise. That's all there is to it. Pretty easy, isn't it?"

Seth pulled awkwardly on the tube.

"Ouch! Not like that. Don't pull it, you fool. Snap your wrist to the right."

Seth startled, scared to have caused her pain. He flicked his wrist and detached the applicator. Bending low, he watched the meter rise. With a smile, Jeremy watched it too. He glanced from the meter, and then to Seth's face, whose lips were pursed in concentration. He obviously wanted to do this right.

In the span of a single breath, the numbers on the meter began to climb, about ten percent, every few seconds. There was no feeling as deep and gratifying as delivering her a disk of insulin. Fifty percent became sixty percent, and sixty percent quickly became eighty. It was heady, an intoxicating sense of security.

"One hundred percent!" Seth exclaimed proudly.

"Yep. One hundred percent. How about that?" With a sigh, Jeremy settled himself and discarded the empty disk. One hundred percent. Thirty days of bliss. Thirty days of freedom from worry. Nothing compared to that feeling.

On hands and knees, Seth backed away from Sam,

as she picked up the book like nothing had happened. She was intent on reading, on doing something normal, but Seth's thoughts were spinning. He turned to Jeremy. "How many disks are left, Carp?"

Sam heaved a sigh. "He won't tell us, Merlin, so don't bother asking."

Jeremy's eyes lost focus. "One," he murmured, before catching himself. The word had slipped out of his mouth.

The room fell silent. Sam slowly lifted her head. She repeated the word with a curious inflection, as if the combination of letters was foreign to her. "One," she uttered softly, meeting Jeremy's gaze. "And I suppose you have a plan?"

"When do I not? That's what San Diego's about, kiddo."

She rounded her shoulders and nodded her head, but he'd seen fear flash across in her face. It hadn't been a trick of candlelight. Sam knew firsthand what would happen to her without proper medication. She'd seen it before, up close, with Peter. Jeremy was instantly remorseful for having told her the truth, though maybe the time was right. Maybe it was time she joined the fight for her life. Maybe it was time she took her health seriously. Hers would be a life of constant struggle, a never-ending quest for pharmaceuticals in a world with a limited supply. She'd never know rest. Could never know rest, lest she allow herself to waste away and die.

Or unless San Diego doesn't work out the way you think it will.

Jeremy scattered the unwanted thought. Yes. It was time Sam joined this fight. It was time for her to see the importance of what he was doing, of staying on the move, of searching the dark corners of pharmacies and convenience stores. It was time she joined him inside those stores, instead of hanging outside with her nose in a book. Jeremy wouldn't be around forever. She would eventually have to do this on her own.

Okay, he though, enough morbid topics of conversation for one evening.

"So," he encouraged them both. "Where were we? I think, last night, Sirius Black escaped Azkaban. Am I right?"

"No," Seth pouted. "That's not where we were. I asked you a question and you haven't answered yet. What was the ocean like when you saw it? Did you see fish? Sharks? Squid?"

Jeremy gazed at the sky. "Nope. Nothing like that. Fish didn't exist, Merlin, not even then. All ocean life was extinct. There were no fish, ocean birds, seals, or porpoises, nothing at all."

"So, what was there? What did you see?"

"Water," Jeremy answered. "Just water. Blue-black water skimmed with oil and peppered with bits of trash. There was lots of trash."

Seth scrunched his nose. "Trash?"

"Why were you even there?" Sam asked. "I mean, why would Grandma and Grandpa take you to the ocean? All the way from Tennessee? It doesn't make sense. I don't get it. Did you go to Florida? I thought that place was dead."

Jeremy shook his head. "Not Florida. California. Grandma and Grandpa took me to the Pacific Ocean. They were scientists back then. Scientists—I might add—who were well respected in their fields. They'd been called to the Pacific to investigate something."

"Was it big?" Seth said. "The ocean, I mean. Could you see all the way to the other side?"

Sometimes Seth's questions were so childlike Jeremy had to remind himself how young he really was, how little he'd seen, how little he knew. He had no concept of what an ocean was like. He'd never attended public school, never seen any photos, or read books. Seth's parents had sheltered their son. And Jeremy wasn't judging them for it. They'd stocked their house with ample supplies. They'd thought to plant gardens and place rain catchers along the top of their roof. They'd done more than some, and less than others. They were the reason Seth was alive today. They'd spent their money on needs instead of wants, on necessities instead of indulgences. They'd been smart. But when Jeremy and Sam had entered that house, Jeremy hadn't seen a single book or magazine.

"No," Jeremy said patiently. "You can't do that. The ocean is too big to see the other side of it. It's larger than rivers, or streams, or lakes." He smiled. "You'll just have to wait and see."

"Wait," Sam said. "Hold on. You said California. But that's where we're headed right now. You just said California was spoiled and full of trash, that the ocean was dead and toxic. If that's true, then why are we going there? Wouldn't it be smarter to try the Atlantic Ocean, or the Gulf of Mexico?"

"Pike, we're not trying to get to the ocean. There's nowhere left to try. The oceans are dead."

She scrunched her nose. "So why California?"

He shrugged. "There's something we need, and it's there."

Fumbling for an answer, he turned to Seth again, silently encouraging more questions. He wasn't yet ready to tell Sam his reasons for traveling to California. He wouldn't raise her hopes prematurely.

Seth's face was scrunched in thought. "I don't get it," he complained. "You said your parents were scientists. What were they sent to investigate?"

Jeremy sighed and folded his hands. "Back then, the Pacific Ocean was called 'The Great Pacific Garbage Patch'."

Seth's imagination was clearly running wild. "Wow," he breathed. "'The Great Pacific Garbage Patch'? So the ocean was covered in garbage? Like you couldn't see the water at all?"

"No," Jeremy countered. "It's not like that. The term 'garbage patch' is just a catch phrase. The trash is there—yes—but it's not on top of the water. It swirls beneath the surface like garbage soup."

"So there's nothing on top? You can't see it?"

"Well," Jeremy ceded, "You can see some of it, I suppose. I did see some of it, come to think of it. Plastics mainly. Lots of plastic. Many things contributed to the death of the oceans, guys, but the Western and Eastern Garbage Patches were a large part of what happened—particularly after the patches converged."

Sam perked at that. "So there was more than one Garbage Patch?"

"Are more than one. They're still there, Pike. Plastic—for the most part—isn't biodegradable. It will take millennia to break it down, if it even happens at all."

"But what did it look like?"

Seth clearly needed a visual.

Jeremy took a breath. "Well, if I squinted my eyes and faced the sun, the ocean almost appeared normal. Only through a microscope could one see the garbage. And that's when my mother and father took me. Most of what I saw was small bits of trash that floated on the surface. The real issue was the water beneath. It was filled with bits of plastic, from large particles to tiny pieces we found when we dredged it up."

"Dredged it up," Sam repeated numbly. She closed her book with a soft creaking sound and folded her hands on the cover. "Okay. We're done with Harry Potter, I think. Tonight there's another story to tell."

For most of history, man has had to fight nature to survive; in this century he is beginning to realize that, in order to survive, he must protect it.

—Jacques-Yves Cousteau

CHAPTER 13
52 Years Prior

JANUARY 3RD, 2124
THE GREAT PACIFIC GARBAGE PATCH
PACIFIC OCEAN

        Representatives from the environmental agencies of four different countries, including the United States, had been summoned to this conference, and it had been a long day at sea for all of them. It was a day of disappointing tests and contentious arguments, and this was about to be the worst one of all. Collectively battered and disheartened by their findings, the team was seated in a small conference room. They were an intimate group of scientists who had been called upon to diagnose a difficult disease. They were here to treat a critically diseased body that had begun showing symptoms over a hundred years ago. The room was an energy field throbbing with anxiety. The scientists leaned forward in rapt attention, foreheads creased, eyes focused on the center of the large round table, where a voice came crackling from a small communications unit.

"Have you concluded your tests, Dr. Colt?" it barked.

All eyes darted to Liam. He nervously pulled from a glass of water before setting it on the table. "Yes, Mr. President...Sir. We have."

Liam felt overly warm, as if the temperature of the room had increased in a matter of seconds. He was about to deliver the worst kind of news to the President of the United States of America. "Sir," he began, "the situation is dire."

An electronic sigh filled the room. Liam could envision him reclining in his chair, the members of his cabinet gathered around him. "Details, Liam," the man said. "I need details. And don't spare the science for those of us without PhD's."

Liam felt frozen. Where would he begin? This was his final assignment for the D.C. Institute of Marine Sciences, and he wanted to be thorough and concise, yet compassionate. He wanted to convey optimism, if he could, yet there was no way to sugarcoat this. This, he was certain, was the end of the line. The situation in the North Pacific was the same as it had been in the South Pacific, and in the North Atlantic and South Atlantic, as well. There was no turning back from this.

He didn't fear to deliver the information, not even to the highest official in the world. He didn't even fear staining his professional reputation. Why fear that? He had no reputation. It had been a long time since he'd cared about things like that. He just wished he hadn't been chosen for this. This was to be his last assignment, and what a thing to end on! The knowledge that this was his final professional act was nothing if not depressing.

People wanted to leave behind a legacy, if they could, retire from their work with a sense of pride and accomplishment. Liam, on the other hand, was leaving without closure, abandoning the pursuits of a lifelong passion as one who had failed or given up. The notion was ridiculous, of course. None of it was true. It was all in his head. But he just couldn't help himself from feeling it. He'd never been good at letting go.

Before they'd made the trip to California, he and Olivia had reached an agreement. This would be the last time they'd venture from their cabin. They knew what the data and tests would reveal, and when that knowledge reached the rest of the world, what remained of civilization would fail. When that happened, they wanted to be home.

Just several days prior, at Pier 45 in the San Francisco bay, Liam and Olivia had reluctantly boarded the Nomad. Olivia had zipped their son's parka around his neck and popped the collar to shield his ears from the wind. Holding tight to Jeremy, she'd peered up at Liam.

"Are you sure about this? About taking him along?"

"It's not that I necessarily want to take him along, Liv. It's that I refuse to leave him behind. I won't split our family apart. We need to stick together, especially now. This won't be a short trip, Liv. The Patch is seven hundred miles offshore. We won't be there and back within a day. And I suspect, once we've investigated it, we'll be asked to examine the Convergence Zone, too. This whole thing could take weeks, despite what we've been told. We can't leave Jeremy alone. Besides," he added, "I can't think of a safe place to leave him. There's no one I trust to leave him with. San Francisco is a disaster zone. There are too many people roaming these overcrowded streets, too many refugees, too many looters and thieves. Everyone in this city is jockeying for position. Everyone is trying to survive. A strange caste system has developed here. Can't you feel it? Can't you see it? It's almost medieval. Those who had the wherewithal to notice the signs and make appropriate plans have assumed the roles of nobles and dukes, while others have been relegated to peasants or serfs. We can't risk leaving Jeremy behind. It isn't safe. People are starving, living in alleyways, dying on street corners, attacking one another. We have to take him aboard, with us."

Standing on the tips of her toes, Olivia kissed him lightly. "Then I suppose," she said, "in this strange caste system of the twenty-second century, you are the King, because no one is better prepared than you."

He'd slipped his arms around her waist. "A King is nothing without his Queen."

"Gross," Jeremy said. "You guys kiss too much."

Liam had laughed and swept his son into his arms.

Son. He smiled. It felt good to say that. Truer words were never spoken. Jeremy was Liam's son in every sense of the word. They'd become a true family in a short amount of time. The adjustment period—if one could call it that—hadn't been difficult to overcome. Liam still wondered at the ease with which they'd connected. He marveled at the comfort they found in one another. Perhaps a secluded life at the top of a mountain could do that to a family, bring it closer together.

He swung Jeremy around to face the sea. "So, big guy. Are you ready for this?" Jeremy's hair lifted with the coastal winds, and his eyes followed the rise and fall of the cresting waves. When he saw the Coast Guard's massive vessel, he reflexively tightened his grip on Liam's neck. "No reason to be scared, son. Nothing to worry about. See that boat? See how big it is? It's almost like a small city, isn't it? You won't even notice we're on the water."

Jeremy's hand cupped the back of Liam's neck. "Will I see any fish?"

"Nope. Probably not. Maybe an albatross though."

"What's an albatross?"

"A bird. A very large bird."

"Bigger than a stork?" Jeremy laid his head against Liam's shoulder. "Bigger than the one that brought me to you and mom?"

"Yep. Even bigger than that."

He'd hugged his son close to his body, cradling him against the blustery winds. Since arriving at their home, Jeremy seemed to be suffering some type of amnesia. He'd locked all memory of his natural parents inside his subconscious. It was an unusual—yet fortunate—coping mechanism. His mind was sparing him the pain of that terrible day. Or maybe he was feigning ignorance. For sometimes, Liam thought, if one pretends at something, one can almost convince himself it's real. Whatever the cause and whatever the reason, Liam was grateful for the way things had worked out. He and Olivia never pressed Jeremy to recall the events of that day. None of that seemed to matter anymore. Those events were in the past. They would stay in the past, and their future was brighter than it was for most people. What mattered now was their love for one another. What mattered was survival, moving on.

The symmetry of the situation had caused Liam— a scientist at heart—to believe in fate. It must have been fate, he told himself, or divine intervention that had woven the threads of this tapestry, for a just handful of weeks after Jeremy's unexpected arrival, Olivia had miscarried their child, and because of the loss, had sunk into a near-debilitating depression. Jeremy was a blessing indeed. Prior to the stillbirth, Olivia had prepared for the baby's arrival by decorating the nursery and purchasing a crib. She'd painted the room a soft pastel green, even ordered a white rocking chair, which had arrived too late and caused a second downward spiral of depressive thoughts.

Liam knew Olivia loved him. He'd never doubted that. Not even for a second. But for those few weeks, he'd been troubled by the depths of her emotional withdrawal. The pit she'd fallen into wasn't one he'd been able to pull her from. Jeremy had been the only person capable of that. He's shone a light inside that dark cave, grasped her hand,

and pulled her toward the light.

He was a lovely child, spirited and alert, observant of the world around him. He followed Liam around like an adoring puppy and had adopted mountain life quicker than anyone expected him to. Liam and Olivia took delight in his newfound contentment, but agreed to always be honest with him. When the time was right, they'd tell him everything. They'd help him make sense of his murky memories, of information that had clearly become jumbled in his mind. He had a right to know the truth about his roots and his parents, even about the macabre way they died. For when knowledge is withheld from children, Liam believed, the secrecy can be more detrimental than the facts.

So their family had flourished despite rough times, and Liam had agreed to take Jeremy along on this final delegation. Not even a directive from the President himself was enough to split up his family.

A 140-foot Cutter class ship had been chosen to take them to the Patch. Liam hoped to reach the designated zone, take his samples, and get out quickly. They had set their belongings in one of the crews' cabins, and though it was small, Liam had insisted they share it. It contained two sets bunk beds, one of which Jeremy had immediately claimed the top of. He'd scrambled up the ladder and planted his backpack in the middle of bed, as if planting a declarative flag on the moon.

They'd met the Captain soon after their arrival, a reed-like man in crisp white. He was friendly yet succinctly professional. "Captain Bernard Walden," he'd greeted them sternly. "Welcome aboard the Nomad." His handshake was firm and his jaw was tight, and though he'd frowned when he first saw Jeremy, he hadn't yet voiced a complaint. He'd walked them about the ship instead, pointing to the galley, dining area, and seaman's quarters.

The ship was impressive, one of the newest line of Cutters, and while on its decks, and with a sense of finality,

Liam had said his goodbyes to the sea. He imbibed of her beauty and smelled of her spice. Olivia had clearly done the same. She'd stood, shoulders slumped, pale hands atop the railing. Her cheeks had been tight with tears. The day had been clear, not a cloud in the sky, and the sun's rays had cast liquid diamonds across the shimmering waves, which had glinted off strands of her hair. She'd thrown her head back and peered at the sun. It was a perfect moment, in Liam's opinion. She and it had been breathtaking.

It was the end of an era, as the saying goes, and it had been a painful ending at that. This was the last time either of them would see the ocean again, and it was difficult to make peace with that. The ocean had been a central figure in both of their lives. They'd committed to her professionally, and personally. She had been their mistress, an alluring siren, a mysterious and intriguing lover. She held endless secrets in her uncharted depths. Without her, life on this planet would end. Without her, life on this planet was ending. It was a tearful goodbye, but a necessary one, and a small part of Liam longed for closure, for once set free, he could return to his home, to his safe haven atop his private mountain, to live.

Society was nothing but pain and suffering now. When he'd arrived in San Francisco, Liam had immediately fought his instinct to return home. The city was like a war zone. California weather was mostly temperate, and thus, had attracted refugees from the Northern states in droves. They wove about the city, searching for food. They were mothers, fathers, grandparents, and children. They were families mixed with dangerous gangs. Were it not for the auspicious fates, Liam concluded, this could have been Jeremy's future. He shuddered to think of the possibilities.

Stadiums and public buildings had been converted into refugee outposts, offering food and drink to thousands of unfortunate souls. Many people were unemployed, their jobs having become obsolete in a matter of months. Oceanic trade affected every facet of industry and commerce, and the fall of China and Japan had only worsened things. Industries with no ties to the sea were soon adversely affected. It was a never-ending chain of devastation and destruction. Crimes against persons reached a historic high. Liam and Olivia had even witnessed a few. The night they arrived, they were whisked to a private government facility, but were awakened repeatedly by the sounds of gunfire. Liam wanted out of here. Fast. And the quickest way out of any situation, he had learned, was often directly through the middle.

So here he was, in the middle of things, speaking to the President through a small comm unit, trying his best to decide where to begin. Rounding his shoulders, he leaned close to the speaker. "Mr. President," he said, his voice thick in his throat, "As I said before, the situation is dire. The Patch has expanded exponentially. The refuse on the surface is visible, yes, but it's the microplastics beneath the water that are causing the most damage. These particles won't biodegrade. Over time, they'll break into much smaller pieces, but will never fully disintegrate. Photo-degradation," he added, "and the churning of the waves has broken the pieces into the size of fish eggs, which are mixing with the water to form a cloudy synthetic soup."

The President's voice was robotic through the unit. "Photo-degradation? For those of us in the back row please, Dr. Colt."

Liam folded his hands and took a breath, but it was Olivia who leaned forward and answered. She nervously drummed her fingers on the table, but her voice sounded strong and firm. "Sir," she began, "we've seen the heart wrenching advertisements and articles: pictures of animals caught in plastic rings, sea turtles choking on plastic bags they mistook for jellyfish, dolphins snagged inside plastic netting, and seals strangled by fishing lines. All of these things threaten wildlife, Sir, and though these images pull at the heartstrings and galvanize people to action, the trapping of individual animals isn't the issue. That's not what's causing large scale extinctions."

Liam easily picked up the thread, tying it back to the original question. "What Olivia says is correct. Crippled ocean life, though a travesty, of course, isn't our greatest concern. Photo-degradation, on the other hand, is. It's the process by which light breaks down plastics. Large pieces are broken into smaller fragments. Follow my logic," Liam said. "Stay with me. Consider this example, if you will: a large piece of plastic is deposited into the ocean. Wave movement and light break it down. As it breaks apart, its surface area increases. And we all know the truth about plastic. As the surface area of plastic is increased, more and more toxins are released. The toxins, which are classified as human carcinogens, have poisoned our oceans irreversibly.

"When I was asked to take part in this mission," he continued, "I was asked to test the chemical properties of the water, specifically within the Garbage Patch. Now that I have, I can tell you with certainty: the toxicity has reached a level I haven't encountered before. In this particular section of the ocean, plastic particles outnumber plankton by a factor of 19. Let me restate it in the simplest of terms: for every pound of plankton, there are nineteen pounds of plastic fragments. This is astounding, Mr. President. Do you know how small plankton are?"

He let the question dangle in the air. The President's breath came soft across the line. Liam had been stunned by the samples they had taken, but it was just as astonishing to hear the words spoken aloud. The group had been methodical in their work. They'd dredged different parts of the zone to be certain, taken samples at each of its boundaries, yet the results at each were the same. Each sample yielded fragments of all sizes and shapes: big, small, and microscopic. Liam had been reluctant—if not frightened—to take them under a microscope.

The President's voice made Liam jump. "The implications, Doctor? What does it mean?"

A man to Liam's right cleared his voice. "Jacob Gagnon, Canadian Department of Fisheries and Oceans, Sir."

"The implications, Jacob. What does it mean?"

Jacob's answer effectively silenced the room.

"The microscopic plastics have irrevocably changed the ocean's ecosystem. Hazardous chemicals are ingested by the smallest of species, by those that dwell at the bottom of the oceanic food chain. Larger animals are mistaking microplastics for plankton, and larger particles for fish eggs. They are eating the plastics instead of real food, and are either starving or are consumed by larger fish, which are in turn, ingested by even larger fish. The process repeats itself until it reaches the top of the food chain."

"Us," President Hall said slowly. "You're talking about us. We're at the top of the food chain."

Liam nodded his head in confirmation. "That's correct, Mr. President. Us. Humans. The issue for us is two-fold. Smaller oceanic creatures are starving to death, which results in less food for larger predators. Many species have become extinct, and the ones that haven't aren't fit for human consumption. It's a slow poisoning that's been happening for centuries. The Garbage Patch, first discovered in 1997, has more than doubled in size since then."

"Not only this Patch," said Lanfeng Tang, from China's Oceanic Administration. "The North Pacific Patch, and the Eastern and Western Patches have joined. The Subtropical Gyre has linked them together. In a similar fashion, the North Atlantic and South Atlantic Gyres have joined to form a Convergence Zone."

The voice from the comm unit crackled with indignation. "Dr. Colt, a gyre please?"

"There are a total of five gyres worldwide, Sir.

Simply put, a gyre is a system of ocean currents, driven by wind patterns and the Earth's rotation." Liam pressed his fingers to his temples. "They're like superhighways connecting one ocean current to the next."

"Okay. So you're saying these 'Patches' have connected. Am I getting that right?"

"Yes, Sir. They are. We've confirmed it, in fact. There are large concentrations of debris and microplastics in each of the gyres, and the gyres have connected to form Convergence Zones."

Liam let the information settle. For his entire life, he'd loved the ocean: the symmetry of it, the rhythm of the waves, the delicate balance of its complex ecosystem. But of late, it was unrecognizable to him. It was toxic and lethal, a deadly poisonous brew. It had waged war on the world it created. Once a rich primordial soup, it was now a consommé of deadly toxins, algae, and chemicals. It threatened every corner of the planet.

He sipped from his glass while trying his best to calm himself. The ship's engines thrummed softly beneath his feet. It was a lot of information for a scientist to absorb, much less a politician or layman. Hearing the facts relayed so succinctly brought to mind the comforts of his cabin back home. His eyes strayed to his son on the floor, playing innocently amid such melancholic talk. Ignorance truly was bliss, Liam thought.

The President, his voice strained and hoarse, finally broke the silence. Liam felt pity for the man. This was a man who'd aspired to greatness, but who'd inherited a dying world instead. He addressed no one in particular when he asked, "What else can I expect to read in your report, or is it safe to say we've covered the most important points?"

An EPA agent gave a breathless answer. "The data we've discussed today covers the chemical elements of the Patch, Sir." She took a breath to steady herself. "But not all plastic floats. Seventy percent of all plastic sinks.

I'm sorry to give such a depressive visual, but in the places beneath the Patches, the ocean floor resembles a landfill."

"Stop," the President said quietly. "I've heard enough for one day. I need to think. I'll read through the rest when I receive your report. What I want to talk about now is a plan of action. What can we do to rectify this situation? Who can we call upon to clean the Patch zones?"

The scientists exchanged horrified glances. Liam could read their expressions as easily as he could a molecular compound. They looked to one another for guidance and support. Any suggestion or idea would be welcome, any theory or conceptualization, any wild supposition, no matter how fringe. Several had slumped in their seats and given up, and some had set their heads on the table in exhaustion. Others were openly weeping. There was nothing left to offer, no viable plan. The time for action had presented itself, but now that time had long passed.

Liam leaned in and cleared his throat. "I'm sorry to say, Mr. President, but there's no coming back from this. There's nothing we—or anyone—can do. There's no amount of money we can pay or spend." Liam felt like he was wilting inside, like the weight of his words was an anvil on his shoulders. "No piece of equipment exists today that can filter thousands of square miles of ocean water, or comb it for microplastic contaminants. Understand, Sir, the oceans are miles and miles deep. Nothing can sift through miles of water, especially at that depth and pressure. The size and scope of this is inconceivable. I'm afraid there's nothing we can do. We couldn't even conceive of a viable way to—"

Liam abruptly ran out of words. There was no other way to state the truth, and as he awaited a reply, his neck prickled. The Captain and his officer had paled.

The President's voice sounded muffled, as if his lips were pressed to the speaker. "Dr. Colt," he said.

"Speak plainly. What are you trying to say?"

Liam felt Olivia's hand touch his knee, and when he met her gaze, she squeezed it softly. He was grateful for her companionship and support. She'd always imparted him strength and warmth, and though he took a breath to steady himself, it failed to loosen the tension in his gut. He met the gazes of each person in the room, of colleagues and friends he'd worked with for years, before telling the most powerful man in the world that the world he ruled was coming to an end.

"Mr. President," he said, "I'm sorry to say, but the oceans are effectively extinct."

Things are never as they seem. A person. A Mark. A statement. They are always deeper than we perceive, like walking in the ocean and suddenly dipping under the surface because the bottom has disappeared beneath your feet. The water appears shallow until you are suddenly flailing around beneath the surface, desperately searching for stable ground once again.

—Kelseyleigh Reber

CHAPTER 14
1 Year Prior

NOVEMBER 17TH, 2175
JUST OUTSIDE OF KNOXVILLE, TENNESSEE

For five long months, they'd been living in this house. For five long months, they'd been combing the countryside, searching for supplies. For five long months, they'd been treating Peter's gangrenous leg, managing his disease, making him as comfortable as they could. They'd been trying to keep things positive for months. They built this semblance of a life as best they could, fortified this house, and planned escape routes should bandits come calling. And for five long months, Jeremy had harbored this fretful, uneasy feeling. He was becoming more restless as each day passed, his inner voice screaming at him to get up and do something!

If only he knew what it was.

Like a Las Vegas casino chip, he flipped the empty disk case between his thumb and forefinger, distracted as rain drummed a steady beat on the windows of the house. Night had fallen on another endless day of foraging— worthless foraging, he reminded himself. His gaze slid from the ceiling to the children, to Meghan, then back to the ceiling again. An ever-expanding water stain was creeping across the far corner of the room. Pointing it to Meghan, he said, "We need to find the source of that leak."

She lifted her head, but said nothing, and he evaluated the angles and planes of her face. She'd put on weight, but she was still too thin. Though the past few months had done her wonders. Her cheeks had filled out and her eyes were brighter. A healthy flush had replaced the once-pallid tone of her skin. When she and Peter had first arrived, they'd been gaunt, exhausted, battered by the elements. Jeremy had worried about their ability to recover, particularly Peter. He was in the worst shape.

Those first few days, Jeremy had encouraged them to rest, eat, hydrate themselves, and then rest some more, and it had done him well to look after someone else. Caring for them had brought him an unexpected measure of happiness. It had made him feel significant again. They prepared starchy meals of beans, rice, and old cans of potatoes, and gathered fresh berries and root vegetables from the woods that hemmed their property. He furnished them water and comfortable beds, clean clothes, and most importantly, a renewed sense of security. His and Sam's generosity helped the newcomers make a slow but steady recovery, and Jeremy was proud of the progress they had made. They'd extended themselves to two strangers, two damaged individuals who'd been circling the proverbial drain.

Meghan and Peter had done little else than sleep those first few days. It seemed like more than a week had passed before either had worked up the courage to come out. And when they did, they were bleary-eyed and full of wonder, fascinated by the opulence in front of them.

They'd been homeless for far too long, Jeremy remarked. They were accustomed to surviving this dangerous world and living among its wreckage. And though Meghan was exceedingly grateful for Jeremy's hospitality, she'd been wary of his kindness for a time. She'd been guarded and overprotective of her son. But as Jeremy had learned from personal experience, time has a way of healing the deepest of wounds, and eventually Meghan softened to him. Her shyness gave way to gentle curiosity, which evolved into unabashed interest. She was awed by the richness of Jeremy's life and astonished by the depth of his resourcefulness. Early on she made it clear to him that she wanted to acquire the same skills.

As time passed, she proved her mettle. She was a diligent student, an industrious worker, a devoted mother, a fighter. Jeremy was proud of her transformation. She'd come a long way from that once-frightened woman holding a gun in a dilapidated convenience store. If nothing else, she'd become his friend. He taught her how to build small cook fires and cook raw food over the tops of them. He shared his list of the most nutritious foods, and the tips for making them last longer, and for the past few months, they'd stocked their shelves. But of late, to find what they needed, they'd been forced to travel farther from the house. Staying in one place was a difficult thing to do. In any given place there existed a finite supply of rations, and they'd vowed not to touch the supplies in the cart. It and its supplies were a safety net to them. It was important to Jeremy to live off the land for as long as they were able.

And it was an incredibly rich land at that. This particular area of the country had been sparsely populated, and thus, was better stocked than most large cities, so they searched it methodically, plotting their course on Jeremy's map as they went, and crossing out places they'd already been. But lately, their need for medication was taking them farther and farther from the house. Jeremy feared overnight expeditions would soon be required.

His frown deepened. The situation troubled him. For several weeks, his apprehension had grown, his fear like a metastasizing cancer in his belly. That familiar voice was whispering again, and as each day passed, it became harder and harder to ignore.

This won't work, it whispered sagely. You know this. Not long term. Not for two children who have the same disease.

The pragmatism of the words lifted the hairs on the back of his neck. He could do his best pretend at stability, but soon, he and Meghan would reach an impasse, and what would they do when that happened? Stability was key for the health and longevity of diabetic children. This house could never be a permanent solution. Besides, he thought, they were barely 30 miles from the ashes of Jeremy's burnt-down cabin. Was this as far as his heart would let him go? Was he refusing to let go and move one? Grasping at the ghosts of his past? He should consider moving on, starting a new life, but if this house wasn't the solution, what was? If not here, Jeremy wondered, then where?

There was a hospital little more than twenty miles from here, but he and Meghan had already cleaned it out. It had yielded a cache of insulin pills, which had already improved Peter's precarious health. He was alert and communicative, his appetite had increased, and his leg had shown signs—though subtle—of improvement. He'd even shown interest in Sam. He would listen to her read, ask her questions about the past. One day, when he and Meghan had returned from a long day of scavenging, he'd caught Sam teaching Peter to read. It was heartwarming to watch. It felt like normal life. A healthy relationship was blossoming between them. But the pills would be an ever-present issue, particularly when their collection started to dwindle.

Which is happening right now, he reminded

himself.

And what about Sam? She didn't need the pills—not yet, anyway. The disks were successfully managing her illness. But how much longer could he depend on that? None of the hospitals or medical centers they'd visited had yielded a single errant disk. Nor had the Urgent Care Centers, or pharmacies. At what point would Jeremy's friendship with Meghan give way to secrets and lies? When would they turn on each another? It was as likely a scenario as it was an inevitable one.

And this, he knew, was the source of his restlessness.

"What are you thinking about?" Meghan asked softly, the flames of the hearth in her eyes.

He shifted uncomfortably. "I really don't know. Thinking about ways to create sustainability, I guess."

"Don't you think we've done that?"

He considered the question, and for the most part, agreed. Over the last few months, they'd known many successes. They'd even discovered two wells. And though only one had been potable, it was more than Jeremy had dared hope for. It was reason enough to stay. But foraging wasn't sustainable. And they'd done little else to create a system that worked.

"I suppose we have," he answered slowly. "But what about food? Our own food? We should be planting crops and growing fruit-bearing trees. How long can we scavenge before we run out of places to look?" He shook his head despondently. "I just think we should be something doing more."

"Something more?" Her eyes slipped to her son, who was sleeping peacefully in front of the hearth, beside Sam. "You've done more for Peter and I than I had ever dreamed possible. And to think I almost shot you." She grinned. "What a terrible loss that would've been."

He smiled despite his foul mood. "You know you wouldn't have shot me."

She held his gaze for a moment too long, a moment longer than was comfortable for him. He quickly looked back at the children. He knew she'd begun to have feelings for him, feelings that had matured and slowly deepened. At the start, she'd shown them in small, subtle ways. At unexpected times, she would touch his arm, or brush against his body in passing. She'd ask kittenish questions through lowered lashes. When he was showing her how to perform a new task, she'd cup her palm to his hand, and say, "Am I doing it right?" or "How does this look?"

But lately, her overtures had grown bolder. And could Jeremy blame her? She was human, after all. She was young and beautiful and lonely, and he was the only living man for miles around. With nutrition and exercise, and the relief that comes with knowing food and water will be found the next day, she'd shed her protective shell. Her eyes had brightened and she'd become more trusting. Her smiles came easier, and often. Like a snake, she'd molted an old layer of skin, a layer of protection she no longer needed, and thus was welcoming adult relationships.

Leaning her head against the cushions of the divan, she tucked her long legs beneath her. "No," she murmured. " I suppose you're right. I suppose I wouldn't have shot you."

Suddenly curious, he arched his brow. "Have you ever shot anyone before?" Funny that he'd never thought to ask her that.

Folding her hands, she met his gaze. "Yes. Once. To protect Peter. And I'd do it again in a heartbeat, if I had to. What about you? Haven't you?"

"No. Burned a few, though."

"Burned a few?"

"Long story."

"Okay," she sighed, accustomed to his evasiveness. "Perhaps one day you'll feel like telling me about it."

One day, he thought strangely. One day.

One day implies more to come, does it not? He glanced at the disk in his palm. There it was: that unsettling pull in the pit of his stomach, that restlessness of spirit trying to communicate something. Stomach churning, he lifted his gaze. She'd been staring at him and seemed suddenly embarrassed. She nervously pushed a lock of hair behind her ear. She really was quite beautiful, young, full of life, and pleasant to be around. But there was something she wasn't, and never would be. She would never be Susan. That was the problem.

How would another man act in a similar situation? He couldn't help but wonder from time to time. An attractive woman, living under the same roof, sharing a household for nearly six months? A woman—mind you— who depended on him for her very survival, who admired and revered him above all others. Most men would find that a heady combination. It was an arrangement that would compel most men to action. But Jeremy wasn't 'most men'. He felt nothing for Meghan, despite the circumstances. Perhaps losing Susan was still too fresh a wound, or perhaps the parts of him that craved companionship and sex had died in that fire, along with everything else.

Again, he glanced at the children. Peter was lying on his sleeping bag, his infectious leg propped against a pillow, his teddy-bear keychain clutched beneath his chin. Though Meghan had recovered and flourished, Peter hadn't. He still faced a steady decline. That wasn't to say he hadn't improved; they'd done much to slow the progression of his illness. But in Jeremy's opinion, it wasn't enough. His condition had been ignored for far too long and had reached a point of no return. For once gangrene set into a wound, there was little one could do to reverse it.

"He's doing much better," Meghan said quietly, as though reading his mind.

"He is," Jeremy conceded, "but the leg—"

"Don't say it. I refuse to have this discussion again."

"Meghan, can't you see what's happening? The rot is slowly climbing toward his knee. Once it passes his kneecap, it won't be long until it claims the whole leg."

Eyes flashing, her fists curled instinctively. "I won't do it, Jeremy. I've told you that. I won't cut it off. Something like that would kill him."

"And this won't?" He could barely keep the anger from his voice.

Her fingers twitched and fluttered, then pulled at a piece of frayed hemming on her shirt. She inhaled a ragged breath to steady herself. "I'm not stupid, Jeremy. And I'm not in denial. Of course I know it's killing him. But that doesn't make what you're saying better. What you're suggesting isn't possible. Not in these circumstances, and not in his current condition. I mean look at him!"

"Yes, Meghan. I am looking at him. I've been looking at him for months."

"No," she argued. "I mean really look at him. When first we met, he was suffering from a wet gangrene. The leg was infected, hopelessly infected—hopelessly or so I had thought. But we've corrected that now. He's doing much better."

"We haven't corrected anything, Meghan. Gangrene is gangrene. Rot is rot. Proud flesh has to be removed."

"Proud flesh? My son isn't a horse, Jeremy." She was silent for a moment before reasoning anew. "You're right. The flesh is gangrene. But it's a dry gangrene, and you know that's better. Dry can be tolerated—if not controlled."

"Oh!" Jeremy said, his temper rising. "Well, he's definitely tolerating it, as you say, but don't fool yourself. It's not under our control. Let me ask you something. If his leg looks like that, what do you think's going on beneath the skin? What do you think's happening to his organs and blood vessels? To his muscles, bones, heart, and lungs?"

She stiffened then swung her legs over the couch. "Okay, Jeremy. I'll bite. What are you suggesting? That not only are you a skilled gardener, but that you're also an adept farmer, a gifted cook, and—oh yes—an accomplished surgeon?" She threw up her hands. "Well bless the Lord in heaven! I've happened across the perfect man! In the end times, I've found the only man alive who is capable of dong everything! So tell me, Doctor Colt, how will you do it? How will you remove Peter's leg in a state-of-the-art facility such as this? With no blood to transfuse, no knives with which to cut, no antiseptics, gauze, lasers, or scalpels—and oh, yes!—with no way to control his pain! Do you know what that would be like for him? We don't have anesthesia, Jeremy! Not a local one, nor a topical one." Her eyes glinted dangerously. Spittle was dribbling over the curve of her lip. "What you're suggesting is absolute madness. It's akin to human torture, and I won't do that. Not in the lowest point of my darkest moment in hell. I'd rather see him—" She stopped suddenly. Her mouth snapped closed.

"You'd rather see him what, Megan? Die?"

"Yes," she spat. "I'd rather see him die. I'd rather see him dead than watch him live through that. Call me a bad mother, if you will. I don't care. I'm not ashamed to admit how I feel."

For a moment, she lowered her gaze to her hands, as if wondering what they were capable of, before cupping her face and starting to weep.

Shit, Jeremy thought. Why was he such as ass? Why were his emotions so close to the surface? He was a ticking time bomb with a very short fuse.

"Meghan, I'm sorry." Leaning forward, he lowered his forehead to his hands. The empty disk was cold against his temple. "I don't know what the hell's gotten into me lately. Lately, I just don't feel like myself.

It's…the pills, I think. They go so fast. And I don't function well without a plan. I just don't know what we're planning to do. What will be our strategy when the pills run out?"

She wept but didn't answer. He felt like a heel. Sliding across the couch, he moved closer to her. Why was he such a damned jerk? He wasn't a good communicator anymore. Perhaps he was just out of practice. Or had he possibly become this callous?

"Meghan," he tried again. "I'm sorry. You're right. We can't do that. We won't consider it or talk about it again. It's barbaric even to think it. I don't know what's wrong with me."

She lifted her face and wiped the tears from her eyes. "Jeremy, I know you're just trying to help, and were our circumstance different, an amputation would be best. I just can't abide that for Peter. Not now." Lifting her legs, she crossed them on the sofa. It was difficult not to notice how close their hands were, or the tears that were glistening in her eyes, or the delicate curve of her throat and bottom lip.

"I know Peter will die," she continued softly, "I'm not daft. Eventually he will. It's unavoidable. But people can live a long time with this kind of affliction."

Jeremy answered her hoarsely. "Yes, with proper medication they can."

"I suppose you think I'm being selfish," she said. "But in my position, what parent wouldn't be? What are my alternatives? If I won't remove the leg, what should I do? Withhold the medicine that prevents his suffering? Do I allow his wounds to proliferate and fester? I can't do that. I won't do that." She cocked her head and ran a thumb across his knuckle. "How I wish I had met you sooner, Jeremy Colt. Maybe if I had, this wouldn't have happened." When she leaned in close, he felt her breath against his forehead. "Maybe if I had met you years ago, we could've built something sustainable then."

Before he could stop her, she had leaned in and kissed him. Her mouth was warm and moist, and though kissing someone other than Susan was unimaginable, the physical act aroused him. It was pleasant, he thought. Pleasant—but wrong. Setting his hands to her shoulders, he gently pushed her away.

"Meghan, you're lovely, but—"

"I know," she breathed shallowly. "I'm not your wife. You don't have to say it. Though you don't speak of her, I can sense your pain."

He lifted a hand to her cheek. "I'm just not ready for something like this. To be fair, I may never be."

"Never say never," she murmured quietly. "One day, you might surprise yourself."

One day. He swallowed. There it was again. He hadn't noticed before, but his fist was clenching the empty disk in his hand. Relaxing his grip, he rubbed his open palm, which was red and dented by the corners of the plastic.

One day, he thought again. One day.

Moving his thumb across the plastic, he scratched the word, engraved on the cover.

Insulidisk, it said. It made no sense. It was a gimmicky word that meant nothing, but it was the thing that kept her alive.

He peered at Peter and Sam, whose bodies were rounded shapes inside their sleeping pallets. Peter had made measurable progress. It was a truth Jeremy couldn't deny. His condition was poor, but he was declining at a much slower pace than before. Jeremy called to memory the morning they'd arrived. Meghan had been pushing the broken-down grocery cart, Peter crumpled in the bottom of the basket. Through the window, she'd appeared exhausted, as if she would collapse in the middle of the street. For several days, Jeremy had known she was there. She'd been watching the house, appraising them from a distance, trying to decide if they were decent people, trying to decide if they were safe.

That was the morning she had risked it all. From the living room window, he'd watched her come, pushing the cart with its rickety wheel, her thin arms trembling with the effort. He'd wanted to rush outside to help her, but his eyes had found Peter instead. The leg, as before, had been lifted and balanced atop a pile of dirty blankets. It was the only thing Jeremy had been able to focus on, and as they approached the house, he had watched it bounce ominously. Instead of running to offer her aid, he'd run to Sam instead. "There are people coming, Sam," he'd said breathlessly, grabbed her by the shoulders and squeezing painfully. Her body had tensed. Alarm had shone in her eyes. "No," he'd added quickly, feeling like a fool. Why did he always have to scare her like that? Nothing scared Sam more than thoughts of other people. "Not bad people, honey. People we can help. People I met in town the other day… the day we went to the library. Remember? The day we first started speaking again." He ran a hand over her hair, smoothed it, and admired the flaxen strands.

"What's wrong with you?" she'd asked, pushing his hands away. "If they're not bad people, then why are you so upset?"

He'd squeezed her arms. "I'm not upset. I just want to prepare you. I need to tell you something. Don't be frightened—don't be shocked I mean. Don't be shocked or upset when you see them. I need you to stifle your reaction."

"What? Stifle my reaction? What the hell does that mean?"

He ignored the curse word and drew a deep breath. "The boy. He's ill—terribly ill. It's his leg. He's—"

"Dad, you're being silly." She'd smiled. "I think I can handle a bad leg."

She'd grabbed his hand and pulled him outdoors, and in silence, the two had watched Meghan approach. Jeremy was proud. Sam had hidden her revulsion well.

She'd fought the instinct to stare openly. She'd been kind and courteous, open to the possibility of helping people in need. It was only after she'd seen the pills that she'd begun asking Jeremy questions. One night, behind the house, she'd found him chopping wood and cornered him there, anger flashing in her eyes.

"Peter's a diabetic? Why didn't you tell me that?"

"Why do you care that I didn't tell you that?"

"You're deflecting," she accused him.

"Deflecting? Good word. Is that our toilet-paper-word-of-the-day?"

"Stop." She'd stamped her foot. "Stop making light of this. You did it on purpose. You kept this from me. When are you going to start telling me the truth? When will you start respecting me?"

He'd dropped the ax and stood there stupidly. She was right. Of course. She was always right.

"I'm sorry, Sam."

She'd crossed her arms. "And how many times are you going to say that? Dad, I don't want your apologies anymore. I just want you to tell me the truth. It's what we promised each other we'd do."

"You're right. We did. And from now on, I will."

She'd dropped her hands to her sides, placated. "Okay. Then why don't you start right now? So Peter's a diabetic. So what? Why wouldn't you want me to know that?"

He had no choice but to tell her to the truth, to tell her the things he and Susan never had. They'd never explained what would happen to her body if she chronically mismanaged her disease. There was no reason to. The disks made it easy. When one ran out, it was replaced with another. Life went on, almost normally. There was no fuss, no hassle. No thought went into any of it. Sam had never visited a diabetic hospital ward, or seen photographs of people in advanced stages of deterioration. She'd been sheltered from the more gruesome aspects of her illness. She simply didn't know what could happen.

Crouching in front of her, he took her hands in his, and though she tried to pull away, he refused to let her go. "Sam, understand, you're one of the lucky ones. You've always had the disks. Peter hasn't. For years, we've managed your illness on autopilot. It was never an issue at home, and as long as we have the disks, it won't be an issue out here. Peter hasn't lived that kind of life. He's had to fight for his health for years, forage for pills on a daily basis. Sam," he added warily, "without the pills Peter will die."

"Without the disks, I will die."

His heart skipped a beat. He wouldn't acknowledge that. "Without medication, anyone in your condition could die. But we won't let that happen. We're smarter than that."

She rolled her eyes. "Dad, I know all of this. I know the risks, and I know how to take care of myself. I know how important the disks are to me. But I still don't understand why you're so upset. Why would—"

Suddenly, her mouth snapped shut. Her eyes narrowed and her hands begun to tremble. "Dad," she said softly, "without medication what happens? You say I get fuzzy or faint. You said I could fall into a coma. What else? What happens after that? It's his leg, isn't it?" She cupped a hand to her moth. "That's what will happen to me."

"No." Jeremy shook his head vehemently. "No. It won't. We won't let that happen to you."

"But that's what happened to Peter, isn't it? That's what caused his leg to turn black. His diabetes did that to him."

"It did. Without proper medication, diabetics can't produce enough insulin, and as a result, their sugars become unmanageable. High sugars cause cells to break down and die."

"Break down and die," she repeated softly. "Die like in rot. That's what happened to his leg. That's why it smells so bad. Because it's rotting off his body."

"I'm sorry, Sam, but do you understand now? That's why I'm such a crazy person when it comes to your health. That's why I'm constantly asking you your number."

He watched her chest rise and fall as she slept. That conversation had meant a lot to him. He remembered thinking that with any kind of luck he'd finally reached her and made her understand. She'd been forced to accept difficult concepts that day, and Jeremy thought she had done it with dignity.

He rubbed his thumb against the lettering on the disk.

"How many do you have left?"

"What?" Jeremy raised his head. Ignoring Meghan's question, he said. "I think you should learn how to properly shoot a gun. We should work on your aim and accuracy. And I think we should plant you a garden out back."

"Plant me a garden out back? What do you mean?"

He sighed. "Meghan, what will we do when we run out of pills?"

"So that's what this is about, isn't it?" She eyed the slim case of plastic in his palm. "It's about you leaving. You're thinking of moving on." When he met her gaze, he was surprised to see tears. "You're leaving because you're running out of disks."

"No." He shook his head. He'd become a decent liar. "I just think there are things you need to learn. And we're being shortsighted if we don't discuss this. We have to have a better plan for locating pills out there."

She rubbed her palms against her thighs. "Well, that's easy. We just keep looking. There are hundreds of hospitals in this state alone. We don't stop trying. We keep after it. We measure our progress as we go. We expand our search grid every time we set out. We mark it on the map.

We never give up."

Search. He flipped the disk, considering the word. Yes. They could. They could continue to search, but what, exactly, were they searching for? A few bottles of pills? With any luck, a case? He traced the word on the cover of the disk, flipped it over, and examined the logo on the back. The words were faded, but clear enough to read.

Bigeye Pharmaceuticals. His eyes widened.

"Search," he murmured absently. "So you're saying we just keep searching."

"Yes." She grasped at his words and held them tightly. "That's exactly what I'm saying. We search forever, if that's what it takes. We search one area until we know it's depleted then move to the next area. It's as simple as that. We've already been doing it for months, haven't we? Tell me, Jeremy, what's changed?"

Numb, he raised his head to meet her gaze. "The pills have changed. Don't you realize that? Every year, they become less potent. They're weaker now than they were six months ago. Some of what we've found is over 30 years old."

Her smile was sad. "You're such a pessimist."

"Yeah," he muttered. "So I've been told."

"But you are. Yes, Jeremy—the pills are weaker. But the United States is a very big place. There are countless places to look."

She was right. Their search grid was enormous. But if they constantly moved around, how could they ever settle down and plant roots? If they adopted the life of a scavenger, how could he give Sam the stability she needed? This vision of life couldn't deliver her that. It wasn't attainable in the long run. What would they do? How would it work? Would he uproot her every six months and move on? Move her somewhere else, and then move her again? How would they ever plant a garden or a grove of trees? How would they ever grow crops? Would they never know the comfort of a permanent home? Were they doomed to live a nomadic life, like wanderers, gypsies, hamsters in a wheel? It wasn't a life worth living. And it certainly wasn't the one he and Susan had planned for Sam.

He glanced about the room, as if it were suddenly foreign. This plan had always had an expiration date. But once it expired, what would be next? If it couldn't be this, then what could it be?

The pitter-patter of rain, so gentle and innocuous just a moment ago now chanted in an ominous voice. It beat against the roof, a two-beat trot of horse's hooves, the sound like opportunity passing him by.

His gaze fell to the disk in his hand, and he cocked his head to read the words.

Bigeye Pharmaceuticals.

The manufacturer. The lettering beneath the name was small and faint. The light was dim. Lifting it closer to his face, he squinted.

Bigeye Pharmaceuticals.
San Diego, California.

If you've managed to do one good thing,
the ocean doesn't care.
But when Newton's apple
fell toward the earth,
the earth, ever so slightly, fell
toward the apple as well.

—Ellen Bass

PART 4

CHAPTER 15
Present Day

One moment he was up and the next he wasn't. It was as quick and as sudden as that. One moment Seth was quietly gliding, the sun glinting off the reflective piping of his backpack. The next he was sprawled across the pavement, bike fallen atop him, saw-toothed edge of the chain mere inches from his inflamed wound. Consciousness had fled him abruptly. His body had folded, collapsed in a heap in the middle of the highway, the screeching of his bike piercing as it skidded across the ground.

Sam screamed.

Jeremy swerved, tottered, and nearly fell.

Dropping his bike in the center lane of westbound I-30, he rushed to Seth's side in a panic. Sweat bloomed across his forehead, dampened his palms and underarms. He was as furious with Seth as he was frightened for him, but mostly he was furious with himself. Seth had lied to him, earlier that morning, with gentle words and an easy

236

smile. He'd said he was fine, that he could go on. He'd convinced Jeremy that his leg hurt a little, that he was mostly tired from lack of sleep the night before.

Jeremy's jaw was tight with anger. Lies after lies, on top of more lies. But it wasn't the lies that angered Jeremy as much as the fact that he had believed them. He was the adult; the responsible member of this expedition, and his failure to heed his intuition had put them in this terrible predicament. Like a fool, he'd miscalculated the severity of Seth's low-grade fever, which had begun to burn two days earlier. He'd treated the symptom with aspirin from the bottle he'd pilfered at the Walmart Supercenter, but he hadn't investigated the root cause of it. Not that he had to—he knew the root cause. Seth's leg was becoming infected.

He should have known it was serious that day, should have demanded that Seth lie down, and rest. No more than twenty-four hours ago, he'd changed the dressing himself. He'd seen it. He'd even remarked at the strange, spider-like webbing of veins in dark blues and reds that sprung from its edges in zigzagging patterns. And the flesh, he remembered, that was a bit too moist, too puffy, and a bit too warm to the touch. He'd cleansed it thoroughly, for what seemed like the fiftieth time that week, but a small amount of puss had oozed from one corner. He'd ignored his fears, pushed them deep inside his belly. Why had he been so naïve? Even the insufficiency of the scab had concerned him. The wound should have closed by then. The wound should have closed, and he should have been smart, should have forced them to stop for a day to monitor it.

But should was a game he always seemed to lose. And now, here they were, in a worse predicament. He could kick himself for being so stupid. He should have been wiser to Seth's deception, but instead, had trusted a nine-year-old boy to diagnose the severity of a serious wound. He'd depended on a child to make an adult

decision and hadn't factored in the other variables. Well—
the other variable, he corrected himself. Sam was the only
thing Seth cared about. His every decision always circled
back to her, which by far, was Jeremy's worst oversight.

Ever since Seth had changed Sam's disk, he'd
become obsessed with the countdown of her meter. He'd
check it in the morning, at breakfast, at sundown. After
she'd eaten. After she'd peed. If she was tired, hungry,
sleepy, or groggy. His preoccupation with it was ridiculous.
Though Sam, for some reason, was tolerant of it, probably
for the same reasons Jeremy was. It meant a lot to Seth.
She meant a lot to him. He would scrunch his forehead,
purse his lips, and gently lift the corner of her shirt, afraid
to glimpse the numbers, yet afraid not to. He'd pace, shake
his head, mutter to himself about the passage of time, and
about how few miles they'd traveled that day. At first,
Jeremy found his fascination endearing, and he figured
Sam probably felt the same. Why else would she condone
behavior she typically found so intrusive from others?
Maybe she knew how badly Seth needed the distraction.
Or maybe, like Jeremy, she sensed how frightened he was,
how tightly he clung to his newfound family. He was
terrified of losing them, of history repeating itself, and fear
is the poison of the soul.

Against all odds, a boy who'd lived in a long-
deserted convenience store, alone, found a place where he
belonged, and people who loved him. In a world ravaged
by an extinction level event, he'd reconnected with people,
found unity and purpose. This second chance meant
everything to him. This surrogate family was his present,
and future, and he clung to it with desperate hands.

So day after day, he pretended at health as he
watched the percentage on Sam's meter decline, which
Jeremy now regretted having shown him in the first place.
It was too big a burden for a young boy to bear, too
stressful for one who'd already experienced such losses.
This entire situation was Jeremy's fault, and the guilt was

tearing him apart.

Staring at his face, Jeremy gently touched his forehead. Shit. The heat from the fever frightened him. The fever was high, and Seth was so small. Jeremy wasn't prepared for this—medically, or emotionally. Panic slowly set in. He froze. Fear turned his stomach to acid. Icebound and cemented in place, he dwelled on the severity of the impossible situation. Every second was a small eternity. What would he do? Where would he take them? How would he treat such a life-threatening illness? The fact that Seth had collapsed in the street meant that the infection was coursing through his blood. For all Jeremy knew, it was shutting down his organs, ferrying poison to his heart at that moment. Had Jeremy the resources to deal with this? Had he adequate medicines, supplies, and shelter? His eyes darted to Sam and his mouth went dry. Forget the supplies. Did he even have the time? His gaze fell to the glow at her belly. There were so many miles between them and San Diego and only one more disk with which to cover them.

She met his gaze, hands clenched at her sides. "Carp, what happened? What's wrong with him?"

Jeremy was aware of pain in his fists, where his fingernails had burrowed into the fleshy parts of his palms. He must act, now, and with conviction of purpose, yet his body was frozen in the middle of the road. He was impotent and paralyzed in a posture of genuflection. He had antibiotics, yes, but how long would they last? Would they be enough? Something this severe could require hundreds of pills, could drain his resources in a matter of days. Was he prepared to give Seth all that what left? What if something happened to Sam? What if something happened and his medicines were gone? He loved Seth, yes; he viewed him as a son. But difficult decisions would have to be made. Would his commitment to Seth overshadow the one he had made to Sam? Was he putting her at risk for a boy he'd just met?

"Dad," Sam pressed, her voice shaking. "What's wrong?"

Jeremy's inner voice began to whisper fervently. It was a familiar voice, a trustworthy one, his father's voice. Pull the trigger, it whispered.

The trigger?

Yes. The mental trigger. Pull it now.

Jeremy sucked in a breath, having nearly forgotten about that. His father had counseled him, on more than one occasion, to create an image he could call upon at will, something that would elicit an immediate response. A mental trigger could be anything, really: a favorite place, an important object, the image of a person one loved. In life-and-death situations, Liam had said, people often find themselves unable to act or think critically, and for this, one needed a trigger. It was a common practice among the Navy SEALs, something he'd picked up while working for the government. During long excursions across dark barren seas, Liam had studied their survival techniques, and this was one he'd brought home to his family.

Jeremy floundered. His mind wasn't sharp. What was his trigger? What had it been? Over the years, as things do, it had changed. As a child, for a time, it was his favorite transformer figurine, which he'd clung to during particularly loud thunderstorms. After that, it was a squirrel that lived in an old rotting tree at the edge of their property. But what had it been after that? He couldn't remember. More importantly, what was it now?

His breath caught. His hands dug into his thighs like claws.

"Carp," Sam hissed. "What's wrong with you?" He felt the air move as she dropped down beside him. "Dad," she said softly, "what's going on?" She set her cool fingers to his wrist. It calmed him. "You're scaring me, Dad. Snap out of it. We have to help Seth. What should we do?"

He could hear the rising panic in her voice, yet he

was still unable to move. The mission was suddenly insurmountable to him. What had he done? What had he been thinking? Travel by bike across the United States proper? This hair-brained scheme could take their lives. He peered intently at Seth. Hell, it had probably taken one life already.

Sam's fingers fluttered against his arm.

"Dad, you're just tired. Your mind is sleepy. You're fuzzy, like I sometimes get. Just pull the trigger, Dad. That's all you have to do." She slapped his arm. "Pull the trigger."

He flinched from the sting of her slap but didn't move. He couldn't remember his trigger anymore. He searched his mind but came up blank. He didn't have a trigger. That was the issue. He'd stoically held things together for so long that he'd ignored his own feelings and needs. He'd concentrated his efforts on Sam and the disks, on Meghan and Peter, on the path to San Diego. For so many months, he'd put himself last. He'd been strong, lifted others, while ignoring his own fears, which had swelled and were threatening to choke him now. He was losing another person he loved. He'd failed as husband, father, and friend, and now another person he loved would die.

Sam seized his arm and squeezed it painfully. "Carp," she said. "Remember what you said. You told me we had to persevere." Her voice cracked and she let loose a sob. "Dad, please. Look at his face. He's gone gray. You have to tell me what to do. I don't know what the hell to do." She slapped his arm and then his face. "Carp! Pull the trigger! Right now!"

Images flashed across his mind like a movie. A trigger: he just needed to find a new one. He'd seen so much violence over the past few months. Hell, over the past few years. First there was the fire, then Seth's dead mother. There were the men who had murdered his wife. There was Peter's rotting leg, and Sam's diabetes, the times she had fainted at the side of the road, dripping in puddles of insulin-induced sweat.

Susan.

He blinked.

And then there was Susan.

Her image rose from the blackness in his mind, the vision finding shape, and brightening. Her face was a ray of sunlight in his mind's darkness: her smooth blond hair, her gentle smile, her blue eyes, the love that had always shone through them. It was Susan. She was his trigger now. She was the spark that ignited his heart. Hers was the voice that whispered to him. Hers was the counsel he sought. It was her gentle hands that pushed him forward.

He would persevere for Susan, and for the life of their daughter. He'd make Susan proud. He'd never give up. Never would he allow someone he loved to suffer so horribly again. Never would he make the same mistakes. Never would he miscalculate a situation so profoundly.

A shudder ran through him, her face like a warming hearth on a cold winter's night. Hadn't her image saved him once before? Hadn't she been his first trigger? And wasn't it fitting that she also be his last? He focused on the details of her face: the broad smile that dimpled her cheeks, the smoothness of her lips, the widow's peak at the top of her forehead that cast her hair around her in perfect falls, the smattering of moles that circled her left eye, which resembled a lop-sided star. His throat pinched. She'd hated those moles, always tried to cover them up. She'd raise a hand to her face, self-consciously, turn her head to the side when meeting new people. Funny, he thought, that she'd considered them flaws, while he'd always found them distinctive and unique. He remembered the first time he'd kissed her, and the day they'd decided they were officially "married", despite the lack of ceremony and proper paperwork. He recalled the day she gave birth to their child. She'd given him everything he could ever hope for, a reason to live, to persevere and soldier on.

Susan, he thought, with a tearing in his gut.

His mind screamed her name. She triggered him. Like a silent film, the images swept through his mind, warming him, chilling him, cutting him to the bone. His best memories were of times he'd spent with her. He'd loved her since he was just a boy.

Susan.

Her name fractured the ice in his joints, loosened stiff muscles, made his heart beat faster. Awareness of her finally broke his paralysis, and with a snap, he turned to Sam.

"I'm here," he whispered, and she fell against his shoulder. Once he'd pulled her up, he focused on Seth. The spell broken, he lifted his body off the ground, and running for his bike, called out, over his shoulder, "Follow me, Sam. We have to find shelter."

He pedaled hard and fast for the nearest exit, Sam hovering close at his rear wheel. They'd made it to Fort Worth, Texas, he realized, and with pride, peered at the top of Seth's head. Despite Seth's weakened state, they'd covered many miles in a short amount of time.

Perceptive as a hawk, his eyes scanned the road ahead. There was an Exxon station, with a 7-Eleven store adjoining it, and though the door was shattered and open to the elements, he didn't have time to be picky. Skidding to the front of the store, he dropped his bike in a heap on the ground, a cloud of dust and sand billowing behind him.

Dry leaves crunched beneath their feet as they entered it. Weeds, grasses, and the familiar fungi had begun their slow invasion of the space. He and Sam moved to the back of the store, where they spread out a blanket and laid Seth atop it. Jeremy regarded his ashen complexion, his slackened jaw, and his sweaty head. Sam was a bundle of nerves. Afraid to even touch him, she rocked on her heels, her nervous hands fluttering at her hips. Her voice was at least an octave to high when she asked, "What should we do?" Her breath was coming in shallow gasps. "Is he going to die? Why didn't he tell us he was sick?"

"Sam, he'll be fine."

"But he's dying, right? The fever means he's dying." Leaning over him, she gently touched his cheek. "We don't even know what his temperature is. What if he doesn't wake up? If he's unconscious, we won't be able to get him to eat or drink anything. And if he can't eat or drink, he'll die."

Jeremy eyed his daughter's stricken face. It wasn't healthy for her to get this worked up. Her eyes were moving rapidly. Her pupils were constricted.

"Sam. You need to calm down," he said. "Listen to me. He'll be fine. We just need to—"

"Dad, look at him. He won't be fine. Do you know what a coma would mean for him?"

"Yes, Sam. I know what a coma would mean."

"What if he doesn't wake up for weeks? How will we help him? Have you thought about that? A coma would be a death sentence for him. We don't have an IV or a feeding tube. We can't give him intravenous fluids. He'll starve or dehydrate." She took a ragged breath. "This could happen to me, you know. What if we can't wake him up?"

She was beginning to work herself into hysterics, the cadence of her speech as fast as her mind was able to shape the images. The tempo of her rocking increased commensurately. It matched the measure and meter of her tumbling words. Setting Seth's arm gently to his chest, Jeremy traded it for Sam's clammy hand.

"Sam, stop." He brought her hand to his lips.

"But we can't lose him, Dad. We just can't. We lost Mom. Then we lost Peter. We can't lose Seth. We just can't."

"Sam, stop. That's enough."

He clenched his jaw. This wasn't working. Her face was red, her hands balled into fists. He needed to refocus her thoughts. Dropping her hand, he seized her shoulders.

"Sam, that's enough! Look at me. Now!"

He rarely raised his voice to her, and the effect was instantaneous. She met his gaze and held it, chin firm, challenging him before she crumpled in defeat.

"Sam," he said gently, "if you want to help him, I'll tell you what to do. Get me a bottle of water from your pack. Pour some of it onto a cloth."

She moved away quickly, happy to be set to task.

"The water from the Caddie River," Jeremy clarified, "Not the fresh water. We need that to drink."

A few days prior, they'd made it to the Caddie River and bathed. The Caddie was a small waterway, fed by smaller tributaries, and the water—when boiled—was clean enough to bath and wash clothes in. Before leaving, they'd refilled their bottles. But they were rationing their drinking water now. And they'd been scouting for additional sources along the way. Jeremy secretly hoped this Exxon would contain a few well-hidden treasures of its own. He could look for bottles that had fallen behind shelves, or for packets of travel-sized medications that had slipped between counters. There were tons of places people forgot to look.

On hands and knees, Sam scooted back to him. Uncapping the bottle, she poured river water onto a semi-clean shirt then stared up at Jeremy, awaiting his next instruction. Reaching toward her, he pushed a lock of hair behind her ear. God, how he hated to see her stressed. She'd experienced too much loss in her life, too much forfeiture of happiness, too much pain. He mustn't lose Seth. It would be the last straw.

"Thanks, Pike," he said, patiently. "This is good. The first thing we need to do is bring his temperature down, but we'll need more rags and water to do it. I'll take any cloth we have: socks, old rags, old shirts, anything."

While she rummaged their supplies, he tore the shirt from Seth's chest. The garment was drenched with sour-smelling sweat, and the smell was rank in the small enclosure. The hemming of the shirt, which was damp and frayed, gave easily to his insistent fingers. He ripped it cleanly from the base to the neck, and then closing his eyes, pressed his hands to Seth's chest. He was burning up. Sam was right. Without a thermometer, they couldn't gauge his temperature. But even without one, Jeremy knew it was high. What would he do? What was proper protocol? He was out of his depth, but wouldn't say so aloud.

Sam pushed pieces of cloth into his hands, and together they soaked them in water. They draped them across Seth's forehead and eyes, tucked strips beneath his neck and armpits. Sam laid a wet sock along each side of his throat.

"To cool his blood," she explained, and Jeremy raised a brow. She pointed to his throat. "That's his carotid artery, right?"

"Yep." He smiled. "Where do you learn this stuff?" Pausing a moment, he pointed to Seth's hands. "I think you're onto something, kid. We should do the same thing to his wrists, don't you think? To both pulse points, to cool the blood."

She nodded soberly. "He's really sick, Dad, isn't he? It's infected."

"Yep. I think it is. And now I need to have a look." Sitting back on his heels, he took a moment of silence to consider his options. "I think we should try coaxing water into his mouth. We need to cool him down and break the fever. And we have to find a way to get aspirin into him."

Sam scooted to Jeremy's pack, where she selected a bottle, and a small wooden bowl. She dropped three aspirin into the bowl, which she crushed beneath the bottom of the bottle. She peered at Jeremy, a question in her eyes. Water was precious. She wanted his approval.

"It's okay," he encouraged her. "Do it. Use it all."

With his permission, she sprinkled the crushed aspirin into the bottle, capped it and shook it till it swirled a cloudy white. They tried their best to rouse Seth and make him drink, but soon, Jeremy knew it wasn't working. Too much of the precious concoction had dribbled over his lips, onto his chin, and down to the floor.

Some is better than none, he thought.

"Now what?" Sam asked.

Jeremy peered askance at her. Though she'd calmed a little, was she ready for this? This part wouldn't be pretty.

"Now," he said, taking a deep breath. "We need to tend the wound, but this is my job. You stay up here; keep refreshing the towels. They'll warm much quicker than you think."

He slid to Seth's feet and removed his shoes, and as he rolled up his cuffs, dread threatened to paralyze him. He was frightened to lay eyes on the wound. What if there was no way to manage the infection? What if it had burrowed too deep? If he couldn't cleanse it properly, there was little he could do to bring Seth out of this.

The smell hit him first, and he cursed himself. He'd noticed a faint odor several days ago. Why hadn't he thought to act then? As he weighed his options, he chewed his lip. What could he try that he hadn't tried already? What could he do with his limited supplies? Sterilizing it with alcohol hadn't worked. Why did he believe it would work this time?

Swallowing his fear, he carefully pulled the bandage free, and then stifled a gasp when saw it. The flesh was inflamed and warm to the touch, and puss was leaking from a corner. But it was the fine red streaks spidering from its edges that set Jeremy's hands to trembling.

Septicemia. His heart lurched. Could it be?

"Sam, the first aid kit, please," he said sternly.

When she brought it to him, she caught sight of the wound, and gasping, dropped to her knees to watch him work. He excreted puss by squeezing the tapered end of the wound, and though some came out, it wasn't enough. He worried about what might be trapped underneath the thick black scab and swollen skin. What if he tried reopening it? Just a bit, he wondered, just enough to make it bleed. Bleeding was a good thing, right? As far as he knew, blood pushed infections out. Blood cleansed wounds. Blood purified. He wasn't a doctor, but the notion sounded right.

Sam winced as he cleaned his pocketknife. "What are you doing?" she asked fervently.

Shaking his head, he remembered something he'd once said to Meghan. "Proud flesh," he murmured. "We need to make it bleed."

"Proud flesh? What does that mean?"

"It's something I explained to Meghan once, when I was talking to her about Peter's leg." Slipping the blade beneath the firmest edge of the scab, he pried up a corner as gently as he could. "I offended her. She hated the term. She even scolded me for comparing him to a horse. But I was right that day, and I think I'm right now. We have to cut away the infected parts of the wound, squeeze out as much of the infection as we can."

She didn't answer him, but as he bled the corner of the wound, she watched. The blood came fast, thick, and dark. Thankfully Seth was unconscious for this. The pain would have been unbearable. Sam winced as Jeremy pushed at the skin, and was forced to look away when he pinched it. He heard her gag when the foulness came forth, and when the blood ran a brighter shade of red, he bathed the entire area in alcohol—the last of the alcohol, he remarked with pursed lips.

Sam caught his sleeve before he applied fresh wrappings. "Maybe we should let the wound breath for a while, let the fresh air get in. It can't hurt."

Jeremy sat back on his heels and sighed. "Your guess is definitely as good as mine." Bending closer, he inspected it, visually and olfactorily. Most of the foulness had dissipated. Good.

"All right," he said. "We'll let the air get in, but we can't let the wound dry out. Let's give it an hour then bind it in wrappings. We want to keep it covered and protected from dust."

Mollified by that, she moved back to Seth's pale face, while Jeremy propped his leg atop a pile of old boxes. Jeremy rolled from his ankles to his rear then crab-walked backward until he felt the cold metal of a shelf against his back. Pushing herself to her feet, Sam joined him. She slid to the floor, set her hands to her knees, and together they watched Seth's chest rise and fall.

"What happened to you back there?" she whispered. "I thought you'd cracked up or lost it, or something."

"Cracked up?"

"Unhinged. Gone crazy or something."

He rolled his head lazily toward her. "Thanks for reminding me about the trigger."

She shrugged. "It just came to me. It was Grandpa's thing. Remember?"

He smiled. "I remember it now, thanks to you." Enjoying a moment of peaceful silence, he let his eyes slowly drift closed. "Do you have a trigger?" he asked sleepily.

"No. I mean, not really, I guess."

"What do you mean, not really? You either have one or you don't."

She picked at mud that had dried to her pants. "I've never really given it much thought. I've never needed a trigger. I've always had you. But if I did have one, I guess it would be Mom. Dad, what are we going to do?"

Jeremy could barely open his eyes, much less think about what they were going to do. "Did you just ask me what we're going to do?"

"Yeah. What are we going to do? What's our plan? What are our three? You should tell me, you know. I'm good at making decisions. I'm not a complete moron."

He smiled in spite of his weariness. 'The three', she had said—more Liam-speak. She wanted to know their three courses of action, so she could weigh the best out of three. The worst decision a person can make is no decision at all, Liam had said, and she wanted to make sure Jeremy was making the right one.

"Forget three," he answered. "Tonight, there's only one." As he stretched out his legs, blood rushed to his feet. "What are we going to do?" he repeated. "Right now the only thing to do is wait."

"Okay. But if we have to wait, let's make the best of it. Let's see what we can find in this disgusting store."

With a nod, he pulled himself up.

"Will he be all right?" she asked, peering down at Seth.

"I don't know, Sam. We'll just have to wait and see. But I do know this: we have to find a way to make him drink. He needs lots of fluids, laced with antibiotics and aspirin." He ran a hand through his sweaty hair. "We'll figure it out. He's strong. And he's young. Sleep and fluids are the best things for him now. We'll arm him with the best tools we've got in our arsenal, but I'm sorry to say, the rest is up to him."

"What did you think of?" she asked him suddenly. "You never answered my question. What was your trigger? What did you imagine?"

"Mom. Same as you. Who else? She was the first trigger I ever had as a boy, and now, as a man, I've come full circle." He set his arm around his daughter's slim shoulders. "It's fitting, don't you think? That I should think of her? After all, when I met her, all those years ago, she was the one who set my feet in motion. It was a night I'll never forget."

Human progress is neither automatic nor inevitable... Every step toward the goal of justice requires sacrifice, suffering, and struggle; the tireless exertions and passionate concern of dedicated individuals.

—Dr. Martin Luther King, Jr.

CHAPTER 16
52 Years Prior

JANUARY 12TH, 2124
KNOXVILLE, TN

Some forty-five minutes ago, their helicopter had landed at McGhee Tyson Airport, and Liam and his family were now stuck in a long line of traffic. Anxious, restless, and eager to return to his cabin, Liam peered at the entrance to Henley Street Bridge. They'd been forced to take a circuitous route that had taken them forty-five miles off course. The Tennessee landscape was bright that night, with the orange light of a multitude of fires. Staccato bursts of gunfire rang out in the distance, in a way that set Liam's teeth on edge. This was it, he thought. He was finished with this. If his family could just get make it back to their cabin, he would never leave it again. Life as he'd known it was over. The country was in shambles. Its people were at war. Those who'd prepared were tucked away in their shelters; those who hadn't were suffering the elements. And those who were predatory in nature, of course, were busy inducing chaos and violence for all.

Just yesterday the Nomad had docked at a San Francisco pier, and Liam had demanded an immediately flight. They were swept, first, to Arnold Air Force Base, and next, by helicopter, to McGhee Tyson Airport, where his jeep had been waiting outside. He and Olivia had said their goodbyes to the sea, and with heavy hearts, had turned from her glistening waters. And though the departure was tearful and gut wrenching at first, they longed for the comforts of home.

Olivia flinched as gunfire crackled in the distance. "Nobody's moving, Liam. This bridge is completely gridlocked."

Strained to see the other side of the bridge, he soon gave up and switched off the car. Jeremy was curled beneath a blanket in the backseat, knees drawn to his chest in a fetal position. He was snoring softly. Kids slept through anything. Liam sighed and turned to his wife.

"You're right. Might as well conserve a little gas."

Opening his door, he balanced himself on the ledge of the SUV, stretching on the tips of his toes to see. This didn't seem like a normal gridlock. It was worse than anything he'd witnessed before, and it set his heart pumping to an unhealthy rhythm. The road before him was bedlam. The bridge was packed solid, bumper-to-bumper. People had strayed from the painted lines of lanes and were now packed tighter than a tin of sardines. There was nowhere for anyone to go. Some were balanced on the lip of the bridge, while others were wedged in the wrong direction. Steam billowed from a few stalled vehicles, while black smoke hissed from the tailpipes of others.

Liam heard screams as a military-grade Hummer rolled over the tops of several compact cars. He ducked his head into the car.

"This is madness, Liv. We'll never get through. We have to turn around, try a different way."

Twisting in her seat, she peered behind them.

"Turn around and go where? We're as trapped as they are. We'll never get out that way."

Though he hated to admit it, she was right. A line of cars stretched behind them as far as the eye could see. He found himself counting them as he tried to think of a way to get home.

"Liam, what does it matter if we're stuck? We may as well relax and make the best of it. It doesn't matter how long we sit here. We have food, water, all the time in the world. We're fine where we are for right now. Let's just sit here and wait this thing out. People have to move at some point, don't they?"

Stretching once more on the tips of his toes, he tried to make sense of shapes in the distance. Something was developing. He couldn't see what. But vehicles that were moving before had stopped moving altogether now. Things had ground to a halt. Dark shapes clustered at the mouth of the bridge, but it was too dark to make them out clearly.

"I don't know," he said slowly. "Something feels wrong. Something tells me we'll never be able to get through." Slipping quietly back into the jeep, he shut the door as gently as he could. "I have a bad feeling about this, Liv." Pursing his lips, he weighed their options. All this planning. All this preparation. What if it had all been for nothing? After all they'd been through, what if he couldn't get them back to the cabin?

"Stop worrying," Olivia said, reading his mind. "We'll make it back home. Have faith."

"Have faith? How can you talk about faith right now? Especially after the things we've just seen? We just left an ocean that's become a landfill, and you want to talk to me about faith?"

"Yes." She motioned to their son. "For him."

Turning from her, he peered out the window. The Garbage Patch had been rough on him. He still wasn't sure how to reassemble himself. He felt as if he'd been blown apart, as if pieces of his body had scattered to the wind. Since they'd left, a melancholic feeling had taken root, and it was now threatening to overcome him. He was having a difficult time shaking it off. Olivia, on the other hand, seemed less affected, or maybe she was just better at hiding her feelings. Not so for him. He'd never excelled at that. He had always worn his emotions on his sleeve. He'd always suffered depressive thoughts, too: anxiety, feelings of foreboding, restlessness. He'd always hovered at the edge of the light, always wished he were somewhere other than he was, always faked his smiles and forced his laughs. He'd always nervously checked his watch. Maybe part of him had anticipated this. Or maybe, like she'd said: he just lacked faith.

Swinging his gaze to the cars in front of him, he startled as a shape detached from the darkness. Olivia sat up, her body rigid. Leaning forward, she clenched her armrests.

"Did you see that?" she whispered.

Of course he'd seen that. Staring at the shadows, he waited for them to move a second time. After a moment, a lone figure made itself visible before scampering around the Ford Raptor in front of them.

"Don't move," he whispered to Olivia, as another figure emerged from the shadows. It crept to the driver's-side door of the truck, where it hovered in silence as if waiting for something. While Liam was finding it difficult to breath, the driver of the truck seemed oblivious to the danger.

In a choreographed movement, the two figures converged on the vehicle, and Liam instinctively moved for his gun.

Olivia stiffened. "Stay out of this, Liam. Don't get involved. You don't know what they intend to do."

"I know exactly what they intent to do. They intend to steal that man's truck."

Liam tensed as he watched one of the would-be

thieves try to open the driver's side door. When it wouldn't budge, he slammed the butt of his gun against the glass, which shattered but thankfully held—until he ran it through with a gloved fist, of course. Stepping up to the ledge of the truck, the man reached through the window and fumbled the lock. Liam felt frozen as he watched the scene. God, he was so damn sick of this shit—sick of desperate people causing mayhem. He was sick of watching them take from others, instead of trying to provide for themselves. He was sick of the violence and savagery, sick of the profound disrespect people showed for one another. As he watched the men struggle through the window, he wrapped his fingers around the handle of his gun. The driver was putting up a decent fight, but he was going to need help if the second man engaged.

Don't just sit here, Liam thought. Pull the trigger!

Glancing at his wife, he reached a sudden realization: he did want to get involved. For once, he did feel compelled to help. He was tired of being a spectator on the bench, tired of watching others play the game and lose. All of his anger and recent disappointments flooded to the surface in an instant. All of his negative feelings about the Patch rushed in, compelling him to move and do something. As the owner of the Raptor leaned against his door, Liam thrust open his own. Startled by the sudden inertia, the thief lost his grip and went sailing through the air. He landed on his back and then righted himself, dropped into a low crouch and assessed his next move. Raising his gun, he issued a guttural threat. "We're taking the truck. Step aside."

Tumbling from his vehicle, the Raptor-owner glared back. "Over my dead body, you son of a bitch."

"Liam!" Olivia repeated, as he slid from his seat. "Do not get involved! Please!"

Funny she should say that, he told himself. Did not three years ago she do the same thing? They wouldn't have Jeremy if she hadn't. Pushing her protests to the back of his mind, he focused on the scene in front of him. Eyes trained on the dueling men, Liam realized he'd forgotten the second thief—until a scream pierced the air from the other side of the truck. The second man emerged from the shadows, rounded the bumper, and stepped into the light. Unfortunately, he wasn't alone. Beneath his burley arm, he carried a small young girl, her sobbing mother close at his heels.

Dear God, Liam thought. This can't end well.

Smiling at his ruthless partner, the gunman returned his gaze to the driver. "See? Like I said, we're taking the truck."

As if to drive the point home, his partner lifted the girl and shook her bodily. She didn't appear to be much older than Jeremy. Her legs pumped furiously, as if she were pedaling an invisible bike.

"Let them have the truck," Liam said. "It's not worth it." Its owner didn't respond, his eyes fixed on his daughter, who was squirming in the large man's arms. Her fists pummeled his thighs like a tiny battering ram. Turning his attention to the thief, Liam held up his gun. "Drop her," he said. "Take the truck. Do neither, and I'll pull this trigger."

Liam was surprised at the strength in his voice. He sounded more confident than he felt inside.

With a sob, the man's wife dropped to her knees. Liam took advantage of the momentary distraction and moved a step closer to the girl. "Did you hear what I said? Put her down. Take the truck."

The moment hung heavy in the air. The child's father seemed paralyzed with fear. "Please," he whispered. "Just take it. Go. Set my daughter to her feet and go. I don't care. I won't try to stop you."

The gunman seemed to be weighing his options. He clearly cared nothing for the child, and was probably envisioning the nuisance she would be. But she was the only leverage he had at the moment and he didn't seem keen on evening the odds.

For a few minutes more, no one moved, and though the thought of disarming made Liam's stomach queasy, he knew, in the end, it was the only choice he had. These men weren't leaving without the truck. And they'd take the child with them if it came down to that. They'd probably take her and dump her in the woods.

Liam lowered his gun, set it on the pavement, then lifted his hands in the air. "Okay," he said softly. "You win. Take the truck. You're free to go. I'm not going to move." He kicked the gun, watched it spin across the road. "I can't stop you now. Just go."

The man with the child sneered. "You're damn right you can't."

The man with the girl edged closer to his partner, swung the child around, and then scrambled for the gun, and with the weapon secured in the waistband of his pants, he shared a meaningful glance with his partner. In a moment Liam would never forget, the man reached a decision and reared back his arm. He tossed the child into the air, and despite her father's efforts to catch her, she fell. Skidding across the pavement, she came to rest several feet from where Liam crouched. Her screams rent the air, but she was clearly all right. Liam released the breath he'd been holding. At least she hadn't hit her head or face.

Both criminals ran for the truck, and when they fired up the engine, no one moved. Where the hell would they go? Liam wondered. The bridge was packed tight; they wouldn't get through, even with a vehicle as formidable as a Raptor.

In awe, he watched them try to get through. The driver pushed the truck to its limits as he tried to ram through the crowd. It appeared as though he was headed for the shoulder and using smaller cars as leverage to do it. Liam heard Olivia exit their car and hazarded a glance in her direction. Her incredulous expression matched his own. She seemed as bewildered by the scene as he was.

Mouth agape, her gaze fixed on the truck, she watched it attempt to create a path for itself. Other drivers were restarting their engines, trying their best to get out of its way. But heedless to all, and considerate of none, the Raptor surged forward relentlessly. When it reached the mouth of the bridge, it nosed through by hoisting two cars atop a small Camry, and as onlookers screamed, Liam felt a sense of impending doom. This fool would get himself—and everyone else—killed, for Liam couldn't be the only person with a gun. Someone—or someones—would stop this madness.

Olivia somehow broke the trance and ran to the woman and her child. Liam watched her squat down beside them and speak softly, so he made his way over to the young girl's father. The man was staring after his truck with wonder.

"All be damned," he whispered. "Look at him go."

"I don't think he'll get very far in this mess."

"Probably not," the man said, turning to Liam. "Name's Tom. I can't thank you enough for what you did back there." The two men stood shoulder-to-shoulder, amazed, as the Raptor climbed the ass-end of an Accord.

"I thought it was best to let him go," said Liam. "I can take you and your family anywhere you need to go."

After a moment of silence, they turned toward the women. Tom's wife was cradling his daughter, who fortunately seemed more frightened than injured. There were several small scrapes along the undersides of her arms, and a long strip of road rash on each of her knees, but a bruised ego seemed the worst of her ailments. Her father swept her into his arms, cradled her there, and smiled at his wife. The gratitude on each of their faces was heartwarming, and it immediately brought Jeremy to mind. He was sleeping alone in the Jeep. Time to go. Setting his hands to his knees, Liam pushed himself to his feet. "Tom, we're parked over there. The Jeep. I meant what I said. If you need to get somewhere, we'll be happy to take you. All we need to do is just—"

An intense popping sound caught Liam's attention. Gunfire, he recognized immediately. He and Tom and the women hit the ground. Liam peered in the direction of the bridge, where a group of men had circled the Raptor. The thieves had made it onto the bridge after all, but had left a path of devastation in their wake. They had crossed the entrance, become wedged between cars, and now, were cornered by angry, gun-wielding men.

"We need to get to my truck," Liam cautioned, flinching at the sound of angry shouting. "We need get out of here. Now. This isn't good."

The little company didn't wait. They ran to Liam's Jeep in crab-like crouches. Liam could see Jeremy staring through the windshield, balancing on his knees, hands gripping the front seats. Eyes wide, he observed the chaos around him, and with mouth agape and eyes puffy from sleep, he met his father's gaze before the world exploded. A great ball of orange-and-yellow fire suddenly filled the night sky. Liam was tossed to the ground, bodily, as if he weighed little more than a bag of soggy leaves. The acrid odors of gasoline and smoke burned his nostrils and clawed at his throat, and a sudden blast of heat warmed his face. The coppery taste of blood flooded his mouth. He pressed his tongue to the inside of his mouth, where he'd bit a small chunk from his cheek. What the hell caused that? He wondered of the blast. He'd hit the ground hard. Everyone had. An eruption of stars glittered behind his eyes. His left bicuspid seemed loose.

The sound of feet scampering across pavement drew his attention to the Jeep. "No!" he said, panicked. "Jeremy, stop! Lay down! Get down on the ground right now!"

As if in the middle of a quaking battlefield, Liam crawled toward his son on hands and knees and fell atop him, a moment before the next explosion rocked the earth.

Together they huddled, until the blasts subsided. Liam lost count of how many there were as he held Jeremy tight and waited. Olivia, he thought. Where had she fallen?

Around him, the scene had devolved into chaos. People were running from their cars in a panic as they tried to escape the dangerous bridge. The fallen were trampled and left behind, the elderly, pushed and cast roughly aside. There hadn't been a blast for a few moments now. Liam scanned the scene for his wife, his gut clenching when he finally saw her. She was laying fifteen feet from where they huddled, covered with debris, curled on her side. She was quiet, dirty, and still.

"Jeremy," he said, lifting his chin. "Are you all right?" Though Jeremy's eyes were round as saucers, he didn't seem to have suffered any injuries. "On your knees then," he said, finding his hand. "Stay close to me. We need to go to Mom."

The two, staying low, scuttled closer to Olivia.

"Liv," Liam said when he reached her. When he cradled her face, her eyes opened, and when her arms circled his neck, his relief was palpable.

"I'm fine," she said, stretching her arms to Jeremy.

"The bridge," Tom muttered in amazement. "It caved in. The entire front section fell in. If we had made it to the entrance, we'd all be dead."

Crouching beside the man, Liam peered at clouds of smoke and debris in the distance. Tom was right. The bridge had cracked in half. "Those explosions must have been cars," he observed.

Tom wiped at blood that had smeared his cheek. "It was the Raptor. Someone's bullet must have hit the gas tank." He shook his head solemnly. "Those cars were packed too closely together."

"My God," Olivia gasped. "All of those people." She had crept closer and risen to her knees, but Jeremy was nowhere in sight. Liam spun around.

"Look at him, Liv." He caught his wife's hand.

Jeremy was brushing dust from the little girl's skirts.

"Let's go home," Liam murmured to Olivia. "We'll leave the car, just leave it right here. I don't think we'll need it anymore, after this. We're thirty miles from the cabin, at best. We'll walk. It might take half the night to get there, but we'll get there safely. Anything is safer than this. We've got water, food, and another gun, too. We'll take Tom's family with us. What do you think?"

He could see the surprise in her face. He was extending their cabin to a family of strangers, which might be a bad idea, he mused. But this was somehow different. Jeremy didn't have friends. He needed this. He hadn't met a child his age in years, hadn't started school, hadn't made a connection. Liam wasn't entirely sure public schools would even open this year. But Jeremy had clearly made a connection now, and it was one Liam wanted to nurture. He watched Jeremy touch the side of the little girl's face, wipe blood from the wound that seeped from her scalp. Despite the maelstrom and chaos around them, he could hear Jeremy's words spoken clearly.

"You okay?" he asked the girl quietly. "You cut your head when that bad man threw you to the ground. My name is Jeremy. That's my Dad over there. There's a squirrel that lives behind our house, in the woods. Have you ever seen a squirrel?"

The girl shook her head slowly.

"We don't have squirrels where we live," the girl's mother said. "Might be fun to see one up close." She grasped her daughter's hand. Liam warmed to her smile. "It'll be an adventure. What do you say, Susan? Would you like to go on an adventure with Jeremy?"

"Susan," Jeremy whispered, repeating the name. She smiled shyly as he wiped blood from her face. "Your moles," he said softly. "They look like a star."

"The two hardest tests on the spiritual road are the patience to wait for the right moment and the courage not to be disappointed with what we encounter."

— Paulo Coelho, *Veronika Decides to Die*

CHAPTER 17
Present Day

OCTOBER 24ᵀᴴ, 2176
FORTH WORTH, TEXAS
1,329 MILES TO SAN DIEGO

It had been a long, painful, unproductive week. Given his limited resources, Jeremy had nursed Seth back to health as best he could, by controlling his fever and keeping him comfortable. At times Seth would rouse and drink tiny sips of water Jeremy had laced with aspirin and antibiotics, but dehydration was always a concern. All things considered, he knew they'd been lucky. It was fortunate when Seth regained consciousness at all, even if those times were brief and sporadic. Mostly he hovered in a dreamlike state, which presented its own set of challenges. Making him eat was one such issue, but making him drink was another. And if the fear of starvation and dehydration wasn't enough to worry about, Jeremy also worried about the medicine itself: the potency of it, their dwindling supply. What if the antibiotics weren't effective? After all, they were decades old. What if their potency had diminished completely? There was just no way to be sure.

Only time would reveal the fruits of his labor.

Potency notwithstanding, he thought, there was still one thing that frightened him more than anything else. After Seth consumed the last of these pills, Jeremy was out of medication altogether: the antibiotics, and most of the aspirin, too. His stores would be empty, and for what? Though both medicines were managing his fever, Jeremy wasn't sure Seth was any closer to health.

He'd suffered through fever after gut-wrenching fever, which crashed over his body in aspirin-laced waves. His clothing was stiff with sweat and salt; his matted hair stuck to the sides of his face. Jeremy and Sam had done the best they could with him. They'd bathed him with pieces of cloth, soaked in warm, soapy water, but it wasn't enough to cleanse him thoroughly. He needed a real bath, food, clean blankets. Hell, he needed a lot more than that, many more things that Jeremy couldn't provide.

His thinness, at this point, was alarming; his body was all sharp angles, planes, and crooks. He'd been youthfully slender before, as boys were, but he was downright emaciated now. Jeremy and Sam fed him chicken soup, or broth from a can—when he was conscious enough to do so, of course, but what he needed right now was meat and starch, something with vitamins, fat, and bulk. Jeremy sighed. A balance bar and a cup of dried lentils would do little to help this situation.

But when Jeremy and Sam weren't tending Seth, they made use of the time as best they could. They foraged and gathered any supplies they could find. The 7-Eleven proved mostly barren, but the U-Storage facility across the street bore fruit. Jeremy took a crowbar to the locks and raised the heavy doors amid the creaking protests of years of grime and rust. Once inside, he and Sam searched the units. There were no foodstuffs among the long-abandoned possessions of the dead, but there were boxes of clothing and socks and tools, even a few sharp knives.

Farther along Sorento Drive, they found a

neighborhood of ranch-style homes, apartments, and a small motel harboring a forgotten cache of water bottles. A vending machine in the motel's employee break room had yielded several packages of stale—yet edible—crackers, and though the food was welcome, Jeremy prized the water. At this point, water was his biggest concern. As long as they were stuck in this place, he decided, he'd do his best to stock up. He and Sam constructed several kinds of rain catchers. It was easy to find the supplies they needed, and Sam had enjoyed the industry of the task. They stretched pieces of plastic across the tops of old pots, placed stones in the centers to add weight. A few, they hung from the corners of buildings: bowls stacked vertically on sturdy lengths of wire, while the simpler designs, they hung from tree branches. Rain gutters ran the length of the 7-Eleven's rooftop, and though the water ran dirty, it could be boiled, strained, and eventually made potable.

These tasks occupied much of their time, and for the most part, Jeremy had welcomed the distraction, as well as the feelings of productiveness. But a week had passed, now, and he was succumbing to fear. His mind was traveling in small tight circles. Anxiety was stealing his sleep. That familiar voice was whispering again, urging him to make difficult decisions.

He sat perfectly still, legs gathered to his chest, while Sam sat silently at his side. Rain was deepening puddles in the road, and sluicing down the windows in thin rivulets, sending worm-like smudges cascading down the glass. A pleasant earthen smell had permeated the store. If circumstances were normal, Jeremy would have considered the day pleasant—pleasant if not for his runaway thoughts. Pleasant if not for the words he wished to say, words that were increasingly difficult to bite back. He could feel them struggling at the tip of his tongue. They would leap from his mouth if he weren't careful.

"What?" Sam asked, leaning into him. She

bumped his shoulder playfully before posing the question he'd dreaded the most. "Come on. What's up? You've got that crazy look again."

"What look?"

"The one that gives you wrinkles across your forehead. You know," she added, "if you wear that face too long, you'll get stuck with it. Come on, Carp. Tell me what you're thinking."

He clenched his fists to keep them from shaking. "Sam," he said slowly, "I'm concerned."

"Concerned." She glanced in Seth's direction. She knew what he was thinking. "He hasn't spiked a fever since late last night. It finally broke and it hasn't come back. He's getting better, Carp. Stop worrying."

"He is getting better. That's true. But he hasn't woken up, or spoken to us yet. He hasn't eaten anything solid."

She turned her face toward the window, and rain. "He's getting better, Dad, a little more each day. You said so yourself last night. Those red streaks beside his wound are almost too faint to detect anymore. You said you could barely see them at all, that his body was beating the infection." She turned to him, her face as innocent as an angel's. "Those were your words, were they not?"

"They were." He hugged his knees and leaned into her. "But that doesn't mean I don't still have concerns. I'm not worried about the infection anymore. By the grace of God, I think he's beaten it. I'm concerned with the time it'll take him to get stronger. It's been a week, now, Sam. A week! I had hoped we'd be back on the road by now. I'd even be happy with a small bit of progress. Small distances would be better than nothing. Anything's better than sitting still. Sam," he added quietly, "we haven't made progress."

"We will. You'll see. It won't be long now."

He shook his head, unable to agree. "I thought so too—at first. But I'm not so sure anymore."

"About what?" She'd suddenly gone stiff at his side.

Twisting awkwardly, he pulled the hem of her shirt above her belly. The numbers were nothing if not ominous. He pointed. "Forty-nine percent, Sam. Forty-nine percent! We've let this disk dwindle to forty-nine percent, and we aren't any closer to where we need to be. I'm concerned that we're wasting valuable time."

She frowned. "How are we wasting valuable time? I'm alive. I'm fine. Nothing's happened to me."

"I know," he answered irritably. "You know what I mean."

"Do I?" She asked, turning to him. Her eyes were suddenly ablaze. "How would I know what you mean? How could I possibly know what you mean? You never tell me the truth—not fully. You give me little snippets or tiny breadcrumbs, but only enough so I'll stop asking questions. What's this invisible clock that's panicking you? And why are we in such a hurry to get to the ocean? There's nothing at the ocean but spoiled water and rotting beaches. You said so yourself. Why the rush? Wouldn't it be smarter to travel a bit slower? Wouldn't it be better if we searched the cities we're passing through? I can't figure out what you're doing. But I will say this: I think you're being stupid. We're flying through these cities as fast as we can, without taking time to forage them. Grandpa Liam would say we were idiots. Can you imagine what he'd think about this?" She brought her hands to her face in defeat. "Maybe it seems like I'm just being stubborn, but I have no idea what you're up to. I can't figure out your ridiculous plan. It makes no sense to me, Dad." She turned to him. "You say you're not so sure anymore. What are you not sure about?"

Jeremy shifted uncomfortably. He wasn't sure how much to divulge. It wasn't that he didn't want to tell her, per se. He just didn't want to get her hopes up.

Or is it something else? The little voice whispered.

Maybe you don't want to speak the words aloud. Maybe you think it's a ridiculous plan, too.

He answered her question, though evasively. "I'm not sure we can sit here much longer, Sam. That's all I'm trying to say."

She stared at him, aghast. "So you're saying we should leave Seth behind?"

"No. I'm just—"

"Stop. Just stop. I can't take this anymore." Standing awkwardly, she peered down her nose at him. "I won't let you do this. Not again. You did this to Peter. I know what you did. You don't think I do, but I do."

"Sam," he said gently, "We couldn't stay there. We were running out of disks. Meghan and I searched that entire area, but all we could find were insulin pills—and crappy insulin pills at that. We never found a single disk. It was time to move on—beyond time, in fact. I was an idiot for staying as long as I did. Maybe if I'd forced us to move along sooner, we'd be in a better situation right now."

"But we left him there. We just left him there. We slunk off in the middle of the night like cowards, and left Peter and Meghan to die."

"To die?"

"I know what you did," she spat angrily.

"Oh really?" He felt his anger rise. "I hatched a plan to keep you alive. That's what I did. That's what I always do. What would have happened if we stayed? Do you ever take the time to think about that? Use your head, Sam. What would have happened? What would have happened to two diabetic kids living under the same roof? What would have happened to two parents fighting for the same medications in a world with a limited supply? Don't you see how stupid that was? Can't you imagine how things would have ended? It was madness, Sam! It wouldn't have worked. Meghan and I would have eventually killed each other. We would have fought one another to save our children's lives."

"I didn't say leaving was a bad decision. I'm just saying that you didn't have to do what you did. Peter is probably dead because of you. We could have just left, but we left as thieves!" He offered no response so she continued brazenly. "I won't let you do it again. Not to Seth. Look around, Dad. Here we are again. Same situation, different boy. Can't you see?"

"It's not the same situation, Sam, and you know it. You don't understand."

"But I do understand. And it is the same." Crouching in front of him, she caught his wandering gaze. "Dad, I don't want to live at the expense of other people. I know you're scared. I know you love me. But we still have one disk, right? Give Seth a chance. Let's wait this out." Straightening, she crossed her arms, in that way that reminded him so much of Susan. "Or don't give him a chance, and leave us both behind. It's your decision, Dad. Do what you want. But me? I'm not leaving him."

"Sam, you're being unreasonable. What if Seth dies? Have you thought about that? What if we sit here for the next two weeks, and in the end, he dies anyway, despite our efforts? Are we supposed to just sit here and watch your meter wind down to zero? What if we do and he dies anyway?"

"So the level of risk isn't acceptable to you. That's what you're trying to say, isn't it? You're weighing his life against mine."

"Of course I am!"

"You're saying his life means so little to you that you won't even give him a chance?"

"A chance?" Jeremy pressed his palms to his eyes. "What the hell do you think I've been doing? Sam, you're missing my point. It's not that Seth's life means little to me. It's that your life means so much." He took a breath. "I care about Seth, but you're everything to me. If Seth dies and you…"

His mouth snapped closed. He couldn't finish the

sentence. It was a vision of the future he just couldn't face.

"Die," she finished brazenly. "That's what you were going to say. If Seth dies and I die, then what?"

Jeremy blew out an exasperated breath. "Don't you see? If I lose both of you, all of this waiting would have been for nothing. Sam, understand: sometimes in life, adults are forced to make difficult decisions, to weigh the consequences, both good and bad, and decide on the best course of action. And sometimes," he added, "there's no right answer. One choice is as bad as the next. But right or wrong, one makes a decision. Right or wrong, one chooses a path. It's something we all have to do." He pushed himself up, and despite her efforts to pull away from him, clasped her hands, held them tightly in his own. "Sam, one day I won't be here. One day, you'll be on your own. You'll be the adult making the tough decisions, and right or wrong, you'll have to make them. It's what being an adult is all about."

"Perhaps. But isn't it also about doing what's right? About being kind and compassionate to others?"

He smiled at her. He couldn't help himself. "You're going to be a much better adult than I could ever be, though I guess, in your eyes, that won't be difficult." Releasing her hands, he let loose a sigh. "I'm just doing my best. That's all I can do. I never said my decisions were right, or good. I never even said they were sane. They're just decisions, plain and simple. They are what they are. They're made by a man who's afraid of losing his daughter." He peered at Seth, lying prone on the floor, while indecision clawed at his belly. Seth's breathing was deeper than it had been before, and in the past few days, his cheeks had gained a healthier hue. He was definitely improving. Sam was right. Turning to face her, he sighed resignedly. "Okay. You win. We'll give him a few more days. We'll wait this out and see how it goes."

"Okay," she said carefully, her chin firm. "But I want you to understand something. I won't be the kind of adult who does bad things to other people. I can't do that. I can't live with myself." Reaching up, she touched his cheek. "I appreciate the sacrifices you've made for me, but over the next few days, I think you should spend some time alone. Consider some of the things you've done." Breaking their contact, she detached the teddy bear keychain from her belt, and turning back to him, pushed it into his palm. "I think you should spend some time thinking about Peter. That's all I'm saying. I'll leave it alone." She moved away from him, quiet as smoke, then stopped, turned back, and took his breath away. "We could have just left him, Dad. You didn't have to kill him."

Jeremy's throat closed as he reached for the memories. "I didn't..." he murmured, but his reply was lost.

Despite his many protests, he couldn't say she was wrong.

"There are times to stay put, and what you want will come to you, and there are times to go out into the world and find such a thing for yourself."

— Lemony Snicket, *Horseradish*

CHAPTER 18
1 Year Prior

NOVEMBER 20TH, 2175
JUST OUTSIDE OF KNOXVILLE
TENNESSEE

"Sam. Wake up."

He roused her gently, his eyes nervously skipping across the room, from shadow to rounded shadow. A slim crescent moon provided little light, but it was enough to do what they needed to do. Leaning closer, he whispered into her ear. "Sam, we have to go. Get up."

Eyes fluttering open, she propped herself up on an elbow, and seemingly confused, glanced about the room. Her eyes found his and she opened her mouth.

"No," he whispered, laying a finger across her lips. "Don't wake the others. You and I going out. It'll be just us. Let's go."

As he knew it would, curiosity got the best of her. She arose slowly and followed him to the hall, padding across the floor on cat's paws. They'd been using the bathroom as a changing area, and a place to wash clothes, and hang them to dry. The plumbing didn't work, but the drain still emptied. She slipped into the room and closed the door.

Jeremy peered out the windows as he waited. Though he was charged with energy, his nerves were somewhat frayed. Was he really doing this? Was he leaving this house behind?

San Diego, he marveled to himself: the headquarters of Bigeye Pharmaceuticals.

Over the past few weeks, he'd been chanting the words as if they were a healing mantra. His mind had whispered them over and over, until they became something of an obsession. The whispering in his head soon became a deafening scream, and it was one he couldn't ignore.

His plan had slowly unfurled in his mind as he weighed the significant pros against the cons. He'd unfolded the maps and measured the distance, whistling under his breath at the scope of the endeavor. He'd considered which routes would be faster versus smarter, which would present the least number of obstacles, and which would avoid the largest of cities. He'd begun to equate time with distance and effort, as he estimated the number of miles they would walk. Could they cross the length of the United States on foot? Indecision had plagued him for weeks. It was an aggressive plan, but was it foolhardy? Would it be a death sentence for Sam?

Leaving the safety of this house was yet another mental struggle to deal with, but as time passed, the idea gained appeal. This, he figured, was the only way to bring Sam the long-lasting stability she needed. Despite the risks and potential perils of the journey, it was the only way to give her a chance. Besides, he wondered, weren't the things worth fighting for the hardest to achieve? The last time he checked patience was still considered a virtue.

As he waited for her, he reflected on the last few

torturous nights. His mind had traveled in endless circles, and he'd spent the majority of his time alone, staring at the Tennessee plains from the porch, the soft sounds of his surrogate family filtering to his perch from the big picture window. Would Bigeye Pharmaceuticals contain insulin disks? They were made there, he reasoned. Why wouldn't it? Was the idea so absurd or outlandish? They were produced there in quantity, packaged, and shipped. From that location they were studied and perfected, experimented with, and manufactured in bulk. If ever there were a more sensible idea, he didn't think he'd yet heard it. It was almost too easy, too simple, too obvious. Well, he thought, frowning, perhaps not easy. Easy was a bit overstated. The journey itself would be perilous and long. Their supplies would only last for so long. But it felt good to have a plan, to be moving his feet. Executing a plan was better than sitting still, and infinitely better than waiting for fate. And though the journey would be difficult, it might also be rewarding, and the prize at the end could be priceless.

And San Diego? He smiled. Of all the places. San Diego was built on arable land. The soil was rich. The weather was temperate. It was almost too good to be true.

He ran his thumb across the lettering on the disk. The empty case had become a talisman. It was never too far from his reach. He kept it in his pocket, twirled it in his fingers. When he touched the plastic, his plan felt real. And the weather, he'd noticed, was beginning to cool. With the searing heat of summer finally behind them, travel would prove much easier. It was now or never. He couldn't shake the feeling. Time was pressing him with insistent fingers. It bullied him with taunts and frightening dreams, and quickened anxiety deep in his belly. It's persistence left him breathless.

He considered, for a moment, what they'd built in this house. They had safe shelter here, and the beginnings of a life. They'd planted and grown a sustainable garden.

The area was rural enough to be safe, yet close enough to roadways to permit easy travel. They'd created a system of survival inside this house, with assigned duties and a division of labor, and thus had created a civilized life. They wore clean clothes and ate with cutlery. Jeremy shared life's burdens with a like-minded and capable adult who reflected on his ideas and provided feedback. He and Meghan were friends and allies who advised and respected one another. It was a support system he refused to take lightly.

The only problem was, it was based on lies. It was as if the foundation of this well-appointed home had sprung cracks that—given time—would bring the entire structure tumbling down.

How long before Meghan felt the need to hoard pills? How long before fear got the better of her? When would she stake out clever hiding places to stockpile pills for her boy? How long before Jeremy did the same? He never divulged how many disks he had left, but a day would surely come when she'd grow tired of guessing. His relationship with Meghan was as genuine and true as the precarious health of their children. Life, in these times, was about survival, protecting one's own to the detriment of others. His friendship with Meghan was never meant to last—not that he didn't still care about her; he cared about her and Peter.

Peter was an amazing boy. Jeremy often wondered what he'd been like before illness had claimed his leg. He couldn't run or play anymore, but amazingly, that didn't cripple his zest for life. Though confined to a chair, he showed interest in the world. He was curious, engaged. He wanted to contribute.

But wanting and doing were two very different things, and though Jeremy cursed himself for thinking the thoughts, Peter was a significant liability in their lives. Though Meghan refused to face the truth, Peter would never heal from his affliction. His path was a slow and agonizing one, a steady decline into pain and madness. He'd never regain his mobility, nor share the workload, nor contribute to the group.

Jeremy pursed his lips. The leg needed to come off. It was poisoning him. And since Meghan refused to see it done, they helplessly watched it corrupt his body. It was a train wreck they couldn't bring themselves to turn from. It disgusted Jeremy. It ruled his thoughts.

But it also set his wheels in motion.

What, he asked himself, were they doing in this house? What events or circumstances were they waiting for? The inevitable to happen? The clock to run out? How long would that take? A year? Maybe two? And in a year's time, if he gave it that long, how many pills would Peter have consumed, only to die anyway? Sam's disks would eventually run dry, and when they did, how many pills would Peter have wasted? How many did it take to stay the wraithlike fingers of a death that had already begun to claim him?

Jeremy disgusted himself with these thoughts. But such is the dichotomy of being human, he reasoned. We think certain thoughts that we consider monstrous, and then hate ourselves for having thought them, when the truth of the matter, in simple terms, is this: life can be ugly, truth can be unpleasant, but difficult decisions have to be made. Jeremy wanted to slap himself for thinking such abominable thoughts about Peter. But he was also human, with instincts and fears. Humans always protect their young. Jeremy could no more suppress that instinct than Meghan would be able to suppress hers. And if their positions were reversed, if Sam was like Peter—a sickly child consuming pills to stay alive—Jeremy would probably act similarly to Meghan. So they must leave this house, he'd concluded weeks ago. Staying wasn't a viable solution. This house, its gardens and beautiful appointments were parts of a false paradise. It wouldn't last. It was never meant to, and delaying their departure only made that more difficult.

So he'd made the decision and picked out a date, and once he had, things were suddenly easier. Making plans and preparations had made him feel industrious. He'd arisen earlier than the rest of the house, planned the route, and prepared the cart for departure. Only a few months prior, he'd unpacked its contents. He and Meghan had done it together, smiling as they outfitted the pantry, as if they'd purchased this new home together, consciously, as if this were a life they'd chosen for themselves.

The supplies from the cart were the remnants of the ark, and thus were many and bountiful. There were bags of rice, lentils, oats, cans of beans, sweet yams, and corn. There were soups, stale crackers, a variety of medicines, bottle after bottle of potable water.

Their passage across the United States would be slow and tedious. Jeremy wouldn't delude himself. And they would have to push the cart as they traveled. They would travel at night, sleep by day. Supplies as rich and abundant as theirs would be taken from them if they weren't careful. But they could make it, would make it. Jeremy felt it in his bones. The plan had sparked renewed energy within him. He imagined the places he and Sam would pass along the way, the sights they would see, the supplies they would find. He thought of the caches of pills they'd discover, which would sustain her when the disks ran out. They would make do. They would live off the land. Like it or not, this was a viable plan, and it made more sense than staying put and doing nothing. It was something Jeremy could feel good about. He had never been a victim, never let life happen, wasn't comfortable letting fate take the wheel. He was an active participant in life, and proud of it. He was a doer, a creator, a designer, an architect. His father had taught him by example.

So he'd re-stocked the cart in the early morning hours, selecting items at will like a bandit. He held each item in his hands and pondered it, wondering how to split it into halves. How much would he take? What would he leave behind? Meghan would be devastated when she discovered him gone, and though he was abandoning her, he wouldn't leave her impoverished. He would be equitable with his provisions. He'd be fair. He would leave her in comfort for as long as he was able. He'd be charitable, yes, though not overly so.

His mind strayed to his first memory of her. She'd been thin and exhausted, at the end of her rope. She'd been dirty and beaten, stretched to the limits of human endurance. But she'd healed since then and grown stronger. She'd learned methods of making life easier, despite her undesirable circumstances. Jeremy hoped the lessons he'd taught her were enough to prevent her from treading the same patterns as before. She and Peter would likely stay in this house. And they should, Jeremy thought. He was leaving it to them. It was his way of rationalizing the things he was doing. The two of them could live a good life in this house. Meghan could tend their fledgling garden, and Jeremy would leave them with ample supplies.

Sam opened the bathroom door, pulling Jeremy back the present. She stepped into the silvery moonlight, crossed the room, and with an arched brow, watched him pocket the disks. He avoided her gaze as they tiptoed past the living room, but couldn't keep himself from peering inside it. Similarly to when he and Sam were alone, the foursome had chosen to sleep together, huddled in this room, yet rolled in separate blankets.

He regarded Meghan's feminine silhouette. She would wake up that morning and find herself alone. Some day after that—probably soon—Peter would die. For a fleeting moment, Jeremy questioned himself. Maybe he should leave her a note, he thought, just a small slip of paper with two words written across it. SAN DIEGO, their final destination. Perhaps he should share that information with her, give her something to cling to when her heart broke in two, some glimmer of hope for when the times became tough.

Though the thought plagued him, in the end, he moved on. This part of his life was done and over with. He'd likely never see Meghan again.

His eyes found Peter, curled tight beneath the sheets. His leg—as ever—was propped atop several thick blankets. It was bad. Horrendous. It would be the death of him. Meghan could call it anything she liked. She could fool herself until the day he died. She could lie to herself, say dry rot was better, but like it or not, rot was rot. Death was death. Gangrene was gangrene. Jeremy shook his head woefully. Leaving her behind was for the best. He couldn't allow her to follow him, nor permit her to drag Peter along.

From the corner of his eye, he caught Sam's inquisitive gaze, and for a moment, indecision plagued him. He stood, frozen, legs shoulder-width apart, his left arm braced against the wall. It was time. They were leaving. He was making his vision a reality, for there was no turning back once he made this decision.

Before he was able to stop himself, he crept into the dark room and crouched in front of Peter. He ran a nervous hand through his hair. What was he doing? They needed to leave. He was stalling and knew it, and the thought engendered panic. Was he chickening out? After all of his planning? Was he doubting a decision he knew to be right? Life was easier inside of this house. Was he a fool to chance the unknown? His heart went out to Peter. Life had dealt him a piss-poor deck. None of this ever should have happened to him. It wasn't his fault. He was innocent, angelic. Had Jeremy met Meghan sooner, he mused, this probably wouldn't have happened to Peter. Jeremy wouldn't have allowed it to happen. But it was too late now. The damage was done.

Jeremy reached for Peter's keychain, which was lying on the blanket. It was a small teddy bear with a bow around its neck. He palmed it, lifted it, brought it to the light. It was old and musty. The fur was matted. The coal-black nose hung loose by ragged threads. He tucked the blankets beneath Peter's chin, while an uncomfortable knot slowly coiled in his belly.

"I'm sorry little one," he murmured quietly. "You'll never know how sorry I am."

Sorry for what? the little voice hissed in his head. For abandoning a defenseless little boy? For leaving a woman who depends on you? Or for putting your own child's needs above another's?

Yes, he thought. Correct on all accounts. He was ashamed of these things, and of course, of many more. He was ashamed of himself for running away, for refusing to stay and find solutions. He was embracing cowardice, deserting people in need. He was ashamed of himself for all of his choices.

As he looked around the room, his eyes fell on Peter's last bottle of pills, and though he felt the weight of the disks in his pocket, there wouldn't be enough to make the journey. The disks wouldn't stretch all the way to San Diego. He'd need the pills, just to bridge the gap. He'd need them to see her over the finish line.

The bottle tantalized him. He wanted it. His jaw tightened. His palms slicked with sweat. It was Meghan's last bottle. She'd spoken of it, just last night. In fact, they'd argued about it. She'd wanted to revisit the hospital in town, but Jeremy had said it was a waste of time. He'd finally convinced her to try Knoxville.

Unable to catch his breath, he moved for the pills. His fingers trembled as they hovered over the bottle. He glanced at Sam and instantly regretted it. Her forehead was creased, a question dangling on her lips. Meeting his eyes, she cocked her head inquisitively. He could practically hear her prickly words.

With sudden decisiveness, he pushed himself to his feet, blocked Peter from her sight, as well as the bottle, and with the sleight-of-hand of an expert magician, palmed the bottle and slipped it into his pocket. Was it his imagination, or had Sam just trembled? Had she heard the pills fall to the bottom of his pocket?

Jesus. What the hell was he doing? This wasn't the action of a sane man. This wasn't the man he wanted to be. Sam didn't need the pills. Peter did. So why was he acting so selfishly? As he scrutinized his precious daughter's face, his conscience waged war within him. Dear God. His breath caught. Her beautiful face, the face that so reminded him of Susan. He would probably do anything for her. No. Correction. He was doing anything for her—right now. He was killing a defenseless child for her. Not by his own hands, of course, but indirectly. He wasn't choking Peter or pushing him off a cliff, but he was killing him. That couldn't be denied. The method didn't matter. In truth, Jeremy's was worse. Peter's death would be slow and agonizing. Meghan would awaken in a panic. She'd be forced to go out and search for pills immediately. Would the leg go first, or would it be his sight? Would he drop into a coma, or stay conscious enough to bear the pain and tough it out?

Meghan would be horrified by Jeremy's last act. He couldn't help but see the bitter symmetry of it. She would have circled back to her first intuition—women's intuition, she would probably call it. She'd curse him bitterly, say she'd always known, likely punish herself for ignoring her instincts. Her initial hunch, after all, had been right. She'd started their relationship with a gun to his head. She'd undoubtedly wish she could end it there, as well.

But Peter still had half a bottle of pills, right? Enough to last until Meghan found more? She kept a bottle hidden beneath the couch in the living room, though she didn't think Jeremy knew about that. Perhaps, he told himself, she kept others hidden, too. Perhaps there were secret locations all over this house. Maybe she'd never trusted Jeremy at all. Maybe she'd feigned her attachment to him, used it as a tactic to get what she wanted, or as a clever deception to get what she needed.

But even as his mind tried to accept the false narrative, he couldn't bring himself to believe it. He was trying to rationalize the worst thing he'd ever done, though he didn't deserve such pardons. He deserved far less, to ponder this last vicious act for what remained of his pathetic, forgettable, and dismal life. It should haunt him by night and plague him by day. He was acting passive-aggressively, dishonorably, and with cowardice. This was a turning point for he and Sam because today he was killing an innocent person. How might karma repay him for that? In what ways would it make him suffer? Would he be the one to ultimately settle this debt? Or would the fates call upon Sam? The thought nearly caused him to fall to his knees. He almost turned back, but didn't. Couldn't. Lifting his shoulders, he tried to exude a sense of confidence he didn't feel inside. Crossing the room in three long strides, he clasped her hand and pulled her toward the door. She came willingly, though woodenly, and together—for better or worse—they stepped into the night and the bitter unknown.

Sam was silent as they walked down the road. Eyes forward, and hands held stiff at her sides, she focused on their path, saying nothing to Jeremy. If she suspected him of something, she didn't give it voice, though she didn't yet know the full extent of his plan. Before he'd awakened her, he'd slipped behind the house and added a few last items to the cart. He'd pushed it down the road, hidden it behind a barn, and she flinched as they approached its familiar shape. Thought her mouth was grim, she still pressed on.

The morning breeze lifted the ends of her hair. The day was tranquil, the sounds soothing: the scraping of tires and boots against gravel, the soft exhalations of her rhythmic breathing. Together they walked as the sun climbed the mountains. Before long, it splashed warmth across their backs. As they continued westward, Jeremy felt transformed. Somewhere in the distance, in the direction he was facing, past the highways, fields, streams, and rivers, San Diego waited with open arms. Somewhere in front of them, the Pacific Ocean gleamed and glittered, as it sent its lifeless waves crashing against the shoreline. They'd make it, he told himself. They would. They must.

He and Sam walked for hours. She didn't say much when they stopped to rest, and nothing when he smoothed their map across the rocky payment. But he knew she'd figured out his plan soon enough. She'd probably reckoned the generalities of it—it was only the specifics she lacked.

She broke the silence only once that day, when she pointed to Neyland Drive, asking simply that they follow it.

"It hugs the curves of the Tennessee River. I'd like to see water, I think," she said.

With a nod, he altered their course. At least she was speaking again. That was something. For that much, at least, he was grateful.

The weeks that followed were much the same. She rarely spoke, if ever, and never unless he had spoken to her first. And she didn't ask questions, as she was prone to do. It was as if her childlike curiosity had died. They traveled at night, and slept in vacant homes, and a few blocks back, he'd smelled water. It was sour and sharp. The river, he surmised.

She finally broke the silence, which startled him. "Wouldn't we find bikes at a university?"

So immersed he was in his own private musings that he hadn't noticed her stop in front of a group of large buildings. Nor had he seen the broken sign on the lawn. It was a school with sweeping grounds, a university. There were bike racks in the front and a bank of seven doors. It was The University of Tennessee, Knoxville.

"Probably rusted heaps of twisted metal by now."

She frowned at that, tiny wrinkles creasing her brow. "You're such a pessimist. You don't know that for sure. We should at least check it out. Don't you think?"

Raising her face, she squinted into the sun. She drew a breath several times as if she meant to say something to him, but in the end, closed her mouth, reconsidering it. They shared an uncomfortable silence as he waited. He owed her his patience, and probably more.

"Pike," she said finally.

"I'm sorry," he said. "Pike?"

"Yeah," she murmured. "Pike. From now on, call me Pike. Pike is a species of fish."

He nodded. "Pike was a species of fish. And why— might I ask—do you want me to call you Pike? Why call you by the name of a long-extinct fish?"

She shrugged, her eyes focused on the road in front of them. "It's my new gang name. You should choose one too."

She closed her eyes and basked in the sun, then lowered her face to meet his gaze. "If we're planning to act like a heartless gang, we should choose gang names. It just makes sense."

With that, she turned, and walked away from him, and with razor-sharp talons, guilt clawed at his gut. Like a child who'd been scolded and rebuked by a parent, Jeremy dropped his head and followed close at her heels. He knew what she meant. It wasn't hard to grasp her meaning. It was the closest she'd come to making a formal accusation, and though she hadn't said the words, he knew what she meant. The disapproval in her eyes ran him through like a sword. Like a knife, it sliced his heart in two.

But people, he had learned, were never one thing. Was Jeremy a good man? Yeah. Of course. Was he a bad one, too? Oh, yes. That, too. One did what one needed to do to survive. Peter wasn't the first person Jeremy had killed, nor would he likely be the last.

Slowly but surely, they'd make it to San Diego. He'd push them. Hard. Probably harder than he should. Perhaps, like she said, they'd find bikes at the University, and if they did, he'd push them even harder.

Perhaps they'd get as far as Huntsville by tonight. Perhaps they'd even cross a state line.

Sometimes, the ocean floor is only a stop on the journey. And it is when you are at this lowest point, that you are faced with a choice. You can stay there at the bottom, until you drown. Or you can gather pearls and rise back up —stronger from the swim and richer from the jewels.

—Yasmin Mogahed

CHAPTER 19
10 Years Prior

MARCH 26TH, 2165
LECONTE MEDICAL CENTER
SEVIERVILLE, TENNESSEE

"Keep to the shadows," Jeremy's father whispered softly. "We're not alone in here."

Jeremy found Susan's hand and squeezed it tightly. In this drafty cold place, he was grateful for her warmth, though the depth of her stubbornness still rankled him. She shouldn't be here. It was too dangerous a risk. Why had he allowed her to come in the first place? Suppressing a sigh, he answered his own question. Allowed her? Who was he kidding? When had Susan allowed people to manage her? She was persistent, headstrong, unrelenting when she'd set her mind to task. She was as obstinate as they came. Jeremy loved her for that. She was a partner to him in every sense of the word, so if danger were in the cards, she would demand to be cut in.

Like Jeremy, she believed knowledge and

experience were akin to power. This excursion, she reasoned, was part of her training. She wanted to be sure she could handle things on her own, in case something happened to Jeremy. After Samantha was born, they agreed on this, on the importance of independence and shared responsibility. Mutual understanding was key. Both she and Jeremy should be equipped to accomplish every task without the other's interference or aid. Though it might be a melancholic worldview, one couldn't argue the pragmatism of it.

"It's just sound planning," Susan had reasoned one night. "As much as I don't want to face the possibility, I can't pretend it can't happen one day. Something could happen to you, and if it did, I need to know how to survive. I need to be able to do everything you can do: aim and shoot a gun, properly forage for food and supplies, build a fire, live in the wild, defend our daughter, our home, and the ark." She'd stated her case while lying in bed, her forehead gently touching his. "I need to come along tomorrow night, Jeremy. Don't shut me out. Let me do this." She shook her head, her hair tickling his shoulder. "This isn't a want, Jeremy. It's a need. Actually, in truth, it's a must. It's something I just have to do. Besides, I've mastered all the tasks around the here. It's time I push past my comfort zone."

Snuggling beneath the covers, he circled his legs around hers. "Mastered all the tasks? I'm not sure about that." She shivered when he pressed his lips to her throat. "I can think of one task that could use a little work."

She'd smiled against his mouth and slipped her arms around his neck. "That was corny as hell, Mr. Colt."

Yeah. It was.

Standing in the dark, he considered what she'd said that night. In the end, of course, he'd relented. He didn't like exposing her to danger, but she made a valid point. She should know how to do the things he did. Nothing in this world was promised them. At any given time they could lose everything. They were one catastrophe away from homelessness or starvation. He should be spending more time with her, honing her skills. So perhaps this mission was a good first test.

Earlier that evening, they'd discussed the idea. Jeremy, Susan, Liam, and Olivia had sat around the fire and planned this excursion, maps of the hospital spread on the table before them. The room had felt so cozy and secure, juxtaposed with the nature of the topic at hand. Orange flames had danced in the hearth, the reflections licking up the fluting of their glasses. The alcohol had pleasantly warmed Jeremy's body, and for a moment, he'd almost felt normal. Everyone he loved was inside that cabin. It was almost like an evening from a child's fairytale. In that moment, he'd wanted for nothing. No one.

But their lives weren't a child's fairytale. Theirs was a harsh reality. Over the past few weeks, as events had occurred, the truth about Sam became clear. She was a diabetic, which was a devastating discovery. The realization had been staggering at first, the diagnosis nearly impossible to believe. Understanding, when it dawned, came rushing at them, but acceptance had crawled a snail's pace. After his initial shock and rejection of the theory, Jeremy went off on his own for a bit, and after considering the situation objectively, the unlikely coincidence had astounded him. It was quite a stretch of the imagination, a long shot if ever there were a long shot. What on earth were the odds of this happening? Jeremy wasn't related to Liam, yet his own flesh and blood presented the same disease. Diabetes had killed Jeremy's biological mother. What were the chances that the perfect surrogate parents had found him, taken him in, and cared for him? The synchronicity of it was awe-inspiring, and after the initial diagnosis, they'd discussed it at length.

The process of diagnosing Sam had been tedious. It had put a strain on the entire family. She'd presented symptoms right after her fourth birthday. After naptime, for example, she'd awaken in a mood. She'd be groggy, uncommunicative, irritable as hell. Fuzzy, Jeremy liked to call it. She'd begun to urinate frequently, and at night, and demanded more water by day. But symptoms like these could be attributed to other things. It was her weight that had been the most telling. Despite the fact that her appetite was healthy, the numbers on the scale had continued to decline. At first, the weight loss was slow. It inched across her body like a slow sunset. Her clothing became slightly looser than it had been, which Susan ascribed to a growth spurt, at first. But soon after that, her face hollowed out. Her cheeks became drawn and mottled with gray, and after that, the situation snowballed. Her arms became frighteningly frail. Her legs became knobby at the knees and ankles. Jutting from her skin were hipbones, vertebrae, and the sharp angles of her shoulder blades and clavicles. Her hair became dull and brittle, before falling to the floor in small blond clouds. Fatigue had accompanied weight loss in equal measure, and soon she was spending most of her time in bed. Jeremy and Susan had been paralyzed with fear as they considered each gruesome possibility.

"It could be any number of things." Susan had said, fear shining bright in her eyes. "It could be anything, Jeremy, anything at all! Cancer. Leukemia. Lupus. A virus. Dear God, what if it's autoimmune? What if it's something that requires a hospital stay? Or something that demands professional care and drugs?"

Jeremy had practically developed an ulcer from the stress of not knowing the answer. It was the unanswered questions that kept him up at night. Susan was right. It could be anything. Something could be eating their daughter alive, and they lacked the proper equipment to run tests. For hospitals didn't exist anymore. They were the last facilities to crumble. When Jeremy was a boy, he could remember the military taking them over. He was born in a hospital, but Sam wasn't as lucky, for it was shortly after Jeremy's tenth birthday that the hospital in Sevierville was finally shut down. The authorities had done their best to keep the doors open, but had quickly given up and moved on. After that, a group of desperate citizens moved in, pillaged the space, and then fought to claim it. A mini-turf war was fought. Half the building was set ablaze. The new occupants killed the medical staff, unwittingly driving out anyone else who might start a new practice. What remained was nothing but a burnt-out shell. The patients' wings were blackened and burned, and the rest was picked clean of anything useful.

Jeremy frowned at the senselessness of humans. The greediness of one small group of people had ensured the detriment of all. But that's how things fell apart everywhere. Society hadn't ended with a pop or a bang. It wasn't one event, or several in synthesis, that sent people scurrying underground. Little by little, civilization had simply languished. It was a wasting away, a slow wilting with time, a slow starvation that became a widespread famine.

The four of them had agonized over Sam's deteriorating health. Night after night, they'd sat up and argued, encyclopedias and medical journals spilled across their knees. They made notes, kept records, charts, and logs, all of which detailed her growing list of symptoms. The complicated nature of the work amazed Jeremy. Many different diseases could be characterized by similar—if not the same—symptoms, and with nothing but a few old books at hand, it was exceedingly difficult to diagnose the proper one.

Weight loss? Well! That could be any number of things. Was the person dying of cancer, or did he simply dislike his green vegetables? The process was maddening if not depressing, but they soon narrowed it down to a handful of suspects, each more frightening than the last. It was only after Sam awakened late one afternoon, screaming and crying, that they finally put the pieces together. Well, Jeremy corrected himself. It hadn't been they. It was Liam who made the initial discovery. And what a discovery it was!

Sam had been groggy and crying, like normal. And who could blame her? She was withering away. Uncomfortable in her starving body, she liked to make it known to anyone who would listen. And as always, in times like these, chaos had ensued. They struggled to find something—anything—to bring her relief. Juice? Crackers? Powdered milk with water, heated over an open flame? Soup? A walk? Freddie the Frog? Coots the cat? At times like these, nothing ever seemed to help, and Jeremy and Susan were nearly driven to tears. It had been one day, after a particularly bitter tantrum, that Liam had crept behind Sam, silently. He'd trapped her tiny fist in his, and with speed and efficiency, and a frown across his face, popped a blood sugar tester into her finger. Lo and behold—five hundred. Five Hundred! The entire family had been stunned to silence. A blood sugar level as high as five hundred could have resulted in a permanent coma.

Things got better after that, for Sam, but Liam had sunk into a deep depression. And though Jeremy found the self-deprecation ridiculous, Liam wouldn't be swayed. He was stalwart in his solitude, dogged in his isolation. To him the misdiagnosis was a personal failure. For more than a month, as he had explained it to the family, he had allowed a disease he suffered from personally to ravage the body of his granddaughter. He had allowed someone he loved to suffer needlessly, without even recognizing the signs. It was all bullshit, Jeremy explained a thousand times. Hindsight was always 20/20. But Liam never forgave himself. He struggled with that until the day he died.

Over the next few months, they slowly coaxed baby Sam back to health. Grandpa Liam put her on a strict diet. He decreased her sugars and dosed her with the proper amounts of insulin, and the effects were nothing short of dramatic. She put on weight almost immediately. She was happier, inquisitive, more alert, more attentive. She regained vitality, energy, and happiness. The family reveled in the success of the treatments and relished the fact that they'd solved it alone, without the intervention of a medical professional.

But the elation had been short lived, for after stabilizing Sam, they were forced to face several difficult truths. It was Liam—of course—who had first brought it up. With brows furrowed, he explained their dilemma. When he and Olivia had stocked the ark, they had only planned to medicate one sick person. While many others in the outside world succumbed to various diseases and afflictions, Liam enjoyed the security of health, delivered by boxes of insulin pills. But there was only enough for one person. There was only enough to keep a middle-aged man alive to a ripe old age.

"Jeremy," he'd said, a haunted look in his eye, "we need to venture out for more pills. My supply won't last us forever." His gaze had fallen to his hands, guiltily. "Not for the two of us, at least."

"Alright. That can't be difficult. Let's start with the hospital. What do you think we'll find there?"

"I don't know. I have no idea. I haven't been there in years. But we need to try, and we need to face the truth. With Sam and I both suffering from this, we no longer have enough pills."

He had seemed to blame himself when he said that, Jeremy remembered, which had bothered the hell out of him, at the time. So here they were, searching for pills. Having first vetted the mission from the comforts of their cabin, they'd developed a plan and then set out at dusk. They'd crept soundlessly through the broken half of the hospital, which had been open to the elements for decades. They edged through the burnt sections first, eager to find solid walls to hide behind. Soil, rich in fertilizing ash, had spawned ferns and tiny plants in the cracks of the linoleum. Like tufts of wiry hair they were. And the place had an odd sort of smell, Jeremy thought, a nausea-inducing blend of burnt materials and mildew.

They crouched in the darkness like cats poised to pounce, darkened hallways spidering before them. Liam had chosen his path already, which he steered them down at a careful pace. He selected a corridor, which Jeremy knew led to emergency rooms and intensive care units. Liam had said the medications—if any were left—would likely be there, but Jeremy wasn't so sure. They proceeded in an awed sort of silence, their footfalls echoing strangely in the drafty halls. They'd attempted this mission at night, and thus, needed flashlights to guide their path. Dry leaves, propelled by the circulating winds, chased one another in annular paths. Shadows weaved with their passing, like ghosts.

Jeremy and Susan followed close behind Liam, to what had once been the nurses' central station, and in response to his outstretched hand, they stopped. His voice was low, his warning severe.

"We're not alone here. There are others nearby."

Jeremy didn't doubt that. He figured many people would seek shelter in a hospital. It was the main reason he hadn't wanted Susan to come. One of Liam's most important lessons pertained to the nature of humans. In times of need, he had said, humans were the most dangerous species on earth.

Jeremy leaned forward. "How many can you see?"

Liam answered by pulling his gun from his waistband and holding it in front of his body, barrel down. Jeremy tried to see, but couldn't. They waited for what seemed like an eternity. Dropping his gaze to their feet, he flinched when he noticed Susan standing too close to the wall. As pulled her from it, he pointed to her feet. "One foot away from the wall," he reminded her. "Bullets ricochet. Remember that." As if a snake had bitten her, she jumped. Her eyes went suddenly wide with fear.

They circled the nurse's station, slipped inside, and then quietly nosed through remaining wreckage that had been repeatedly pillaged by others. After finding nothing of value, they moved on, following signs toward operating rooms and supplies. The supply rooms had been badly plundered, the contents strewn about in careless piles. Most of the equipment they found was useless to them, or to anyone else for that matter. High tech equipment, now obsolete, made ghostly shapes beneath dirt-smeared tarps. Test tubes, lengths of rubber, and piping littered the floor like eels. And if the supply closets were bad, the hospital pharmacy was worse. The destruction here was total. It was as if a battle had been waged within. Bullet holes peppered the walls in strange patterns. Empty shell casings littered the floor. But if something could be found, Jeremy figured, it was here, and so they spent hours searching its depths. They each chose a corner, separate from each other, and sifted through the rubble with meticulous care.

When his eyes grew tired, Jeremy rested them on Susan. She had formed a pile of trash to one side, and on the other, a tiny collection of items she wanted to keep. His let his gaze travel the room, as he mentally performed the safety rituals he'd been taught as a boy. It was important to locate any nearby exits and choose a few places that would offer concealment, should any strangers come calling. It was a ritual that was now instinctual to him, and one he still needed to instill in his wife. He returned his gaze to the crap in front of him, which he'd heaped into piles less orderly than Susan's. His search had yielded nothing of use, and he was beginning to feel the sharp edges of anxiety. Susan stood up, dusted her khakis, and moved across the room to join him, her mouth grim. She'd been no more fortunate than he, or so it seemed.

Liam, having also found nothing of use, motioned them into the next set of rooms, where they repeated the same daunting task with less passion. Wash, rinse, repeat, ad nauseam. Leave this building and then try the next.

They searched three separate care centers that night, but in the end, had little to show for it. They had amassed a collection of decent enough wares: clean needles, towels, two bottles of antiseptic, a bottle of antibiotics Susan had found in a patient's overnight bag. And the coup de grace, of course: three bottles of insulin pills. The booty was small, but at least they'd found something. It was more than they'd had before.

Just as the sun was brightening the eastern sky, the three gave up and headed for home. The sky bled purple, blackness giving way to indigo and eggplant, like a growing bruise that mirrored their sentiments. Jeremy was the first to break the silence. There was no denying the failure of this mission, and he worried about his father's state of mind. Liam was taking things much too personally, lately, and lacking in his characteristic determination and exuberance. He was bordering on obsessive-compulsive behaviors. Jeremy peered at the rigidity of his body, taut as the high E-string of a guitar. He was alert with wiry energy, it seemed, but his hands were balled into fists at his sides. Jeremy hated to see him like this, though seeing his perspective wasn't difficult. Liam had spent years planning for every eventuality. He'd been meticulous with it. It had been a second job. But he'd never conceived of something like this, and Jeremy sensed a seething anger within him, boiling over like steam from a pot. It was an emotion Jeremy feared he'd turn inward, for the depth of Liam's love for Sam knew no bounds. If she ran out of insulin before living a full life, Liam would never forgive himself. So only one question remained, and it was one that kept Jeremy awake most nights: how far would Liam go to save Sam? What was he willing to sacrifice?

"Didn't find much tonight, did we, Dad?" Jeremy asked, and then winced at the absurdity of the question.

Liam's mouth was grim. "No, son. It wasn't a good night. We'll just keep looking tomorrow, I suppose."

"That's right. We'll try again tomorrow," Susan

said quietly. She seemed determined to see things positively. "There are plenty of hospitals in the area," she went on. "Plenty of hospices and care facilities, too, not to mention Urgent Cares and after-hours clinics. We can expand our search grid to Knoxville and Pigeon Forge. We can pack overnight bags, if we have to, and try Nashville, Mississippi, Georgia, and beyond."

"I think we'll probably have to," Liam said, his eyes fixed on the ground. "Whether we like it or not, this is now our fulltime job. But we need to think of a better way to do it, and when we do, we'll—"

"Freeze, old man."

The voice had been hissed from Jeremy's left, somewhere in the dark, from behind an old building, the raspy sound intruding on the burgeoning dawn. Susan instinctively stepped in front of Jeremy, a selfless act that would later amaze him.

"Drop your weapons," a male voice ordered them. "Raise your hands where I can see 'em. Do it now."

Jeremy eyed his father sidelong, and then mimicked his three-quarter turn toward the man. Two shadows emerged from the darkness.

Only two, Jeremy thought. Just two. Not bad.

"I said drop your weapons." The man's command was soft and insistent, which was more effective than a yell would have been. Jeremy immediately complied. Lowering to a crouch, he set his gun on the pavement, but curiously his father didn't move. Liam turned and addressed the men confidently.

"There's nothing at the hospital worth taking. I assure you. I know you were there. I heard you, too. But unlike you, I had the decency to move on. I only ask for the same in return." Jeremy's heart threatened to leap from his chest. "I'm not putting down my weapon, so make your choice."

The response seemed to surprise the smaller gunman. "Why don't you show me what you found old man, and I might be willing to broker a trade."

Liam shook his head. "I don't broker trades."

With a sharp click, the man cocked his weapon, lowered it, and aimed it at Liam's chest. Jeremy's panic threatened to overcome him. His mouth went dry. Sweat bubbled from his pores. His father was acting like an idiot. Was he too depressed to reason properly? Give these men what they wanted, Jeremy thought. It wasn't as if they'd discovered a treasure. None of what they'd found was worth their lives.

Jeremy's gaze tunneled on the gun. Without thinking, he dared a step forward.

"Wait!" said Susan, lowering her pack to the ground. "We found a few things you might want." She rummaged her bag with trembling fingers then held up the bottle of antibiotics. She shook it, gently, like a baby's shiny rattle. "Antibiotics. See? A rare find. It's yours. I'll give it to you if you let us move on."

The smaller man advanced half a step. "And?" he asked, his eyes probing the open flap of her pack.

Jeremy flinched as the man moved closer. What on earth was wrong with him tonight? Had he lost his nerve? He was suddenly so frightened he wasn't able to move. Like fingers scrabbling at the edge of a cliff, his mind clawed for a way out of this. Each idea was sillier than the last, each scenario worse for his family. Susan's generosity would matter little to these men, who would likely strip them of their possessions and clothing, shoot them, and leave them for dead, anyway.

His father must have agreed, for in a flurry of movement, Liam raised his weapon, and without offering a word or explanation, buried two bullets in the would-be thieves' heads. The echoes from the blasts were concussive forces, and in a heap of arms and legs, the men fell to the pavement. Their scalps gleamed wet in the pale morning light, their blood black, and glistening like oil.

"Dad?" Jeremy asked, astonished at the act. As far

as he knew, Liam had never hurt a man, much less shot or killed him. He hadn't thought his father was capable of that.

"Let's go, Jeremy."

"Dad! Wait! What the hell?"

Liam turned quickly, catching Jeremy off-guard. "We don't have time for this." When he turned to Susan, his eyes narrowed. "And we can't spare anything for anyone anymore. Not antibiotics or anything else. Given the way our lives have changed, we can't spare a bottle of damn Tic-Tacs. It's every man for himself out here, and from what I've seen tonight, to find the things we need, we'll have to venture farther from our home—as everyone else has been doing for decades."

Jeremy peered at bits of bone and brain that had splattered unceremoniously onto the road. He tried to swallow but couldn't. "But did you have to kill them, Dad?"

"Yes, Jeremy. I did." Liam moved closer and grasped Jeremy's hand. "It is only when we hesitate, Son, that we fail. We must act boldly, without fear. This dangerous world doesn't reward the meek, or the ones who sit and do nothing. Be strong. Be decisive. Do what needs to be done."

Jeremy squeezed his father's hand and frowned. He flipped it over to massage the weathered palm. The aftermath of his waning adrenaline threatened to manifest itself as tears. What would he have done if his father had been shot? What would any of them have done? Drawing a ragged breath, he smoothed his father's hand in his. Jeremy had always considered his father's hands beautiful. Though he'd spent his profession life inside a lab, Liam's hands told a very different story. Maybe they were lab hands once, Jeremy thought, but they became the hands that created this life, the hands that shaped Jeremy's childhood home. They were beautiful, calloused, weathered, yet soft.

They were also shaking, and had thinned noticeably.

"Dad, your hands. You're shaking."

Peering into his father's eyes, he allowed his suspicions to rise to the surface. For several weeks, he had denied the truth, though the truth was as plain as the nose on his face. People often fooled themselves; saw what they wanted to see. Funny, he thought absently. People believe what they wish to believe, while ignoring what truly is.

As he held his father's hand, Jeremy's fears spread wings and took flight. The truth was standing in front of him, now, and the scattered pieces came shifting into place. Many times, over the past few weeks, Jeremy had seen his father standing in the kitchen, still and stoic, frowning as he stared at a bottle of pills. He would gaze through the large picture window in the living room, remove the cap, shake the pills into his palm, roll them in his fist like dice. He would peer at the pills for a moment, then at Sam, playing in a square of sunlight on the floor.

Liam didn't blink, but stared at his son. "I just shot two men," he said carefully. "I suppose I'm a bit shaken up, is all."

Beneath the pale light, Jeremy stared at his father, whom he hadn't really seen for some time. His father's face seemed drawn, almost pinched, not gaunt, though he'd lost a bit of weight. His cheeks had hollowed. His jawline was distinct. The flesh beneath his eyes had puffed and deepened with color.

No, Jeremy thought. Not this. This was something he just couldn't face. This sort of thing happened out there, to other people. Not to people who had planned. Not to them. Liam was nothing if not a stubborn man. He was deeply devoted to his family and life. But was he too devoted, Jeremy wondered suddenly. So devoted as to martyr himself?

Jeremy somehow found his voice, which cracked. Susan stepped forward and laid a hand on his back. "Dad," he whispered. "You don't have to do this. Please tell me you're still taking the pills. We can figure this out. We'll find another way. Please don't sacrifice yourself for Sam."

PART 5

I cannot tarry longer.
The sea that calls all things unto her calls me.

—Kahlil Gibran, The Prophet

CHAPTER 20
Present Day

NOVEMBER 8TH, 2176
ODESSA, TEXAS
1,010 MILES TO SAN DIEGO

Sam's rear tire was the first to run flat. Jeremy crouched low, inspecting it with a frown. There must be a pinhole leak, he surmised, a small rupture that had been leaking for miles.

She'd awakened earlier that morning, hands trembling, as she gently roused Jeremy from a deep and dreamless sleep. She'd pointed to her belly, her eyes haunted.

"Zero percent," she'd whispered softly. "We're down to the last one."

He'd wordlessly fished the last disk from his pocket, his dread so profound it nearly threatened to overwhelm him. He'd injected the thin tube and pressed down the plunger, while trying to keep his hands steady. "Thirty days," he'd muttered, like she didn't know that.

She hadn't replied, but had turned toward Seth, appraising him with a discerning eye. "He slept through the night," she said. "Finally. And he didn't wake up with sweaty clothes this time. I think it's a win. I think he's doing better. I think he's finally beaten the infection."

"Yep. Seems so. That's good," Jeremy said, as he fished a container from deep inside his pack. "Why don't you take this outside, by the fire. Heat up a kettle, make some oats for us to eat."

She'd scrunched her nose at the suggestion. "Oats again? They're gross, Carp. They taste like cardboard, especially since we used up all the Splenda."

"True. But it's the best I can do." He thrust his chin in Seth's direction. "And it's what he needs to put weight on his bones. We need to make sure he eats five times a day, at least, until he regains a bit of strength."

She'd acknowledged the request and gone outside, toward the collection of wood they'd piled high the night before. He waited for her to crouch down beside it, pull out her lighter and ignite a small flame before edging closer to Seth. He wanted to perform a closer inspection, but wanted to do so in private. Seth's neck, he noticed, was cool and dry, as were the collar and underarms of his shirt. Sam was right. He was healing. It was a positive sign. He wasn't drenched in sweat like he'd been the nights before, which was a vast improvement—to put it lightly. For the first week, the infection had raged, and though he'd been fever-free for close to seven days now, his body still worked to expel the toxins. Several times a night he'd awakened, hair plastered to his scalp, wet clothes clinging to his body. Shivering and stumbling like a newly dropped fawn, he'd peel of the clothes and leave a soggy pile by the door.

He was eating again, too, and robustly. His cheeks had regained a healthy pink hue. And though he still slept both day and night, his breathing had evened and deepened. But the wound was what interested Jeremy the most. The fear of relapse was a constant concern. With bated breath, he examined its edges. The laceration was now covered with a thick black scar, and the surrounding flesh was flat and smooth, and finally cool to the touch. Much better.

Satisfied, Jeremy rolled to his heels and settled himself on the ground. While staring at Seth, he let his mind wander. His fingers drummed a stead beat on the floor as he considered where they were versus where they needed to be. A significant amount of time had been lost, but Jeremy refused to think about that. They'd been lucky. Things could have gone differently, and worse, and though he'd been careful to appear competent in front of Sam, he really hadn't known what to do about Seth. He'd only done what seemed right at the time, applied the kinds of treatments that made the most sense. It was a miracle Seth had healed at all, given the poor circumstances and lack of resources at hand. It was the medicines that had done it, Jeremy mused, not his efforts.

Medicines that are now all gone, he thought, frowning.

He reached out to tousle Seth's hair. Once Seth had awakened, things quickly got better. Jeremy had missed his goofy smile and silly questions, and was reminded—once more—of the importance of family. Thankfully Jeremy had listened to Sam when she convinced him to give Seth time to heal, though his gut still clenched when he considered their predicament. Two weeks had been lost to them, and though Jeremy had watched Seth slowly improve, he'd clawed at the walls like a wild caged beast. Two ridiculous and excruciation weeks; he would panic anew if he allowed himself to ponder it. Though they'd seen the worst and come out the other side, they were unfortunately left to manage the consequences. But it was done and behind them. No use worrying about it now. For once, Jeremy was proud of himself. He'd shut his mouth, and let Sam lead, and he was fairly certain she was grateful for that. He may have even earned a few brownie points.

Though the fever had drained Seth to the point of exhaustion, once his temperature normalized, his strength returned rather quickly. He began to eat solid food again, take short walks, drink copious amounts of rainwater. And once he'd cultivated the taste for food, his appetite became insatiable. So much so that Jeremy worried about their supplies. Mealtimes had also become debriefings. They were times of intense interrogation and discovery. Seth wanted to know everything. He had no recollection of the time he'd been ill, how'd he'd gotten to the 7 Eleven, or how much time had passed. Space and time were entirely lost to him. He'd query Jeremy and Sam for hours, with a nervousness that set Jeremy's teeth on edge. When he was ill, as he'd explained, a week felt like a day, and when Jeremy told him how much time had passed, it was as if he'd suffered a punch to the gut. With eyes ablaze, he'd pushed himself to his feet, swayed, and turned in small circles. It was as if he were seeing the convenience store for the first time.

"That's not possible," he'd argued fervently. "Two weeks just isn't possible. It's really been two weeks?" He'd held his hands in front of his face then examined the sagging waistband of his pants. "I'm thin," he stammered. "I mean, really thin."

"You've always been really thin," Sam had tried to joke. "But now, to me, you're just scrawny. You're the size of a tiny toothpick."

His eyes had gone wider at the sound of her voice, darted to her face, and then dropped to her belly. Tottering to her side, he'd fallen to his knees, lifted the corner of her shirt and gasped aloud. "Twenty-four," he'd stammered, as though he would cry. "You're down to twenty-four percent." He was a deer in headlights as he turned to Jeremy.

"It's okay," Jeremy lied. "She'll be fine. Let's focus

on you right now. Let's get you better and get back on the road. That's the best way to help Sam now."

"But how much farther do we have to go?"

"You let me worry about that."

He'd shaken his head. "But how many miles?" he'd insisted, his face stricken.

"Stop," Jeremy said. "We'll make it just fine. Right now, we need you to relax and get better. The quicker you get better, the quicker we'll make up the time. We'll push ourselves harder, if you want to do that. We'll cover more ground to make up the difference. Can you push yourself harder for Sam?"

He'd nodded, though Jeremy had still seen guilt in his eyes. "Yeah. Okay. We'll push ourselves harder."

And push himself harder he did. Guilt seemed to bring Seth's goals into laser focus, because regaining his strength became his fulltime job. He ate dutifully, and often. He stretched his muscles and took long walks, kept the rain catchers empty and the pots and pans clean. He tended the water purification at sunrise, double straining it, and boiling the contents.

"Wait till it cools," he'd chastised Jeremy. "You can't pour hot water into plastic containers. The chemicals get into the water. It causes cancer."

Jeremy had suppressed a smile but played along. "Thanks for the tip. Where'd you learn that?"

"Everybody in the world knows that."

Proving himself was important to Seth, demonstrating his worth and resilience. Perhaps it was the benefits of youth, Jeremy thought, or Seth's deep affection for Sam. But in a few short days, they were back on the road, and from there, central Texas came and went in a blur. He'd pushed them—harder than he probably should have, but there was considerable ground to cover.

And time, unfortunately was always ticking.

Though they stopped more frequently than Jeremy would have liked, they soon regained their former rhythm. Seth would pedal, red-faced, cheeks puffing, his eyes fixed on the road. He attacked the miles aggressively, as if punishing himself for a personal failure. Jeremy was the one who forced them to rest, despite Seth's whines and protests. The last thing he wanted to do was to wear Seth out, or stress his body past the point of repair. He needed his strength right now. They all did. Now more than ever before. For the path, of late, had become treacherous and challenging. The eastern half of the United States sat lower than the western half. The gentle gradient was sly at first, so gradual, in fact, that they barely noticed it. But once they did, it was all they could think about. The effort required to travel the same fifty miles was noticeably greater than it had been in the east, evident in their unquenchable thirst, their sweaty clothes, and the constant burning in their thighs.

And it will only get harder from here, Jeremy thought. New Mexico and Arizona will be higher still. The oxygen will be thin. The temperature will increase. It will take all we've got to see it through.

But despite their setbacks, they'd made excellent progress, and Jeremy was starting to feel human again. Until now, he thought grimly, as he stared at the tire. They were fifteen miles outside Odessa, Texas, and Sam's rear tire had gone flat. She'd swerved, dangerously, and then yelped through a skid, pulling her bike to an ungraceful stop.

"Shit," Jeremy swore aloud. He was such a damn fool. He should have foreseen this. Of all the foolish things he'd ever done in his life, this had to be among the top two or three. How could he have been so careless? How could he have forgotten something as important as this? His thoughts returned to that U.T. supply closet, with its rows of gleaming bikes, over a thousand miles away. He could punch himself for being so stupid. If only his father could see him right now. Oh yeah, he sneered inwardly, how impressive you are. Piss poor planning at it's finest.

Great work.

"You said a bad word," Seth muttered absently, his eyes fixed on the flattened piece of rubber.

"Dad?" Sam asked, her voice quiet and small. "What do we do? How will we go on?"

Jeremy's mind raced as he met her gaze. She'd been quiet since early that morning, he'd noticed, withdrawn and introspective since he'd inserted the last disk. Reality must weigh heavy on her now. He could see its effects in her posture and bearing. Her head hung lower. Her brow was stitched with concern.

In an attempt to downplay the seriousness of the situation, he rolled his shoulders dispassionately. "We find a tire shop. It's as simple as that. A new inner tube would suffice. Or a whole new tire, if we can find a bike store. It's really no biggie. We can figure it out." He forced a smile that he didn't really feel. "We'll figure it out, Pike. Don't get stressed out. In fact, when we find the right kind of store, we'll take advantage and stock up. We'll grab several tires—one for each bike."

He'd never been good at selling false optimism. The edge in his voice always gave him away.

"Yeah," Seth added, sensing Jeremy's desperation. "We'll each get one, and wear it on a string. We'll wear them on our backs like sombrero hats." Turning in a half circle, he peered at a sign in the distance. "But it's sixteen miles to Odessa. Is that a town?"

"Sixteen miles?" Jeremy asked.

"Yeah. Sounds really far."

"Nah. Sixteen miles is nothing."

"Nothing? But Dad, sixteen miles? How will we get the bikes there? Are you saying we have to push them?" She sneered at her bike like it had disappointed her. "How will we push this thing sixteen miles on a piece of flat rubber? Can't we do better than that?"

She made a good point. That would take too long. There had to be a more efficient way to cross the distance.

He could ride to Odessa himself, he considered, leave the kids here and return with a tire. But what if it took too long to find a store? Or what if one of his tires went flat? They'd put miles and miles on these tires already; having not had a flat was just pure dumb luck. They should have lost several by now, statistically speaking. Biting his lip, he glanced at the sun, which was low and heavy in the western sky. None of these ideas were worth the risk to him. He couldn't leave the children alone on this road, not without knowing for sure when he'd return. The sun was setting, and though Odessa was only sixteen miles away, he didn't know where to go once he arrived. He'd need to find a bike shop, a sports store, or a Walmart—and one that wasn't pillaged, at that. The whole thing could take hours, or longer, even days.

Taking a breath to steady himself, he contemplated the situation anew. Okay. He could figure this out. It wasn't difficult. They would stay together, as a team, get the bikes as far as Odessa city limits, stash them, find a map, and then begin a thorough search. Each moment was precious to him. To Sam's point, efficiency was key. He chewed the inside of his cheek. "Let's remove the tire and assess the damage to the rim."

Sam backed away as he flipped the bike over. Balancing it on its handlebars, he removed the tire by releasing the clamps. The rubber held tight to the rim. Jeremy broke a sweat as he wrestled it off, revealing a deflated tube inside the tread. Removing it disdainfully, he stood to appraise the damage. The tube was limp, like an eel in his hands. And though it had worn thin, it wasn't completely destroyed. Only a pinhole leak existed on one side.

"Got a hair tie?" he asked Sam quietly. There had to be a way to get the bike to Odessa, for she surely couldn't ride on the rim. Pulling the elastic from her ponytail, she passed it to him, and with the blade of his pocketknife, he sliced it in half before looping the ends around the ruptured tube and tying them together in a secure double knot. Widening the pinhole with the tip of his knife, he inflated the tube and frowned at the taste. With the elastic tied to one end of the tube, the other end trapped air well enough. Could it hold for sixteen miles? he wondered. Setting the tire down, he glanced at their surroundings. If half of the tube could hold air well enough, all he had to do was fill the remaining half. But with what kind of material? What would suffice?

Stalled cars ran the length of the freeway on both sides. Could he find something useful inside one of them? Some kind of filler or packing?

"What are you thinking?" Seth asked him cautiously.

Jeremy set his hands to his hips. "Half of the tube is inflated, but we can't leave the other half flat against the rim. We can't afford to damage the rim or we'll ruin the bike permanently. But we have to get the bikes to town somehow, so we have to find something with which to pack the rim. It should be something soft, smushy, cushiony, something that yields against pressure. It should be something we can easily stuff inside the rim."

Seth didn't skip a beat, but turned toward the edge of the road. "What about grass and leaves?" He pointed. "Or mushy roots? Something like that?"

Jeremy arched a brow. "Okay. Not bad, kid. Let's give it a try." He followed Seth to the shoulder of the road. "But there isn't much grass along a major interstate, and we've reached the edge of the desert."

"Okay. But what about weeds?" Seth crouched at Jeremy's feet. "There are plenty of weeds out here. Look at these."

Jeremy shrugged. It was as good a plan as any he had heard, so together, they pulled fountain grass by the roots. There were tufts of low scrub brush beneath a corroded sign, and piles of dried leaves, surrounding old vehicles. Sam found a yellow flower and pushed it behind her ear, and when she smiled, Jeremy smiled back. He was grateful for the small pleasures life saw fit to deliver these days, for the beauty of her smile, for Seth's inquisitiveness. The three of them were a strong support system, and Jeremy was once again thankful for Seth. Waiting for him had been the right thing to do. It was as if, by waiting, Jeremy had regained a part of himself he'd thought lost, like the universe was offering reciprocity. Some might call it karma, he mused, or an exchange of goodwill for doing something right. Whatever it was, it felt healing, and good. Despite their dire circumstances, they had—and always would have—each other. Jeremy felt a lump in his throat. In this moment, Susan would be proud of him, of his commitment to their daughter, but also to Seth. Jeremy peered at Sam through blurred tears. He would never let her die—not while he lived. He'd do anything to ensure her safety, and he was certain, now, that Seth would, as well. Come hell or high water, they would make it to San Diego—even if they had to walk the remaining miles on foot.

Seth made a basket of the shirt he was wearing, in which he collected the greenery and roots, which Jeremy used to pack the deflated portion of the tube. Pulling the tread over the rim was difficult, but the finished product seemed sturdy enough. He pushed and pinched and squeezed at the rubber. Not bad, he thought. Not bad at all, particularly for a nine-year old boy. Righting the bike, he sat gently on the seat, and leaned his full weight on the tire. He bounced and pedaled, traveled slowly down the road. The going would be tough, not smooth. Their solution was decent, but not exactly stable. It was hard to maneuver, even harder to steer, but it was manageable. Jeremy thought it would hold.

"Okay," he said. "I'll take this one, guys. Sam, you take mine. Seth, grab yours."

"No," Seth said, shaking his head in disagreement. "I'm the lightest. You said I was scrawny, remember?" He kicked the tire and shouldered his pack. "I'll take this one. It has to be me."

Jeremy couldn't find fault with his logic. "Okay. Let's go, but we're taking it slow. Let's try to be smart about this. You take the lead, Merlin. I'll watch from behind. And if you feel like something's breaking, jump off. Don't push it. I'll take anything we can get out of this. Four or five miles is better than none, and anything is better and faster than walking."

Seth nodded determinately, and wordlessly swung his leg over the seat. Before long, his face was streaming with sweat, but he never voiced a complaint. Not once. Their pace was excruciating; the setting sun boiled. But Jeremy considered each mile a small victory.

When they finally reached Odessa city limits, they hid the bikes, and then poked around the town. A burnt-out convenience store yielded brochures of apartment rentals and local maps, which listed shopping centers in the immediate area. Seth wanted to visit the Walmart, of course, for he harbored an emotional soft spot for the place. And if it yielded nothing useful, Jeremy figured, the mall was only a short distance away.

Seth chattered away as they walked, talking of gardens and trees, and the various kinds of plants they would cultivate in San Diego. He spoke of the type of home they'd choose for themselves. "If you think about it," he said, "we could choose anything! A house so huge we could each have a wing! I hope it overlooks the ocean," he added wistfully. "And if it does, we could find an old pair of binoculars. We could watch the waves from our house on the hill, look out for dolphins or whales or something." Catching Sam's reproachful gaze, he quickly corrected himself. "I'm just saying, one day there could be dolphins, and if there are, we'll be the first to see them. Maybe we could supervise the sea, like it's a job, and tell everyone when it comes back to life."

Jeremy hated to disappoint him. "That's a lovely

dream, Seth, but it won't come true. Not in our lifetimes, at least."

"But why?"

"Pessimist alert," Sam muttered beneath her breath.

"Are you saying the oceans will be dead forever? Forever's a long time, Carp," Seth said.

"It's hard to say, Merlin. No one really knows. But when the oceans die, everything dies, and it takes a long time to recover. This happened once before, millions and millions of years ago. Scientists called it The Permian Extinction, while others refered to it as The Great Dying." Jeremy mopped his sweaty head with his sleeve. "And if this extinction is similar, recovery will take millions of years."

"Millions?" Seth was aghast as he chewed on that. "So you're saying everything is dead? How do you know? How can you be sure? If the ocean's as big as you say it is, how can everything be dead? Couldn't something be alive out there?"

"I suppose." They'd reached the entrance to the Walmart Superstore. "I suppose something could be alive, Merlin. My dad once said life always finds a way. It's possible that some species made a go of things, like a small kind of snail, or squid."

"Or jellyfish," Sam added with a frown.

"Or jellyfish. Amazing things happen after extinction level events. Other species emerge from the wreckage and thrive in the new environment. Creatures we couldn't imagine in our wildest dreams could emerge and make the new earth their home."

"But what will happen to us?" Seth asked, as he snatched a handful of oats from his pack.

"Humans might not make it this time. After The Permian Extinction destroyed almost all wildlife, crabs, lobsters, and small ground rodents evolved into larger species of reptiles, which eventually evolved into dinosaurs."

Seth's eyes danced at the images. "So you think there's gonna be dinosaurs?"

"Maybe. Who knows? No one can say for sure. But whatever emerges, it will take a long time. You won't be around to see what comes next."

Jeremy smiled as he nudged open the rusted double doors. Simple conversations were nice. Normal. It was pleasant to be peppered with questions like these, with things that didn't pertain to medicine or mortality. Seth was very special boy. Jeremy watched him step aside and hold the door for Sam, his movements echoing hers as he watched her. He was deeply committed to seeing this through. He'd shown grit and fortitude, loyalty, and allegiance. He would do anything for her survival, despite the cost.

As they entered the store, Jeremy let his mind wander. How deep was Seth's commitment to Sam? How much would he sacrifice? How far would he go? Would his sacrifices rival Susan's? Would they match the sacrifices his father had made? Commitment that complete and selfless was rare, for no one had sacrificed the things Liam had. And apart from Jeremy, no one likely ever would.

A man who was completely innocent, offered himself as a sacrifice for the good of others, including his enemies, and became the ransom of the world. It was a perfect act.

—Mahatma Gandhi

CHAPTER 21
10 Years Prior

MARCH 27TH, 2165
SEVIERVILLE, TENNESSEE
THE ARK

"Did you know about this Mom?"

Jeremy was furious. So furious, in fact, that he hadn't spoken to his father for the entire journey home. Shaking Susan's hand from his shoulder, he'd abandoned them both and walked alone, lumbering up the mountain, seeing red. He was the first to return to the cabin, and with fists clenched, threw open the door. Dirt and grass fell from his boots as he trudged straight into the living room. Olivia was busy, bent over the hearth, while Sam still slept in her bed. Olivia had clearly been busy. The rich scents of hand-ground coffee, maple oats, and freshly squeezed juice hinted at her industriousness. A bowl of fresh dewberries from the shrubs by the stream had been set beside four mugs and matching saucers. There was powdered cream in a crystal saucer, and a silver-handled spoon with which to ladle it. The scene felt wrong, the space too warm, the arrangement too polite and civilized. It was inconsistent with Jeremy's foul mood and with what he had witnessed that morning. Their family was in trouble. This felt like pretend.

His abruptness startled his mother. Her eyes flew open and dropped to his boots. "Forget something, Jeremy?" she asked with a frown.

Ignoring his boots, he repeated the question. "Mom, I asked you a question. I asked if you knew about this."

"About what?" Confusion knit her brow. "Tell me what's happened." She slowly crossed the room to stand in front of him. "Did you not find anything useful out there?"

Jeremy's hand trembled as he pulled it through his hair. "I'm not talking about that. I'm talking about Dad. Did you know about his Mother Theresa act?"

She flinched. Recognition flickered across her face. "Come sit down. Let me pour you a cup of coffee." She peered at the door, which he'd left wide open. "Where are Susan and your father?"

Jeremy's patience was running thin. He was angrier than he'd like to admit, yet an unwelcome weariness was beginning to take its place. His shoulders were suddenly heavy as stones, his boots too solid and dense on his feet. "Mom, just tell me the truth. Dad stopped taking his pills, didn't he?"

She bit her lip before answering, which made her appear to be spinning a lie. "It's not that simple, Jeremy. Sit down. You must be starving. You must be—"

"Jeremy." Susan strode into the room, angrily, Liam quietly in tow. "You're acting like a spoiled child. Let's discuss this together, as a family."

Rubbing his eyes, Jeremy sank to the divan. He didn't have the energy for this. Not now. They'd been out all night, and had returned with little to show for their efforts. Not to mention the two men his father had killed. I wonder if that will be discussed at family time. He massaged his brow, and then met his father's gaze, lifting his hands in resignation. "I'm out of fight, Dad. I've got nothing left. I've seen too much for one evening, I think. But I need to understand this decision you've made."

His father slipped out of his boots wordlessly then crossed the room and perched on the divan. Without a word, he poured himself a cup of coffee, ladled powdered cream with the dainty little spoon, and when he met Jeremy's gaze, it was difficult to breathe. Liam was clearly out of sorts. Confusion etched fine lines around his mouth, which was odd; Liam was rarely confused about anything. He was a self-possessed man of action, a caretaker who always knew what to do. But this situation had him flummoxed. He was flying by the seat of his pants, so to speak, a behavior that set Jeremy off balance. Liam had no idea what he was doing, and improvising wasn't his strong suit. He was facing a situation he hadn't planned for, and the lack of forethought was tearing him apart.

The full-bodied aroma of coffee did little to clear the fog from Jeremy's head. Sitting forward, he fixed his gaze on his father. "Dad, what you're doing isn't necessary. Last night, if I recall, inside this very room, you said we could figure this out as a family. We agreed to find a solution, together, but we never agreed on this."

Liam was never one to beat around the proverbial bush. "Son, we don't have enough insulin."

"Well, isn't that the news of the day? When did you figure that out?" Jeremy shook his head. "Isn't that what we've been saying for weeks?"

Liam held up a hand. "There isn't enough for both Sam and I. So what do we do about that?" He slurped from his mug, a faraway look on his face. It was as if he pondered his own question. "Think about the people out there," he said slowly, "the foragers, pillagers, criminals, and gangs. When people have next to nothing, Jeremy, they conserve what little they have. It's called rationing. It's the smart thing to do. All I'm doing is rationing our supplies. I'll resume my dosage once we find more pills."

"We're not talking about bags of rice, here, Dad. We're talking about something you need to survive. If you don't take the pills, you'll die."

"Who said I've stopped taking pills? I'd be dead or in a coma in a matter of days. All I've done is decrease my dosage, Jeremy. You're making too much of this."

Jeremy poured coffee with hands that trembled. "Right. I'm making too much of this. Great. So instead of dying in a matter of days, you'll be dead in a matter of months. Wonderful. Because a matter of months is so much better. Thank you for considering our feelings on this." He dropped his head to the cushions, his eyes slipping closed, despite his anger. "This is absolute madness," he murmured to himself. "One family member dying in place of another. How did we end up here?"

"What's the alternative, son? All we can do is accept what is. Jeremy, be honest with yourself, and with me. What would you do if you were in my position? You would do the same thing, and you know it. To deny that truth is to lie to yourself. Admit what you know to be true."

Jeremy didn't have a response for that. Well, to be fair, he did, but he was too damned stubborn to say the words aloud. If he were in Liam's shoes, he would do the same thing. Any parent would. It was a natural-born instinct, an impulse so strong it overpowered logic and reason. Ignoring the question, Jeremy asked a different one. "How long can you survive on a smaller dose? What will it do to you? Long-term, I mean?"

Olivia gripped her husband's thigh desperately. Jeremy had forgotten she was there. Tears had pooled and spilled down her cheeks, and he suddenly felt like an ass.

He hadn't considered her feelings in all of this. Smiling at her husband, she fondly squeezed his leg. "Let's focus on the positives, shall we? We've diagnosed Samantha. That's half the battle. And now that we have, we can put our heads together. We can develop a plan. And as flimsy as our plan may sound to us," she added, "at least we have one, which is better than nothing. Anything is better than not knowing."

Susan picked up the thread of her enthusiasm. "I, for one, will never stop foraging. Remember what we said last night. There are hundreds of hospitals in this state alone, hundreds of clinics and urgent care facilities. Let's put together an exploration schedule. Let's log where we go to avoid retracing our steps." She peered around the room and brought her mug to her lips. "What else is there to do but try? We can't sit around here feeling sorry for ourselves. Let's get out there. Let's solve this problem."

Jeremy was grateful for Susan in that moment. It was time to face facts. She was right. It was time to accept what was, and then act upon it with courage. Liam would do what he wanted to do, despite Jeremy's or anyone else's objections. He'd convinced himself it was the right thing to do, and Olivia had chosen to back his decision. She must have come to terms with his logic—or realized there was little she could do to change it. The only way to make him stop was to find a long-term solution. "Okay," he acquiesced. "I guess I understand. But like Susan said; let's solve this problem. We won't give up. We'll never stop looking. Not until we find a viable solution. I'll make you a commitment right now, Dad, if you make a commitment to me in return. Promise you'll never take less than half a dose. You can cut it to half, but never less than that. Can you commit to that? That's what I'm asking."

Liam nodded. "Consider it done."

"Okay."

An uncomfortably silence followed his words. Liam dropped his gaze to his hands guiltily.

"Oh for God's sake, Dad. What aren't you saying? Can we please air out this family's laundry right now?"

Liam pulled a bottle of pills from his pocket. "There's one more thing I should tell you." He rattled the bottle then cupped it in his palm. "Over the past few years, the pills have changed. I've been forced to slowly increase my dosage." He took a breath to steady himself. "You have to understand: though diabetics are insulin dependent, insulin doesn't behave like a drug. The body doesn't acclimate to a specific dosage, and then demand a higher one to achieve the same effect. It just doesn't work like that. So the only explanation for what I've experienced is that the pills have weakened over time. A dose that was effective for me three years ago, is no longer effective for me now."

Jeremy swallowed. "So you're saying half a dose isn't really half a dose anymore."

"I'm saying that taking what amounts to half a dose still won't leave enough for Sam."

Susan had gone stiff at Jeremy's side. Her response was clipped and businesslike. "This just confirms what I said before. We need to be out there every week—every night, if that's what it takes." She wagged a finger at all of them. "I won't lose my daughter to this. I'll travel all the way to New York City, if I have to, or to the smelly Florida Keys. I don't care where we go."

Jeremy slid closer to rub her back. She was practically hyperventilating. A small cry escaped her lips as she leaned down over her knees. "This wasn't supposed to happen," she murmured. "This was our unlikely paradise. I'll never forget the first time I saw it. We had everything we needed inside this house, enough for us, and enough for Sam."

"We still have everything we need," Jeremy said, smoothing her hair and rubbing her back. "We'll figure it out. There must be a way."

She lifted her head, her cheeks smeared with tears.

"You're not listening to what he just said. You missed the point he was making. If what he said is true, the pills will eventually become useless to Sam—maybe not now, but one day they will. It doesn't matter how many we find if what we find doesn't work anymore. And I'm worried about foraging, too. Foraging will be our new way of life, but what happens when it's just you and me? We can't leave Sam alone in the cabin while we venture out into the world. I'll be damned if I take her out there. And it isn't safe to go out alone, particularly after what happened last night."

"What happened last night?" Olivia asked.

Liam and Jeremy exchanged worried glances before an inappropriate laugh bubbled from Jeremy's lips. He had no idea where it had come from, or why. Nothing about what had happened was funny. Perhaps he was just overtired, he thought, or stressed by these new revelations. Or maybe he'd finally lost his mind. Whatever the case, he suddenly couldn't hold back. He barked a laugh, which soon gained momentum. Beside him, Susan's shoulders began to shake. Rolling to her side, she lost all control. Liam and Jeremy soon followed, and while hearing Liam laugh felt good, it also made composure that much harder to regain.

"Mom," Jeremy choked, "I'm sorry about this. We really shouldn't be laughing. Nothing about what happened is funny."

"Oh," Susan said, pointing at her father-in-law. "But it is. It's the funniest joke I've heard in years. Billy the Kidd over there shot two criminals in the head last night."

Olivia sucked in a breath. "He did what?" She peered at her husband in awe. "You killed someone last night?"

"No. Not someone," he replied. "Someones." The corners of his smile suddenly bled to a frown when he saw the incredulous expression on her face. "I'm sorry, Liv. It isn't funny."

"No. It isn't. I fail to see the humor in this."

"I don't think we actually find it funny," he said. "I just think we're coming down from an emotional high. It's the incredulity of it all—the absurdity that our lives have suddenly become. The truth, simply put, is that it's harsh out there. You haven't been out there for quite some time. Things have changed, Liv. The tone has changed. Many more people have died and starved. And those who haven't are vicious and heartless. Savagery is the only way to survive."

"People are desperate, Mom," Jeremy added. "It's the aftermath of the apocalypse, and everyone is searching for the same exact things. Susan is right. We can't forage alone."

Liam pulled his wife into his arms. "I'm sorry, honey. We're punch-drunk here. What I did isn't funny, but it was something I had to do, and if I'm being honest with you, I'd do it again. We're not rejoicing in the act of killing. Trust me. It's nothing like that. It was more of a rude awakening. Last night we discovered the truth about things—about how things are for other people, I mean. The bottom line is this: we have to protect ourselves. Those men would have killed us if I hadn't killed them first. They were toying with us. They would have taken our packs in an instant, if I'd let them, and left us for dead without a shred of remorse. And if you think about it," he said with a shrug, "what they did makes perfect sense— mathematically speaking. The fewer people who are left in this world, the longer the supplies will last for those who remain. It's the basic principle of conservation. Those who have persevered will find bounty and abundance, but only if they act savagely against others."

He pulled the new bottles of pills from his pack, and Olivia's eyes lit up. "So you did find something. It wasn't a total loss."

"We did," Jeremy said, "But don't get too excited. We had to visit three different facilities to find those pills.

It took too much time. Our plan sucks. We have to think bigger and better."

Peering over the rim of her mug, Olivia answered casually. "What if we take a different tack? What you did last night, if you boil it down, was search for a needle in a haystack. Why don't we work smarter instead of harder?"

"Explain."

"Go back to the hospital tonight," she suggested. "Well, maybe not tonight. The three of you look exhausted. But maybe tomorrow night, or the night after that. But this time, look for something else. Try to locate the old patient records."

"Why would we do that?" Susan asked.

"Because if we can create a list of diabetic people, we can focus our foraging on them. We can do it better, smarter. Get a list of diabetic patients. Get names, addresses, and ages, if you can."

A slow smile dawned across Liam's face. "You're a genius, Liv. That's brilliant."

"It's not brilliant, Liam, but I do think it's better. But it brings up other important considerations. We need to ask ourselves what kind of people we want to be. Who are we? How do we want to act?"

"I'm not sure I follow, Liv," Susan said.

Jeremy did. He knew exactly what she meant. Setting down his mug, he set his palms to his knees. "She's saying that this is a different kind of plan. This is scavenging on a completely different level. When we steal from hospitals and urgent care centers, we're taking medications that would have otherwise spoiled. If we visit people's homes, we're stealing from them." He rolled his neck, which was stiff and sore. "What we're doing right now isn't hurting anyone." Peering at his father, he winked. "Well, what Susan and I are doing isn't hurting anyone. This, of course, would be totally different."

"I'm not comfortable with this," Susan said, shaking her head. "Think of it in a personal terms. What if someone came here, to our cabin, intent on taking what's ours? What are we saying? That we plan to do that? That we're comfortable stealing from the hands of other people? That we plan to break into their homes by force? Like carry-a-gun-and-steal things by force?"

"No," said Liam. "I don't like that, either. I agree with you. We would never do that. But logically speaking, many of those patients are probably dead. Diabetics need insulin, yes, but they also need water and food, which we can all agree are in higher demand. It's possible—probable, even—that many of the people on this would-be list have already died from thirst or famine, or even flu for that matter. We just don't know. For all we know, there could be bottles of insulin pills wasting away inside hundreds of empty houses, never to be found or consumed by anyone. If we tweak this idea just a bit, it's brilliant."

"Okay," Jeremy said. "Let's compromise, then. We do it Mom's way. We compile a list of diabetics and visit their homes, but we only take from the dead. We do this humanely. We do it with respect. We only take from empty homes." He glanced at each solemn face. "Do we agree?"

The other three nodded and Jeremy felt sudden relief. He let his head fall to the cushions, his adrenaline waning, leaving him exhausted. He felt hollow inside. And though the topic of conversation was unsettling at best, it felt good to have developed a worthier plan.

"Hi, sugar," Susan cooed, as Jeremy's daughter stepped into the room. She was standing barefoot in a small square of light, a blanket clutched beneath one arm, its edges trailing behind her like a bridal train. The sun reflected from her pale smooth hair, and added sparkle to her soft blue eyes. She was innocent and beautiful, so much like Susan. It broke Jeremy's heart to look upon her. He offered her a hug, but of course she refused, moving instinctively to her grandfather's side. She padded to his chair and he lifted her up. She molded herself to his chest.

Children are instinctual creatures, Jeremy thought. Sam had always been drawn to her grandfather. Theirs was a special connection. It was something that transcended biology. Perhaps she sensed his desperate love, or his willingness to sacrifice anything for her. As she curled her arm around his neck, Jeremy moved his gaze to his father. Liam had shown a different side of himself tonight. He'd taught everyone a different lesson. Dear God, Jeremy thought, in awe of the man. Will he never run out of special wisdom to share? Liam had always touted the importance of planning, but last night he demonstrated the importance of strength, of protecting the ones you love at any cost. He'd acted bravely, and without hesitation.

As Jeremy stared at his father and child, he vowed to protect them with the same tenacity Liam had shown last night. To keep Sam alive, he would do anything. He'd go to the ends of the earth, and back again.

Well, he thought smiling, maybe not that far, but certainly to the ends of the country. But it would never come to that, now, would it?

Water is fluid, soft, and yielding. But water will wear away rock, which is rigid and cannot yield. As a rule, whatever is fluid, soft, and yielding will overcome whatever is rigid and hard. This is another paradox: what is soft is strong.

- Lao-Tzu (600 B.C.)

CHAPTER 22
Present Day

NOVEMBER 27TH, 2176
BOWIE, ARIZONA
512 MILES TO SAN DIEGO

When they crossed New Mexico's southern border, they followed I-20 to the long-awaited I-10, pedaling fast through the charming yet barren cities of Luna, Las Cruces and Deming. Jeremy loved the flat expanse of the desert, which was cupped in the palm of majestic mountains, visible in every direction. The landscape was dramatically different than Tennessee. It was brown instead of green, sparse instead of lush, yet uniquely beautiful in its own right. The air was clear and dry. The sky overhead was immense and blue, so big it was strangely humbling. Land sprawled as far as the eye could see, which imparted to Jeremy a sense of security he hadn't experienced in months. Nothing could surprise them out here. Nothing hid. Nothing could spring from behind a large elm, or hide behind the crest of a hill. Visibility was absolute.

But it was hot.

Heat was the trade off. The southwestern heat was punishing and thick, and wafted from the pavement in shimmering waves. It sapped moisture from his eyes and burned his throat. But it was a dry heat, right? Bah! Right! Nuts to that. Hot was hot. Melting was melting. Though thankfully dry heat had its advantages. The aridity wicked sweat from their shirts and cooled their backs. The gentle breeze—when it actually blew—was a comfortable fan of air across their faces.

Sam and Seth had never seen the desert, and Jeremy found himself enjoying their reactions as much as he enjoyed the landscape. They oohed and awed at the peculiar plants, at the unique colors of the sand and sunsets. They pointed at spikey yucca, with strange center stalks pointing straight toward the sky, their tips crowned in creamy white flowers. Seth likened smaller cacti to hunched porcupines, while Sam gushed at their delicate fuchsia flowers. There were regal fields of Joshua trees, which reached for the heavens with gnarled arms. Sunset quickly become their favorite time of day. The sunsets in the east, at the tops of the Smokey Mountains, had always been beautiful and breathtaking, but were incomparable to the sunsets in the west, particularly when clouds carpeted the sky. The sun would dip below the horizon, and shimmer across the desert's velvety sands. It would alight the clouds with fire, painting the sky a rich pallet of oranges and reds, which would eventually fade to pinks and purples, culminating in a sweeping amaranthine field. Sometimes the little company would choose those moments to stop and rest and enjoy the view, and drink small sips of water. They would sit and limber sore muscles at the side of the road, content to exist in this peaceful place.

Once, Jeremy recalled, they'd even tried to sleep beside that lush landscape, beneath an overhead blanket of gleaming stars. The memory brought a smile to his lips.

"Why coop ourselves up in some rotten old house?" Sam had said as she marveled at the setting sun. "We haven't seen anyone else for weeks. If we exit the freeway, we'll just waste time. Why don't we camp out here? No one is crossing these roads, but us. No one has enough water to make the trip. And if we stay out here and sleep by the road, we can wake up early, save ourselves an hour, start from the same place we stopped. Think about how much time we would save."

That first night's attempt was an utter failure. Truth is rarely as beautiful as fantasy. They'd circled their pallets, built a fire in the center, eaten a hearty meal of oats and lentils. Jeremy had passed around crumbling tablets of Vitamin C, while Sam read pages from The Deathly Hallows. They enjoyed the sounds of the gusting winds, which whispered their secrets across the flat sands—until the coyotes appeared, of course. That first low howl was all it took. Seth leapt from his blankets and scampered to Sam. She closed the book, held him tight, and shivered.

"What the hell was that?" Seth whispered, eyes wide.

"Language," Sam admonished him lightly.

"Coyotes," Jeremy muttered, awestruck by the sound. "It's the sound of howling coyotes. I'll be damned."

It was amazing to discover coyotes living here—amazing that they still lived at all, he supposed. It had been so long since they'd encountered wildlife that fear battled with their reverence and awe. They had encountered no dogs or cats along this journey, no squirrels, or chipmunks, or rats, or field mice. But to Jeremy the coyotes made sense. Desert animals were accustomed to this environment, having acclimated to it a long time ago. They were conditioned by thousands of years of evolution. Arid lands were a home to them. Their world, he supposed, was the least bit changed by the death and starvation of the oceans.

Though Jeremy would have loved to stay and catch a glimpse of just one coyote, the children would have none of it. They scampered about to pack their belongings, shoved blankets and books into their packs with haste, and food and water into their panniers. In a matter of moments, they'd packed the entire camp, while Jeremy struggled to stifle his laughter.

"Okay," he'd agreed as he stretched out his legs. "I suppose we'll have to find a house. Probably safer that way, anyway. I mean, Coyotes are one thing, but what about snakes? Don't snakes and tarantulas hunt at night? And I suppose there'd be scorpions too, wouldn't there?"

Sam had yelped while groping for her flashlight, while Seth tap-danced in the middle of the road. The memory was precious. Jeremy had tucked it away. And yes, he thought, remembering, New Mexico was beautiful. He'd enjoyed every moment and the memories they'd made. But now that they'd reached the barren lands of Arizona, things were starting to unravel again.

They'd spent more time in Odessa than Jeremy cared to admit. Finding a solution to their problem hadn't been easy. The local Walmart hadn't borne fruit. There had been no bicycles or bicycle parts, no inner tubes, tires, or oil for the chains. The store was nothing but a burned out shell. Someone had erected three tents in its center, but Jeremy hadn't lingered to find out why. The Sears, down the road, hadn't helped much either, and The Sports Authority had proved much the same. Having failed at several other stores after that, Jeremy finally agreed to check the small green one. It was a mom-and-pop shop, a specialty store, ugly green with pink framing. From outside its weathered doors, it hadn't looked promising, but Sam had been close to tears by then, so Jeremy agreed to check it out. It had been their fifth day in that ruined little town, and the stress of their predicament had begun to affect her. She had started to wilt like a dying flower, while

Jeremy secretly panicked inside. He was barely able to conceal his fears. He was short of temper, tense, and irritable. His movements were jerky and fitful, and a permanent frown pulled the corners of his mouth. Seth tried his best to bolster Sam's withered spirits, but even he had succumbed to repeated disappointments.

They had entered the store and picked through the rubble: helmets, empty water bottles, piles of multi-colored biking shorts. Apart from a few panniers, which they took, they found little to help their situation. There didn't seem to be a single tire in that store, and it was only after they nearly gave up that Jeremy remembered his mother's sage advice.

Stop looking for a needle in a haystack, she whispered. Work smarter, Jeremy, not harder.

With sudden hope, he pushed himself to his feet and rifled through piles of old mail and unopened bills, behind the front counter of the store. He was looking for ledgers or accounting journals. How crazy it was, he remembered thinking, that the owner hadn't used computers to manage such things, but the lack of technology, in the end, was a blessing. Triumphant, he emerged from behind the counter.

Sam had been less than optimistic about his discovery. "What's so great about that?" she complained. "A pile of mail and old papers? Big whoop." She tossed a water bottle to the floor with disdain. "Is there a map to a bike warehouse in that stack? 'Cause that's the only thing that would get me excited."

"Nope. It's better than that," Jeremy countered. "It's the address to the shop-owner's house. You remember what grandma used to say, don't you? Stop looking in obvious places. This guy owned a bike shop, didn't he?" When Sam shrugged her shoulders, Jeremy lifted a hand. "Come on. Hear me out. This is going somewhere. All we need to do is find the shop-owner's house. There's bound to be all kinds of stuff over there, because if the man sold bikes, he owned bikes, too. Doesn't that just make sense?"

"I suppose." Muttering to herself, she pushed herself to her feet and followed him soberly to the man's modest home. By then, her tire had flattened completely, the grasses and weeds having lost their buoyancy. Jeremy feared irreparable damage to the rim, but thankfully, their efforts were handsomely rewarded. The house, when they reached it, was vacant of course, but replete with bicycles and bicycle parts.

The rim of Sam's bike, as Jeremy had feared, had been destroyed and bent beyond repair. And though he'd tried to fit a new tire to the rim, he'd given up quickly amid a torrent of cursing. It was Seth who pointed to the bike-owner's car, behind which two new bikes were wedged. A rack on the east-facing wall of the garage housed boxes of tires and plump inner tubes, and Jeremy replaced old items with new. As Seth had suggested just days before, they fashioned backwards tire-necklaces and wore them like sombrero hats.

Framed photos lined the mantel of the man's fireplace. Their benefactor, it seemed, had been a father and a husband, and Jeremy thanked him for his contributions. They spent a night beneath the man's roof, and awakened the next morning to set out.

After Odessa, they followed a rigorous schedule. They'd lost a week and were crumbling under the pressure. The ominous rattle of their last bottle of pills offered Jeremy little to no comfort. Why had he been so stupid? He should have experimented with the pills when he'd had more disks. It had been a long time since Sam had taken them. It was difficult to say how effective they would be. How many would it take to lower her sugars? How many would be required in an emergency situation? He scolded himself. He'd never know now. He should have done something when the conditions weren't extreme. With a sigh, he pushed the thought aside. At this point, 'should' and 'would' were ridiculous concepts to ponder. Better to strategize about what would come next.

New Mexico had been a welcome respite. The beauty and stillness of its peaceful landscapes had done wonders to enliven their spirits, but the rigors of Arizona were upon them now: the unforgiving heat, the ever-increasing elevation. That, he thought grimly, and their dwindling supply of water.

Water had become a pressing need. Since Fort Worth, they'd encountered no rain, and though they'd foraged a few bottles, their supply was dwindling. Jeremy would have to start rationing soon. But how could water be safely rationed when those who drank it biked fifty miles a day? The two ideas were diametrically opposed. The Arizona sun was hot and punishing. A tight ration schedule could quickly result in dehydration. It was a riddle without an answer, and it plagued him constantly.

The southwestern states had battled water rights for years. For back then, the Colorado River had been the most metro-dependent river in America, and when the oceans soured and society began to crumble, people horded as much as they could find. Water became the currency of the west. It was the main reason for the migration of its people. Water refugees became the norm back then. Over nothing more than a few of bottles of Evian, convenience stores were held at gunpoint. While people on the east coast starved, people in the west died of dehydration. Nothing could survive this cruel heat without water.

"Dad," Sam said, "you promised,"

"Promised what?" They'd finally found a place to hunker down for the night, an adobe-style ranch, just a mile from Interstate 10. They had just eaten their last can of soup, and Jeremy was trying not to dwell on water. "I'm sorry, Sam. Promised what?"

She sighed. "You promised you'd be honest with me. You promised you wouldn't keep secrets from me anymore."

Jeremy set down his bowl, cursing inwardly. Jeez. Was he that transparent?

"I didn't realize I was hiding anything."

"Oh please. I can read you like a book. You've got that funny look on your face again, and that crease you get in your forehead. And you get tiny crinkles around your eyes and mouth."

"I get crinkles and creases because I'm an old man."

She tightened her lips to avoid grinning. She wouldn't allow him to deflect with poor humor. "Oh yeah. You're old. No one's denying that." Stretching out flat on her stomach, she peered up at him. "So let's have it, old man. What's the problem now? What's got your panties in a bunch?"

He frowned. "Oh, I don't know. Let's see. Maybe it's the meter on your belly running low, or the week we lost in Odessa. Or maybe it's the heat or the food in our packs that seems to be drying out more and more each day. I don't know, Sam. Take your pick." Her mouth twitched and he instantly regretted his words. "I'm sorry, guys. I'll tell you the truth. I'm worried about water right now. If you haven't noticed, it's damn hot out there, and we haven't found water since Odessa."

Sam spooned a ball of rice into her mouth. "Okay, so what's our plan? You always seem to have one. In the infinite wisdom of Jeremy Colt, how do we find an elusive underground spring? How do we find that magic well? That vault of water bottles, hidden in a bank?"

Jeremy flinched. Did she see him like that? As someone who could always solve her problems? Astonished and speechless, he stared at her. She met his unwavering gaze. Dear God! She actually thought he had answers. The revelation was both humbling and frightening, and for a moment, he fought back a smirk. She had just let her teenage-mask slip. Only a bit, perhaps, but enough to show the truth. Though she hadn't meant to, she'd confessed her dependency. She trusted him, he realized with a start. She thought he actually knew what he was doing. Dear God, how he hated to rain on that parade.

"I don't think we'll find a hidden spring here, Sam. You've been reading too many Harry Potter books."

"Okay, so what then? What do we do?" This from Seth who had curled his body closer to Sam's.

Jeremy popped a rice ball into his mouth, and tried to make light of a crappy situation. "We start rationing. That's what." The two of them were simultaneously aghast. "Just a little bit, guys. It won't be so bad. And there are a few more things we can do, as well. We can travel at night, when it's cooler outside. I, for one, am sick of the sun. It's killing my perfect complexion."

Neither one of them cracked a smile. "Makes sense," Sam said, "But the nights are still hot. We'll still have to drink."

"I know. That's what worries me the most. We'll have to slow our pace to search for water."

"We can't." She lifted the corner of her shirt for effect. "I'm at forty-three percent. We're running out of time." Turning away from him, she scoffed. "Though you still haven't told me what this journey is all about. What's this oasis you're taking us to? A rotten ocean and a deserted old town? What's in San Diego? A store full of hundreds of boxes of disks?"

"Yeah," Jeremy replied quietly. "Kind of. That's about the sum of it, Sam." He caught her gaze and held it fast."

She instantly brightened and rose to her knees. "Really? Okay. Then let's follow your plan: sleep during the day, travel at night. Doesn't sound complicated to me."

He spread his hands in supplication. "That's all I've got, unless you've got something better. But traveling at night won't be easy, guys. Sleeping during the day is a hard thing to do. Our bodies won't want to do that. While the idea sounds easy, the execution will be tough. I know from experience, Sam. Your grandfather and I used to forage at night, when the human body is trying to sleep. We'll be pushing ourselves while wanting to rest."

Seth rolled to his ankles. "But we'll be in San Diego in just a couple of weeks. Can't we suck it up and just get there?"

"Suck it up?" Jeremy suppressed a smile.

"Yeah. I mean we've made it this far. Just a little farther to go. Let's suck it up, and get there already. If we need to bike when we're tired, let's do it."

In that moment Jeremy couldn't have loved Seth more. He let his smile stretch wide across his face. "Okay. Then let's start sucking it up right now."

"Right now?" Sam frowned. "But we just got here, and we've been riding all day. You want us to ride all night, too?"

"Nope. But we need to do something to shift our circadian rhythms. That means forcing ourselves to stay awake tonight."

Seth groaned, lowering his head to the floor. "Okay," he muttered. "But how do we do that? 'Cause I'm already really tired."

Sam plucked the idea from Jeremy's head. "By staying active. That's how. By finding something important to do. If we're short on water, we forage for water. We take all night, if we have to."

So they did. They finished their meal and stretched their tired muscles, and fighting their bodies' instincts to sleep, they laced up their boots and stepped outside. It was as good a plan as any, Jeremy thought. At least it was different, a welcome change of pace.

The night air was crisp and clean, and though tired, they tried to make the best of things. They walked and talked about water and fish, and explored all manner of homes. The world was full of tiny treasures, and like pirates, they claimed them for themselves. They were cautious, though not overly so. Jeremy didn't think many Arizonians still inhabited this place, for hunkering down in the middle of the desert wasn't a good idea. Arizona was nothing but an afterthought now, a stopover at best, a blip on the map. Animals and insects had reclaimed this land.

With the encroaching dawn, they returned to the house, blacked out the windows and made up their pallets. Their efforts had been handsomely rewarded. They'd found six bottles of water and a box of stale crackers. Seth had jettisoned his navy T-shirt, trading it for a lighter one that didn't smell as bad, and Sam found a pair of hiking boots that didn't pinch her toes.

The Arizona days were as quiet as the nights, yet sleep teased and eluded Jeremy. He tried his best to match Seth's rhythmic breathing, but his eyes kept snagging on a slice of bright sun, peeking through a gap in the curtains. Shifting quietly, he stared at the ceiling fan above. Dust had gathered along its blades, and like the lace hemming of an elegant dress, an impressive spider web connected each plank. He focused on the delicate gossamer threading, was hypnotized by its quivering movements in the air. What moved the web? The breath from their lungs? Air that seeped through cracks in the house?

Breath from their lungs would find those blades. Molecules would strike other molecules, he mused, which would in turn strike other molecules. It was chaos theory, something from Liam's vast curriculum. It was the theory of the butterfly effect. It was the supposition that even the smallest change had far-reaching effects on future consequences. So what effect was Jeremy causing now? What decision had he made recently that would irrevocably alter their course? What significant breath had he exhaled? What word had he uttered that would change their future?

It was at once a comforting and debilitating thought, and he pondered it as sleep claimed him. His dreams were psychedelic and bright. It was a strange stream of unconsciousness, born of extreme exhaustion, worry, and fear. In the first dream, he was a sailor aboard a ship, surrounded by cresting black waves. The sun pierced the clouds and glittered across the water, as he stumbled about the decking like a drunkard. He lifted bottle after bottle of water to his parched lips, only to taste brine and the salt of the sea. The next dream brought him to the solitude of the desert, where he flew over the mountains on the wings of a hawk, searching for prey but finding none. He was a furry brown spider burrowing into cool sand, only to boil with the rising sun. He was a man once again, standing beneath seething sky. The clouds were smoky black and choked him. He found himself sputtering and fighting for air.

Throwing back his blanket, he shot to his feet, and spinning around, tried to adjust to his surroundings.

Sam was already awake. "What's wrong?"

Seth rubbed his eyes beside her. He raised his face and squinted into the dark. "What?" he asked, his voice hoarse. "What is it?

"Get your things," Jeremy whispered. "I smell smoke."

"You must do the thing you think you cannot do."

—Eleanor Roosevelt

CHAPTER 23
Present Day

NOVEMBER 27TH, 2176
BOWIE, ARIZONA
512 MILES TO SAN DIEGO

"I don't see fire," Sam said, raising her hand to her nose. She whirled around and stared into the bright sun. "I smell smoke, but I don't see fire. Where's all this smoke coming from?"

"Over there." Jeremy pointed. "It's coming from the south. We have to get out of here. Now."

"But how do you know where it's coming from?" Seth complained. "And if we can't see the fire yet, why are we worried about it?"

"Because fire moves fast. It follows the wind. We need to get past it before it traps us on this side of Arizona."

Seth rubbed his eyes. "But I still want to sleep. We haven't slept in almost two days."

"I know, Merlin. We will. We'll start our plan tonight. I promise. But for now, show me what it means to suck it up. That's what you said last night, didn't you? If we don't get past this fire right away, it could end up permanently blocking our path."

After donning their gear in haste, they started pedaling back toward I-10, the smoke becoming thicker as they approached the exit.

"How does something like this happen?" Seth asked, calling out the words over his shoulder as he pedaled. "How does a fire start all by itself? I haven't seen people lately. Who started it?"

"Not who started it, Seth. What. It was probably a storm—lightening, or something. And since there aren't firemen anymore, there's no one around to put it out. This thing will rage on until it burns itself out, or runs out of fuel, whichever happens first."

"What fuel?" Sam asked, skidding on a patch of scattered sand. "What's in the desert, anyway, other than sand?"

Jeremy pulled in front of her bike, blinking his eyes against the gritty soot. "What fuel, you ask? What fuel? What about all those dry grasses and roots? That stuff we crammed inside your tire? That's the only kind of fuel this fire needs to burn. It's a forest fire, Sam. It feeds on nature."

Seth frowned, not buying it. "But there isn't a forest out there."

"Then you can call it a wildfire or brushfire, if you like. It's a fire. And it's big. That's all we need to know."

When they pulled onto the freeway proper, Jeremy felt a scratching in the back of his throat. He could only see a short distance in front of them, two or three miles at the most. Everything beyond that point was obscured. I-10 gently curved around Doz Cabezas Mountains, and from here, Jeremy could see thick clouds of smoke, billowing into the clear, blue sky. He heard Sam cough behind his back. Time to move.

"Pedal faster guys. I think it's just beyond the curve of that mountain."

"Dad," Sam choked. "If it's just beyond the curve of that mountain, why the hell are we heading that way? Shouldn't we choose a different path?"

He answered by leaning his weight onto his pedals, shooting forward, and beckoning her to follow. There was no other path, and they couldn't turn back. There was nowhere else for them to go.

The closer they came to the edge of the mountain, the thicker and murkier the air became. It was a swirling gray that eclipsed the sun, shrouding them in soot, making it difficult to breath. This close to the blaze, soot and ash were the only things visible to them, but it was the parts they couldn't see that frightened them most: the roaring in the distance, the ever-increasing heat.

"Stop," Jeremy gasped, pulling his bike up short. "Guys, slow down. I can't breath."

The children stopped, almost gratefully. As they heaved, coughed, and wiped their eyes, the flames roared in the distance like dragons. Kicking down his stand, Jeremy rummaged through his pack, and stripping off his shirt, began to rip it into shreds. He uncapped the water he had pulled from his pack.

"Dad, what are you doing?" Sam asked warily.

Ignoring her, he doused the pieces of cloth in water, distributed them, and tied one to his face. "Like this," he pointed out, his voice muffled. "Tie it around your nose and mouth."

"But Dad, we can't. That water is for drinking."

He lifted the cloth from his face to speak. "No one's drinking anything if we suffocate. Once we get around that mountain, the air's gonna get really bad. I know this water is for drinking, Sam, but we need clean air just as much." He dropped the cloth into place on his face. "Now follow me. Do as I say. Tie that cloth around your face."

"I'm scared," Seth said.

"Yeah, Merlin, me too. But we have no choice, so

we'll have to be strong."

Turning from their terrified faces, he bent to retrieve his pack, for if he waited much longer, he'd lose his nerve. Surging forward like a bat out of hell, he pedaled toward heat and smoke and fire, and prayed they'd find a clear path.

With the curve of the mountain just ahead, he swerved, shielding his eyes from the searing heat. From here, he could see massive plumes of smoke ahead. Hopefully the flames were contained to one side. If the fire raged on one side of the road, he could find a clear path on the other. He couldn't let this thing trap them in Arizona. It could rage for days. They hadn't the time. Nor was there another convenient path to San Diego. They'd committed to this road. Doubling back wasn't an option. It would cost them hundreds of miles, possibly more, which wasn't acceptable to Jeremy. He'd taken so many stupid risks on this journey. What if he failed them at the last state line?

Just as his handlebars were beginning to singe his hands, he rounded the corner and confronted the blaze. To his dismay, it surged up both sides of the mountain, trapping the street in between. Smoke blocked his view in every direction, while embers jumped and danced in the air. Something exploded to his right. Sam screamed.

"Dad, we're heading right for it," she gasped, leaning over, coughing, and swerving dangerously. "We'll never get through this. If we try, we'll die."

He slapped at chunks of debris that were flying through the air. Swirling pieces feathered into his hair. "We have no choice. We have to try. There isn't another way to San Diego, Sam. We've committed to this. We have to see it through. Do you know how many miles off course that would take us?" He pointed to an ember, burning a hole through her shirt. "Ride," he growled as he slapped it off of her. "Ride. Fast. Push yourself. Get it done. We have no choice but to get ourselves through it."

The three of them sped beneath a dragon that roared, its breath exploding in a torrent of flames. With a whoosh, Jeremy heard the sounds of Joshua trees, bursting into flames, while a canopy of glittering sparks rained upon their heads. He could barely see twenty feet in front of his face, and the air quality was deteriorating rapidly, as much from the heat as from the ash. Peering over his shoulder, he saw Sam, but not Seth. Slowing, he watched for Seth's bike to reappear, and knew a moment of panic when it finally did. An ember had ignited a small patch of his hair, which Jeremy doused with water from his pack.

"Seth," he screamed. "Move faster!"

He pushed the back of Seth's bike angrily, propelling the boy into motion. The sound of the fire was deafening in his hears, while the smoke stole the breath from his lungs. It was as if they had landed on a distant planet. Walls of flames rose high on both sides, and Jeremy suddenly worried for their tires.

A sudden explosion threw debris into the air. A stalled car, Jeremy realized. There were probably more, containing remnants of oil and gas in their tanks.

We're in hell, Jeremy thought. This is what hell is like. Will we never catch a break on this journey?

The air was becoming too hot for his lungs, and he found himself panting beneath the thin strip of cloth. This is it, he realized. We're dead on our feet. We've been breathing this air for too long. He slapped at cinders that were flying around his head. Susan, he thought miserably. I'm sorry. I failed our daughter. I've led her to her death. We're so damn close, but we just can't make it. How much farther can this torture go on?

Almost as if she had answered his call, a bright patch of sun shone through the thick gloom, but when he put on a burst of speed, he heard a popping sound. His rear tire had just exploded.

"Sam!" he called out, seeing her shape through the gloom. "Look up. Clear sky. We're almost there!"

He pushed himself, and his bicycle, too, from a black inferno into a clear blue sky. And he didn't slow down for half a mile, at least. Downwind of the blaze, he let his bike fall to the ground. Rolling to the pavement, he righted himself. Seth was suffering a fit of dry heaves, while Sam seemed to be coughing up a lung. But they were alive. Thank God. They'd made it in one piece.

"Dad," Sam choked. "Your pants!"

Smoke was curling from his left pant leg, which he slapped, patted, and then doused with water. He didn't give a shit about himself, or his clothes. He was more interested in a spot on her arm. When he pushed back her sleeve, he couldn't help but wince. It was a second-degree burn, though thankfully not worse. "Does it hurt?" he asked as he turned her around.

She pointed to a blister at the side of her neck. "No more than this does." She pointed at Seth. "Never mind me. Go look at him."

Jeremy moved toward Seth, but was stilled. "No," Seth said. "I'm okay. I'm sucking it up."

For several more moments, Seth coughed into his fist, before the three of them silently peered at the fire. It was a miracle they'd made it through at all. They'd been lucky. The devastation it wrought was astounding. The fire consumed brush, grasses, and trees indiscriminately. It must have started in the south, Jeremy thought, for it crawled a steady northward pace as it swept its way east.

"Wow," Seth breathed, touching his finger to his scalp. "How long do you think it'll burn? Will it just go on like that forever? Burn everything it touches?"

"Not forever," Jeremy said, rubbing soot from his pants. "But for a very long time, I'm sure." Frowning, he crouched to examine the ruptured tire. The places where rubber had melted to metal had cooled in strange lumpy shapes.

"Use your sombrero," Seth pointed out smugly. "I told you it was a good idea."

Jeremy sat down hard on the pavement and laughed. "My sombrero. Yep. Thank God for my sombrero." Swinging the tire from his neck to the ground, he began to tug on the cooling metal clamps. "So, Seth," Jeremy asked with a smile. "How was that for sucking it up?"

The boy's smile was white against ash. "Not bad, I guess. But I think I'm done now. Can we just find a place to lay down and take a nap?"

Sam stretched out across the pavement, close to where Jeremy worked. "I'm not sleeping until we're far away from here."

"Agreed. And I wouldn't mind taking a bath either. I stink."

Sam raised herself up on an elbow. "Speaking of a bath, can I get a sip of water?"

With a flick of his wrist, Jeremy fit the plump tire to the frame, before pulling his backpack closer to his feet. With belly clenched, he peered inside. If they were low on water before, this was worse. They were getting close to desperate now. He peered at the sky. The sun had lowered. It must be late afternoon. He'd take them as far as the nearest town, find a place to sleep, and then forage for water. But he wouldn't say a thing about it now. Let them have all the water they wished, for he refused to show them how little was left, or how much he'd spilled on their shirts.

Pasting a false smile across his sooty face, he handed his daughter one of their last bottles. "Drink up," he said, as confidently as he could. "Because we've almost reached the California border. Maybe I'll do all the 'sucking it up' from here."

It is good to have an end to journey toward; but it is the journey that matters, in the end.

—Ernest Hemingway

CHAPTER 24
Present Day

DECEMBER 11ᵀᴴ, 2176
YUMA, ARIZONA
172 MILES TO SAN DIEGO

That's the thing about a desert landscape. For a long time, its simplicity is comforting; its purity is cleansing to the soul—until it becomes a big bore, that is. At a certain point, one cactus becomes the next. One sienna field ranges into another, for as far as the eye can see. Monotony tugs at the imagination, and while beautiful at first, leaves one wanting more. The desert is a question that begs an answer. What lies beyond the sandy dunes? How many more miles must we travel?

And where, Jeremy wondered, can we find more water?

That was the question on his dry parched lips. Though his initial plan of sleeping by day and traveling by night had stretched their supply beautifully, it hadn't prevented the inevitable. They were quickly running out. Particularly after encountering the fire. And bicycling at night presented a new set of challenges. It was actually much harder than one might expect. Perhaps it was the body's natural rhythms, Jeremy thought. The body wanted to rest at night. It didn't want to exert itself, or handle stress. Or perhaps it was the depth of silence surrounding them, or the lack of ambient light. When he'd birthed the plan, he hadn't considered these things. He wasn't alive when large cities had thrived, but in all the books and magazines he'd ever read, light had blazed in the cities of old. 'Light pollution', he'd once saw it named. The darkness of the desert at night is absolute, and it was something he hadn't expected. Stars reflected off shiny pieces of sand, while the moon guided them inexorably forward, but when its solemn face slid behind a bulbous cloud, they could barely see anything at all. And at times like these Jeremy led the children forward, slowly, a flashlight awkwardly clenched between his teeth, his worry for the batteries a stone in his belly.

They couldn't see a thing until it was directly in front of them: pockets of sand that curtained the road, thick tumbleweeds, scraps of rubber, or rusted cars. The road was a never-ending chain of accidents waiting to happen. It was a dangerous way to travel, he knew, but he also knew that they didn't have a choice. The alternative was that much worse. If they continued to travel by day, he reasoned, they would run out of water before reaching California, and though November had come and gone in a flash, December had proved just as hot. This was the Earth's new climate. This was normal now. Cold and snow were relegated to its past, or to the highest peeks of the Colorado Mountains, to Canada, Alaska, or possibly Siberia. The sun had inherited the rest.

He mustered what moister he could and licked his lips. These past few days, he had rationed himself harshly, and he was beginning to feel the effects. His lips had cracked and begun to scale, and his urine was dark, a concentrated yellow. He knew he was playing at a knife's edge with this, as he was suffering the early stages of dehydration. He couldn't allow it to worsen. These minor discomforts were the early symptoms. Confusion and fatigue would likely come next, while unconsciousness and unresponsiveness would be his end. If that happened, all three of them would die.

He pulled his bike to a stop and slumped, his tongue thick against the roof of his mouth. The last exit was a mile behind them, and an old apartment complex was in front. "That's it for tonight," he croaked. "I need to rest. We all do. Let's stop, stay here for the night."

Swinging his leg over his seat, he peered at the building in front of them. Was it vacant? Safe? There had to be close to seventy units inside, and hopefully rations of food and water. His pulse quickened. It was promising. If they could just locate a few bottles of water…

"Dad," Sam said, "This is bullshit." Pulling a bottle from inside her pack, she frowned and handed it over. "It's not that bad. You're making too much of this. We still have water. Just drink. If we have to stay here for a while, we can. There's bound to be water somewhere around here, even if it's an old reclamation plant. We'll double-boil it, strain it. It'll work. And it'll get us the rest of the way to San Diego. You're pointlessly killing yourself. It's dumb."

He was certain Sam and Seth were thirsty, but they weren't as thirsty as he. He'd reduced his quota so they could have more. "We can't stay, Sam." He pointed to her belly. "Your meter. What's it say?"

She hesitated because she probably knew, and she was probably trying to spare Seth. Thrusting out a defiant hip, she lifted her shirt and scowled. "Two percent, okay? I'm down to two percent. But you've got the pills, so let's not freak out."

He hadn't missed the false bravado lacing the edge of her voice. Had there been a spark of fear in her eyes? Uncapping the bottle, he allowed himself a sip. The water was cool on his battered throat, and though heavenly, he permitted himself just a small sip. "Yep," he replied. "We've got the pills. But there's only one bottle, so let's be smart."

As they walked their bikes across the parking lot, Jeremy swore he could hear her mind spinning in her head.

"Carp," she asked him tentatively, "you've put a lot of faith in San Diego, don't you think? What if we don't find what you're hoping to find? Shouldn't we slow down and look for pills?"

Though he shook his head, his belly clenched at her words. Had he put too much faith in this foolhardy plan? "We're 172 miles from San Diego, Pike. If we push ourselves, that's four day's time—three if we really push ourselves. The fire wore us out, but it also forced us to move faster, which is good. It was actually a small blessing in disguise. I say we push ourselves, just to get there." Turning to Seth, he winked a dry eye. "And I seem to remember someone advising us to suck it up."

Sam stopped suddenly, kicked her stand to the ground. Jeremy turned, brows arched. She looked angry. "Dad," she said. "I'm sick of this. You've put all our eggs in one basket, and I'm afraid you've set us up to fail. What if we've made this trip for nothing? What if we've completely exhausted ourselves and there's nothing waiting at the end of it?" She scratched a burnt patch of skin on her palm. "What if we had taken our time, instead? Explored each city we passed through? Think about it, Dad, in the thousand or so miles we've traveled, how many disks do you think we might have found along the way? How many bottles of pills in those homes?" When he didn't answer, she pulled Seth against her hip, hugging him without giving it a second thought. "That's it." She shook her head. "I'm done. I won't travel another mile with you. Not until you tell me what you've banked my future on."

Jeremy's anger swelled out of control. "Did you just say 'what I banked your future on'? Is that what you think of me? Please tell me you're joking, Sam. You think

I'd risk your life on nothing but a whim? A hunch? Some wild intuition?" When she didn't respond, he thrust his hand into his pocket, felt the shape of the empty disk case and flipped it over to her. He'd been carrying it in his pocket for months, since the moment he'd decided to move forward with his plan. It had become like a coin or a bottle cap to him, like a lucky talisman one might hang around a piece of yarn. The absence of it was strangely discomforting.

She held it up to the light and squinted. "Yeah? So what? What am I looking at?"

"Turn it over," he demanded impatiently.

She did, and peered at the lettering on the back. "Bigeye Pharmaceuticals," she said out loud, regarding him with narrowed eyes. "So what? That's the maker of the product. What about it?"

"God, Sam, you're impossible. Look what's printed below the name."

"I can't see it," she complained. "It's dark out here." Seth pulled her arm down closer to his face then pulled his flashlight from his pocket. "San Diego," he murmured when he shone it across the plastic. "It says San Diego."

"San Diego?" The words had been a mere breath on her lips. Her head snapped up; her voice trembled with excitement. "The manufacturer is in San Diego." She hadn't phrased the words as a question. "Do you really think they'll have disks?"

He allowed himself a second small sip of water before his body demanded that he take a large one. "Yes, Sam. I think they'll have disks. And there's something else I think you should know. The technology of the disks was introduced to the world when it was already beginning to collapse. Few people were fortunate enough to receive an implant like the one you have in your belly right now. Your mother and I researched this subject extensively. Don't you remember how much time we spent at the library? Before everything fell apart, nanotechnology was used for many things, but the disks were still fairly new. So the answer to your first question is no. I don't think we've passed a string of disks along the way. I don't think the manufacturer had time to sell them, much less distribute them across the entire country. Your mother and I went to great lengths to obtain the ones we did. We met with dangerous contacts, brokered and traded many valuable things. The disks were hard to come by. So that begs the answer to a question, doesn't it? If we can't find hundreds of disks out there, where the hell are they? If they were produced in bulk, but never sold or shipped, where might that supply be now?"

As she put the pieces together, she blinked. "Okay, so maybe we haven't. Maybe we haven't passed hundreds of disks, but I'm sure we've passed countless bottles of pills."

Jeremy nodded. "I'm sure we have, too. But therein lies the second problem. Over the years, the pills have lost their potency. Though a similar encapsulation method was used, it wasn't as effective as the disks. Stopping at every town and city along the way would be similar to walking on a treadmill. We would be gathering pills—yes—but losing precious time. I had to make a decision, Sam, and I thought the best one was to get us to San Diego. If we get there and I'm wrong, we'll just search for more pills."

Her eyes filled with tears and he felt his throat constrict. He had thought this news would excite her.

"So you're saying one day the pills won't work at all?"

Crouching in front of her, he grasped her hands. For once, she didn't pull away. "I don't know, Sam. We can't know for sure. But the disks are better. That much I know. The technology was wildly advanced." A lock of windblown hair had loosed itself from her messy ponytail. Tucking it behind her ear, he cupped her small face in his hands. "We'll figure this out," he assured her softly. "I won't let you down. You know that. I won't let anything happen to you—not while I'm alive and still breathing. If we don't find disks in San Diego, we'll come up with something else we can do. I've only been doing what I think is best. That's all a person can do. But know this: Grandma was a genius at locating pills, and I remember all of her techniques. If we need them, Sam, I'm confident we'll find them."

She dropped her gaze to her feet. "So that's what happened to Grandpa, isn't it? He stopped taking pills. For me. He took fewer so I could have more. That's why he died. Am I right?"

"That's right. It was just something he wanted to do. You couldn't have stopped him. None of us could. He loved you more than he loved his own life. So let's do this for him. Shall we? Let's honor his sacrifice. Let's make it mean something. Do we have a deal?"

"We have a deal." She rounded her shoulders and wiped her tears. She was gathering her strength like Susan use to do.

Jeremy watched her drop the plastic case into her pocket, and then lifted his gaze to the towering building. "What do you guys say we try to find some water? There's bound to be something inside this old dump."

And thankfully, that night, they did. At one time this had been a retirement village, and one thing Jeremy had learned over the years was to count on the wisdom and foresight of elders. They tucked away all manner of things. It was a relief really—one less thing to worry about. They drank their fill and gorged themselves, on stale balance bars and old boxes of crackers. The spoils, to Jeremy, were impressive, and for once he let himself relax. Sam read from a book. They slept on the floor. And despite their earlier conversation, they were able to find a bit of normalcy and peace. They didn't speak of her meter again, or of the hundred-or-so miles of road in front of them. There was a nervousness in the energy between them. They'd reached the end, but wouldn't say so aloud. But there was also hope and faith. He could feel it. They believed what they needed would be provided to them.

Jeremy fell asleep on his side, facing Sam. Her hand was resting at the edge of his blanket. He reached out cautiously, not wanting to disturb her, and when sleep finally claimed him, he felt the warmth of her hand as she placed it atop his.

The next morning, her meter had fallen to zero, and when he passed her the last bottle of pills, his stomach lurched. Was it the bottle he'd pilfered from Peter, or was it the one he had found beside Seth's deceased mother? Life was random, seemingly aimless, like molecules scattering from a butterfly's wings.

Not I, nor anyone else can travel that road for you.
You must travel it by yourself.
It is not far. It is within reach.
Perhaps you have been on it since you were born, and did not know.
Perhaps it is everywhere—on water and land.

—Walt Whitman, *Leaves of Grass*

CHAPTER 25
Present Day

DECEMBER 16ᵀᴴ, 2176
SAN DIEGO, CALIFORNIA

The San Diego hills rose majestically in front of them, but simultaneously wreaked havoc on their thighs. As the first rays of sun were streaking across the morning sky, they finally reached the city limits and yelled out a warrior's cry. They were exhausted, though, Jeremy in particular. In the days that followed the expiration of her disk, Sam had weakened considerably. The intensity of the physical exertion, coupled with a poor diet and lack of proper sleep, had been too much for her battered body to handle. The night before, in a frightful moment, Jeremy had watched her attempt to pedal forward, and fail. She had wobbled on her bike precariously, and then slumped across the handlebars in defeat. The end. Seth had stifled a scream, while Jeremy dashed to her side, panicked and frenzied.

"Seth," he'd called out, his voice shrill, "I need help. Pull yourself together." Shrugging the heavy pack from his shoulders, he'd quietly passed it to the frightened young boy. "You'll have to take this, while I carry her. I'm sorry, Seth. It's too heavy for you. You'll just have to make do somehow." Seth had accepted the burden wordlessly.

Lifting Sam's body into his arms, Jeremy had let her bike fall to the ground with a clatter. It was useless to him now, but he'd whispered his thanks. Like a rose on a grave, he'd left it where it lay. It had done its job dutifully.

He'd propped Sam against his chest, while Seth splayed her legs across his bike's handlebars, and they'd ridden like that for the last fifty miles. Seth had accepted the weight of both packs, and though he hadn't complained, Jeremy knew he was struggling. The remaining distance was an uphill climb, both backbreaking and murderous to their legs. He couldn't imagine how Seth was getting through it. Jeremy's own legs burned from the effort. His eyes were bloodshot and swollen. He clenched his teeth against his many discomforts: the hard edge of the bicycle seat, pressing painfully into his groin, his trembling arms that he had to keep taut, the unbearable thirst he wasn't able to quench, the bottle of water that was just out of reach, strapped to the underside of the frame. He wouldn't allow himself to stop and drink, wouldn't sacrifice a moment of precious time.

They'd ridden all night, wordlessly, until dawn, saving their breath for the last few miles. Sam was somewhat lucid at times, though for most of the journey she wasn't. She remained in a deep and immersive sleep. That was the lie Jeremy told himself, at least, for he wouldn't allow himself to face the truth, that she walked the fine line between sleep and coma.

He'd braced her arm between her belly and his, in a way that showcased the numbers at her wrist, and as night progressed, he watched her numbers rise. Her sugars were unacceptably high. Though he and Susan had never been sure, they'd suspected her of suffering the worst kind of diabetes. While the bodies of some produced small amounts of insulin, Sam's didn't seem to make any, and only two days prior, much to Jeremy's dismay, her body had fallen into diabetic ketoacidosis, which meant the pills were useless to them now. After ingesting them, her sugars would fall, but the dosage required to accomplish such a task would empty their bottle in less than a day. As such, he and Seth didn't rest or stop, didn't speak or complain, only focused and pedaled, alone in their private visions of hell.

Jeremy tried his best to keep Sam alert, by engaging her in mindless conversations, and by keeping the wind in her face and hair. He didn't allow her to eat anything, either, a desperate measure that felt cruel and inhumane. It was a trick his father had mentioned years ago, something to be used in critical situations. Maybe it had helped, Jeremy wondered privately, though it only seemed to weaken her further.

"Ten more miles to the ocean, Pike," he said softly, trying to liven her spirits. "Can you believe we actually made it? When we get there, what do you expect to see?"

Sometimes she'd answer by grunting acknowledgment, or with a fluttering of fingers against his wrist. When she didn't, he took comfort in her rhythmic breathing, which at times was the only thing that proved she still lived.

Seth struggled behind him stoically, and though they stopped once for water and a small bite of food, each idle moment felt like an acceptance of defeat. Neither of them could stay still for too long.

As night slowly progressed into day, she became less responsive in his lap. "See Pike?" he begged of her. "I wasn't wrong. It wasn't wrong to attempt this journey. The things we could have done didn't matter after all, because everything that happened would have happened anyway. The pills," he muttered maniacally. "They don't work anymore. Searching for more wouldn't have helped. Don't you see? So we need to forgive ourselves. No." He shook his head. "You need to forgive me, for doing this to you, for taking you so far from your home and life, for gambling on nothing but faith. But," he countered, "Peter's leg happened because the pills didn't work, so maybe I hastened what would have happened anyway. The leg, I mean. Peter's leg was a sign, a sign that somehow I missed. I should have tried harder to understand it. I just didn't see the truth fast enough. And when I finally did, I didn't listen to my gut. I should have listened and acted instead of hesitating, instead of allowing us to sit in that house for months. We should have left sooner, and that's on me. For if we had, we'd be there by now." He blinked back tears and firmed his chin. "It's my fault, Sam, and I can't forgive myself. If I had acted sooner, you'd be safe by now. If I hadn't hesitated—like Grandpa used to say—we'd have our home by the sea. We'd have trees and gardens, rain catchers along the roof." A sob suddenly tore from his chest. "Stay with me, Sam, just a little bit longer. Do it for me, for Seth, and for Mom."

The sky was brightening into a kaleidoscope of purples when they finally crossed into the city of San Diego. Streaks of amethyst knifed through the blackness. Lilac brightened deep pockets of eggplant. Casting a glance at Seth over his shoulder, Jeremy picked up speed.

"Seth?" he called out, glancing quickly at the boy, whose cheeks were red and puffing with air. "We're almost there, son. Suck it up."

When Seth raised his face, Jeremy's breath caught in his throat. There were tears glistening in the boy's brown eyes. "Sam?" he asked breathlessly, the word cut short by a gut wrenching sob.

Jeremy couldn't muster a reply. Returning his gaze to the road ahead, he bore down with a strength he hadn't thought he possessed, and when the ocean materialized, he let loose a low howl. "Sam," he screamed, shifting her slightly in his lap. "Open your eyes. We made it! We're here!"

Her eyes fluttered opened and her mouth twitched, the corners lifting into a thin smile. "We made it?" she questioned him faintly.

"We did! Look," he said as she tried to raise her head.

"It's beautiful," she murmured. "Like diamonds on silk."

Once she had seen the water, her head fell back, her eyes slipping closed as she fell into sleep. Like a frail doll she was, her eyelashes splayed across delicate cheeks. "You did it, Dad," she mumbled to him softly, the words so faint he had to lower his chin just to catch them. "You got us here. We have to tell Mom. We have to take her down to the beach."

Her words were slurred and nonsensical. Jeremy fought to keep his voice from shaking. "Of course we will, honey. We'll go get Mom. We'll get her and have ourselves a picnic by the sea."

She smiled at that and Jeremy's heart skipped a beat. Banking left, he steered onto Sunset Cliffs Road, his bike skidding dangerously on patches of sand. The ocean was breathtaking and vast. It was a beauty he'd long thought gone from this world. Waves blanketed the shoreline in refreshing salt sprays. The sea was a glittering quilt of winking stars and sparkling gemstones. It was like diamonds, he said to himself. As usual, Sam was right. Though the waves were lifeless and the water empty, the sight of it lifted his spirits nonetheless. In that radiant moment, there was only one thing he could have found more beautiful than the ocean itself: the tall glass building in the distance, beckoning him, shimmering at the edge of the cliff like a beacon.

Bigeye Pharmaceuticals. They'd made it at last.

It was a contemporary building of steel framing and glass. Glass—not reflective like the pink-and-gold of a Las Vegas Casino—but clear and limpid, transparent on every side. It was a lighthouse to Jeremy, a flare in the dark, shining bright beneath a slowly rising sun.

He sped toward it breathlessly, the sounds of Seth's spinning tires close at his heels. Pulling his bike to the edge of the lawn, he whisked Sam into his arms and ran. He needed to check her vitals first, to gauge how much time she had left. She'd made it this far, he counseled himself. "Please," he prayed aloud. "Hang with me, Sam. Stay with me a little bit longer."

Her head lolled against his shoulder before falling dangerously limp across his arm. No, he thought, crazed. Stay with me. If she fell into a coma, he might never get her back. He couldn't allow that happen. Lowering her to the grass, a sob tore from his throat, as he searched her pockets for the near-empty bottle. Seth dropped silently to his knees beside him, tears streaming down his face and onto his shirt. Jeremy saw him reach for her hand and draw it close. The bottle was stuffed into a pocket of her khakis, and when he removed the cap, his heart skipped a beat. There was only a handful left, little more. He pushed them past her lips, but she wouldn't swallow them. She was too far-gone, not lucid anymore. They fell from her lips and rolled onto the grass.

Jeremy's panic swelled. "No," he whispered. He could bring her back from this. This couldn't be it. This wasn't the end. They'd come so far and been through so much to fail five feet from the door. He wouldn't allow it. He shoved the bitter pills into his mouth and did his best to emulsify them, before pushing the paste into her mouth. He coated the insides of her cheeks and her tongue. "Just a little bit longer," he begged of her. "Please. You can't leave me. Don't do this to me."

He poured what little water he had into her mouth. If he could just get the medicine into her bloodstream, she just might make it, though barely. Scooping her up, he sped for the doors, his mind beginning to wander as he ran, back to that very first morning, back home, to their trip to the burnt-out hospital. It was the morning his father had murdered two men, and he remembered it with crystalline brilliance. What question had he asked Liam? Oh yes. That's right. "How long can you survive on half a dose of pills?" Though his father hadn't responded, the answer had revealed itself soon enough.

Sixteen months.

Liam had died in sixteen months. He was an older man by that time, of course, and his age coupled with the poor medication had destroyed his body in sixteen months. His death had been slow and agonizing. He hadn't lost a leg or suffered a gangrenous wound, not in the ways Peter had. His pain and atrophy had hidden themselves in places his family couldn't see. His deterioration was internal and private—which was exactly the way he had wanted it to be. It allowed him to simulate health a long while, to keep up appearances and suffer alone. Jeremy could only surmise that by then Liam had discovered the truth about the pills: they were weak, and with time, would continue to spoil. He must have determined how ineffective they were, for he decreased his dosage significantly, and in secret. The human mind makes extraordinary leaps. It tethers together strange pieces of truth to form false conclusions and faulty deductions. Then it acts on those conclusions with tenacity and vigor. By taking more of the pills for himself, Liam believed he was killing his granddaughter. That was the conclusion that ultimately killed him. It was madness, twisted. To Liam, it was love.

Toward the end, he lost weight quickly, and once his pain became too great, he simply allowed the inevitable to happen. But Jeremy also remembered that he was happy. The closer he inched toward death, the more content and untroubled he became, it seemed. What he did for Sam had been a personal choice, and it was one he had made willingly, a sacrifice. He was alive when Sam first learned to read. He loved spending quiet evenings beside the hearth, watching her lips make sense of the letters.

Sacrifices beget other sacrifices. Acts of love are links in a never-ending chain. Jeremy and Susan owed Liam so much. It was his sacrifice that finally forced them outside. He was the impetus that drove them from the cabin to search for the alternatives that led to the disks. It had been his blessings, his selfless gifts that ultimately saved her life.

But what would become of that sacrifice now? Jeremy cast his eyes about the ground. The large double doors were locked and chained. Inclining his head toward a stone on the ground, he nodded at Seth. "There. Pick it up. Throw it against the glass. Hard. Do it now."

Seth complied with a scramble. He picked up the stone and backed several paces, reared back his arm, and loosed it with a snap. With a sharp clatter, stone crashed through glass, the sound a sharp contract to the waves against the cliffs. Jeremy widened the hole with a kick, and the two of them pushed through the opening awkwardly.

"Where?" Jeremy screamed as he spun in endless circles. "Where do we start?"

They ran to the reception area first, and stopped, for had Jeremy not been holding Sam, the sight would have felled him to his knees. Beside the front desk, a billboard stood, the twenty-foot image of a beautiful woman, posing in a white bathing suit, her hair blown back by the wind. The advertisement was old, faded, and blanched, but the familiar green glow at her belly was clear. Jeremy nearly lost himself. A seed of happiness sprouted in his belly, the feeling so intense he could barely hold it in. He'd been right all along. He'd gambled and won.

Seth saw it too and spun wildly around the room. "But where?" he moaned. "Where are they?"

Jeremy set Sam down on the reception case glass and pressed two fingers to her throat. He stilled, holding his breath as he listened. Her pulse was faint and fluttering, but there, and though her breathing was ragged and shallow, she breathed. She lived. She hadn't left him yet. There was time. For where life still existed, a fight could be waged. Jeremy stood and peered around the room.

"Where?" Seth said. He was sobbing now. "Carp, what do we do? Where are they? This place is too big. We'll never find them."

Jeremy wiped the tears from his eyes and peered around. There was a set of double doors behind the reception platform, which he sprinted toward, Seth close at his heels, their footfalls echoing in the empty room. The doors concealed two long hallways. Seth banked left, and Jeremy, right.

Some of the doors were open, some locked, and Jeremy searched each room with trembling hands. This was the end of the line, his final move. His plan would succeed in this building or it would fail. He would save his little girl, or he would lose everything. His thoughts were jagged and sharp behind his eyes, his memories bright and electric. There was Susan and the morning of Sam's birth. Jeremy's mother had been so calm that day. She was Jeremy's rock. He'd never forgotten her strength. As everything else in the Colt household, Sam's birth had been a family affair. They'd staged a tub of water in the baby's room, an old kiddie pool with plastic sides and a bright blue bottom. He remembered his father pacing the halls outside, and Susan's fear of the burgeoning pain. She'd clutched his fingers with an iron grip, and he'd continued to say the wrong things. "Women have been doing this for thousands of years, Suse. For thousands of years—and without epidurals."

"Not this woman!" she'd screamed, her face red. "This woman needs the drugs! Now!"

He remembered that day so fondly. Susan had always been strong in Jeremy's eyes, and true to form, she hadn't wavered in this. People always say the birth of a child is life's greatest gift, and after experiencing it firsthand, Jeremy knew it to be true. He would never forget his daughter's birth. It brought his family closer together. With quiet assurances and a gentle touch, Olivia tended mother and baby with skill—or the intuition only a woman possesses. She'd seemed to know all the right things to do, though later she confessed that her confidence was an act. She'd laughed through tears and shrugged her shoulders. "A woman's body will do what it's supposed to do. All I did was cheer her along."

Jeremy thought of that beautiful day, and of all the days that had followed since then, of the things his family had endured along the way: the planning and secrets, the wins and losses, the countless tears and sacrifices. There had been Liam's death, and then there was Susan's, and it had all led up to this moment—Sam's moment. Nothing would matter if he lost her now. He couldn't face that, couldn't bear it, couldn't live. He couldn't lose them both in the span of one year.

His body thrummed with nervous energy, and as he searched one empty room after the next, a sob tore from his throat. He thought of the sparkling sea outside, just below the cliffs on the bluff. He imagined its shimmering surface, like diamonds, and the silence of its depths below. He pictured the miles of empty water, turquoise slowly fading to black. Nothing existed in that void. Nothing lived. It was a bathtub full of water, and a graveyard of bones.

He imagined the smooth ocean floor with its majestic hills and valleys, and the jutting whalebones in castles atop the sand. He thought of the millions of fallen shark teeth and the bits of trash, peppering in the sand. Plastic entombed with precious bones. It wasn't right. It didn't belong down there. But maybe, he thought for a moment, I do. For if I lose Sam, I lose everything. Perhaps I should join the old bones, just die. The thought, though macabre, held a certain appeal, for if she died, he couldn't go on. He would find a small boat and oars, he promised himself, and row past the breakers, beyond the shoreline.

He'd cast himself over the side of the boat and sink to the bottom, join the silence of the dead. Perhaps his bones would settle with the teeth, and be captured in a sandy tomb. It was fitting really. It was where he belonged. He'd done monstrous things to get them here, and after all was said and done, it may have been for nothing. She might die anyway, and it wouldn't have mattered. He belonged in the depths of those barren waters.

He shook the thoughts from his head and focused, sprinting from the last empty room in the hall, catching sight of a set of double doors at the end. Entrance to these required a thumb or palm print, pressed against a rectangular scanner. He cursed. Slapping it in anger, he cried out a howl and flung himself against the solid doors. How was this happening? After all this shit? How was any of this possible?

Startled by the sound of Seth's running feet, he turned, his hopes suddenly dashed in an instant. Seth stopped short, his empty hands held high. It was as if he had wilted or sunk into himself. Tears were streaming down his cheeks. Jeremy whirled in anger, slamming his shoulder against the impenetrable fortress, certain the disks were inside it. It only made sense that they would be, of course, for this was the elusive vault of treasure—his treasure—the treasure that always seemed just out of reach. He howled with rage, hurled his body against the door.

"Wait!" Seth screamed. "The counter!"

"The what?" Jeremy turned and growled. "What counter? What are you talking about, Seth?"

"The counter! You laid her across the counter out front, but there was something beneath the glass."

Jeremy froze.

The unconscious mind works in baffling and mysterious ways. People see thousands of images in a day—hundreds of thousands, yet often don't process the images until later. The concept is the scientific theory of dreams. Dreaming, scientists believe, is the mind's attempt to organize images. And so, Jeremy's mind organized. It replayed the images like a movie: their entrance into the structure, both wild and chaotic, the beautiful figure of the cardboard woman, the pallid tone of Sam's sunken cheeks, the dustiness of the counter where he'd lowered and left her body, the oblong cylinder, just inside the glass, resting on sapphire velvet.

He drew a breath.

Dear God! It had been there. He just hadn't seen it.

Racing back to the reception area, he pushed through the doors and ran to her. She was breathing, though barely. He gently lifted her up. And when he saw the case, he wept openly. Setting her down, he turned toward Seth, who pressed a stone into his palm and slowly backed away. With a nod, Jeremy slammed the stone into the glass, battering it until it finally broke. He lifted the applicator from its cushiony bed, and kneeling beside her, lifted the corner of her shirt. The applicator clicked into place with a satisfying snap, and as he pressed the plunger, he held his breath. Seth's hand found his as the numbers began to rise.

The sea is nature's vast reserve. It was through the sea that the globe as it were began, and who knows if it will not end in the sea! Perfect peace abides here. The sea does not belong to despots. On its surface immoral rights can still be claimed, men can fight each other, devour each other, and carry out all earth's atrocities. But thirty feet below the surface their power ceases, their influence fades, their authority disappears. Ah, sir, live, live in the heart of the sea! Independence is possible only here! Here I recognize no master! Here I am free!

-Jules Verne, *Twenty Thousand Leagues Under the Sea*

CHAPTER 26
Present Day

JANUARY 25ᵀᴴ, 2177
SAN DIEGO, CALIFORNIA
THE PACIFIC OCEAN

"Guys, it won't hurt you."

From his blanket atop the sand, Jeremy called out to them, smiling as they scampered to the water, and laughing when they ran from the incoming waves. "It won't kill you, goofballs. You can dip your toes in."

As usual, they ignored him. It was as if he wasn't there. The game, he supposed, was much more fun. Turning his gaze to Sam, he smiled. She looked amazing, so healthy and strong. He could barely believe the transformation. Her burns had healed, and she'd put on weight—at least ten pounds by his estimate. For a girl that slim, ten pounds was noticeable. But there were other changes as well—emotionally. She was happier now, more secure, exuberant. It had been a long time since he'd seen her like this, even longer since he'd felt the same way. The morning he'd found the disk in the case was the most gratifying of his life thus far. The moment her meter had risen to 100%, he knew he'd saved her, that life would go on. He and Seth had wept by her side, unabashedly, and then begged her to wake up and talk to them. When she did, their lives had begun anew. They'd moved her to a small square of light in the sun and Seth had coaxed her into drinking some water, while Jeremy ran to retrieve the crowbar.

After two painful hours and a stream of curse words, he managed to break through the facility's security doors, and the reward, in the end, was breathtaking. Row after row of unshipped disks were waiting for Sam, just beyond the locked doors. There were cartons, boxes, cases, and crates—more than enough to last Sam a lifetime.

But that's the thing about the end of the world, all of the stuff that remains, the surplus. Sam was one of the lucky ones. No. She might be the last lucky one—the only one of her kind, at least. The thought was humbling and demanded gratitude, but it also brought to mind unsettling images. At that very moment, across the United States, how many street-wars were being waged? How many people were killing one another? Fighting over food, water, or shelter? How many mothers, emaciated and worn, were pushing ailing children in the baskets of broken-down shopping carts? In this strange new world, things had changed irrevocably. Certain things were more valuable than diamonds. Sam was now a very wealthy woman.

The disk had immediately stabilized her health, as had the life they built on the highest peak in Point Loma, San Diego. When the three of them set out to choose their new home, the children's' choice had surprised Jeremy. He'd expected them to choose a monstrous mansion, or a French chateau in the suburbs, or maybe a posh penthouse in the gas lamp district, or a sprawling manner overlooking the blue waves. Their choice, however, had been simple and cozy, and Jeremy was proud that he'd allowed them to make it. He'd retreated from that decision entirely, for it had been his job to save their lives. He'd let them decide how best to live them.

They chose a small house at the top of the highest rise, a yellow, one-story ranch, built in the late 1950's, hidden beneath overhanging cedars and elms. Truth be told, it was reminiscent of their cabin in Sevierville. Perhaps Sam had chosen it because of that, or because of the big picture window that faced the bay, or the cozy fireplace in the small living room. Whatever her reasons, she'd chosen well. The view from the windows was spectacular, different from the one in the Smokey Mountains, yet no less glorious or magnificent.

The house itself was small and old. "Big love grows in small spaces," Sam had said, and now that they were here, Jeremy couldn't agree more. Once they moved in, they planted their garden, though the grounds had been lush already. Fragrant lemon trees, boughs heavy with ripened fruit, had already matured on the property's western border. They added to these spinach, kale, and tomatoes, cucumbers and broccoli, and various root vegetables. They even planted a row of dwarf peach trees, a small fig tree, and a blueberry bush. The soil was black and rich with nutrients, and already, their seeds had begun to sprout. They harvested fruit from neighboring yards— but only from the places where no one was home.

Seth—like he had said he would—had scavenged the neighborhood for binoculars, and on the clearest days, in the early dawn light, he would hold the convex lenses to his eyes and scan the sea for signs of life. From the bay window, he could see as far as Tijuana, Mexico. At some point Jeremy would find a telescope with which to view the stars and beyond. But for now, they had everything they needed, and more.

The house had needed work, and more than a little. The cleaning and dusting had taken four days. Old food had dried and spoiled on the kitchen shelves, and Jeremy had dragged the smelly refrigerator down the street. It hadn't rained lately, so water was a constant concern. It was something that would require a permanent solution, but Jeremy refused to let that worry him now, for the life they were living was deliciously regular. Their sore muscles and burns had healed, along with their battered spirits. It would take time to recover from what they had seen, and from all the things that had been done to them, but the human spirit is nothing if not resilient.

They weren't alone in San Diego. Jeremy wasn't stupid. That didn't make sense. The land in this area was too rich, too lush. Life was too easily sustainable. Jeremy scavenged alone, and at night, and though he hadn't crossed paths with people, he hadn't tried. There were too many other important things to get done, too many things to find, to collect, and to grow. There was a life to embrace, to love, and to live.

Jeremy dropped his head to the sand and listened to their giggles, contentedly. He let his eyes close. Sunlight danced behind his lids in strange patterns. Sometimes, still, he would awaken in the night, sweating and frightened, unsure of where he was. He would panic if the children weren't sleeping beside him, for of late, they slept in separate rooms. For the first few nights, after their arrival, they slept as they had before, in the same room, beside each another, each rolled into his pallet. But as comfort set in, each took his own room, and Jeremy had struggled to retrain himself to the coldness and loneliness of sleeping alone.

Though life had calmed, there were times when anxiety still struck him, when he couldn't believe they had actually made it, when his heart beat wildly and he lost his breath. There were times when he felt like he'd been a bad father. Sam was right. He had gambled her future. He had put all her eggs in one very small basket. His decisions, at times, had been reckless and irresponsible, and he wondered if luck hadn't yielded the results. Things could have gone much differently, and worse. There were so many forks along the road they had travelled. Any one could have led to her death. But it hadn't, and it was best not to dwell on such things and move on.

He turned his face to the spraying salt surf. He was certain Susan would have liked San Diego. She always loved the Smokey Mountains of Tennessee, but perhaps she would have liked this better. Jeremy and the kids didn't have an ark yet, but they were working hard to build a new one. And Susan, he knew, would be proud of that. Pushing himself on an elbow, he smiled, as Sam and Seth crouched low on the beach. They were inspecting something, a shell perhaps, or a bit of sea glass. Sam felt his gaze and came scampering over.

"What did you find over there?" he asked.

"A crab!" she gasped, out of breath. "Can you believe it? Well, at least I think it's a crab. It's ugly. I can barely see its legs. Its shell is tiny and it lives in a hole. It burrows into the sand when the tide rushes out."

"It's a mole crab, Sam," he said with wonder. "That's amazing. You actually found life. Seth must be proud."

"Wait. A mole crab? That's a terrible name."

With a grin, he shrugged. She was still into names. "I don't know what to tell you, Pike. That's just what they're called."

She wrinkled her nose. "I'm sure I can come up with something better than that."

Turning her face, she peered across the water. They didn't normally spend any time at the beach, but today was special. It was Seth's birthday—or so he had said. There was no way verify that information. "Ten years old," he'd stated triumphantly. "One year closer to Sam." Jeremy didn't know if he was telling the truth, or just using their ignorance to catch up with her. Nevertheless, he and Sam played along.

"I like it here," she said suddenly, her voice soft.

"Yeah. Me too."

"Mom would've liked it, too."

"I was just thinking the same thing before you

came over here." Staring at his daughter, Jeremy took a deep breath. "I'm glad you like it, Sam, because it's yours. Every last thing in that house is yours—yours and Seth's."

"Yours, too," she said, turning to face him.

"Yep. Mine too."

"Mole crab," she said with disdain. "Terrible name. But I guess not everything's dead, is it?"

"Nope." He squinted into the sun. "Guess not."

"Think we'll see any fish? Seth is over there looking for fish in the shallows—looking for shadows of fish, I should say. He says you can't see them because they swim too fast, that you have to find their shadows instead."

Jeremy laughed. "No. We won't see any fish, I'm afraid. Nor will your children, or your children's children. But maybe your children's children's children's children will."

"My children?"

Jeremy sucked in a breath. The words had just slipped out of his mouth. He hadn't given thought to their meaning, or considered the promise they held. With a shrug, he pointed toward Seth. "Yeah. Sure. All it takes is a man and a woman."

She turned, peered at Seth and raised her hand to her brow. Jeremy delighted in the smile that split her face. "Eeeeew, Dad! Stop! That's disgusting!"

As she scampered away, Jeremy laughed out loud. At their age, four years was quite a gap to bridge, but as time marched on, things would change. Their friendship would likely deepen into love. A lump suddenly rose in his throat.

This is it, he thought. I've actually done it. I've acturally done what I thought was impossible. This was what Susan and I wanted for Sam—a happy life, a home, a lifelong companion, the possibility of children, a family of her own.

He smiled. Maybe not such a bad father after all.

Maybe even Liam would be proud.

As he basked in the sun, he thought of his wife, of the first time he'd seen her as a beautiful woman and not just a girl with moles on her face. She'd been bathing in the stream that ran behind their house, and he'd watched her guiltily—until she'd caught him, of course. She'd screamed, then laughed, and then run to the trees, only to return to the same spot the next day. That memory always brought a smile to his face. It captured the spontaneity of her spirit, her vitality, but also the amazing serendipity of life. People come into our lives when we need them. The trick is remembering to cherish the time and give thanks to the powers that put them in our path.

As Jeremy watched his daughter scan the beach for mole crabs, he couldn't help but think of the human soul. Perhaps humanity would survive after all. Turning his face to the glittering water, he basked in the breeze and the feelings of peace. Humanity was decent at the survival part. It was the preventative stuff that needed a bit of work. If man had focused on initiatives that worked to protect and conserve what was given to him, there may have been a different outcome for everyone.

Humanity had failed the magnificent sea. But would man fail himself in the process? Only time could answer that question, he thought. Perhaps man's ingenuity would see him through any cataclysmic event, his resilience, his drive to succeed. Or maybe it would be his undying devotion, his willingness to sacrifice for those he loves. In the end, maybe that would save him.

ABOUT THE AUTHOR

Julia Shupe resides in Las Vegas, NV with her husband Nat, and their three cats; Tiger, Fred, and Baxter. She is the author of the Sentinels of Kiln series and will soon be releasing another science fiction novel as well as a thriller series.

www.Juliashupe.com
@Juliashupe33
https://www.facebook.com/BarrenWaters/

BOOKS BY JULIA SHUPE

Barren Waters

SENTINELS OF KILN SERIES
Woven Realms
Woven Quests
Woven Destinies...*Coming Soon*

VANESSA STONE SERIES
Carved in Stone

Made in the USA
Middletown, DE
24 February 2022